SKIN GAME

CARA McKENNA

Second edition

Originally published in 2011

Edited by Kelli Collins

Cover design by Cara McKenna

ISBN: 978-0-9977834-8-3

THE GATHERING

CAMERA 0001

THE FINAL CONTESTANT ARRIVES in the forest clearing—a slender, dark-haired, pale-skinned man in a tweed blazer and a straw fedora. Irises so blue they must have a patent pending from a chemical plant off the New Jersey turnpike. He takes a Sharpie from a khaki-clad crew member and scrawls *Ian* on a Hello-My-Name-Is sticker and slaps it on his lapel. The others mill uneasily, making small talk, but this man strides, duffel bag slung over one shoulder, a sideshow huckster scouting for rubes.

His eyes settle on the easiest mark in the group, and one of the youngest. A girl, early twenties, a blend of exotic ethnicities, kinky black hair pulled back in a sparkly clip. Her name badge reads *Leah*. She's the picture of store-bought bohemia, but she's bundled tight in Midwestern naivety under the skinny jeans and tunic top and chunky plastic jewelry. Her strange amber eyes pan the site as if searching for an escape route. Everyone was allowed to bring what they could carry, but she seems to have arrived for the battle unarmed.

Not far from her stands a tall, wiry black man with graying dreadlocks. *Greg.* His arms wave emphatically as he speaks to a younger guy—fit body, overly enthusiastic smile, a camouflage shirt bearing a sticker with the name *Brad.* He says something funny and earns a loud laugh and a high-five from the man next to him, a fellow twenty-something dressed all in black and called *Javier.* He's brimming with competitive energy, his hyper-curly black hair making him seem electrified, the polar opposite of the man seated to his left.

Camped out on a log, in the center of the group but unmistakably disengaged, is a kind-looking fellow, perhaps just shy of thirty. Dirty blond hair overdue for a trim, soft face, prominent nose, watchful, melancholy eyes. *Rory Hobbs*, he's labeled, in tidy capitals. The Sharpie-wielding crew member approaches. Nicknames or first names only, he says, and our man Rory politely obliterates his surname. He swallows frequently, doing an imitation of calm patience that won't be winning him any acting awards. His eyes dart to the woman standing opposite him across the clearing's unlit fire pit.

Chloe, her label says. Her posture tells us she'd prefer to be dressed in a tailored suit and ball-stomping heels, but the hiking pants and boots and vest say she's more interested in winning than in looking good for the viewers. Her honey-blonde hair and salon-perfect highlights beg to differ, but she pulls her wavy mane into a ponytail and pushes her mirrored aviator shades to the top of her head. There's a hefty-lensed camera hung around her neck. She raises it to snap a shot of the huge man busy hitting on her.

A mercenary—that's what he looks like. Six-four, easily. Buzzed hair, three days' stubble, sharp hazel eyes like a raptor. The arms crossed over his chest are as thick as Chloe's thighs and his body language says he'd be happy to have the thighs in question wrapped around his hips. His sexual interest is about as subtle as the hunting knife sheathed at his belt or the writing across his neck. The tattoo reads *Mother*, though his attitude suggests the artist ran out of ink before he could add *fucker*. His name badge reads *Daisey*.

The man standing behind him is dwarfed in comparison. Five-seven or -eight, compact, Asian, with a short, naturally spiky mohawk overgrown by a few weeks. *Pike*, he's called. His face is as hard to read as his age, the expression landing somewhere between cool apathy and fierce vigilance. There's a backpack at his feet and a sturdy plastic case in his hand. He turns as a girl nudges him, pointing at the case.

The young woman nods as he tells her it's supplies. She smiles brightly, dark eyes sparkling. She's small, just over five feet, but her tank top showcases the accomplished arms of a climber or rower. Her frame pack looks punishing though she doesn't show a single sign of strain. Of everyone in the initial group of twelve, she seems the most relaxed. Her creamy complexion is as luminous as the shining brown hair she's pulled back into pigtails. *Mac*, her name tag says.

Beside her stand two other twenty-something girls. The one labeled *Amanda* is doing a fine impression of sunny optimism, her anxiety given away only by the aggressive snapping of her gum. She's dressed to hike in shorts and a tee, mouse-brown ponytail threaded through the back of her baseball cap. The girl beside her is fair-skinned with a sunburned nose and flaming red hair piled into a messy bun. *Marissa*, she's called. She's got her skinny arms locked over her chest, looking as fed up as a woman trapped in a lunch-hour line at the DMV.

A loud whistle cuts short the twelve-way orgy of scrutiny as a stunning black woman in a cropped khaki blazer and matching jodhpurs strides to the center of the clearing, glossy jackboots crunching across the dirt.

"Hello!" Her voice is magnified by a tiny headset, and she trains a smile as blinding-white as a stage light over the scattered competitors.

"Welcome to Alaska. More importantly, welcome to The Ant Farm, as we're calling this group for the next couple of weeks. A social experiment in reality-show format. Uglier than *Survivor* and the Stanford prison experiment put together, we hope, and the only audience will be a handful of the world's leading social psychologists. There are over eight thousand cameras hidden throughout the landscape, but we're going to ask you all to try to forget they're there."

The number earns scattered murmurs and an impressed whistle from Daisey.

"My name is Lenora, and I'll be serving as your emcee for the duration of this experiment. Your jobs will be to focus on the tasks we set you," Lenora goes on, speaking with the perfect diction of a QVC spokeswoman. "Seven challenges in all—for those who make it to the end, that is. As I'm sure you're all acutely aware, there is a five hundred thousand dollar prize for the final man or woman standing. To clarify, that's five hundred grand, *after* taxes. And just a note, we had a last-minute no-show for the original pool of twelve, so an extra welcome to our lucky alternate."

The blue-eyed devil in the fedora, Ian, smiles indulgently.

Leah, the H&M-ad-come-to-life, rakes her gaze around the site again, looking frantic. She opens her mouth to speak but Lenora beats her to it.

"I've been informed that we've received your waivers and you've all passed your physicals, so let's jump right in. You're now going to be broken into your initial teams. For the first Objective, as we're calling the challenges, you'll be in four teams of three, each team designated by a different color." She waves a fistful of bandannas. "Please wear your colors on your head or around your neck so the doctors can keep you straight on tape. You'll also each be wearing a wireless mike."

A staff member holds up a box filled with little black devices.

"We ask that you keep them clipped to your collars at all times, except when you're bathing or otherwise undressed. Anyone who fails to keep their mike on for a minimum of twenty-two hours per day will be disqualified.

"Now by random selection, here are the teams. Red Team—Brad, Amanda and Javier." The three lively twenty-somethings jog forward to collect red bandannas and microphones and clap one another on the back.

"White Team—Chloe, Rory and Greg." Our resident man-eater and mild-mannered nice guy join the dreadlocked fellow in accepting their white bandannas.

"Blue Team—Marissa, Leah and Pike. Please come forward." Hidden cameras catch stoical Pike's expression darken as he approaches, taking in the two young women he's been teamed with, neither looking especially athletic in build or dress.

"And the Black Team—Mac, Ian and Daisey." Thank goodness for name tags, or we'd all assume the tiny, grinning woman is Daisey, and the hulking man-beast Mac.

"And there you have it," Lenora says, clapping her hands with finality. "The first Objective will be a foot race, and the last person to finish will be eliminated—as will his or her teammates." She pauses for the hushed whispers that ripple through the crowd. "So it may behoove you to watch your partners' backs on this trip."

Pike swallows deeply, eyes darting from waif to waif.

"That said, don't get too attached. Between each Objective teams will be switched up, and, in some cases, it'll be every player for him- or herself.

"Now, you've got a little while to get to know your new colleagues, so grab some lunch and some shade, and I'll meet you back here at sixteen-hundred hours to kick it all off." Lenora flashes her smile again and departs with squishing hips.

OBJECTIVE ONE

THE RACE

MAC

TYING THE BLACK BANDANNA over her pigtails, Mac gave her teammates a good looking over. It might be too soon to tell, but she suspected she'd hit the jackpot. She'd already been confident in her own chances in the upcoming race challenge, and now any reservations she'd had about her would-be partners had flown out the window with a little luck of the draw.

Ian, she read on the first man's name tag. He wound his team color around the band of his fedora without taking it off. He was just shy of six feet, she guessed. Slender, and dressed more for an evening at a Prohibition-era speakeasy than a wilderness excursion. Still, he looked youngish and sturdyish and his cool, watchful expression suggested he might just be the sharpest tack in the entire campsite. He was goddamned good-looking as well, and Mac bet he knew it. He caught her eye with one of his Listerine-blue ones and winked, pure evil. He wandered off toward the tables where the crew was setting up a buffet lunch.

Mac frowned at his back and took a seat on a log beside the other man, the one she'd wanted to throw onto the dirt and devour the second she'd seen him. Sweet Christ. She was mired in sex withdrawal and he was a syringe of something hard, ready to send her into one damn beautiful relapse.

"Daisey," she said, reading his name tag. She looked up at his drill-sergeant face, trying to square it with the moniker.

"Mac," he read, and gave her a curt nod of his just-about-shaved head.

"I think I won the teammate lottery," she said, appraising him. *Well* over six feet, and built like a man's idea of manliness. Hers too. "I bet you'll do very nicely."

"I come in handy." There was a slow, thoughtful Southern twang in the words, and Mac had to fend off an urge to hump his leg. Her journey had started a week ago when she'd left New Mexico, and this was the farthest she'd ever traveled in her life. She was deep in adventure mode and Daisey looked like the personification of Alaska, rough and huge and uncivilized. Yet another new challenge she'd gladly tackle, no monetary motivation necessary.

Ian swaggered back to them, stripping the meat off a barbecued rib. With red sauce smearing his pale fingers he had the air of a gentleman axe-murderer, the kind a girl might happily follow down a dark alley. He took a seat on the ground as Mac turned back to Daisey.

"What did you do to earn those?" she asked, giving his nearest muscly arm a poke.

"Day job. Used to be a marine 'til I got kicked out."

"For what?" Mac asked.

"I got a problem with authority," he said, sounding pleased about this.

"So what do you do now?"

"Underwater welder," Daisey said. "Most dangerous occupation on the planet."

Ian swallowed and broke his silence. "Sounds like a job for a man with something tae prove." He aimed his eyes pointedly at Daisey's crotch. "Or something tae compensate for."

Daisey's brows shot up like a rifle being cocked, and Mac did a double-take at Ian's Scottish accent.

"Let's play nice, boys. Teammates, remember?" She stood before either of the men could, clapping her hands to her thighs. "Who wants a soda?"

"I fancy a beer." Ian nodded languidly to the cans arranged in an ice-filled tub by the nearest buffet table.

Not to be out-testosteroned, Daisey nodded. "Make it two."

"We need to be ready to race in a couple hours, kids," Mac said, hoping the years of training her brothers had given her in man-corralling would prove sufficient this afternoon. "Let's stick with soda, how about that?"

Ian gave her a pitying look. He stood and skirted her to grab two beers from the cooler, tossing one to Daisey. Mac wasn't about to wreck the truce inherent in the gesture.

"I bet you just both failed some little behavioral psycho-whatever test," she said, deciding to be amused.

"And I bet you're dying tae join us." Ian sat and leaned back, sounding as if he meant more than just drinking with the two of them. He cracked the can and took a deep draught.

Mac squinted up at the midday sun. "You're right, actually." She went to the catering table and grabbed herself a beer, sitting to make a triangle with Ian and Daisey. "Fuck the cameras." She enjoyed the cold prickle of the liquid as it slid down her throat. "If you two get sloshed and wreck this for me, I'll be damned if I'm going to lose *and* be sober for it."

"Atta girl." Daisey leaned over to tap his can against hers and Mac took a long, thorough gander at his bare arm, wanting to sink her teeth in like an amorous pit bull and never let go.

"So, Mac," Ian said, catching her off guard again with his heavy brogue. "What's that short for, eh? MacDonald? MacClure? MacKenzie?"

"You can guess for an hour and you'll never get it." She took another drink.

"MacCarthy? MacGrath?"

"Machiniak," she said.

"Polack," Daisey said, not quite an insult but not far off.

She rolled her eyes. "And what sort of a name's *Daisey*, anyway?"

"Irish."

"American," Ian corrected, definitely an insult.

"Watch yourself, pretty boy." Daisey's eyes flicked to Ian's hat, his tweed blazer, his black dress shoes.

"A Polack, a Scotsman and a Yank-Mick walk into a social experiment," Mac said, hoping to diffuse the manly tensions—clearly her role in this team. "So what do *you* do, Ian?"

"I smoke a hell of a lot," he said, pulling a metal case out of his breast pocket. "You mind?"

"Kind of."

He nodded, getting to his feet and wandering a few paces toward the woods to light up.

"Cute," Daisey said, implying the opposite. He turned to Mac. "What about you? What do you do?"

"I run an outdoor adventure company with my three older brothers, in New Mexico," she said with a smile. "Rafting, hiking, camping, climbing, all that stuff."

"Hunting?"

"Nope. But it looks like you've got us covered on that count," she said, taking a sip and pointing with her pinkie at Daisey's knife.

He nodded back. "There's more where that came from."

"Where you from?"

"Outside Biloxi."

Ah. Mac thought she ought to send the state of Mississippi a thank-you note for his accent. "And you live there now?"

"Between jobs, yeah. I do a lot of welding on rigs in the Gulf. Go home for a week every couple months."

"Got a woman willing to put up with that schedule?" Mac asked, shameless.

"Even if I did, she'd never stick around for the rest of my bullshit." He finished off his beer and crushed the can in his fist. "What about you? Your brothers let any guys within ten yards of you?"

"Not lately." She gave him a conspiring look as Ian returned, fragrant as an ashtray. "Jesus, you smoke Marlboro Extra Tars or something?"

"I roll my own," he said, distracted as he scanned the other teams. "We putting bets on the losers?" He glanced back at Daisey and Mac. "Got my dosh on Fu Manchu and the bulimia twins." He nodded to the Asian guy named Pike whom Mac had spoken with earlier. His two female teammates combined probably weighed less than Daisey.

"Well, it won't be us that goes down first." Daisey pointed at Mac. "She runs an outdoorsy thing with her brothers," he told Ian. "And I'm ex-military. You're our weak link, cancer-boy, and I still think we've got all these yahoos beat. There's our biggest threat." He nodded toward the red-bandannaed group on the far side of the site, two guys and a girl, all college-aged, all fit and looking capable of giving Mac's team a run for its money.

Ian nodded, eyes narrowing.

Mac looked around. "My ego's not riding on this, but I can't say I've got much faith in those three." She pointed to the flawless thirty-something blonde woman with the camera slung around her neck. She was flanked by a fair-haired man who looked remarkably like an accountant, plus a more likely competitor—the wiry African guy named Greg. "I give that woman until the bugs start biting," Mac said. "Who wears lipstick on a wilderness expedition?"

Daisey smiled widely and crossed his powerful arms. "Beats me, but I'll tell you where she can leave it. And it ain't the rim of a coffee cup."

Mac rolled her eyes. Ian just smirked, seeming focused somewhere outside their trio, outside the entire group. Seeming like a viewer, not a participant.

Mac turned to him. "I caught you smiling like that when that Lenora chick said there was an alternate. Was that you?"

He nodded.

"How come you look so smug?"

"See that lass?" He pointed across the clearing to the funkily dressed girl with dark, curly hair and the weird pale eyes.

"Yeah. I think her name's Leah."

"Her bloke was meant tae be here too," Ian said.

That explained her conspicuous lack of supplies and orphaned expression. "How do you know that?"

"I ran intae him at a petrol station, hour before the deadline. White as a sheet. Said he could'nae go through with it. Said his lassie flew in separate, she was counting on him, but he did'nae want tae go."

"But why wouldn't he at least show up and give her whatever stuff he brought for the trip?" Mac asked. Daisey echoed her with a "Yeah." "Or at least *tell* her. Nobody's here against their will."

"Poor sod ran intae some car trouble," Ian said, eyes glittering. "Guess he never made it. Cannae complain, personally. Pure dead brilliant, that luck."

Mac's skin crawled. "Yeah, what a fantastic stroke of good fortune."

Daisey glanced between them, hard to read.

Mac gave Ian a final cold glare before standing up, and he met her venom with a tight, lip-biting smile. She strode across the campsite to where Leah and Pike and the red-haired girl stood, making small talk.

"Hi," she said, looking between them.

"Hey," Pike offered, cautious.

"Don't worry, I'm not trying to infiltrate you," she said affably. "Could I borrow Leah for a second?" Mac gave them all her finest cheesy, disarming grin.

Leah followed her to a spot by the fire pit and Mac could *feel* Ian's attention on them. Good. Let him sweat…if he was capable of such a human function.

"I don't mean to be nosy, but you look like someone who didn't plan on being here alone."

Leah's amber eyes widened. "Yeah. My boyfriend was supposed to be here. The crew said he called right after the deadline, that his car broke down, but I doubt it." Her voice turned bitter. "He's been acting weird since last week about the whole thing."

"That sucks. Let me guess—he was bringing the gear?"

Leah nodded. "He drove up, I flew. He had our stuff and all my outdoor clothes. And nobody's allowed in now that the experiment's started. Awesome." She held out her arms to showcase her woefully inappropriate wardrobe. "And all this was his idea in the first place."

"Men can be real shits." Mac's gaze snapped reflexively to Ian. "Listen, I don't have a ton to offer but I'm sure I could lend you a shirt or two, and I've got an extra canteen."

Leah looked about ready to give her a kidney in return. "Seriously? Just a shirt would be amazing. I look like a moron." She plucked miserably at her stylish top. "At least I wore flats."

Mac glanced down at Leah's espadrilles and winced with sympathy blisters. "Follow me. We'll see what I can spare."

She led Leah back to her team's corner and Mac had to hand it to Ian—if he was worried that she'd said anything about him, she couldn't read it on his face.

Daisey gave the two women a skeptical look. "No fraternizing with the enemy."

Mac brushed past him. "Put it back in your pants, soldier." She rooted through her frame pack and found a couple of shirts and a pair of wool socks and a spare jog-bra for Leah, plus her extra water jug.

"You are a *lifesaver*," Leah muttered, hugging the supplies to her chest. "I owe you so bad. Let me know if you need anything. Not that I've got much to offer."

"Just be glad you're not the ref in a dick-measuring contest," Mac said loudly, casting a glare at her colleagues.

Leah laughed, the smile turning her pretty face from haunted to warm in an instant. She thanked Mac again and went back to her team.

Daisey rounded on Mac. "What the fuck was that?"

"It's called human decency."

"No, it's called giving the competition a leg up," he said, and as much as Mac wanted to smack him, she wanted to knock him down and molest him far worse.

She stared condemningly at Ian. "Well, my best guess is that our team already screwed her, big-time."

"I have'nae screwed anyone yet," he said innocently, then flashed his unreal eyes up and down Mac's body. "But I'm taking reservations—"

"So the least we can do is help her," Mac concluded, talking over him.

Daisey shook his head, baffled. "This ain't a Girl Scout jamboree. This is *Lord of the Flies*."

Ian nodded his agreement. "Sympathy's as good tae you out here as sunstroke. Best you start thinking of everyone as the enemy."

"Including you two?" she asked.

Ian cracked a grin. "You're damn straight."

LEAH

THE BORROWED ATHLETIC BRA wasn't a perfect fit, but it beat running around in the woods with her boobs bouncing every which way. Leah rejoined her team as they were getting lunch. She put on her best game face, swallowing a truckload of fear and anger and heartache and focusing on the task at hand.

"That's an improvement," the Asian guy named Pike said, pointing a serving spoon at the tee shirt she'd changed into. Also tight, but she wasn't about to complain.

Leah nodded. "That was really cool of her."

Pike glanced over to Mac and her teammates. "Yeah. What happened to your stuff? Didn't you bring clothes or supplies?"

She felt tears boiling up but clamped a lid over the urge. "It's a long story."

Pike took her hint and dropped the subject.

Marissa, the third member of the Blue Team, poked through an aluminum tray of rice and beans. "God, do you think all the food's going to be like this?"

Pike's expression was cagey. "I think the cuisine might be the least of your worries."

"Where do you think we'll sleep?"

He shrugged.

Leah smiled at the man across the buffet table who surrendered a pair of tongs they'd both made a grab for. Kind brown eyes, soft features, sad smile. She heaped three ears of corn onto her plate, not spoiled for vegetarian choices at this banquet. "I was picturing tents," she offered.

"*Tents?* Oh *God.*" Marissa tossed her red hair.

Pike's irritation broke through his cool crust. "What did you think you signed up for? *The Real World, Frontier Alaska?*"

"The ad thing said it was a behavioral experiment. I thought we'd be in a lab. Or like, at a college."

"It said, 'come prepared for rigorous outdoor activity'," Leah quoted, immediately feeling stupid since none of the hiking gear she'd carefully selected was here to back up her bitchy tone.

Pike went quiet, seeming uneasy. He took his food and wandered away to sit on a bench near the fire pit. Leah hurried after him, leaving Marissa to sigh over the fare.

"We're screwed, aren't we?" she asked in a loud whisper, sitting beside him.

Pike nodded, glancing back at their teammate. "Likely." His deep voice belonged to a man quite a few inches and pounds bigger than him. "What were you going to spend *your* grand prize money on?"

"I dunno. Student loans, probably. It wasn't even my idea to be here. What about you? What did you want the money for?"

"I was going to pay off my mom's mortgage, for starters," he said.

"That's sweet."

Pike shook his head. "More like necessary. You ever had a Korean mother?"

She smiled. "No, that's the one ethnicity I'm not."

"Well, they expect a lot."

"Can I ask how old you are?"

"Thirty-one," Pike said. "What are you, like nineteen?"

She snorted. "Twenty-three, thank you. So…any guesses about who'll win?"

His black eyes darted around, making an inventory. "A few. But I'm withholding my judgment until we know what these people's definition of a 'race' is. Given that intro, I'll bet it's theatrical." He dug into his potato salad.

"I bet it's a woman who wins," Leah said, smiling smugly but not really meaning it. She just wanted the banter to keep going so she could ignore how terrified she was. The fact that their team seemed doomed to an early failure was actually a bit of a relief.

"Could be a girl," Pike said. "The one who gave you the clothes— she seems up to it, if she can survive her teammates."

"Mac," Leah said.

"Right, Mac."

Marissa finally joined them, looking predictably petulant. "What are you guys talking about?"

"The weather," Leah said. She could practically feel the storm clouds rolling in now.

CHLOE

PIECE OF CAKE.

Chloe tapped her chicken leg against the sturdy paper plate, calculating. She remembered her high school track coach's favorite adage. "Don't burn all your fuel in the first lap. You win a race with your brain, *then* your body."

Too right. Her team might not finish first in the initial challenge, but they wouldn't lose. She just had to keep pace until the field narrowed and she was relying solely on the one person who'd never let her down—herself.

At her side, the Australian named Rory looked close to tears.

She nudged him with her elbow. "You okay?"

When he spoke, his voice was as soft and sincere as his face. "Oh yeah. Just ready to get started. I can't stand all this not knowing."

He sounded a lot calmer than Chloe had expected. "You look anxious."

"I always look that way," he said, offering a sheepish grin. "People are always asking me if my dog died or something."

Greg, the lanky black man, approached with a tower of three soda cans stacked between his palms.

Rory accepted the center one. "Cheers."

"No thanks," Chloe said. Last thing she needed was a sugar crash when the race began, and that could be any minute now.

"I'm surprised they're letting you bring the camera," Rory said, nodding at the battle-weary Nikon resting against her ribs, "considering the Bible-sized stack of waivers they made us sign. It gave me the impression they wanted us all to keep mum about this thing."

"They said we could bring anything we could carry."

Rory frowned. "I wonder if anyone brought guns." She caught his pale brown gaze drifting to the florally named meathead across the way with the knife strapped to his hip.

"It is just a friendly competition," Greg said in his heavy African accent. "I doubt anyone would bring firearms."

"You know, I bet we're the only American-free team," Chloe said, looking between them. "I'm Canadian. Rory, you're Australian. Greg, what are you?"

He grinned broadly. "I am American actually, as of six years ago. Though I grew up in Zimbabwe. And he's not Australian." He pointed with his can at Rory, who nodded.

"Cheers for that."

"I have watched enough cricket in my fifty-one years to know a Canterbury man when I hear one," Greg said with a friendly laugh.

Rory's smile brightened his hangdog expression.

"You don't sound English to me," Chloe said.

Rory shook his head. "I'm not. I'm from New Zealand."

"You know how to swing a bat?" Greg asked.

Chloe tuned out as they began to talk about cricket. She finished her food and set the plate aside, wiping her fingers on her pants and lifting her camera. She aimed the lens around the site.

She targeted Daisey first, activating the zoom to scrutinize his pack while pondering Rory's comment about guns. There'd been no metal detectors or bag searches when they'd checked in with the crew, so it was possible…and intriguing. She made a mental note to include Daisey in her list of potential allies. They'd spoken earlier at length. Former marine, built like a tank and salivating to get between her legs. A handy combination. A disgusting thought, though—Chloe wore the pants in the bedroom, and she wasn't interested in wrestling that beast for them.

Still, leverage was leverage, and control was sacred. She couldn't control the cancer eating away at her mother back home, but if she kept this game and these strangers under her thumb, she could damn well afford to give it a good fight.

The jury was out on the fellow next to Daisey, the pale guy with the hat and the stubble. His walk said he owned the place, but posturing didn't mean a thing without some hard assets to back it up. Plus he smoked like a chimney, and no man did that if he wasn't secretly a nervous wreck.

The Bobbsey Triplets, as she'd nicknamed the team of younger kids, had the bodies but not the bloodlust. They were too happy. Too excited. Looked too prepared to blow the grand prize on a binge-drinking trip to Cancun.

The one who really interested Chloe was Pike. He had the air of a man playing chess, or better still, a robot programmed for the job. And he'd brought a specialized case. Some kind of equipment. Maybe something navigational, or for communication. Hell, maybe firearms. The man with the least to say probably had the most to hide, and she hoped he was hiding something valuable. Something she could cash in on. Though thanks to his teammates, chances didn't look great that Pike would make it far enough in the competition to be of use. Shame.

"Okay, folks!" The black woman with the ridiculous jodhpurs, Lenora, strode down the hill from the tented area the crew occupied. Chloe lowered her camera.

"It's time to get started! The instructions for this first Objective are simple. All three of your team members need to reach the bonfire we've set up, fifteen miles from here."

Chloe grinned down at her freshly broken-in hiking boots.

Lenora continued. "You don't have to make it there as a group necessarily, but the person who's last to arrive and be counted...? Your entire team will be eliminated. Each team will receive a map and a compass, and each individual will be issued an emergency alert button with a GPS tag. You get lost or badly hurt, you push the button. You and your team will be eliminated, but the safety crew will find you and get you back in one piece, and I think we'll all agree that's more important than the money. Understood?"

The group of twelve nodded and murmured their collective agreement, though Chloe would sooner compete with a broken arm than admit defeat and push that stupid button.

"Each team please appoint a member to be the navigator. Those folks, head to the tent to collect your maps and compasses."

Chloe volunteered herself immediately. No way she was trusting anything important to anybody else's hands. Neither Rory nor Greg put up any resistance. She smiled. Just how she liked her men to behave.

She and the other navigators converged on the crew tent. Among them were Pike, the small, pig-tailed girl named Mac, and a young guy named Javier who looked pumped and ready for a Dartmouth kegger.

Mac's and Pike's compass lanyards were tangled and Chloe heard the former say, "Well, we're off to a smooth start."

"You know anything about orienteering?" Pike asked.

"Only tons. I'm a trained mountaineer. I'll see you at the bonfire," Mac added good-naturedly as she freed her compass.

Chloe grinned. She added Pigtails to her short list of future best friends.

PIKE

"HERE GOES EVERYTHING."

Pike hadn't meant to mutter it quite so loudly, but Leah gave him a commiserating nudge in the side and he returned her smile, if halfheartedly. "Sorry."

She shrugged. "*I'm* sorry. I know I'm the obvious weak link in our group."

Though he was inclined to agree, Pike mustered some polite optimism—not his strong suit. "Anything could happen in fifteen miles."

She nodded solemnly. Pike confirmed their orientation and pocketed the compass.

The map was straightforward enough. It included terrain and elevation and it looked as though this trek was a test of endurance more than strength or climbing ability. Still, his teammates' shoes alone made him feel about as hopeful as a man with no arms signing up for a swim meet. Life had repeatedly taught him it was wise—if a bit depressing—to expect the worst. It kept one prepared and eliminated the possibility of disappointment.

"We better stay close," he said to Leah and Marissa.

"Agreed. I get lost almost daily on the subway," Leah said. "Direction is not my strong suit."

Around the camp, the other teams were gearing up. Pike's eyes flicked to the Black group, to Mac. He frowned, sad he'd likely never get a chance to be on her team for one of these crazy trials. If they were allowed to stick around for a meal after they lost, he'd try to at least talk to her a little more. Maybe get her number. The gigantic dude at her side was tightening the straps of his pack. The pale Scottish guy was spit-shining his shoes. Talk about priorities.

Lenora reappeared and everyone perked up, alert.

"It looks like we're ready to get started. When you reach the bonfire, be sure to collect a token from the crew member stationed there. That will be your proof that you completed the Objective. All right? Any questions?"

"Is there a time limit?" someone shouted.

"No time limit, but I suggest you complete the race before dark if you didn't pack a flashlight. Luckily that won't be until about twenty-three-hundred hours, which gives you all nearly seven hours. Plenty of time. Anything else? No? Excellent." Lenora pulled a starter pistol from her belt and aimed it at the sky.

With a pop, they were off.

The first fifteen minutes were a mess, everyone clumped together in one current. The crowd eventually thinned as paces leveled out.

Teams were sticking together for now, and that meant the slowest people set the speed for their groups. In the Blue Team's case, that was Marissa.

Pike felt as if he were reliving every bad date he'd ever been on, guerilla-style. Pouting, complaining, freaking out, all piled on top of a hike through the Alaskan wilderness. He slapped at the midsummer mosquitoes feasting on his sweat-sticky neck and arms, an inadequate outlet for his angst. At least they didn't have to worry about scaring a bear; Marissa's constant whining announced their presence at least once a minute. Leah rolled her eyes so frequently Pike thought she must be developing a tic.

"Hey, guys."

Pike looked to his left an hour into the race to find Mac trudging toward them. She was smiling as always, a streak of perspiration darkening her tank top. He tried to ignore how good she smelled as she neared.

"What are you doing back here?" he asked.

"I needed a pee break."

"Where are your teammates?" Leah asked.

"They're not much for the whole solidarity thing," Mac said. "Before we even left, Ian traced two copies of the map. They're so confident I think they're just racing each other now."

"What's with him?" Leah asked. "The guy with the hat."

"Ian? You ever read *Othello*?" Mac asked.

"Ages ago."

"Well, he's Iago. I'm sure their entries are right next to each other in the *Encyclopedia of Colossal Assholes*."

"What about Daisey?" Pike asked.

Mac smiled in a way that made his heart sink a little. "He's a sasquatch. But I'm glad he's on my side."

"I'll bet."

"I better get a move on," Mac said. "I'd like to find at least one of them. Who knows how lost they might get in that cloud of testosterone."

"Just follow Ian's smoke signals," Leah said.

Mac grinned. "I'll see you guys at the finish line."

"Yeah, good luck." Pike offered a half-assed smile as she jogged ahead, frame pack bouncing on her shoulders.

"I can't believe they didn't stick together," Marissa said after Mac was out of earshot. "That's so rude. What's the point of splitting up?"

"I'm sure it has its perks," Pike muttered.

The competitors were scattered so far apart he couldn't hear or see signs of any other group. Once Mac disappeared, he glanced at his watch. They could be making *worse* progress, he admitted. If another team got lost, they might actually stand a chance. For all her complaints, Marissa kept marching. Leah, too, though she was limping. Had been since three miles in. Dear God, twelve more to go.

A half hour later, an annoying noise grew behind Pike. Funny how he could handle people screaming in agony but the sound of sniffling drove him up the fucking wall. He turned to fix the offender with a glare but when he saw the tears streaming down Leah's face, the bitchiness drained right out of him.

He slowed until she was walking beside him. "Hey."

She met his eyes with her reddened ones and wiped her cheeks. "Hey."

"Is it your feet?"

She shook her head and forced a smile. "Nah. I know I'm a wuss, but I promise I'm not crying over blisters."

"Oh."

She sighed. "You want me to tell you? It's pretty pathetic."

"Sure," he lied, opting for diplomacy. "I mean, what else are we going to do on this death march?"

"My boyfriend was supposed to be here, but he didn't show. He's the reason that Ian guy's here, as an alternate. I came here for *him* and he ditched me."

"So you're angry?"

She laughed and gave him a patronizing look. "You're a genius, Pike."

"Are you going to dump him? Here." He dug a clean napkin out of his pocket and handed it to her. She honked her nose into it.

"Oh yes. You're looking at a bona fide long-distance, one-sided breakup." She dabbed at her nose. "Dignified, huh?"

"My best friend back home is a girl who cries when the store is out of her brand of soap. You're cool. Cry all you want."

"Thank you. I will."

Pike nodded and spent an uncomfortable moment debating whether or not he was supposed to hug this stranger. He settled for an awkward and probably inadequate clap on her arm.

"Thanks."

"Sorry," he said. "You know, on behalf of my gender."

"Did they put you in charge of heading up the complaints department? That must be a thankless job."

Pike nodded and distance formed between them, emotional first, then physical. He tried to keep himself triangulated between Leah and Marissa, the meat in a petulant sandwich.

Left, right, left.

He slapped another bug, though in truth Leah troubled him far worse—open displays of weakness always grated on his nerves. Strength had nothing to do with size or muscles or one's willingness to take or throw a punch. It was all about self-control. Emotional control. The lack of that was more distressing than normal, coming from this woman. Lost, a bit abandoned, rattling around in this group with her role unclear. Pike had spent his entire life until his late twenties being that person, bundled in uncertainty like a thick, itchy sweater. Leah was the sniffling, limping definition of *uncertain*, and that old sensation unnerved Pike worse than just about anything.

He made a decision to quit wishing he knew where everyone stood and began assigning roles. In their threesome he was the obvious leader—oldest and most prepared. Settling into that title, he decided to see Leah as a charge instead of a burden. He shifted his course to walk next to her.

"So," he said, breaking a long silence. "What are you, anyhow? You know, like ethnically?"

She looked to him and smiled weakly. "Bit of everything. Dominican and Mexican and Jewish and Irish. And Italian, I think."

"Wow."

She nodded and turned her gaze back to the ground. "Spicy."

Pike held his tongue, thinking that aside from her exterior—her skin and hair and clothes—she smacked of middle-American blandness.

"I'm adopted," she added, addressing Pike's unasked question. "Right when I was born. But I know a whole bunch about my birth mom's history, and a tiny bit about my dad's. The town I grew up in was like ninety-nine-point-nine-percent white, plus me and, like, one Indian family."

"Black sheep?"

She laughed. "Try paisley sheep. But it wasn't that bad. Most people didn't make a thing about it."

"Huh."

She squinted at his face. "Are you all Korean?"

"Nah, only half." Only enough that he'd spent his childhood looking too Asian to ever be accepted by the white kids, his name too white to qualify him as one of the Korean kids. He'd entered young adulthood as a semi-recovered screwup, a maladjusted scholarship kid surrounded by middle-class hyperachievers. Striving to be one thing, but still with the mistakes of his youth following him around like a nasty odor. Even the city he'd grown up in no longer knew its own identity, confident only in the fact that its time had come and gone.

At twenty-eight Pike had finally found someplace he fit, assigned a rank and title and a clear description of who he was expected to be. Sweetest fucking feeling in the world, the relief of fitting somewhere, being someone, knowing his place.

He cleared his throat. "You live in New York City now, right?" he asked Leah. "Anybody can blend in there."

"I guess. Still, it's pretty easy to feel like a nobody in a place that huge."

Pike nodded, knowing that sensation too. He felt it here in this experiment, uncertain if he'd prove a strong competitor or a complete joke. "Give it some time," he told Leah. "You'll figure it out."

"Yeah."

They fell silent once more. His mind glazed over as the hike wore on. Four and a half hours in, Leah was still limping dutifully along, tears long gone. Pike felt blisters forming inside the fist wrapped around the handle of his case. Mercifully, Marissa had lost the will to whine back around mile ten.

So much for his dream of another team getting mixed up—the route was practically a straight shot. Rocks and fallen branches and small creeks interrupted the landscape, but they were nothing. Must be a wheat-and-chaff sort of test. Pike could feel himself being sifted right out of the running. At least they must be within striking distance of the end by—

A scream cut through the air.

"Oh my." Leah's yellowy cat eyes scanned the surrounds. "It's a girl."

Pike cupped his hands around his mouth and bellowed, "WHO WAS THAT?"

A man's voice answered, maybe a quarter mile away. "OVER HERE!"

Pike veered to the left and his teammates followed. After a couple of minutes he could see colors, the clothes of the team full of college kids. Two were on the ground, a girl and a guy. Pike saw red, and not just from their bandannas.

He jogged over. "Shit, she okay?"

She wasn't, he could tell. The girl had a huge gash on her calf and was bleeding fast. Too fast to wait around for the safety crew, even.

"She tripped and cut herself open on a rock," one of her teammates said. He had his hands clamped over her wound.

"Did you push your button for help?" Leah asked.

"No!" the girl blurted. "I'll be okay. I just need it to stop frigging bleeding."

Pike knelt and opened his case, rooting through his supplies. "Amanda, right?"

She nodded.

"Let me get in there."

The guy holding her leg let Pike apply a tourniquet above the gash. She moaned.

"Sorry, it's got to be tight."

"Does anybody else think she needs to just push the damn button?" Leah asked.

"You two just go on ahead, okay?" Pike was amazed this day could actually be getting crappier. He handed Leah the map and compass. "I'll catch up. Just go."

She gave him a skeptical look but turned back to the trail. Pike heard Marissa mutter, "Bitch needs to push her goddamn button," as they walked away.

The girl whimpered. Pike wasn't used to his patients complaining over flesh wounds and it made him anxious. Then again, it was nice to treat someone who hadn't just had a limb blown off.

"You'll be okay. I just have to close you up now."

"*What?*"

"Calm down, I don't mean stitches. Not here, anyhow." He wrapped her leg tight in gauze, then duct tape—he'd never found a better fix out in the field.

"Try to stand up."

He and her nearest teammate each took an elbow.

Pike eyed her carefully as she tested her leg. She didn't look like any soldier he'd known, but she had that glint in her eye that he knew all too well. "You won't quit, will you?"

She shook her head.

He turned to her partners. "Listen, you guys—just go. I've got the kit, I'll look after her. Go up ahead and tell the crew she'll need medical attention when we get there. I promise I'll get her there safe."

The guy now covered in her blood gave Pike a cold look. "One of us should stay with her."

"You don't seriously think I'm going to sabotage her, do you?" Jesus, what was wrong with these people?

"I'm just saying, it's probably a good idea."

"Fine," Pike said. "Knock yourself out." He got Amanda to wrap her arm around his neck and they began to limp forward together. The Hispanic guy, Javier, jogged on ahead and the other remained, trailing behind a few paces.

They'd only been walking a couple minutes when another body came crashing through the foliage from farther along the trail. Mac again. Pike's heart gave a little murmur.

"Oh man. I knew that scream was no good. You guys okay?" Mac's eyes flicked from the girl's leg to Pike's bloody hands. "Did she push her button—"

"No!" Amanda said.

"We're cool. Just slow." Pike considered smiling at Mac but decided it wasn't worth the energy to fake cheerfulness at this point. "Don't worry."

"Nothing I can do?" she asked.

He shook his head. "We're pretty near the end, right?"

"Three miles, I think? Maybe less."

"Go on," he said, nodding up the hill. "We're cool."

Mac hesitated then shrugged. "I'll see you up there."

"See you." Pike sighed. Left, right, left.

Thirty minutes later, the only sight that could have made Pike's day any worse appeared.

"Oi!" Ian shouted, jogging down the incline toward them, slipping something yellow into his pocket. Daisey was hot on his heels.

"What?" Pike spat.

"Hate tae be the bearer of bad news, but your red-haired lassie, she threw in the towel."

"Marissa? Seriously?"

"Seriously?" Amanda echoed, perking up against Pike's shoulder.

"Oh man, that is *sweet*," the Red Team dude behind them said, and Pike heard him clap his hands in cocky triumph.

Ian nodded. "Pushed her button for the rescue crew, I heard. Said she was dehydrated or something. So you're done. Sorry."

"I'm sure you are. Here to rub it in?" Pike looked between Ian and Daisey.

Daisey shook his head. "He is, maybe. I just thought I'd help. We got nothin' to lose now, thanks to your girl. I'll take the cargo," he said, nodding to Amanda. "I'll be faster."

Pike sighed. "Fine. Knock yourself out. Just take it slow, she's lost a lot of blood."

Daisey didn't offer a shoulder—he hoisted the girl bodily into his arms. Pike felt his balls wither and drop off.

"Go on ahead," Daisey said, probably draped in close to two hundred pounds between the girl and his pack, but looking unburdened. "I've got her."

"Here." Ian held a piece of paper out to Pike. "We made an extra map."

Pike frowned at it. "Is this like a fake or something, to get me lost?"

"What'd be the point of that?" Ian asked. "You're already out."

"Yeah, right." Pike took it but didn't plan on using it. He crumpled the map and thrust it into his pocket. He had a pretty good sense of where to go now, and the bonfire smoke in the distance was visible through the thinner sections of canopy.

"I'll see you," he said coldly to the two men, and walked on ahead.

"Hell," Ian said. "I'll walk with you."

"Great." Pike made sure his tone conveyed his extreme lack of interest.

"So that's what's in the mystery case, eh? You a doctor?"

"A medic, yeah."

"Army then?" Ian asked beadily.

Pike nodded.

"Very intriguin'."

Pike cast him an openly distrustful look.

"Dun'nae be like that. I'm jest being friendly."

"No offense," Pike said, "but you don't strike me as a helpful guy."

"Well, you're done, mate. I've no reason tae feck with you. Of everyone here, you and your girls are the only folks I got nothing tae worry for, right?"

"Shouldn't you be busy kissing the asses of the people who can still help you, then?"

"Arse-kissing ain't my scene," Ian said.

Pike let the conversation slide. Ian walked a few steps ahead, setting the route. Pike kept his eyes on the smoke, checking that he wasn't being led astray. But in ten minutes' time, he spotted the fire and the clothing of the players who'd finished, fifty yards up the hill.

"See? I told you I was'nae playing Pied Piper with you." Ian smiled over his shoulder in a self-satisfied way, revealing a pair of sharp canine teeth. "Let's finish this, eh?"

"PIKE!" The shout came from up the hill. He squinted to make out Leah's borrowed red shirt, her arms beckoning him with frantic sweeps.

Ian's eyebrows rose innocently. "I hope no one's hurt."

"PIKE! HURRY *UP!*"

He couldn't argue with a woman when she was screaming like that.

He sprinted, dodging roots and rocks and branches, his chest heaving by the time he reached the summit, visions of fresh medical emergencies flashing through his mind. Then Leah took his breath away entirely. She was grinning.

"Come on! Hurry!" She grabbed his wrist and yanked him forward, drawing him through the competitors sipping bottled drinks and eating off paper plates. Several people clapped as he passed by. As if he needed sarcasm on top of the day he'd had.

"Yeah, thanks." He shot the peanut gallery a glare then looked to Leah. "Why are you smiling?"

She dropped his wrist but hurried on. "Why wouldn't I be?"

"Because we're done."

"I know! So why aren't *you* smiling?"

"Because I wanted to win!" he said, slowing to a normal pace.

"Jeez, Pike, I know third's not great, but at least we're not out. What happened to the girl you—"

"Whoa, what? We lost, didn't we? Didn't Marissa quit?"

Leah slowed to stare at him. "What? No. We finished together. Almost an hour ago. She's right there." She pointed to the edge of the clearing, where Marissa was drinking a soda and talking to the spindly African dude.

Pike stopped completely. "That Ian guy said we were out. And Daisey."

"Well, they're wrong. Come on—you have to get a tag to prove you made it."

Pike gave up trying to solve the mystery. He followed Leah to the crew table, where a khaki-clad staff member handed him a yellow plastic token, like a poker chip.

"Woo!" Leah did a triumphant dance, blisters forgotten. "I can't believe it!"

Pike shook his head, feeling drugged. "Me neither. I have to go find Ian."

He threaded back through the people and trees and spotted Ian popping a beer tab, staring out into the woods.

"Hey!" Pike's fist tightened, though he'd suppress his urge to punch Ian until he could pinpoint exactly what the guy had done to deserve it.

"All right there, Hippocrates? See you got your golden ticket." Ian pointed his can at the yellow chip in Pike's hand and smiled broadly.

"What the fuck, dude? Why'd you tell me my team lost?"

"So you'd finish, mate." Ian slid a cigarette from behind his ear and tucked it between his lips.

"You better start making sense, because I am *all* out of patience for you and your fucking riddles."

Ian lit up and took a deep drag, jetting the smoke off to the side. "What d'you think would have happened when you got tae the top of this hill with that lass draped on your arm, eh? I'll tell you. Her two teammates would have come down on you hard and whisked her off tae the finish line, thinking you were still a threat." Ian ashed his butt in the direction of the crew. "And you'd have let them, because you dun'nae want this bad enough tae stop them. Jest like you did'nae want it bad enough tae make her use that bloody rescue button even after you closed her up."

Pike gave him a long, searching look.

"And because you've got two weak links on your team who dun'nae even want tae be here. You're a medic. You've got mercy. And it makes you soft." Ian smiled again.

"That's only your opinion," Pike said coldly, not wanting to analyze himself deeply enough to find out if Ian was right.

"Aye, and it's true. I know. Got a brother jest like you."

"So what's your thug Daisey going to do? Dump her in the woods so he can finish ahead of her?"

"Nae need," Ian said. "We all finished ages ago. Fairst. Me and him went back for you when Mac turned up and said what was going on down there. You and the lassie you helped and her mate, you were the last ones."

"Great, so you won. What do you care if I get eliminated or not?"

"Your team's rubbish." Ian shrugged. "No offense tae you."

"None taken."

"The others—the injured girl and her lads, they're good. Strong. Maybe clever, maybe nae. But I'd rather be up against you three than them, you follow?"

Pike shook his head, incredulous. He gave Ian a deadly look straight in his creepy-ass eyes before turning away. "You care *way* too much about this." He stalked off in the other direction, gulping fresh air, face burning with a hundred emotions, none of which he wanted anyone witnessing. Least of all this jackass.

Behind him came Ian's shout. "Oi! You're welcome!"

Pike clenched his fists and the yellow plastic bit into his blistered palm. He decided right then he wouldn't drop out of this contest until he watched that asshole go down, hard.

MAC

SHE SHOULD HAVE BEEN TIRED. Five hours of hiking after an early start, pushing ten p.m. now—no matter what the Alaskan sun suggested—and a couple beers in her belly. But Mac was as keyed up as a kid on Christmas Eve.

Their team's reward was a good one. Since Daisey had finished first, they'd be sleeping in the best digs available for the night—a fully equipped cabin, complete with a hot tub and real beds. The other two remaining teams were stuck in tents, and rain didn't look beyond the realm of possibility.

Daisy had earned himself an extra prize. He got to pick his two teammates for the next day's challenge, whatever that would be. Gym class all over again. Mac was confident he'd keep her around. She had a lot to offer. More than he probably realized... She'd have to have a little *chat* with him about that this evening.

The White Team had finished the race together, Daisey had told her, a half-hour behind him. Chloe, the calculating blonde, was fitter than Mac had guessed, and she apparently didn't give a shit about getting sweaty or bug-bitten. Ian and his smoke-addled lungs had arrived twenty minutes behind them, and a half-hour ahead of Mac, who'd doubled back when she'd heard the scream. They hadn't known there was a prize for the second person to finish. Chloe had just happened to be the first in her group to grab her yellow token, but now she had dibs on the folks left over after Daisey finished his selection for the next Objective.

Mac smiled. The way it worked out, Daisey wouldn't get to pick Chloe for his team. Aw, so sad.

Around the time the sun finally decided to set, Mac glanced up to find Pike approaching. She'd noticed him tossing strange looks her way all night, since Daisey had returned with the injured girl and the losing team had gotten a helicopter escort back to Fairbanks. He crossed in front of the bonfire and passed a group talking over the classic rock playing from Greg's crank radio.

"Hey, Pike. Glad to see you're still with us."

"Thanks." His deep voice was weary as he crouched across from the stump Mac was sitting on. Swirling a can of beer, he looked anxious in the residual firelight. "Not celebrating with your teammates?"

"I have to bunk with those thugs tonight. I could use a little breather first."

Pike glanced around. "I need to ask you something."

Mac sat up, curious. "Shoot."

"You seem all right," he said, and met her gaze.

"Thanks." She smiled, confirming that this tough-to-read man had come to flirt. Game on. "You're not so bad yourself. The way you helped that girl was really cool. I thought you were going to get screwed over for it, but I'm glad you didn't."

"Right…well, listen. Were you in on that?"

Her smile drooped. "In on what?"

"On Ian and Daisey's little scheme back there."

She frowned outright. "I honestly don't know what you mean, Pike."

"When you made it up here and told them somebody was hurt, and they went back. What did they say they were up to?"

"We'd all finished by that point. Ian said they ought to go back and see what was going on."

"And that didn't strike you as suspicious?" Pike asked.

She smiled, apologetic but impatient. "Ian's a jackal. I figured he was interested in carrion. Look, Pike, you're going to have to let me in on the joke, because I seriously don't know what you're getting at."

"Ian told me Marissa quit. That my team was disqualified."

"He did? Why?"

"So I wouldn't suspect he and Daisey were up to something when they took over with the injured girl and sent me on my merry way. Because, as he said, if I'd known I was still in the running, I'd have let the other team win."

"Would you have?" Mac asked, still trying to untangle the logic.

"I don't know. Maybe. You didn't know about any of that?"

She shook her head. "Can't say I'm surprised though." She slid the can out of Pike's hand and stole a sip. "Why'd Ian want you guys to win so much?"

"Because he knew we were the weakest team. And because he knew *I knew* neither of my teammates really want to be here."

A bell of comprehension dinged in Mac's head. "I see... We're already getting like that, are we?"

"Looks that way." Pike took his beer back and drained it. He swallowed and Mac noticed the strange texture of the skin on his neck—a big scar, long-since healed but surely a doozie in its day.

"Well, what's done is done. I'm not saying you should send him a thank-you note, but try and be happy you're still in the running." She pulled the bandanna from her hair and toyed with it. "A one-in-nine chance at five hundred grand must be a nice consolation, even if you got tricked into forfeiting your ethics."

He blew out a long breath. "I dunno."

"It's a game, Pike. A psychological one by design. And the stakes are high for some people. Me included, and Ian, clearly. It's going to get ugly. You're a medic or something, right? Have you been in a war zone?"

He nodded.

"Well, I'm sure you've seen worse then. I mean, take a wrong step here and some creep like Ian plays you. At least you didn't get your foot blown off, right?"

"I guess," Pike said. "But I still want to punch the guy."

She shrugged. "Get in line. But you never know… You two might have to work together sometime. And you could do way worse, as teammates go. He's for damn sure got to be a better ally than an enemy."

"Maybe."

"As for me, I have to go drink champagne with the guy now. And I bet he's a *real* gracious winner." She stood and dusted her butt off. "And I know what he did was shitty, lying to you. But I'll tell you what, I'm glad he did. I'd keep you around too." She gave his arm a friendly pat. "I'll see you for breakfast in the morning, if they feed us."

He nodded. "G'night. Good luck with your bunkmates."

"And good luck with the wild animals. I almost envy you campers, out here with just the bears to worry about."

Pike smiled tightly and gave her a limp wave, heading toward the little tent city the crew had erected. She watched his back, wondering if he was wise or doomed, adopting such a surly outlook. Their chat certainly hadn't been the flirtation she'd been hoping for, but no matter. That urge could be satisfied elsewhere.

Mac walked a quarter mile down a lit gravel path to the cabin they'd won for the evening—modern cedar frame, front and back decks. She could see Daisey's back through the picture window, a champagne flute in his hand, body animated as he spoke.

She pushed in the front door and kicked her boots onto the slate floor tiles. Nice. She peeled off her socks and reveled in the cold stone against her brutalized soles.

Daisey's voice boomed from the next room. "Best hurry up, kid. Runnin' out of bubbly fast."

She padded into the den area, a rich person's vision of a hunting lodge. Ian was lounging on a plush leather sofa, a mounted elk's head leering at Mac from above him. He held up his glass in greeting.

She pointed to the doors opposite the window. "Those the bedrooms?"

"Yep," Daisey said. "There's only two. Cute, huh?"

Mac pondered this as she poured the last generous draught of champagne into a glass. She took a sip and gave Daisey an up-and-down so thorough it probably looked sarcastic. "I'll bunk with you."

He raised his eyebrows. "That's a very intriguin' offer, Machiniak, but Ian here already made the team sacrifice. Said he's happy to crash on the couch."

Ian smiled at her, the gesture slippery with self-satisfaction.

She sneered. "How very chivalrous."

"I would'nae want anyone tae feel uncomfortable."

"No, obviously not." She looked back to Daisey. "What's this I heard about a hot tub?"

Daisey nodded toward the hall opposite the front door. "Soak it up while you can."

She raised her brows lewdly, snapping her gaze between his face and the bathroom door.

He laughed. "You afraid of drowning or something?"

"Go on, Mr. Underwater Welder," Ian said. "The lass clearly needs her pipes sealed."

Mac shot him a withering look.

Daisey drained his glass and set it on the coffee table. "C'mon then."

She stuck her tongue out at Ian and followed Daisey down the hall to an expansive, gleaming bathroom. Two rooms, nearly, with a sunken area housing the hot tub, a sleek electric fireplace and a bar.

"Wow."

"I know," Daisey said. "It's like that stupid-ass *Cribs* show."

She ran her hand over the glass shower cubicle and the smooth marble countertop. "This room is probably worth more than my house."

"Hell," Daisey said. "This room is worth more than my hometown."

Mac eyed the toilet. "Oh gross, a bidet. Who lives here, do you think?"

"Someone who thinks they're too good to clean their own asshole. And someone who can afford a helicopter. I didn't see no roads."

"Damn." She wandered down to the hot tub and messed with the settings until it began filling with steaming water. "Oh my feet are going to love this."

Sitting on the rim, she sipped her champagne and flexed her toes in the water. "There's no way I'm ever losing a challenge. The payoff's way too good." She stood to tug off her sweaty tee shirt and drop her hiking pants.

She looked up and found Daisey watching, face neutral. If she'd known she'd be sharing a Jacuzzi with this obscene specimen of manliness, she'd have packed something more alluring than jog bras and cotton boy shorts.

"It's been a long day, Daisey. I'm bug-bitten and blistered and exhausted. At least have the decency to leer and make me feel like a woman."

He laughed. He stripped off as Mac eased herself into the nearly too-hot water. She sat on the contoured wrap-around bench and stared at Daisey's torso. She felt a growl rising in her throat, the sound of a dog gearing up to take down a rack of ribs. Daisey kicked his jeans aside and she drank him in, lingering over the bulge in his underwear.

"Get your eyes off my junk, little girl."

She met his gaze with overdone innocence, batting her lashes. He sank into the water, groaning his satisfaction. Mac hoped she'd hear that noise again before too long.

He stretched his huge arms along the rim of the tub, flicking the water with his fingers. "So tell me 'bout yourself, Machiniak."

"Not much to tell. I live about forty minutes from Santa Fe, in the same house I grew up in. With my three brothers and a sister-in-law."

"Cozy."

"It's a big-ass house. Used to be a ranch. We converted most of the stables into bunks, for the guests who come for the wilderness trips."

"Is it one of those retreats for rich folks?"

She shook her head. "Only if they're the sort of rich folks who like shitting in gen-u-ine outhouses."

"Gotcha."

Mac slid the elastics from her pigtails and shook out her hair. She dunked her head and let the water run down her neck and collarbone. She studied the tattoos on Daisey's arms and chest, a collection of your standard blue-collar and service fare.

"You get first pick tomorrow," she said.

"That I do."

"You ought to consider keeping me handy. I'm the next best thing to military-trained."

"Is that why you're lookin' about two breaths from sucking my dick? This just some ploy to stay on the winning team?"

"Nope. That's just because I'm about two breaths from sucking your dick. Sir," she added.

Daisey laughed, a soul-deep sound. His eyes crinkled at the edges, the lines giving him away as one of the senior members of the relatively young group—late thirties, possibly forty.

"Anyhow," she said. "Any dick-sucking that may take place here tonight is completely unrelated to the competition."

"You watch that dirty mouth of yours," he said, still smiling.

She countered with an evil grin. "I'll be too busy. You'll have to watch it for me."

Daisey sighed. "Little girl, I got at *least* a decade on you. Hell, munchkin, I prob'ly got fourteen inches on you, and another ten you wouldn't know what to do with if you had the chance. You best ditch this hot tub for a cold shower. I ain't lookin' to break anybody's heart."

"Who said it's my heart I'm looking to have broken?"

He shook his head. "You ain't used to hearin' no, are you?"

She shook hers back, lips twisting into a sly smile.

"Well, heed a warning when you hear one. I don't play nice, and mountain adventure scout or whatever it is you are, you still can't handle me."

"How do you know what I can handle?" She sipped her champagne. "I haven't even seen it yet."

Daisey closed his eyes and clenched his jaw, failing to hide a smile. "How old are you, Mac?"

"Twenty-five."

His eyes opened. "Fine. Come on over and take a look then." He beckoned her with an impatient hand.

She crossed the little pool, delicious apprehension zinging through her body. Something in his expression darkened as she neared.

"On your knees, girl." Daisey nodded and she obeyed, swallowing. She sank down, bubbling waves dancing just below her breasts.

Daisey reached both hands into the water. Beyond the roiling current, the black shape of his shorts slid down his legs. He rested his arms back along the rim of the tub. "Go on, then. Have your way."

Mac met his eyes with one more challenging glance, then dipped her hands into the water. She ran her palms over thighs nearly as big around as her waist and licked her lips, hungry. She found him with her fingers, stroking the side of his hard shaft, measuring his length. Damn, he hadn't been exaggerating. She wrapped her small hand around his cock and her fingertips didn't even meet her thumb.

"Whoa."

He chuckled, looking down at her, some mix of wicked and smug plastered all over his face. "What you gonna do now, little girl?"

She gripped him tight, weighing his heavy dick in her hand. Hard, thick as her wrist, long as an Alaskan summer day. Shit, she didn't have the first clue what she was going to do with him. He knew it as well as she did.

Daisey grabbed her hips in his huge hands and spun her around, pulling her backward onto his lap. He draped her legs on either side of his and took her hand, plunging it into the water between her own thighs where his dick stood, rock-hard, hot enough to make the searing water feel tepid. He pumped her fist with his, tight and rough.

"Like that," he ordered, showing her the harsh movements he wanted before he let her go it alone. His broad hands reached up, sliding the thick straps of her bra down to half-pin her arms in place. She sucked in her breath as his fingers took her, pinching and tugging at her nipples, no mercy. She moaned, losing herself in the sensations, the intimidation, the heat flooding into her core. She pressed her pussy against his shaft as she stroked him.

"Harder," he barked when her grip slackened. She was dying for him to reach between her legs and rub her clit. Those big fingers on the tiny nub, as rough and mean as his voice. She wanted to feel that huge cock forcing its way inside her, the worst and best fit imaginable.

"Fuck me," she murmured.

"You think you can take me?" he asked, right in her ear. He plucked her nipples, pumped his hips beneath her, driving his cock deeper into her grip.

"Yeah, I can."

"You got a condom that can?"

Shit. "No. Do you?"

"No."

A voice came from behind them. "I do."

Fuck fuck fuck.

Mac yanked up her wet bra and turned. Ian was leaning casually in the threshold, the tumbler in his hand swirling something amber.

Mac hoped her face couldn't get more flushed than it already was from the hot tub and the hand job. "Jesus, you're creepy."

"Creepier than fecking a bloke whose fairst name you dun'nae know, in a building that's prolly riddled with cameras?"

Mac's stomach did a flip.

Ian nodded. "Aye, I may be that creepy. You got room for three in this wee celebration, eh?"

Daisey finally spoke. "Get your punk-ass out of here before I beat it for you."

Ian put his hands up, ice cubes tinkling. "My mistake." He turned to wander back into the dark of the hallway.

Daisey pushed Mac off his lap and stood, water dripping down his body, heart-stopping erection still at half-mast. She stole a hungry glance before he yanked his briefs up. He shut off the taps and jets.

"Sorry, girl. That kinda killed the mood." As he said it, a ribbon of wrapped condoms flew through the door and slid across the tiles. He ignored it. "Maybe some other time."

No no no! Now! Right now! "Yeah," she said. "Maybe."

He tossed her a towel and she joined him on dry land. Fucking Ian. Fucking cameras... Mac scanned the room, wondering if he was right about those. She didn't really give a good goddamn right now.

"What *is* your first name?" she asked Daisey, trying to distract herself from the embarrassment burning her cheeks, the frustration clenching her pussy.

"You'll find out when it's time for you to scream it for me," he said, running the towel over his stomach.

Mac's blush shifted from humiliation to pleasure. "I guess I will."

"What's yours, anyhow?"

She smiled and pushed the tub's drain lever down with her foot. "Guess you'll find out when you're ready to beg for me." She wrapped the towel around her trunk and strolled past with one last lewd glance at the bulge in his wet shorts.

The air in the den was cool and dry. Ian was lounging on the big leather sofa with his feet propped on the coffee table, perusing a hunting magazine. Mac glared at him.

"My last name's Kilpatrick," he said, not looking up. "Case you were curious."

"I wasn't," she said snottily, but sat down on the chair opposite him. She was restless, antsy from the sexual deadlock. "You never take that hat off, do you? You hiding a bald spot or something?"

Ian lowered the magazine and lifted his fedora, revealing a healthy head of wavy black hair and a sharp widow's peak. Daisey wandered through in his underwear and closed himself in a bedroom without a word to either of them.

"You figured out who you're going to sabotage next?" Mac asked Ian coldly.

"Sabotage?" He replaced his hat. "That's an ungrateful way tae think of it. You should be thanking me for keeping your mate Pike in the running."

Mac swallowed, not really wanting an answer to her next question but knowing it had to be asked. "Did you do something to Leah's boyfriend's car?"

Ian shook his head, expression placid. "It was'nae broken though. He jest wished it was, so he could quit before he started. He told me it would'nae start, but he was lyin'. All *I* did was promise tae give his girlie the supplies. But as it happens, I'm a forgetful man."

"You're a sociopath."

"Nae, I'm an opportunist. And a good one. See, your mate Pike, I like him too. Dead useful. I fancy having a man around who could stitch my back up, after I get stabbed in it."

"Which you'd no doubt earn," Mac said.

He nodded. "No doubt. Plus those two lassies with him, they're dead weight. No threat. Thanks tae me we're down three decent competitors. Hate my methods, but dun'nae tell me you're nae happy with the results."

Mac took a breath and considered it. "No, I like the results."

Ian smiled all the way to his sideburns. "Exactly. You stick with me, I'll give you the payoff."

"You told me everybody here's the enemy."

"Aye, maybe I did. But I may take a fancy tae you."

"I don't want anything you've got to offer."

His smile dropped and his brows rose. "No? Well, you come by my bed some night and I'll scratch that itch you cannae reach." He nodded in the direction of Daisey's closed door.

"Fuck you."

"Shut your eyes and picture him, if you like. I'm nae bothered. But jest remember, I'm the man who can get things done for you."

"I'd need a fifth of bourbon and you'd need a *generous* prosthesis to make that disgusting scenario convincing," Mac said, tasting acid in her throat. She got up and stalked toward the spare bedroom. "I hope you sleep wretchedly."

"Nae as wretched as some. Give my best tae your right hand."

Mac made a final flustered noise and slammed the door behind her. Trying to get the last word with Ian Kilpatrick wasn't worth the effort.

OBJECTIVE TWO

THE MEAT LOCKER

CAMERA 1269

DAWN ARRIVES just before four a.m., weak sunlight winking through the trees to reveal six small tents arranged in a circle. Four contain sleeping competitors. Two are empty.

The soft-faced New Zealander, so far from home, is sitting cross-legged on the ground with his back to the dying bonfire. Rory. The sort of man you'd trust to look after your cat or your grandmother, if you had only his looks to go by.

In front of him on a log is the skinny wannabe bohemian camouflaged in Mac's borrowed clothes. Leah's the breed of girl who'd make the perfect meek assistant to a volatile fashion editor, if it weren't for the fact that she'd crumble the first time a steaming latté was hurled in her direction.

Quite a pair.

RORY

HE HADN'T SLEPT A WINK. It felt like jet lag, though the multi-leg trip from Ashburton to Fairbanks crossed the dateline and only skewed him by a few hours. No, this restlessness was a product of the sheer bizarreness of the first day's activities. He hadn't expected to find anyone else awake when he'd given up and crawled out of his tent, but there Leah had been, sitting on a log and staring into the dying embers of the fire. They'd been making small talk for an hour or more.

Tired of watching Leah massage her heels through her canvas shoes, Rory patted his lap. "Give me your feet."

She shook her head. "No way. They totally stink and they're probably all covered in blister juice."

"C'mon. Give 'em here." He scooted forward in the dirt and grabbed her ankles, slipped her filthy espadrilles off and plunked her stocking feet on his crossed calves. Between mosquito slaps, he rubbed her arches.

"So," she said, watching him. "Is this what you expected? The game?"

He made a face and swatted another bug. "I didn't really come here expecting anything in particular, except a shot at twenty years' worth of my salary. What about you? Is it what you were picturing?" He caught himself. "Well, I mean, aside from your bloke not being here."

"I guess. I was picturing *Survivor*, kind of. I guess it's about right. Except I wasn't planning on being so unprepared." She sighed. "I spent a whole week ordering exactly what I thought the right clothes would be, and had them all shipped to his place in Seattle. Then I show up dressed like an idiot, wanting to look so hip after my first year in New York."

"So you guys are long-distance?"

She nodded. "I don't recommend it. And trust me—if I had a cell signal, he'd be in *no* doubt of how officially over we are now."

Rory tactfully resisted the urge to whoop. "That was pretty shitty. If you're right about him chickening out."

"He's one of those people," she said, stretching her neck from side to side. "He gets all super-jazzed about one thing or another, and he's obsessed for a month or two. Like playing the drums or learning how to brew his own beer. Or becoming a video game designer. Then he gets distracted by something new and never follows through."

Rory nodded. He knew the type of guy she was talking about. He was willing to bet the jerk could be distracted by an exciting new woman as easily as a hobby.

"This whole thing," Leah went on, "it was part of his newfound obsession with psychological experiments, after he saw some documentary. I should have known this would happen. The fact that I even showed up should be a study in persistent, chronic stupidity."

Rory flexed Leah's toes, feeling a little jolt of triumph against all the shit-house blokes of the world—the satisfaction of rubbing the feet of one of their inequitably attractive girlfriends.

"I'm buggered if the next Objective-thing starts this morning," he said. "I don't think I've slept in about thirty hours. Not since I was on a plane."

"What do you do back in New Zealand?" she asked, sleepiness in her voice.

"I work at a café."

She yawned, and Rory wanted to lie down with her and breathe in whatever her hair smelled like.

"Do you enjoy it?"

"More than I should," he said. "I have a degree in music, but when I finished school I never quite got 'round to doing anything with it."

"What sort of music?"

"I studied composition. I play guitar and piano and a few other things. Or I used to. Now I'm just sort of…floating. Floating toward thirty with no orientation."

"Floating sounds nice," Leah said. "I'm just trying not to drown."

Rory smiled to himself. "What did you make of your teammates?"

She made a sputtering noise with her lips. "Well, Pike's cool. He comes off kind of snarky and irritable, but he's a good guy." She lowered her voice. "Marissa's frigging obnoxious. All she does is complain. And I'm not talking about bugs and blisters, either. I mean like, the food. The *accommodations*."

"Charming."

"What's that Chloe woman like?"

Rory considered it and laughed. "*Ooh*, barracuda." He air-guitared the Heart riff for Leah's amusement. "She scares the shit out of me. But she's bloody fit and determined, I'll give her that."

She smirked. "I bet you would."

Rory blushed, thankful it probably didn't show in the dim light. "Yeah, right."

"Why not?" Leah asked, sitting up straight. "You're cute. And she seems pretty, you know…liberated."

He shook his head. "Trust me, I'm even less her type than she is mine."

"What's your type?" Leah asked, biting her lip and squinting, just a touch devious.

Rory wondered if she was sizing him up as some easy rebound conquest. He wondered if he ought to work a little harder to feel insulted by the idea.

"Well, I'm one of those blokes with about twenty female friends, and any time I get the bollocks together to ask one of them out, they always say something like, 'Oh, I couldn't—that'd be like dating my brother.'"

"'I value your friendship too much,'" Leah offered.

"'You're a top mate, but I'm really looking for someone a little more *focused*.'" Rory shook his head, rubbing Leah's heels with his thumbs. "Translation, 'Your nose is too big and your paycheck's too small.'"

"Aw, I like your nose." She grinned. "I think it makes you look British. What do they call that? Distinguished."

Rory looked down to hide his smile. He knocked her feet together a couple of times before he opened his mouth. "If you're trying to flirt with me, you're doing a rubbish job of it."

Leah's lips parted, ready with a retort, but a loud crackle of feedback from some unseen speaker cut through the air.

"GOOD MORNING!" boomed Lenora's magnified voice. "I HOPE YOU'VE ALL SLEPT WELL."

DAISEY

DAISEY LITERALLY FELL OUT OF BED, legs tangled in some stranger's six-hundred-thread-count sheets.

"What the fuck?"

He staggered into the cabin's living room in his shorts. Ian opened a window to let in the broadcast that had flashed Marine Recruit Brian Daisey back to his first day of basic training for a few confused seconds.

"...SO PLEASE REPORT TO THE CLEARING FOR BREAKFAST AND INSTRUCTIONS BY OH FIVE HUNDRED."

"What the fuck time is it now?" Daisey asked.

Ian pulled a pocket watch out of his pants. "It's half past one in the afternoon in Greenwich."

"It's four thirty-six," Mac announced through a yawn, stepping out of the other bedroom, wrapped in a sheet.

"I call the shower," Ian said, and strolled off toward the bathroom.

Daisey ran a hand over his head. "Five a.m., huh? Weird how it feels that early, even three time zones behind."

Mac nodded, combing her fingers through her sleep-matted hair. "Shit, it'll take us at least five minutes just to walk down there." She padded toward the bathroom and cracked the door, shouting to Ian. "Is there soap in there?"

He shouted something back that Daisey couldn't make out. Mac stalked back to her room and emerged carrying a toiletry bag.

"What are you doing?"

She paused long enough to shrug. "I might not get another chance at a hot shower for a week, co-ed or otherwise. The cubicle's plenty big enough for two."

"With *him?*" Daisey jerked a thumb at the door as though the Devil himself were behind it.

"Youngest child and only girl," Mac reminded him. "I've seen plenty of gross stuff in my time, Daisey. Plus they could be taping us on the toilet, for all we know. The world will keep turning if Ian sees me naked."

She knocked on the door again and Daisey could hear the din of the water. "I'm coming in. Look wherever you want, Kilpatrick, but if you touch me I'll break your teeth."

Daisey narrowed his eyes at the door as it closed. He fished through Ian's duffel bag, hoping to find his cigarettes and possibly hold them for ransom, but the fucker must keep them in his jacket. All Daisey found were a couple changes of clothes, a notebook, a few basic tools, a flask and two bottles of whiskey. He headed to his room to dress and pack.

He glanced between Mac's and Ian's matching wet hair as they walked down the dusty path to the camp area ten minutes later.

Mac yawned. "They better have coffee."

"It's a psychological test," Daisey said. "They'll probably give us decaf then document us freaking out."

Ian looked over, a brow cocked above one freaky-ass blue eye. "Who's on your team then?"

"Not you, pretty boy."

"What about me?" Mac asked, grinning, a child gunning for a ticket to the carnival.

"You'll have to wait and see."

He caught that predatory, flirtatious look pass over her face again, the one he'd gotten all too acquainted with in the hot tub. Cute girl but too damn hungry. Like a kitten with a cougar's appetite.

Ian halted, letting Daisey and Mac drift ahead a few yards. Daisey squinted over his shoulder as the guy lit a cigarette.

"He looks different with his clothes off," Mac said, and Daisey hated the hot little flare that ran up the back of his neck.

"And I don't?"

Mac looked him up and down and shook her head. "No. You look just how you're supposed to. Ian doesn't. He's in way better shape than I'd have guessed."

Daisey thought about this, nodding. "When I was in the woods with him yesterday, he was pissing me off so I did one of these." He faked a left hook within a few inches of Mac's face, making her flinch. "His hands came up like *that*." Daisey snapped his fists up, tight to his chin and jaw.

"Boxer?"

He nodded.

"And he's got a tattoo across his upper back," she added. "Some kind of Roman numerals."

"Kind of souvenir a man picks up in prison."

"You don't know that," Mac countered.

Daisey shook his head. "There's something wrong about that guy."

"Duh."

"I aim to figure out what," he muttered.

"Can't be hard." Mac turned and shouted, "Ian! Where did you learn how to box?"

The prick took a deep drag and blew the smoke to one side. "From my filthy uncle Jack."

Mac slowed and Daisey reluctantly followed suit. "Oh yeah?" she asked as Ian reached them.

"Aye. He ran the local bookie's. Only thing he liked more than getting pissed was watching lads beat the livin' shite out of each other."

Daisey looked at Ian's hat and dress shoes and clothes, unwilling to imagine the man underneath could actually throw a punch.

He paused only a beat before he lunged and took a swing.

Ian jerked his head back and blocked Daisey's fist with his forearm, quick as any man he'd scrapped with in the service or on a rig. Ian's other hand flashed to his pocket—and Daisey's mouth dropped open at the blade suddenly glinting a foot from his face.

Ian went dead still. His lips twitched his cigarette to one side and he blew the smoke toward Daisey.

"Jesus," Mac said. "Chill out, guys."

Daisey dropped his fists. "Just wanted to check." He used the calm, cocky voice he reserved for when some sad sucker caught him in bed with a not-quite-as-single-as-she-let-on woman. The perfect diplomatic mix of apology and fuck-you.

Ian snapped his switchblade closed and pocketed it, running his hands primly down the front of his jacket. He smiled at Mac, ashed his cigarette to one side before saying, "Funny fecker, your mate Daisey."

They began walking again.

"How did you get an illegal knife through airport security?" Mac asked.

"Did'nae need tae. You can buy any-bloody-thing in Alaska."

The camp came into view. Daisey's stomach growled as his hackles lowered. "Bacon."

Mac clapped. "I see coffee!"

The others were all there, dressed and looking tired, milling around with Styrofoam cups and paper plates heaped with scrambled eggs and bagel halves. Daisey scanned the choices—the people first, then the food. He'd better hold off on deciding on teammates until he knew what the next challenge was all about.

He loaded a plate with bacon and eggs and found Chloe sitting on a log with a cup of coffee between her slender hands.

"Mornin'," Daisey said, and took a seat beside her.

She turned, and he could see his face with its five o'clock shadow reflected fish-eye style in her mirrored sunglasses. "Mornin' yourself, cowboy. How was the Ritz?"

The hot tub flashed across his reptile brain. "Ritzy. How 'bout the tents?"

"No complaints." She slid her shades to the top of her head and Daisey noted faint lines around her eyes, making her a well-rested forty or a sleep-deprived thirty. Her irises were cold, gray-blue, eyebrows near-black despite the highly convincing blonde hair.

"Looks like we're on separate teams again," Daisey said.

"That we are. You know who you're picking yet?"

"Thought I'd wait and see if they tell us what sort of bullshit we're up against."

She sipped her coffee. "I bet the Objectives get harder each day."

"I bet you're right."

"If you want someone who's easy to mold, I recommend Rory. He's tougher than you'd guess. Physically." She nodded to where he was sitting, so close to Leah their hips were touching.

"Looks doomed to me," Daisey said.

She shrugged. "Greg's good too."

Daisey watched Greg's salt-and-pepper dreadlocks bounce as he chatted animatedly to the half-Asian medic. "He must be nearly fifty."

"Fifty-one. But he's a long-distance runner, and he's very cooperative."

"Who do you want?"

Chloe pursed her wide lips a moment, seeming to contemplate whether or not to tell him. "I want Pike. And that Scottish motherfucker."

Daisey made a skeptical noise in the back of his throat. "Watch what you wish for. We've been out here less than a day and that shit already pulled a knife on me."

Chloe fixed him with a snotty look. "Yeah, and I'm sure you didn't deserve it. Anyhow, I want that one where I can keep an eye on him." She flipped her sunglasses back down and drained her coffee. "What about that Mac girl? She any good?"

"Yeah, she's good. A little soft-hearted, but she's smart and damned up to it, physically."

"I'll bet." Chloe's mirrored eyes stared blankly at him. "I'm surprised she stopped gagging on your hu-*monnn*-gous cock long enough for you two to chat." She smirked then stood, tossing her cup into a trash bin as she headed toward the tents.

Daisey watched her hips as she walked away, wanting to spin her around and kiss her filthy mouth even more than he wanted to fuck her. Which, compared to his usual M.O., was practically a proposal.

The speakers crackled on again just as he stood.

"Looks like everybody's had a chance to get some breakfast." Lenora strolled into the clearing, dressed again in her aviatrix-on-safari getup, adjusting her headset mike. "Everyone sleep all right? Ready for the next Objective? Wonderful. I won't tell you the specifics until our teams have been formed, but it *is* another endurance test."

Daisey heard a low groan and looked over to see Leah cast her feet a mournful look. Rory gave her shoulder a squeeze.

At least they'll lose together, Daisey thought, knowing neither he nor Chloe would be short-listing them.

"Mr. Daisey," Lenora said, and his head snapped to attention. "Would you please select your two teammates?"

Daisey crossed his arms. The first choice was easy. "Mac," he said, nodding to her. She kept her face neutral, nodding back. He weighed the other options. Endurance. Pike was a temptation, but Daisey didn't want to give the guy a chance to pay him back for yesterday's deception. "Greg," he decided, and the older man pumped his fists in triumph.

"And Chloe," Lenora said. "Your picks?"

Chloe had returned from the tent with her frame pack on her shoulders, born ready. "Pike and Ian."

Daisey caught Pike sending an apprehensive glance in Ian's direction. Cancer-boy wasn't making himself many friends.

"All right. That leaves Rory, Leah and Marissa as the third team."

The losing team, Daisey corrected in his head.

"Please be ready to go in five minutes. The crew will lead you to where the next Objective is taking place."

Greg and Mac shouldered their bags and joined Daisey as he wolfed down the last of his food.

"I wonder if it will be more walking," Greg said.

Mac stole a piece of bacon off Daisey's grease-darkened plate. "Fine with me."

"No bandannas this time?" Daisey asked, then turned as a whistle sounded. They joined the other teams, following a pair of crew members into the woods. He looked to the left, to Chloe and Pike and Ian. She'd stockpiled the brains, medical and criminal, but Daisey had versatility on his side.

After close to an hour's easy hike, a vast clearing came into view. There was a building at one end, big as a gymnasium, corrugated metal walls streaked with rust. The crew made a beeline for it.

"What do you think this place used to be?" Mac asked.

Daisey could see industrial remnants all over the ground. "Oil operation."

They tromped through clumps of wildflowers and weeds to the entrance of what had probably been the workers' bunkhouse and rec area a few decades ago. Lenora was standing by the main door. Daisey hadn't heard any helicopters, and he wondered how they'd gotten her here so quickly, so fresh and relaxed.

"Welcome to your second Objective." She flashed her toothpaste-ad smile at the group. "Follow me." She led them inside, the old building echoing with their steps and murmurs. They stopped in a wide stretch of hallway with doors running along both sides.

"We're calling this challenge the Meat Locker," she said. "A test of your stamina under extreme conditions. For each minute your team is in its assigned room, the temperature will drop one degree Fahrenheit. All you have to do is endure. If it gets to be too much, there are panic buttons. Simply push yours and we'll let you out." A crew member began distributing buttons like the ones from the day before.

Another helper handed Lenora a plastic box. It rattled as she opened the lid. "Everyone needs to swallow one of these," she said, and held out the box to reveal what looked like nine white pills. "These are sensors that will monitor your core temperature. If anyone's sensor drops to eighty-eight degrees, you'll be yanked out, regardless of whether you've pushed your button or not. That's flirting with profound hypothermia—we're talking risk of heart arrhythmia. Not worth the money, I'd say. On the bright side, I trust the frostbite will get you first." Lenora offered the tiniest hint of a smirk.

The red-haired girl spoke up. "Do we lose if we push our button first?"

"It's not as simple as that," Lenora said. "I'll explain the elimination method once the Objective is over. I will tell you now, however, that the team that stays inside the longest as a group—all of those members will be safe. I'll also tell you, you will have no way of knowing if the other teams are still standing."

It was about sixty degrees in the building now, Daisey guessed. That meant it would take an hour before they were sunk down in the sub-zeros. What a bitch it would be to stay until the bitter end only to discover all the other teams had broken up a half-hour earlier.

"Any other questions?" Lenora asked. "No? Good. Watch your teammates' backs, please. Once a person's core temperature drops even to the mid-nineties, rationality can fly out the window. If somebody seems unresponsive, you'll have to push their button for them. All right? I suggest you all take a couple of minutes to bundle on the layers. Leave anything you're not wearing here in the hall."

Daisey dropped his bag and pulled out the warmest thing he'd packed when preparing for a cool Alaskan summer—a sweatshirt. He tugged it on over a thermal shirt and found his work gloves, a random choice he was grateful he'd made.

"Hey. Leah."

He turned and found Mac holding out a fleece jacket, trying to get the other girl's attention. He grabbed her arm and yanked her back.

"Ow—Jesus, Daisey!"

"You're not pulling that Girl Scout bull again." He squeezed her so tight he knew it must hurt. She held his eyes and finally relented, jerking her arm back and rubbing it.

"You don't want to win this, do you?" he asked.

"Sure I do. It's possible to win *and* be a nice person."

"Let her boyfriend over there worry about it." Daisey looked to where Rory was digging through his pack. "Plus, letting her lose now would be the kindest thing and you damn well know it. She's not gonna win. Better she goes sooner than later. Now put your fucking jacket on, little girl."

Mac glowered. "Thug."

"Like you don't love it."

Lenora's voice cut in. "Okay everyone, let's get started."

IAN

IAN WOUND A SCARF around his neck and pushed a pair of leather driving gloves into his pants pocket. He flashed Daisey a final cold smile as he followed Chloe and Pike and a crew member down the hallway.

"Everyone got your buttons and mikes? Swallowed your sensors?"

They nodded at the crew guy.

"All right then. Good luck." He pulled open a door, one of three that didn't match the others in the corridor. Thicker, paneled in aluminum. Presumably highly insulated.

Chloe stepped inside first. "Oh fuck *me*."

Ian followed after Pike, nearly knocked down by a wall of heat.

"It's a hundred degrees in here," Chloe said.

"A hundred and ten," the crew man said, and closed the door behind them.

Pike unzipped his thick fatigue jacket and tossed it across one of the ancient bunks that lined the back wall. "Awesome."

Chloe went further, stripping down to her bra and panties so fast you'd think *that* was the Objective.

"Oi, woman. Wait 'til we need tae think up ways tae get warm."

"Shut up, Ian. Get your clothes off, both of you. Don't let anything get sweaty."

"She's right," Pike said. He kept his pants on but ditched his shirt and shoes and socks.

Ian lost the blazer and scarf but kept the rest. He was planning on working against nature, not with it. Looking around the room, he found it retro-fitted to insulate. A glance at his watch said they were two minutes in, putting the temp at one-oh-eight.

"Well, we've got the means tae make fire, but nae enough ventilation." He grabbed his lighter from a pocket and flicked it open and closed.

Chloe looked at him long and hard. "What else have you got up your greasy sleeve?"

"Fags," Ian said. "Jest the necessities."

"Like the knife you pulled on Daisey?" Chloe asked, raising a brow.

Pike's narrow eyes widened.

"Self-defense," Ian countered. "You seen the way he looks at you? You might want tae try it yourself."

"I'm not worried about Daisey," she said, wandering away to explore the space.

Ian watched a bead of sweat slip down her spine.

"Especially not for this challenge," she added. "He grew up on the Gulf Coast and probably served in the other Gulf. I bet he's never even seen snow. Mac's from the southwest. Greg's from fucking *Zimbabwe*, then Atlanta. I'm from Montreal." She turned to them. "You're from the north," she said to Ian, then looked to Pike.

"Detroit."

"Nice. See? We've got this in the bag." Her lips curled into an evil smile that made Ian's collar feel tight.

"There's no wind," Pike said. "We could probably make it to minus twenty, maybe lower. Or some of us could." He frowned at Ian's clothes.

"I came prepared," Ian said vaguely.

The first half-hour passed in bored waiting. As the temperature dipped to near seventy, Chloe and Pike pulled some of their layers back on.

Chloe kept pacing, looking restless, arms crossed over her chest.

"You ever been inside a cell, sweetheart?" Ian asked.

She met his stare with a haughty look. "I'm a photojournalist. It's in my job description."

"Ever been inside a *padded* cell?"

Her eyes narrowed a moment and she shook her head.

"You've got the walk down pat."

Pike sighed. "We've got at least another hour to bicker, kids. Don't blow your loads now."

Ian grabbed his blazer off the bunk and slipped it on, pulling a pack of cards from the inner breast pocket. He tossed them on the floor.

Chloe glanced around then dragged the mattress off the nearest bunk. Pike did the same on the other side and they sat.

Pike shuffled. "What are we playing?"

"Reverse strip poker," Chloe suggested. "It'll make adding layers more fun."

Pike began dealing. "We'll play crazy eights."

"I wonder what the other teams are doing to pass the time," Chloe said, arranging her hand.

"Complaining," Pike replied. "In Marissa's case, anyhow. I so fucking hope she goes home after this." He set a ten on top of Chloe's.

"If Greg goes out fairst," Ian said, "I can tell you exactly what Mac and Daisey will be doing in their little walk-in honeymoon freezer." He caught Pike twitch and made a mental note.

"I don't get it," Pike said, picking up from the pile. "He's such a douche." He slapped an eight down. "Diamonds."

"You like her?" Chloe asked slyly.

"There's no point liking anybody here." Pike looked irritable, and not on account of the heat. "We're in competition, and we'll all be going back home in a week or whenever. I didn't come here to get laid. I came here to get rich."

"I showered with her," Ian said, tossing down a jack. He gave Pike a long, cruel look, a pale substitute for blowing smoke in his face. "Jest this very morning."

Chloe laughed. "How on *earth* did you talk her into that?"

"Did'nae. She jest about broke the door down. She's a very forceful lassie."

Pike rolled his eyes.

"You've got a rubbish poker face," Ian said.

"Good thing we're playing crazy eights then," Pike muttered.

"Well, dun'nae worry—she's still hell-bent on fecking Chloe's not-so-secret admirer."

Chloe took a card. "Mac and Daisey? Like a beagle going after a Great Dane."

Ian shrugged. "Good luck tae her. If she's walking like a wee cowgirl tomorrow morning we'll know she got her way."

Pike made an exasperated noise.

"She looks nice with her clothes off," Ian said casually, jamming the knife a bit deeper before dropping the subject. "What about you, Chloe? Who are you dying tae shag in this group?"

She shrugged. "I'd probably fuck Lenora first. Might give me a leg up."

Ian laughed.

Grinning, Chloe looked up from her cards, gaze traveling all over the room. "And if you're good I'll let you watch," she said, addressing the unseen eyes behind the hidden cameras.

A few games onward the temperature turned officially cool. Ian did some math and guess they had a half-hour before it got rough. Perfect.

He stood between hands and wrapped his scarf around his throat, pushed his hat tighter against his head. Pulling the gloves from his jacket, he dropped them next to his seat, ready for when they dipped closer to the forties.

Pike shook his head, looking fed up.

"Aye?"

"You look like you're dressed for a Sunday drive in a Stutz Bearcat. Where are your hiking clothes?"

"I dun'nae like all that sporty shite. Plus I've got something a hell of a lot better than layers, if you fancy it." Ian rummaged in a pocket and tossed Pike a tiny plastic bag with a dozen cheerful yellow tablets inside.

Chloe leaned over. "What's that?"

"Uppers?" Pike asked, eyes wide. "You aren't serious."

Chloe took the bag and squinted at the pills. "Is this Ecstasy?"

Ian shrugged. "Find out."

She made a face. "Jesus, Ian. I figured you were sleazy, but I clearly underestimated you... Can I have one?"

"Be my guest."

Pike grabbed her wrist. "Can you say 'uncontrollable sweating'?"

"Mental clarity?" Ian countered. "Energy, endurance? Diminished pain response? A deep sense of well-being and inner peace?"

Chloe yanked her hand from Pike's and took a tablet out, looking it over.

"You'll thank me when we hit the single digits," Ian said. "And do it while you've still got enough spit tae swallow." She did, and he took the bag back and popped one himself.

They went back to the cards for another twenty minutes, trading insults and theories until their fingers were too cold to continue.

Ian blew out a plume of steaming breath, wishing it were smoke. Then he felt the first effects of the pill kicking in, triggering that blessed race in his pulse.

"Ooooh," Chloe said a minute later. "I think mine's working."

Pike glared at Ian. "You pull a stereo out of that jacket next and start playing house music, and I *will* murder you."

"Jest trying tae win," Ian said, holding his hands up innocently. "It's nae even cheating. There's nothing in the waivers about chemical aids. Or weapons, come tae that. I jest want every advantage."

Pike shook his head. "Just keep your clothes on, fuck-wits. And for the love of God, don't start rubbing up against each other."

LEAH

RORY'S NECK SMELLED WONDERFUL.

Leah forced herself to focus on it, even as her fingertips and toes screamed in pain.

She was standing with her chest against his, arms wrapped around his middle under his coat. His hands, balled in the sleeves of his sweater, were cupped over her ears, reminding her of how it sounded when she'd duck beneath the bathwater as a kid. Her breath steamed against his skin, making it warm for a moment before the dampness cooled. Leah wriggled her toes inside her shoes, socks stiff with frozen sweat.

She whispered against his throat, "How cold now, do you think?"

His three days' stubble brushed her temple. "No idea. Maybe ten degrees? I'm no good with Fahrenheit."

Marissa hadn't spoken in a half-hour, not since they'd first all agreed it had officially become cold. It was the most pleasant and charming she'd been since Leah had met her.

Rory took his hands away for a moment, blowing into his cupped palms and putting them back over Leah's ears. It didn't help, but she let him think it did.

He was bigger than she'd thought before. And firmer. She squeezed her arms tighter around his waist, liking the solid feel of him. Her boyfriend—her *ex*-boyfriend—was tall and skinny, like an indie rocker. Rory wasn't as tall, maybe five-ten, but he felt strong. She registered her first rush of warmth in the last forty minutes. She liked his smile and his big nose, and his voice with that interesting accent. If by some miracle they didn't all get sent home, she'd definitely kiss Rory tonight.

"What's your last name, Rory?"

"Don't think I'm supposed to tell you."

"Mine's Bernstein," she said. "Now tell me so we're even."

She felt him laugh. "Hobbs."

"Can I look you up when we're back in the real world?"

"I'll make it even easier." He told her his e-mail address, an easy one to memorize.

"If my fingers don't fall off in here," she said, "I'll be sure and write to you."

Behind her, Marissa cracked. Breaking her silence, she staggered to the door and pounded it with her fists.

"Oi, use your button." Rory let go of Leah to jog to Marissa, turning her by the shoulders to face him.

"You sure you want out?" he asked.

She nodded her head, fast and maniacal in short, stiff motions. She whispered something Leah couldn't hear.

Rory put his hands in her pockets, coming out with her button. He pushed it and dropped it back in her coat. He returned to Leah.

"I guess that's it then," she said. "Think anyone else dropped out yet?"

"I don't—" Rory turned as the door opened and a crew member took hold of Marissa's arm, leading her out before closing it again.

"Good riddance," he muttered, and Leah heard his teeth chattering. "Anyhow, I'm not sure it's going to work the same as the last challenge. I mean, if the entire team goes out with the first person to give up, why would they have us stay in here, enduring as individuals?"

"Maybe the first team with all its members eliminated loses," Leah guessed.

"Maybe. Yeah, that's not a bad guess."

"If we don't lose and get shipped out of here, I'm going to make a move on you later," Leah said.

Rory laughed. "Oh. Okay." He looked nervous behind the shivering, but didn't pull away.

"Did I just totally weird you out?"

He shook his head, smiling.

"I'd make a move on you now," she went on, "except if we kissed it might be like licking a flagpole in the winter."

"What, like they'd find us glued together by the face when they open that door?"

Leah started laughing, the impulse turned convulsive by the chills racking her body.

"You're really rubbish at seduction, Miss Bernstein."

She smiled and hugged him tighter. Just then something to her left rattled, and a mild but steady breeze oozed through the room.

"Bugger *me*," Rory said, squeezing his eyes shut. "Bloody wind chill. That's brilliant. Fucking sadists."

He left her to investigate. The current was coming from a vent high on the far wall. Rory tugged on one of the bunk beds but they were bolted to the floor.

"Shit."

They surveyed the room for something tall enough to aid in blocking the wind, coming up short. They did the next best thing, leaning a mattress against one of the bunks, making a laughably ineffective buffer to stand behind.

"Is it just my imagination," Leah asked a short time later, "or is the wind getting worse every minute?"

"F-feels real to me," he said. "Makes the one-d-degree drop multiply like fivefold. How are your toes and f-fingers?"

"They frigging hurt...but don't let me think about it. Distract me."

Rory caught her eyes a moment and she could see him trying to translate her request, to filter it for romantic intentions. She wished she were up to that kind of levity, but the heat of their flirtation had blown away in the breeze.

"Let's jog in p-place or something," she said.

Each second became a torturous eternity. It felt as though another hour passed as they hobbled on frozen legs but Leah bet it was ten minutes, if that. If Rory weren't here, counting on her, she'd have given up by now.

Soon the paralyzing cold became so bad they couldn't speak, and the starkness of the physical pain became unbearable. Shivers turned to convulsions and Leah cracked. The pain in her toes and ears and hands was too much, going from freezing to numb to scalding until she felt as if her skin would split open.

"H-h-h-have t' g-g-get out." She forced the words through quaking lips, thick, white breath rising between their faces.

Rory nodded, expression too strained to reveal his feelings about giving in. He got his button out as Leah did and they pressed them together. She entertained a momentary panic that maybe the electronics wouldn't work in this extreme temperature. The few seconds it took for a staff member to pull the door open played out like a lifetime.

Leah shuffled out into the hallway, so cold she didn't even feel relief.

"Congratulations," the staffer said. "You both made it to minus-twenty-two degrees Fahrenheit, plus wind chill."

She nodded, not sure how to even qualify that number. She joined Rory in looking around, flexing their joints and trying to figure out who else might've thrown in the towel.

They staggered on stiff limbs down the hall to the corridor where everyone had left their bags. Greg was there, slumped by a wall, dreadlocks trembling, teeth chattering as loud as shaking dice. A staff member with an unopened first-aid kit was crouched by him, pressing his hands around a steaming Styrofoam cup and whispering to him. Greg nodded his replies, his mouth seeming stuck in a grimace.

"Is he ok-k-kay?" Leah asked.

"Yeah, he'll be fine," the staffer said. "It'll take everybody a while to shake off the effects. But his core temperature's good. Don't worry."

She nodded and looked to Rory. His once-bloodless cheeks and nose and ears were flushed bright pink. "How do you f-feel?" she asked him.

"G-glad to be out of there."

"The others who dropped out are in the yard," the staffer said. "You're welcome to join them if you feel stable."

Rory and Leah exchanged a look. "Yeah," she said.

The staff guy nodded toward the door they'd entered when they'd arrived at the complex.

Rory fell into step beside Leah. "That m-means Greg and Marissa aren't the only ones who quit. Who do you think...?"

"No clue," she said. "Ian, maybe. He didn't have the clothes for it."

With an effort that looked comically punishing, Rory pushed the metal door and it opened with a labored, rusty squeak. Leah spotted Marissa first. Sitting on a metal utility box, she seemed to have mostly recovered, a blanket draped over her shoulders and a cup in her hands. She looked up as they approached. Leah raised a shaky hand.

"Hey," Marissa said, then sniffed, clear snot quivering under one nostril. "You guys held out a long time."

"Who else is out here?" Rory asked.

Marissa nodded to the edge of the building. Rory headed around the corner and Leah followed.

Daisey stood a few meters out in the prairie, stretching his huge body. Mac was on the ground, hugging her knees to her chest and staring at her stocking feet, flexing her toes.

"Hey," Rory said, and they both looked over.

Mac smiled. She was shaking faintly but that warm friendliness was there as always. "Guess you didn't need my clothes," she said to Leah.

"Guess not."

"That's all of you then," Daisey said.

"And all of you," Rory countered. "Greg's in rough shape."

"He went out first," Mac said. "You see Ian or Pike or Chloe inside?"

They shook their heads.

"Jesus. Maybe they murdered each other," Mac said.

"Don't get your hopes up," Daisey muttered, a bruised ego coloring his words. "I hope they stay in there another hour."

"Proved my theory wrong then," Rory said. "Ian must be warm-blooded after all."

"They said it was negative twenty-two when we came out," Leah said. "And there was wind. Did you guys stay in long enough to get the wind?"

Mac nodded. "I started freaking out like two minutes into that."

"Must be getting dangerous in there," Rory said.

"Can't imagine what you two did to keep warm," Daisey said, too pissed to keep the bitterness out of his remark.

Leah ignored him. She wiggled her toes inside her shoes. They still hurt—a prickling burn in the skin, sharp ache in the bones—but she was relieved to find she could move them. Her face felt sunburned but she sensed her body thawing, slowly but surely.

No one said anything for ten minutes or so, not until the squeak of the door announced another emerging competitor. Everyone seemed to hold their breath until Pike appeared around the corner. He gave the group a cursory nod.

"Well done," Rory said, weariness making it sound insincere.

"Th-thanks." Pike's voice hitched. "How l-l-long you guys been ou-out here?"

"Ten, fifteen minutes?" Leah guessed, pointing to her and Rory.

"Ages," Mac said.

Daisey didn't offer a reply.

"It's just Ian and Chloe in there now," Mac said.

"Th-they drove me out," Pike said. "M-much as the cold d-did."

"Like forced you out?" Mac asked, brow furrowed.

"N-no. Y-you'd have wanted to escape th-them too, if you'd b-been on that team." He wiped his dripping nose with his sleeve.

"I'm going to check on Greg." Mac slowly stood and wandered toward the entrance on unsteady feet, as if the yard were paved with hot coals. Leah saw Pike's eyes follow each step.

The group loitered outside for another five minutes before the door squealed again. This time it was Lenora who strode around the corner. Her white teeth glinted in the sun, as though the effect had been added in post-production.

"The second Objective is complete," she announced. "Would you all please come inside so I can explain how the elimination is going to work?"

Leah walked side by side with Rory at the back of the weary procession as they followed Lenora to the wide corridor where their bags waited. Greg had made it to his feet but still looked shaky. Ian and Chloe were out, sitting shoulder-to-shoulder on the floor with their backs against a wall. Chloe's eyes were streaming and her mouth was twisted into a grin as if she'd just about died over the funniest joke ever told. Ian was smiling too, looking predictably self-satisfied even through his obvious chill. They each had a hand on the other's thigh, fingers caressing fabric. Leah caught Daisey's eyebrow pop up at the sight, nostrils flaring.

"Well done, everyone!" Lenora's perky voice rang like a gong in the dim, echoing space. "Let me explain how we'll be determining who goes home this morning."

Morning still…Leah felt as though this challenge had lasted an entire week.

"Chloe, Ian and Pike stayed in the Meat Locker longest of the group."

Leah heard Daisey add "Suckers" in a loud whisper.

"Very impressive," Lenora said. "No one on your team will be going home today."

Chloe blinked her wide eyes, rubbed her shoulder against Ian's like a cat.

Leah leaned in close to Rory and muttered, "Do you think they're drunk?"

He shrugged.

"As for the other two teams," Lenora went on, "you'll both be losing one member."

Leah and Rory glanced at each other.

"And it may not necessarily be the first person on your team to have dropped out," Lenora said. "It will be up to the team members to vote for who's going home. Whomever receives the most votes is packing their bags. In the event of a tie, the person who dropped out first *will* be eliminated. Understood? So Daisey, Mac, Greg, Rory, Marissa and Leah, please stay here to cast your votes. Chloe, Ian and Pike, you may head outside."

Pike left first, seeming eager to escape the theatrics. Ian made it to his feet and hauled Chloe up by her armpits. He wrapped a jovial arm around her shoulders and steered her giggling toward the exit.

"Gather around," Lenora said.

The six present competitors stepped close and Lenora handed each a square of cardstock and a Sharpie. "Just write down the name of the teammate you wish to see eliminated."

Leah could barely get the cap off her marker but the decision was simple. She scrawled Marissa's name in jaggy letters across the card, folded it and handed it to Lenora. The others did the same, Greg managing the feat last, limbs still twitching.

They stood in awkward silence while Lenora conferred with two staffers.

"Okay!" she said, beaming with over-the-top professionalism. "One team came in with a decisive vote. Marissa, you will be going home."

Leah felt Rory push his arm against hers. Marissa's face was blank as she gave the barest twitch of a nod.

"As for the other team, we've had a tie, one vote apiece."

Greg didn't react but Mac and Daisey turned to look at each other so quick, Leah thought she heard a whip crack. They shared a meaningful, tense stare.

Lenora went on. "And that means Greg will be going home, as he dropped out of the Objective first. Greg and Marissa, please gather your bags and follow Ryan out through the back." She waved a gracious hand at the clean-cut, beige-clad young staff member standing military-style to her right.

Mac hurried to Greg, putting her hand on his arm. Leah wondered if her face and words were full of apology or polite regret. In any case, Greg gave her a quick hug, picked up his bag and followed the staffer down the hall. Marissa was on his heels, her face stony as she left, no goodbyes or hugs or handshakes offered on either side.

Leah felt and heard Rory release a deep breath as the losers disappeared around a corner.

Mac had her eyes on the floor, expression troubled, jaw set. Leah glanced to everyone in turn, Mac and Daisey and Rory, realizing with a feeling of deep drunkenness how bizarre all of this was. It was disturbing how easy it was forget where they were, what they were doing here, that this entire scenario was ridiculous and choreographed and ringmastered. Just the opposite of normal life, it was so simple to get caught up in the present here, to focus on the now and overlook reality.

Rory tapped her chin a couple of times. "You all right?"

"Sorry…yeah. Just got lost in my head for a minute." Leah huffed out a breath. Daisey and Mac were heading for the door, bags in hand. Rory gathered his things and they followed, Lenora behind them.

They joined Pike and Ian and Chloe at the edge of the grassy plain.

"So five are gone already," Lenora said. "And here are our final seven. Well done, everyone. You'll be camping here for the night. Chloe, Ian and Pike, you're invited to sleep in one of the three-bunk barracks, if you're wanting a mattress under your backs tonight. You earned it, not giving in until minus-forty-one degrees and an eight-mile-per-hour breeze. As for everyone else, it'll be tents again.

"It's currently," she checked her watch, "just past oh nine hundred hours. And a balmy seventy-three, I'm happy to report. Lunch will be here at noon, so you should use these next three hours to get your bodies back on track. No challenges until tomorrow, so relax. A table with tea and coffee will be set up shortly. If anyone has medical concerns, you may talk to any one of the staff members or myself.

Understood? Great!" Lenora clapped her manicured hands, way too cheerful amid all the weary, cold-stiffened souls.

"Oh," she added, a seeming afterthought. "As you may have noticed, there's no tidy way to divide seven, so you're all on your own for the next Objective."

Tense energy rippled through the group as Lenora grinned and waved, before strolling back toward the building.

No one spoke until two staff members came around the side of the barracks, a buffet table carried between them. More khaki-uniformed people followed bearing big metal carafes, stacks of cups, folding chairs, the makings of a marquee tent. The competitors seemed to come back to life as cups of coffee were passed around and butts found seats. The staff members disappeared until lunch, leaving the final seven subjects to a morning of quiet speculation and tingling, thawing extremities.

Leah and Rory unfolded their chairs a few meters from the erected tent, soaking up the sun in shared silence. From somewhere behind the burning of Leah's skin and the ache in her joints, another sensation emerged, a sting in her sinuses, before two hot tears rolled down her cheeks. She looked up to find Rory's brown eyes fixed on her face, round with concern.

"What's wrong?"

She laughed, tears doubling. "Sorry."

"What is it?"

She took a deep breath, all the relief in her body replaced with sudden, paralyzing grief. "It should have been me who went home."

"No," Rory said. "You lasted ages longer than her."

"Not like that. I mean... God, I just want to go."

Ian strolled past in a cloud of smoke. "So go."

Rory fixed him with a cold glare. "Fuck off, mate."

Leah laughed through a sniffle.

"You mean go home?" Rory asked her.

She nodded.

"You can't mean that. I mean, we just made it through another challenge. You're doing brilliant. You outlasted Daisey and Mac and Greg, and they're really good."

"Yeah. Once again, I made it through another round without even meaning to." She closed her eyes and rubbed her hands over her face. "Shit, I should have voted to eliminate myself."

"Don't say that. That would mean it was all a waste, us keeping each other going in there. And it didn't feel like a waste to me."

She met his worried stare. "No, and it wasn't. I'm sorry. I just feel so…so frigging wiped out right now. I look around at everybody, at the landscape even, and I just…" She shrugged as dramatically as she could manage. "Why am I here? I feel like I'm stuck in some exhausting dream and I can't wake myself up."

Rory's gaze darted over her face, lips pursed into a hard line.

"What?" She reached over and touched her fingertips to his nose. She'd miss that nose when she left.

He smiled tightly. "I don't want you to go. I fancy you."

She looked down at her lap, his words warming her more than the sun or the air or the hot coffee hugged in her palms. He reached over and slid the cup away, setting it on the ground.

Leah took in the details of him as his face neared, his three days' worth of blond stubble, the faint lines creasing his forehead and bracketing his mouth, the thin scar that bisected his left eyebrow. She memorized him in a heartbeat before his warm lips pressed against hers and her eyes shut.

The kiss wasn't a bolt of lightning or a crashing wave. It was easy—the most natural thing in the world. They pulled away after a few seconds and Leah ran her fingertips over his lips, then angled her head. He brought his mouth back to hers and she knew how to kiss him, as though they'd been doing this for years. It was sweet for a minute, PG-13, then she felt his fingers tangle in her hair. He turned and she did the same, their knees locking between the two chairs. He tilted his head and took her. His tongue parted her lips, slid against her own, and a flash of warmth coursed from her cheeks through her neck, heating her breasts and belly and lower, between her legs. She sucked a breath through her nose, shocked.

Rory kissed like a different man. He kissed like a man who'd never lost in a fist fight.

She was vaguely aware of someone whooping a ways off, egging them on, but the noise dissolved as Rory devoured her.

She'd thought he was sweet before, but now she knew better. Behind the thoughtful nice guy lurked a second Rory. Fascinating.

She imagined this other Rory pushing her onto her back and spreading her thighs with his hips.

She wanted in on the secret.

CHLOE

CHLOE SUCCUMBED to an almighty yawn, covering her mouth with her hand. It was dinnertime, though the sun was still hours from setting. The Ecstasy had officially worn off and the manic energy that had been surging in her veins since that morning in the barracks slumped, leaving her listless. She moved pilaf around on her plate with her fork.

Pike looked up from his own dinner, that disapproving-mother look he was so good at tightening his features.

"We won, Pike. You can quit with the sour faces." She yawned again as Ian sauntered over looking perfectly awake. He snapped a folding chair open and sat down with a beer, popping the tab and lifting the can, presumably to toast their victory.

"And *you* can quit with the camaraderie," she added to Ian. "It's creepy coming from you. And we're all on our lonesomes tomorrow." Thank goodness. The promise of self-reliance had Chloe breathing ten times easier.

"You'll miss me," Ian said, then turned his attention to his beer. Chloe gave his profile a good, long study. Too goddamn handsome for his own good. And far too handsome to trust. Or waste.

Chloe turned as Pike muttered, "Thank God."

She looked up to see Rory heading in their direction. "Thank God for what?"

"For some company that's not suffering from chemical withdrawal or a personality disorder." Pike stood and jogged to grab two cans from the ice chest and met Rory as he reached their little corner of the yard.

"Hey, man. Good to see you're still here."

Rory's eyebrows rose but he accepted the beer. "Sure."

Pike opened his own can and tapped it against Rory's. "And thank fucking God you guys gave Marissa the boot."

Rory broke into a guilty smile and his posture relaxed. "Sort of a no-brainer, that one."

Ian piped up. "If those lassies had any brains they'd have gotten rid of you."

Rory's eyes narrowed in his direction. "Oh?"

"You're the only one in that group who's any kind of threat."

"Is that meant to be some kind of compliment?"

"Jest saying, your little mate Leah missed a trick. Guess she likes *you* more than winnin'. No accountin' for taste."

Rory rolled his eyes. He seemed to recede back into some invisible shell, setting his unopened can on a tree stump. "I came to talk to Ian," he said, folding his arms over his chest as though the very idea gave him the chills.

Chloe thought she caught Ian's pupils dilate for a split second as his brain rewired, switching off antagonist mode and flipping on the scheming curiosity.

"Alone," Rory added.

Pike wandered toward where Daisey and Mac were playing some kind of don't-flinch punching game…the weirdest foreplay Chloe had seen in a while, and tempered by that same edgy vibe that had been crackling between the two since the elimination.

She looked up to find Rory staring pointedly at her.

"I'm not going anywhere."

He made an exasperated face and she retaliated with a shrug of profound indifference.

"You've got something private to say to Ian," she said. "How can my being here possibly make that any more tragic?"

"Fine." He turned to Ian. "Leah said Mac said you've got condoms."

The corners of Ian's lips curled, evil. "Oh, well well well."

"So do you?" Rory asked.

"I may…"

"Is there any chance I could have one? Please?" He looked ready to gag on that tacked-on nicety.

"Mebbe. What do I get in return? Free show?"

Rory made a disgusted face and turned to leave. "Fucking forget it."

"Oi, calm yourself, Kiwi. Jest fecking with you. What've you got tae trade? You got any flares? Anything with gunpowder in it?"

Chloe blinked and made a mental note as Rory shook his head.

"Shame." Ian reached inside his blazer and came out with a plastic square. "Here you go. On the house."

Rory's brown eyes snapped between Ian's face and the condom. "What's the catch?"

Ian grinned. "No catch, mate. I'm an old romantic from way back."

Rory took the condom, skepticism tattooed across his face.

"Plus I'm going to feck you over the second I get the chance, so consider it an apology gift in advance." Ian's wicked smile broadened and he forfeited their staring contest to fish for a cigarette.

Rory cast Chloe a look and turned away.

"Check it for holes," she said, meaning it to be more helpful than bitchy. "And have fun."

He shook his head as he left them.

Ian lit a smoke and laughed. "That's too fecking funny."

She watched Rory's retreating back. "I think it's sort of sweet."

"Aye. Good luck tae 'em. They're both wasting their time here. Let 'em have a consolation prize."

Chloe nodded, sleepiness creeping over her again. She watched Daisey and Pike showing Mac some self-defense move, Daisey lunging at Pike with a sheathed knife and Pike twisting down the attacking arm in slow motion.

"He fancies her," Ian murmured, and Chloe turned to find his gaze on the threesome as well.

"Daisey or Pike?"

"Pike."

She nodded, having already suspected as much. "Did you mean what you said before? Did you actually see her naked?"

He nodded and blew out a long jet of smoke. "Aye. I'm a prick, nae a liar."

"You are so a liar. Your lying during the first challenge is the only reason Leah and Pike are still here."

Ian made a grudging face and Chloe countered with a grin.

"So did Mac lose a bet or something, have to strip for you?"

"Prolly jest did it tae get Daisey riled up. Looks like it's working. Anyhow it's keeping his mitts off you for a change, so count your blessings."

"Amen to that." She stared out over the yard for a minute, breathing in Ian's secondhand smoke, that sweet, forsaken stench.

She picked up her camera and caught Ian in the viewfinder, took a few pictures of him, those eyes squinting in the sunlight, probably too blue to ever print accurately.

"Ian," she said at length.

He raised his black eyebrows at her and she snapped another shot then set the camera down. "What do you do? Professionally?"

He blew a couple of smoke rings and made her wait. "What d'you think I do?"

"Between the cheekbones and pills and the height and the lack of a soul, I guess I've got my money on model."

Ian smirked, turning his attention back to his vice.

"Do you think it's a coincidence that everybody here is single and straight and decent-looking?" Chloe asked.

"Leah was'nae single when she got here."

"No, but she was supposed to be here with her lover... You think maybe these so-called scientists are really just pervs out to tape a bunch of strangers banging each other in the woods?" She glanced reflexively at Ian's crotch as he watched the others. "I bet we were cherry-picked for just that reason. I bet those psych tests they gave us show we're all hot-blooded nymphos or something."

Ian gave her an appraising look. "I bet any group of semi-anonymous strangers thrown together in competition end up wanting tae feck each other's brains out."

Chloe giggled, blaming the sound on some residual chemical still swimming in her blood. "And I bet *you* tomorrow's challenge is like a battle-royale orgy."

"Oh aye? And how do you decide who wins?"

"Last one to come?" she offered with a shrug.

"Sounds like it's stacked against us lads. And who do you think would go out fairst?"

She scanned the bodies around the clearing. "Well, I think Mac would go off if Daisey so much as cut a fart too close to her."

"Right. And who'd last the longest?"

"Me."

"You sound pretty sure of yourself," Ian said through another plume of smoke.

"Nothing turns me off more than losing," Chloe said and checked her watch. Early, but she wanted a solid chunk of sleep to reset her body clock. "I'm off to bed."

"Aye. You'll want tae be nice and rested for the orgy."

She stood and gave Ian's face a final study. "Get some beauty sleep yourself, Ian. I want you looking handsome when I fuck the holy hell out of you tomorrow in the great name of competition."

"Pretty threats."

She smirked at him and spoke in a throaty, action-movie-one-liner voice. "I don't make threats, Ian. Only promises."

One side of his mouth tweaked into a skeptical grin. "You bite, lassie?"

"Only if you piss me off."

"Aye. I'll be sure and do that then."

She turned to head to the barracks. "Sweet dreams, asshole."

RORY

REAL OR IMAGINED, Rory felt half a dozen pairs of eyes on his back as he neared the little green tent, Leah's shoes parked outside the flap. The condom wrapper was damp from his sweaty palm and he blotted it on his pants.

He swiped his knuckles across the nylon entrance. "Knock knock."

"Who's there?" Leah's voice sounded from inside, bringing his blood to an instant simmer and pushing everyone else from his mind.

"A bloke who just sacrificed the last of his dignity for you."

The flap unzipped and his heart skipped a few beats. Leah's face smiled out from inside, so pretty he was tempted to write it off as a mirage.

"You got it?" she asked.

He sat down at the edge of the tent and handed her the condom, unlaced his boots outside.

"Was he a prick?"

Rory raised his eyebrows. "That was rhetorical, right?"

She laughed.

"Chloe said to check for holes. Don't think I didn't."

Leah held up the square and squinted. "I think we're good."

Rory folded his legs into the small space and pulled Leah down beside him. They lay on their backs staring at the green ceiling, the stretched-out shadows of leaves painted across it by the evening sun. He snaked his hand between their hips and laced his fingers with hers.

"What a fucking weird day," he said.

Leah nodded, curly hair bouncing against the blanket spread over the tent floor.

"It's nice to see you perking up though," he said.

"I'm going to push my button in the next challenge."

His head swished against nylon as he sat up, fear like a punch to the gut. "What?"

"I'm going to go out. I want to go home."

"You can't just give up. That was just talk, what you said earlier. Wasn't it? You can't actually go."

She laughed. "Why not? This is misery, and it's voluntary."

"Misery?" He swept his eyes over her body then dipped his chin to gesture at himself.

"Not you," she said. "Not us, right now. But this whole thing. It's fucked, what's going on here. I never really wanted this to begin with and my brain's not like these other people's—Ian or Chloe or even you. It's not worth it to me, fighting for this. Even if I wanted the money that badly, other people here seem like they *need* it—like they're practically ready to maim somebody for it. I just want to go already. And this competition...doesn't it feel kind of creepy?"

He considered it, what he felt about this experience underneath the pleasant, hazy sensation Leah gave him. "Yeah. It's a bit... It's dodgy. And it's weird that the so-called doctors or whoever are investing so much money. For the prize and the setup and flying us all here, just to tape us competing in a bunch of games."

"And not only taping the games." She held the condom up. "It feels *off*, the whole thing. If this was for TV, I could see it being so…dramatic. But it's for some psychiatrists in a room somewhere. It feels sketchy. Plus, I'm going soon anyway, no matter how hard I try. There's seven of us left and let's be honest, I'm not going to win."

"If I went out," Rory asked, "would you fight for it then?"

She shook her head. "I don't want it. Not bad enough to do all this. I'm the only one who didn't come here for themselves. Even if I managed to win somehow, I wouldn't deserve it. You deserve it. Mac and Pike deserve it. The decent ones, who want it bad but aren't stepping over other people to get it."

"Why don't you deserve it?" he asked, leaning over and tracing a finger along her collarbone.

She shrugged. "I just want to go home. It's worth it to have met you, but my intuition is practically shouting at me to get the fuck out while I can. Before things get weirder than the frigging Meat Locker. Before they start asking us to risk something worse than hypothermia. That probably sounds paranoid… But anyway, I'm done talking about it."

"Make me a promise," Rory said.

"What?"

"Promise me that if I go out first, you won't give up. That you'll stay and try to win."

She shook her head. "It's not going to happen that way."

"What if it did? Would you promise me that?"

She looked down and sighed. "Fine. And you can't just hit your button before me… But if for some reason you lose and I stay, then okay. I'll try."

The fist strangling his heart loosened, if slightly. "Good."

"Let's not talk about the stupid competition anymore though. Not 'til the sun comes up tomorrow at four a.m. or whenever. For the rest of this day, let's pretend we're on a date that went totally awry."

He nodded, guessing he could pretend to stop thinking about it even if he couldn't do that for real. "Sure. I just took you out for a buffet dinner in the wilds of Alaska. Girls love that, right?"

She smiled, melancholy fading. "You know what I'd *really* love? A shower."

"We can arrange that. Sort of."

Her lips pursed. "What do you mean?"

"We walked over that bridge on the way here. Over the river."

"I dunno," Leah said, suddenly shy and goddamn adorable. "It could be all full of leeches or something."

"Not a river. Come on. We've got hours of light still." He got to his knees, shuffling to the open tent flap to lace his boots back up. Leah reluctantly followed suit. Rory zipped the mosquito netting shut and grabbed his towel and soap and took Leah's hand. Fifty yards across the prairie he saw Daisey nudge Pike with an elbow and nod in their direction. Mac and Pike turned, faces brightening with identical surprise. The side of Pike's mouth twitched and he turned away, more discreet than the thumbs-up Mac offered.

"Oh God," Leah muttered, but Rory could feel her excited, happy energy.

They walked a quarter mile back toward the previous day's camp, tramping into the dappled shadows of the woods and finding the low vehicle bridge along a long-disused and overgrown road. They stood on it and leaned on the crumbling concrete rail, staring down at the wide river, slow and clear with a pebbly floor.

"Perfect," Rory said.

"These woods could be riddled with cameras," Leah reminded him.

"Maybe. But they can't have put them *everywhere*. Just near where the Objectives are happening, I bet."

Leah giggled. "And maybe in the tents."

"Well, I don't give a shit if you don't."

"I guess I don't really give a shit," she said. "And I feel disgusting. Fine, let's do it."

"We can get your clothes washed too. You can borrow something off me to sleep in when we get back to the campsite."

"You sure know how to get my motor running, talking about hygiene and laundry," she teased.

"Just wait until we start swapping recipes." He took her hand again and they left the bridge, walking along the river for five minutes until the road was out of sight and they came upon a nice stretch of bank, a clean rock slope that led gently down to the water. Rory crouched by the river's edge and trailed a hand in the current.

"How is it?"

"Not freezing…but not warm either."

"Worth it to get clean," Leah said.

He stood and faced her. "We doing this the modest way? Avert our eyes 'til we're in?"

"I sent you in search of condoms, Rory. I think us getting naked's probably a foregone conclusion." He caught a faint blush in her tan complexion and felt his own cheeks mirror it. "Eventually, anyhow. Maybe let's keep our undies on," she said.

"Fair enough."

They stood in silent inactivity for a moment, each waiting for some unknown sign. Finally Rory set the towel on a rock and tugged his sweater off, unlaced his boots and kicked them aside. Leah watched.

He laughed. "This strip show's feeling a bit one-sided."

"You've got way more layers. I'm waiting so the grand unveiling will be simultaneous."

"I see." He pulled his shirt up and off, wishing Daisey's bare biceps hadn't been Leah's last glimpse of civilization.

She yanked her own top off, revealing a bra she must have worn with enticing her ex in mind, not hiking. It was stripey and lacy, cute and sexy at the same time, like Leah. Rory did his level best not to stare and failed miserably.

Leah giggled, covering her big smile with a palm.

"What?"

"Nothing. I just haven't been ogled like that in a while."

"Is everyone in Manhattan blind or something?"

She made a face. "It's different there. *Everybody's* gorgeous. Unless you're a supermodel you get rounded down to troll. Or at best, invisible."

"I'd notice you," he said, dead serious.

"Thanks."

They exchanged a pair of shy looks then Rory turned his attention back to undressing. They stripped down to their underwear together and his stolen glances turned into a prolonged study. "Damn."

"It gets worse," Leah said, looking down at the panties that matched her bra. She gave him a nervous glance and whispered, loud and falsely secretive, "It's a thong."

He blinked and Leah laughed again.

"I'm not really a thong person," she admitted with a smile. "And having hiked in one now, I can't say it's a mystery why L.L. Bean doesn't make them."

Rory offered a laugh, his stomach turning at the knowledge that said thong hadn't been selected for his benefit. Then, twisting the jealousy into smug triumph against Leah's mystery man, he let the ugly feeling go.

"Should I turn?" she asked, making a goofy face. "You wanna see my butt?"

"Course I do." Rory made a twirling motion with his finger. "Go on. Unless I massively bugger this chance up—which, knowing me, I could—we're both going to see everything anyway. Go on."

Leah bit her lip, the most endearing gesture in Creation. She turned and Rory resisted the urge to drop to his knees and scream

Hallelujah to the heavens. He kept mum, waiting for her to turn back around. When she did, he put a fist to his chin and nodded, feigning scrutiny.

"Well?" she asked.

"It's all right," he said, trying to sound like a snotty connoisseur.

Leah put her hands to her hips. "All right?"

"It'll do."

She laughed and rushed at him, swatting his shoulders and arms with a few good whaps.

"Ow, kidding. Your butt's fantastic."

"Let's see yours then," she said, tugging at his arm until he turned around. "No thong?" she teased. "Briefs, though. Very nice. I hear they're making a comeback."

"They never went away in New Zealand," he said and faced her. "We're very fashion-forward."

Their bodies were close, a mere foot apart. Rory studied hers with open fascination. She was the same color all over, the same smooth, even caramel sort of shade. She had moles, a sprinkling of dark freckles along her collarbone and a few on the rest of her body. She had a tiny waist and arms, a smooth swell of the world's most feminine potbelly—not as if she were pregnant, just a wonderful little imperfection. Rory wanted to run his palms over it but held back, knowing women weren't always happy about that kind of thing.

"You're looking at my stomach," she said, poking his chest with an accusing finger.

"No, I'm not. I'm looking at your crotch."

She snorted. "It's okay. I know it's there. I've had it since I was like four. My mom always said it'd go away, but here it is." She drummed her fingers on her belly.

"I like it."

"You know what?" She lifted her chin and smiled at him. "I do too."

Rory put his hand out and lay it on her cool skin, running it over her stomach and ribs and up her arm. He took a step, erasing the distance between them.

Her slender arms wrapped around his neck and they kissed, wasting no time. He pulled her close by the waist until their chests and stomachs were pressed tight together, until the lace trim of her underwear glanced his skin and his cock flooded with heat, composure abandoning him completely.

She welcomed his tongue, his mounting aggression, welcomed the firm pull of his hands. His palm drifted lower, cupping the smooth, bare skin of her butt. He kissed her the way he'd been dying to when they'd been hugged together against the cold that morning. He felt her hips swivel, rubbing her mound against his hard-on and dissolving any composure he had left. He pressed close. Her body was eager, pressing his right back until they stumbled together, an intrusion of gravity and the lumpy terrain into their cloud of hormones.

Rory smiled as they broke away. He caught her gaze flash to where his cock was demanding attention behind his underwear.

"Don't forget to do your laundry," he said, the quip ruined by his unsteady voice.

She nodded. "Of course not. Let's get that out of the way."

Rory licked his lips, watching Leah crouch to pick up her shirt and pants and socks. He shook himself into coherence and followed suit. They waded into the current together and the cold water redistributed Rory's blood, reacquainting him with sanity.

"Oh, brrr," Leah said.

"This is nothing. Just think about the bloody Meat Locker. This is like a Jacuzzi compared to that."

She laughed, wading deeper. "I heard Mac and Daisey got it on in an actual hot tub in that fancy cabin they stayed in last night."

"You're hitting below the belt there, Bernstein. Me and my icy cold river's not enough for you Manhattan women?"

She grinned. "Try Ohio. And of course not. I love your river."

They made it knee-deep and rinsed their sweaty, stinky clothes. Trudging to shore, they wrung out the garments and slung them over some low branches to drip-dry. Rory tried unsuccessfully to keep his eyes off Leah's breasts, her hard nipples behind the striped cotton. His gaze floated up to her expectant face. Busted.

"Sorry."

"Don't be. You're making me glad I came armed with such ridiculous clothes." She glanced away, not hiding a nervous smile. "Plus I'm checking you out too." She stared pointedly at his crotch.

"I'm feeling compelled to explain the scientific phenomenon that is shrinkage."

"No need. I got a good look earlier."

"Pervert." Rory stepped close and pulled her against him by the hips. Wet legs, dry chests, cold hands, warm lips.

"You ready for that shower?" she asked.

He nodded. He took her hands and they padded down the bank, lazy, cool water washing over their ankles, shins, thighs. Rory sucked in a breath as they made it waist-deep and his balls ran for cover. He looked over to find Leah making a face, mouth round, eyes rolling up. Her descent slowed to a halt.

"Come on," he said, tugging on her hand.

"Give me a second to adjust."

For a heartbeat, he considered being nice. Then he scooped her into his arms and charged forward, ignoring her kicks and screams until they were both in up to their shoulders.

Leah recovered from a protracted gasp and slapped his arm. "You fucker."

He let her down, slowly, her body sliding against his until her feet found the pebbled river bottom. "You would have taken ages, otherwise."

She did a poor job of glaring at him before it melted into a grudging smile. She smoothed cold, wet palms over his face, pushed his hair back. Rory wrapped his hands around her shoulder blades and stared at her irises a moment. What was that color? Yellowish greenish orange. Like a certain type of autumn leaf. Like the chutney from his favorite Indian takeaway. He kept these similes to himself and kissed her. She kissed back and his blood commenced to circulate, slow as tar. He kept his eyes closed and listened to the water, the birds, to the tiny noises she made against his mouth.

He let his palms drift lower, down her spine to her butt, lower. His mouth left hers as he bent and got his hands behind her knees, hoisted her up until her legs hugged his waist, arms around his neck. She dipped a hand in the river then he felt cool water trickle down his scalp and temples as her fingers combed his hair. Cold, everywhere, except that mouth.

They kissed for ages, until rustling leaves and crunching undergrowth brought Rory back to reality. He felt Leah's body freeze and they both stared up at the edge of the woods where the noise was coming from.

"Guys?" someone shouted. A man.

"Yeah?" Leah shouted back.

Pike appeared between the trees. He had his eyes pointed up into the canopy as though he'd expected to find them exactly this way.

"Is everything okay?" Rory called.

"Lenora's gathered everyone together. Some announcement about the next challenge. You'll probably want to get back."

Rory lowered his mouth to Leah's shoulder and sighed. "Bloody buggering Lenora."

She laughed and unwrapped her legs and started toward the shore. "Please keep your eyes where they are, Pike."

Pike turned around and began meandering back toward the old oil operation. Rory tugged his damp pants and shirt on and Leah cinched his towel between her breasts. They got their shoes on and walked fast, catching up with Pike at the bridge.

"Thanks, mate," Rory said.

Pike shrugged. "Fucking timing, huh?"

"They probably did it that way on purpose," Leah said. Rory studied the heavy, wet curls plastered against her neck, the droplets of water dotting the arms hugging her wet clothes to her chest.

They reached the prairie to find all the other competitors assembled, plus Lenora and one of her clean-cut henchmen. The staff had taken away the marquee and chairs in their absence. Mac turned as they neared and Rory saw her stifle a smile. She had an open beer can in each hand and passed one to Pike as he reached her.

Everyone took a moment to assess Rory and Leah. Daisey and Chloe offered near-identical raised eyebrows and smirks. Ian smiled openly and adjusted his hat, expression unnervingly saccharin.

"Thank you, Dr. Pike," Lenora said. "And thank you both for joining us," she added to Rory and Leah, face not giving away any sign that their showing up dripping wet, Leah dressed in lingerie and a bath towel, was the least bit unorthodox.

"As I mentioned earlier, you're all on your own for the third Objective. However, you will be getting to the location as a group tomorrow evening. You'll be taking a hike through the woods then walking to the next destination via an old service road, about thirteen miles all together." She waved a hand beyond the barracks. "We'll be starting at midnight, so I suggest you all leave by eight tomorrow evening. I've got one map here—"

Chloe was stepping forward before Lenora could even finish her sentence.

"If someone would be in charge of it...right, thank you, Chloe."

"What are we doing until eight?" Mac asked.

"Anything you wish," Lenora said, with the air of a teacher who'd just announced a free period to a group of fifth graders. "Breakfast will be available at seven, lunch at noon. No more surprise announcements, I promise, so feel free to do as you wish." She clapped her hands, ridiculously delighted. "Sleep well. And enjoy each other's company tomorrow. At least one of you won't be here by the time the third Objective's through."

Rory glanced at Leah.

With that cheerful pronouncement, Lenora turned on her heel and marched back toward the barracks.

"Beautiful fuckin' timing," Daisey said with a chuckle, and Rory turned to discover the remark was directed at him and Leah. He didn't feel like wasting the breath it would take to figure out if the guy was being apologetic or plain old mean. Leah hiked up her towel in his periphery.

Pike cleared his throat. "Sorry. She made it sound like maybe the next challenge was about to start."

"No worries," Rory said.

"Even if it had been," Ian piped up, "it'd serve you two right, missing out while you're carrying on your lurid wee affair in the woods."

"Fuck off, Ian," Pike and Mac said together, Pike sounding weary, Mac bored.

Rory looked at Chloe. She was dressed in flannel bottoms and a stretchy, low-cut camisole thing, hair pulled back, face looking plainer than normal. "I'm going back to bed," she announced.

"You got the next twenty-some-odd hours to sleep," Daisey said. "Right now we've still got beer and sunshine."

"I don't trust a thing that bitch says. She tells us we have nothing to do until tomorrow night at eight, I bet you anything there's a catch." She folded the map in tidy quarters and started toward the barracks, blonde ponytail flapping with each purposeful stride.

Daisey kept his gaze nailed to her back, jaw set.

Rory looked to Leah, finding worry in her eyes. "Hey," he said, nudging her shoulder with his. "Let's head in."

LEAH

RORY WAITED until they were a few yards on to put his arm around Leah's back, and the contact eased all the tension Lenora's little speech had introduced. She watched the tent getting closer with every step and felt her heart speed with excitement. Happy excitement, but dark as well. Her feelings for Rory and what was going to happen tonight weren't about revenge...revenge was merely an extra spice flavoring the thrill. His arm fell away as they reached their campsite and he took her wet clothes and tossed them over the unoccupied tent that would have been Leah's.

"After you," he said, voice tight with nerves or eagerness.

She pushed off her shoes and opened the netting, crawling inside the tiny dome and tossing aside the towel. She waited with held breath. Rory unlaced his boots and joined her, kneeling and tidying his things strewn around the tent floor.

Something about the fact that it was still bright as day made it all seem realer. More real than any of the other odd surprises this trip had thrown at them.

Rory had left all his damp clothes aside from his underwear outside and she took in his body again. It was winter on the other end of the globe in New Zealand, and his skin was pale, just a bit of color on his neck and face and arms. He had a nice body. A very nice body. She grinned at him, ditching the last of her shyness.

"What?" he asked, grinning back.

"You're really quite sexy." She reached out and squeezed his closest arm. "Between working at a café and having a degree in music, I wasn't expecting this."

"I'm in a social rugby league. Keeps me in shape I guess. Or bruised, anyhow."

"That's like football without the helmet or padding or common sense, right?"

"Sort of." He lay down on his side, facing her. He felt close, his energy, his skin, his face.

"Close the flap, Rory."

He didn't need telling twice. He tugged the zipper down on the outside world, on what might happen tomorrow, on Leah's half-made decision and on all the bullshit that constituted the bizarre reality of the day.

When he lay back down, Leah didn't waste a second. She ran a palm up his warm, bare arm, his shoulder and neck. She rubbed her thumb over his cheek, studying his eyes.

"You're sure about this?" he asked.

"You think I'd make you go groveling to *Ian* for a condom if I wasn't a hundred percent sure I wanted this?"

He nodded. "Fair enough."

"I've wanted this since you rubbed my stinky feet."

"Me too. I want this a lot." He kissed her, light and a touch shy, worlds away from the man who'd held her in the river. He pulled away.

"And I don't just mean I want the sex," he said. "I want *you*. I think you're really...cool. God, that sounded lame. I dunno. I really fancy you, like more than I thought you could fancy someone you've only known for a couple days."

"A couple extremely bizarre days," she amended. "I think we can round it up to a week, given the weirdness factor."

He nodded. "Good. I wouldn't want you thinking I'm easy or anything."

She smoothed his soft, damp hair back from his forehead. "Don't worry, your reputation's safe with me."

"And I think you're really pretty." The words tumbled out of his mouth. "Like, *really* pretty."

"Thanks."

They shared a long silent moment, faces close and smiling. Leah caught something change in his eyes, nerves fading to make room for heat. His mouth took hers again, deep this time, and rougher. His tongue slid between her lips, hot and wet and sure. He led the kissing, his growing aggression thrilling her just as it had before. Leah rolled onto her back and he took her hint, bracing his arms beside her ribs and his knees between hers. His palms pushed beneath her back and she felt his weight, the heat of his chest, the graze of his stiff cock against her thigh. She'd been dying to touch him in the river, aching with curiosity to hold him. She snaked a hand between them and cupped his bulge, rewarded by the moan that heated her lips.

She whispered against his mouth. "Wow." She ran her fingers up and down his heavy length through the cotton.

"I want you so bloody bad."

She squeezed him tight, earning another moan. "I can tell."

He balanced on one arm, reaching between them to push his waistband down and release his cock into her palm. He was hot and smooth. Uncut. Leah eased the skin down and palmed his head, hoping he couldn't tell she wasn't entirely sure what she was doing, only having ever been with circumcised guys before. His affirmative grunts said her ignorance wasn't showing.

His broad hand slid inside her panties. Two fingers passed teasingly over her clit to find her lips and part them. She felt them slip easily over the wet folds.

He sucked in a breath. "Oh God."

Warmth rushed through her body and pooled against his fingers. He was more frantic than masterful, stroking her lips, wetting her clit, hips pushing his cock deeper into her grasp. After a minute his hand left her pussy, slick fingers easing her grip on his erection. He moved back to angle his dick to her, pressing through her underwear. His palm slid beneath her as he thrust, and she felt his fingers fumbling with her bra.

"The hook's in the front. Here." She weaved her arms between his and undid the clasp, watched Rory's pale brown eyes widen in the tent's dim light. He freed his hand again to palm her bare breast, his touch feeling so wonderfully different than her ex's she wanted to burst into song at the sensation. He stroked one nipple and lowered his mouth to the other, the caresses as firm and hungry as the pressure of his dick between her legs. She cupped the back of his head.

His whisper cooled her wet skin. "Touch me."

"Where?"

"Anywhere. I just love being touched."

She started with his scalp, raking her nails through his hair. Then she stroked his neck, his strong shoulders, the damp skin of his back. She ran her palms over his hard ass, kneading and fantasizing about how it'd feel when he was inside her, that moment surely so close. He moaned, hips shifting to force her legs wider until she brought her knees up beside his ribs, welcoming the delicious threats his cock was making.

"I want you, Rory."

His groan vibrated through her chest.

"Now."

His mouth broke away and he stared into her eyes a moment, the look almost too intense to return. He leaned back on his haunches, looking for the condom. Leah studied his cock, stiff and thick, curving up to nearly touch his belly. She reached out to touch it, grazing the smooth, deep pink skin of his head with her fingertips. She watched his stomach contract at the touch, loving the power she had over this man.

He found the condom. Leah sat up and shrugged out of her bra. He pushed his briefs off then eased her panties down her legs, his eyes zigzagging, lips parting. She brought her knees up and he slid the wispy, cutesy item off. She could see his hands shaking as he ripped the plastic open and she put out her hand.

"Here."

He handed it over and she slid the rubber out, pinched the tip and rolled it down his cock with a slow hand. He got back on his hands and knees, the skin of his thighs sticky against hers as he pushed her legs open again.

"Are you ready?" he asked.

"Yeah."

He reached between them, guided his cock to her lips. His breathing was sharp and shallow and fast in the small space, drowned out by Leah's groan as he pushed in.

He eased in slowly, one thick inch at a time until their hips met.

Leah released her held breath, letting her body relax around his. She remembered his request and touched him, memorizing his back and arms and sides with her palms. She held his hips as he began to move—short, slow, controlled thrusts. She wanted more. She wanted that rough version she'd so far caught only glimpses of.

Leah pulled at him, body begging, and he responded, cautious hips speeding up, pumping her deeper.

She ran her hands over every inch of skin she could reach. He changed, giving her what she craved. "God, you feel wonderful."

"Touch me." His body turned greedy, thrusts fast and deep, voice harsh. "Fuck, touch me."

She rubbed his chest and stomach and breathed in his smell, sex and sweat, the musky scent of his deodorant, latex, the green, grassy wildness of Alaska all around them. She'd never had sex in this much daylight before and loved every detail it offered—the flush and glint of his damp skin, each tiny line and freckle on his face, the view between their bodies—Rory's cock withdrawing and disappearing inside her in fast, steady strokes. She joined in the motions, moving her hips in time with his to sharpen the smack of skin on skin each time he pushed deep.

When she muttered his name, he responded as if she'd cracked a whip. He made it faster, harder, losing some of that self-control that made this a performance and turned it into what it was—two relative strangers fucking each other senseless in a tent.

Glorious.

Screw you, idiot ex-boyfriend. Screw you, brain, second-guessing everything all the time. This was the most spontaneous and freeing experience of Leah's life and she wanted to arch her back into it and wallow and roll around until she was caked in irresponsibility.

Rory's skin burned hot, his energy chaotic and wondrous. His eyes were wild, so unlike how he was the rest of the time. Leah grinned, thrilled that she got this secret Rory all to herself. She hoped he'd win. She hoped he'd be the last one standing at the end of this crazy experiment and that the money would make him happy, let him follow some dream he might have on hold.

He laughed through his desperate panting. "What are you smiling at?"

"Nothing. Just happy, that's all."

"I want to make you come." He shut his eyes as if the very idea hurt. "What do you need?"

"It's easiest if I'm on top," she said.

Rory nodded, turning them over and wedging them into the corner of the tent. He scooted them to the middle on his back and Leah sat up, wild hair grazing the nylon above them.

"Do whatever you need," he said, crazed eyes staring up into hers. "I want to feel you come so bloody bad."

Locking a foot behind each of his knees, she put a palm to the ground on either side of his chest and started to rock. She drew herself nearly all the way off him, then took him deep. She might not be exceptionally experienced, but she knew this one position well, knew exactly what worked for her.

Rory felt new and exciting, thick and amazingly hard, his length changing her rhythm, making the strokes longer, the thrill and pleasure darker. The angle rubbed her clit against his pubic bone and shaft as she rode him. She felt his hips shifting beneath her but he was good—he let her control the motions even as she could sense him dying to thrust. His breath came in throaty whimpers, sounds that made her feel radiant with power. He held her breasts, palms cupping, thumbs stroking her nipples so she thought she'd catch fire.

She groaned. "God, keep doing that."

The pleasure grew and changed. It went from a warm, vague, happy sensation to a razor's edge, a mean, hot, needy streak connecting her clit and belly and breasts. She watched Rory's face, his half-open eyes, panting mouth, pink cheeks.

"God, Rory."

"Please," he muttered. "Come on me, please."

"I will. I will." His face faded to a blur as she got lost, sucked into the ache in her pussy and the collective heat of them. Strong hands clamped her hips as the spasms started, keeping her riding as her coordination waned. She pushed herself down onto his cock, hard, taking him deep as the climax came to a head. She heard his voice, whispers she couldn't make out.

She'd closed her eyes and that handsome face was there when they opened, still in thrall, brows contracted in some painful-looking breed of worship.

She bent her arms, collapsing against his slick chest as she caught her breath. He gathered her hair and pulled it back from her face, his lips planting soft kisses on her temple.

She groaned, happy. "Thank you."

"You're welcome."

She smiled, unseen against his jaw. "Your turn."

Rory shifted her until they were side by side, propped on their hips. He slid his cock from her and eased the condom off.

"Touch me," he said. *Begged.*

She ran her hand down his chest and stomach to hold his hard dick. She gave him a couple of light strokes then put her hand to her pussy, making her palm wet before she wrapped her fist back around him.

"Yeah," he breathed. "Stroke me."

She gave him slow, tight pulls until his hand covered hers and sped up the friction.

"Like that. Just like that."

"You feel so good, Rory. You're so big. You felt so good inside me."

He moaned as though the words burned him. "Don't stop. Please."

She loved his voice, his body, that mix of commanding and desperate, aggressive and helpless. "Get on your back, Rory."

He turned and she got to her knees beside him, only missing a beat. She kept her right hand pumping as the left found his balls, cupping and squeezing, the touch tensing his entire body and making his arms tremble. She worshipped him with her hands, recording every sensation for tomorrow or the next day, whenever they were forced to say goodbye.

"God, stroke my cock. Make me come," he begged. "Make me come. Just like that. Please."

She tightened her hand, milked him with a few strokes more before he came undone, hips rising off the tent floor as the first spurt lashed his belly. She stroked until he was empty and his groan died and his body settled back against the blanket. Then she did something she hadn't before, not with either of her former lovers.

She leaned in and licked him clean, loving his taste and smell, the moan he mustered.

He made a noise, a sigh mixed with a cough. "Oh God."

She swallowed and laughed, wriggling her body up alongside his to sling an arm across his chest. She felt his heart pounding against her wrist and she kissed his shoulder.

"Awesome." Smiling, she settled her head on his arm.

He smoothed her hair from her face and cleared his throat. His mouth opened and closed, tiny, uncertain sounds, but he didn't share whatever words teetered there.

She spoke for him. "That was fantastic. Thanks."

He laughed. "Nobody's ever thanked me for sex before. Twice."

"Well, trust me, that was worth its own parade float."

He was quiet a minute. "I know we were mostly having a laugh earlier, about there being cameras in the tents...but there could be."

"Fuck the cameras," Leah said. "Or wait, no. I hope there *are* cameras."

"You got some secret exhibitionist streak in you?"

She shrugged against him. "That was the hottest sex of my life. I hope the whole goddamn world got to watch it."

OBJECTIVE THREE

TWENTY-ONE QUESTIONS

CAMERAS 3240, 3249

AN HOUR PAST Alaska's summer dawn, the first competitor stirs in her bunk bed. Chloe swings her legs to the floor and stands. Stretching, she frees her ponytail and finger-combs her long hair, ties it back again. After casting a glance at Ian's sleeping form in the bunk across the room, she turns away to peel off her camisole and replace it with an athletic bra. She slips on canvas flats and gets her things packed into her bag. Grabbing a large water bottle, she gives Ian a final study before pushing the door open, walking down the silent corridors and out into the yard. Crossing the prairie and squinting into the bright sky, she disappears into the edge of the woods for a minute. When she returns she surveys the grass, seeming to find a patch that meets her standards.

A trance-like exercise routine has her full attention when the second waking soul emerges. Daisey's heavy, lazy footfalls as he crosses the yard are the textbook contrast to Chloe's graceful, precise movements.

"Mornin'." Stopping ten feet from her, he tucks his hands into his pockets, waiting patiently until she sets her hovering foot on the grass and acknowledges him.

"You're up early for a man who told me to consider sleeping in this morning."

"This fucking Alaska sun won't let me sleep. What're you doin'? Wax on, wax off?"

"It's Tai Chi."

"I thought that was for folks like Pike's grandparents," Daisey says.

"I can do worse, if you want."

"Worse like what?"

She stares at him a moment then steps close. She brings her knee to her chest, extreme slow motion, tilts her hips, raises her fists to her shoulders and blows out a long, serene breath. Fast as a whip-crack, she kicks, hitting Daisey hard enough in the head to send his hand flying up to cup his ear. She keeps her foot extended by his shoulder, perfect control.

He squints an angry eye at her then plays dirty, hooking his arm under her leg and toppling her to the ground, landing on braced arms with his knees between her thighs, their crotches dangerously close.

"Get off me!" She shoves him hard in the chest until he rolls over onto his back on the grass beside her. She sits up and gives him a spirited whack in the ribs.

"Ow." It comes out as a laugh and he rubs the spot before folding his arms under his head.

Pike strolls into view carrying a towel, looking even more angsty than usual this early in the morning. "Is this some kind of beat-each-other-senseless challenge?" he asks, gaze shifting between them. "Wish I got that memo."

"Chloe's just showing off her Tae-Bo skills," Daisey says, sitting up.

"Tai Chi," she corrects, standing and reaching behind to brush grass off her back. "And kickboxing."

"Your ancestors into all that crap?" Daisey asks Pike. "All that slow-mo *Karate Kid* action in the park?"

"I'm half-Korean, genius."

"That a yes?"

Pike shakes his head and aims himself toward the woods.

"Moody motherfucker," Daisey mutters. "You takin' a leaf out of Rory and Leah's book?" he asks, louder.

Pike nods, not breaking his stride.

"Oh Pike," Chloe says. He turns this time and catches the water bottle she tosses at him. "If the river looks clean, would you fill that for me?"

"Yeah, sure."

"Thanks."

Daisey looks up at her as Pike disappears. "Got anything else you need fillin', Chloe?"

She rolls her eyes. "Not by you, redneck."

"Oh darlin'." He claps a hand over his heart. "You're killing me, here."

"I would if it won me that money, believe me." She puts her bare foot to Daisey's chest, giving a couple of firm pushes before she abandons him to start back toward the camp.

"What if you had to bed me to win it?" he calls.

She turns and stares at him, a curious smile curling her wide lips. "I'd drink a handle of gin and fuck that shit-eating grin right off your face. Then I'd take a decon shower and dance my ass all the way to the bank."

"So you're telling me there's hope?"

She does a little hip-shaking move as she walks away. "For five hundred grand, I'm anybody's whore, *darlin'*. Even yours."

MAC

MAC FUMBLED FOR HER WATCH on the tent floor beside her sleeping bag. Six-ten.

"Fuck."

She'd nodded off around two but now it was bright again, too bright to sleep. It might be baking back in New Mexico but at least a girl could get some shut-eye.

She tugged on hiking pants and a tank top that did nothing to hide the chunky straps of her athletic bra. As if anybody here would care. Least of all the man she was looking to entice.

It was cool and damp outside beneath a clear sky—nice weather for passing a free day. She was surprised to see people up. Daisey and Pike were out in the yard, standing in that manly military way, feet planted at shoulder width and arms crossed, looking as if they were psychically sniffing each other's crotches to figure out who was outranked. Daisey had size and seniority on his side, but Pike sewed injured soldiers back together for a living, which had to count for something with an ex-marine, no matter how dishonorably Daisey may have been discharged.

"When d'you go back?" Daisey was asking as Mac neared them.

"Not sure," Pike said. "I completed my active duty in June, but I'll probably sign on for another tour when I get back. Need to see how this whole mind-fuck plays out." He nodded at the landscape to mean the entire Ant Farm experiment.

"You'd take the Middle East over Michigan?"

Pike shrugged. "I like visiting my mom and everything, but where she lives in Detroit, it's all the same senseless bullshit and violence, except people are killing each other over designer watches and nobody's paying me to be there." He turned and waved at Mac, offering a smile.

She returned the smile and nodded at Daisey before her attention got drawn back to Pike. He must've bathed as his black hair was wet and even spikier than usual. He had on a fatigue-green tank top and Mac's eyes got stuck on his arm, the lean, locked muscle a surprise distraction from Daisey's less-subtle breed of sex appeal.

"So, yeah," Pike said. "I'll probably end up back there. The weirdest thing is that I miss the *smell*. The dust."

"Shit, I don't," Daisey said. "I did a tour in Iraq—no thank you. I'll trade you for a fish-stinking oil rig any day."

Pike shrugged again. "Gets me sort of excited."

Daisey cocked an eyebrow at him. "You got bloodlust or something?"

"Nah. But I get anxious when I'm sitting around. Over there, I always have to be ready to go. It chills me out, like I know what my job is and I just have to do it. It makes me punchy, waiting around, doing nothing."

A silent laugh flared Daisey's nostrils. "Today should be a fucking treat for you then, Doc." He turned to the right. "What'cha doin' up so early, Miss Mac?"

"Stupid sun."

"Me too. No coffee for another hour, either."

Mac looked to Pike. "You get cleaned up in the river?"

He nodded.

"How was it?"

"Good, once you escape the mosquitoes. I think Chloe's down there now."

Mac caught Daisey swallow at the thought and resisted the urge to roll her eyes. "I've bathed with creepier things than mosquitoes on this trip," she said, pleased with the squint she earned from Daisey. "I meant Ian, actually."

This time both men winced.

She turned toward movement in her periphery. "Oh, speak of the Devil."

Ian crossed the yard. He disrupted their scruffy trio of tank tops, dressed for an underground gambling circuit—blazer, slacks, scratched-but-still-shiny shoes, hat tucked under his arm.

"Beautiful mornin', eh?"

All three offered their resounding indifference.

"I miss anythin' good?"

Mac shook her head. "Just the same thing that'll be going on all day. Absolutely nothing."

Ian set his hat on his head, licked a finger to check where the breeze was coming from and pulled out his cigarette case and lighter. He stepped through the circle to stand downwind behind Daisey and lit up. "Well, we'll jest have tae make this day intae one big getting-tae-know-you campfire jamboree. How'd you fancy your tent, Mr. Too-Good-for-the-Barracks?" he asked Pike.

"Fine. Looks like you and Chloe both failed to drip poison in each other's ears then."

Ian smiled and blew out a jet of smoke. "There'll be plenty of chances, yet."

MAC RETURNED from a cold but much-needed dunk in the river in the early afternoon. As she neared camp, a weird noise greeted her—homesickeningly familiar but totally out of place here in the wilderness.

Beatbox. She crossed the scrubby prairie at a run.

Rory and Pike were standing together, four open beer cans beside them on an ancient, disused utility box. Rory had his hands clamped over his mouth, huffing and hissing a rhythm as Pike rattled off lyrics Mac knew as well as other people might remember lullabies. With a painful ache, she missed her brothers, her home, the desert, the cracked linoleum of their cavernous, messy kitchen.

She stood with her arms crossed over her chest, nodding along for a few bars then jumping in, matching Pike's deep voice with her girlie one, chanting the words with identical delivery until Pike lost his flow and let her solo for the rest of the verse.

"Whoa," Pike said. He and Rory stared at her. "That is *weird.*"

"What?" she asked, knowing damn well.

"That you know Rakim. Aren't you twenty-five?" Pike asked. "Where'd you learn that?"

"My oldest brother, Tim. He's forty-three and he's always been obsessed with hip-hop. He pretty much raised me."

"Huh."

She laughed. "If KRS-1 was a lanky white dude who did a few too many bong hits when he was younger, that'd be Tim."

"Wow."

Mac shrugged. "And what about you? You're only like thirty, aren't you?"

Pike shrugged right back. "When I was in kindergarten I used to hang out on the sidewalk in front of my house and practice Moonwalking for like, hours at a time. Then this crew of break-dancer dudes from the next street sort of adopted me. Like a mascot."

She put her hands to her hips. "No. *Way.* You still have any moves?" She stared at Pike to demand a show.

"Yeah, sure. But not in tall grass wearing hiking boots."

"Oh we can fix that." She ran off toward her tent, grabbing the blue tarp lashed to her pack and dragging it back across the prairie. After spreading it out as flat as she could manage, Mac stood by expectantly.

"Wait wait wait," Rory said. "This is an accident waiting to happen." He left them and returned with four tent pegs and a rock. "You mind, Mac?"

She put on a hillbilly accent. "C'mon now, Rory—that be mah weddin' tarp-o-lin."

"That's a brilliant Daisey impersonation."

"Go ahead," Mac said. She and Pike held the plastic tight and Rory banged a peg into each corner.

"Better." Rory tossed the rock aside and wiped his hands on his pants, cupped them back over his mouth and got a beat going. Pike pushed his boots off and peeled away his socks, stepped barefoot onto the rumpled plastic, face full of skepticism.

"Warm me up, Mac," Pike said. "Get the party started."

Mac kicked her shoes off and stepped onto the rustling blue dance floor in her socks. Pike snorted as she busted out a way-too-hoochie-tastic Sprinkler.

"Dear God, make it stop, white girl."

Mac got her shoulders and hips jerking in the most horrifying Harlem Shake she could muster. "Come on. You know you can't step to the dance-off shit I be bringin'."

"Promise me you don't actually do that in real life."

She ramped it up, segued into some moves that sent Rory into hysterics and wrecked the beatbox for a few seconds. "Oh Pike, I am so hijacking your flight to Detroit and taking you clubbing in Santa Fe when we're done with this contest."

"If I dance, will you take that threat back?"

Mac nodded, adding some booty-shaking that further incapacitated their DJ. She hopped off the floor to catch her breath, looking between the men expectantly. Rory got his shit together and went back to beatboxing.

"All right, all right." Pike stepped to the center of the tarp, smoothed it out and took a deep breath. He got his bearings and started to dance—sucked all the smug teasing out of Mac's brain and replaced it with awe.

Pike could *dance*. Not just for a soldier-boy in his thirties, either. He had body-popping, crazy-ass kung-fu moves. Mac could hear Rory struggling to keep the rhythm going, suppressing shocked laughter.

Mac turned as Leah appeared beside her, mouth wide open. "Holy crap."

"I know." Mac shouted to Pike, "Bring it, Detroit!"

Pike danced for another minute or two, until the pegs began tearing up the corners of the tarp and the dance floor turned dangerous. He finished with a funked-out Sprinkler that put Mac's to shame. She and Leah clapped and whistled and whooped and Pike took a bow.

Ian arrived in his cloud of smoke, Chloe a few steps behind him. "Did we miss an announcement?" she asked. "Is this tonight's challenge? Final seven talent show?"

Pike lifted his tank up from the waist to wipe his sweaty face, and Mac did her best to not notice his abs. "Well, you totally shut me up," she said, smacking him on the shoulder as he stepped onto the grass. "I cower before your skills."

He smiled as genuinely as she'd ever seen him manage. "I think your performance was better, frankly. You must know what you're doing if you can turn it around and make it that awful."

Mac gave him a theatrically withering look, so happy to feel some of the familiar camaraderie she thought she'd left behind with her brothers. "I'll have you know you're looking at the under-ten tap dance champion of New Mexico, 1991."

"You remember any of it?" Pike asked, and Mac offered a couple of over-enthusiastic windmills.

"If you can tap dance, you could definitely break-dance," he said.

"My big-ass trophy's still on the mantle...though most of the glitter's fallen off. I've also been spotted in a club or two," she added haughtily.

"Well, let's see it," Pike said. "Your real moves."

"I need some fly dude to mack on," she said.

Pike looked around, pointed to Ian. "Lemme borrow your hat."

Ian tossed it to him like a Frisbee and Pike perched it at a just-so, Justin Timberlake angle, let his belt out a couple of inches so his pants hung lower and tucked the front of his tank behind his buckle. He took a couple steps toward Mac with his arms loose and gestural, club-dude swagger if she'd ever seen it.

"Wait, wait." Chloe stepped forward and handed Pike her aviator shades.

Mac stripped her shirt off and did her best to hoochify her hopelessly straight hair, pointing to Rory when she was ready. He cupped his palms over his mouth and gave them a beat.

Mac let the woods and sunshine fade away, replaced it with the strobey, sweaty darkness of her favorite cheesy dance club, the forty-five-minute bumpy commute each Saturday that was her only escape from the never-ending fresh air and wide open spaces of her normal life. She offered up a few of her choicer moves, the ones that usually earned her some spirited *'Oooh, girl!'* shouts from the half-jealous, half-shocked Hispanic girls in the crowd. Pike played the part of annoying club guy almost too well, but even pretending to be a lousy dancer he was damn good.

Mac stopped to catch her breath, wishing she was at her usual spot now, that tacky warehouse full of noise and excitement and a promise of romance that never quite panned out once the lights came up.

Leah clapped and Pike joined her.

"Thank you, thank you."

Rory nodded his approval. "You've got quite...swivelly hips."

"Yeah," Pike said. "That was pretty sweet."

Mac laughed. "I've got some old-school moves, if you'd prefer, MC Pike. I do a mean Running Man."

Pike offered a fine one himself and Mac joined him for an encore, not caring that they surely looked idiotic. Ian snatched his hat back and wandered off just as Daisey arrived to replace him. Daisey stopped at the edge of their group, arms crossed, brows raised with curiosity or skepticism.

"What's happening, white kids?"

"Half-white," Pike corrected, panting and smiling. He handed Chloe back her glasses.

"Little body-poppin', little breakin'," Mac said, holding her arms up and giving Daisey a quick demo. "Do you dance, Daisey?"

"Hell no."

"Then stop crowding the floor." She waved him away a few paces, earning a grin from Pike. Daisey and Chloe left and the dancing went on a while longer, until Rory brought the tempo to a close. Mac caught him exchange a glance with Leah.

"Think I need a water break," Rory said and he and Leah wandered off toward the tents, leaving Mac and Pike alone with their heaving diaphragms.

"I have a sneaking suspicion that water break's going to take about four hours." Mac turned to aim a grin at Pike. "Well...I have to admit, I was *not* expecting that from you, army-boy."

"I'm quite a hit in the infirmary."

Mac gathered up the cans and walked them to a box set up for empties. She grabbed a fresh beer and tossed it to Pike, cracked one open herself. "How did you end up a combat medic, anyhow? Were you a marine first?"

He shook his head and took a drink. "I was a doctor first."

"Oh."

"I couldn't stand it, once I was out of med school. By the end of my first year of residency I was ready to kill myself."

"How come?" She led him to a cluster of empty folding chairs and they sat.

He wiped a dirty hand across his forehead. "Everything. Politics, people's attitudes and egos, the patients. Like everyone around me was either miserably ill or a cutthroat workaholic. I had loans and I was living with my mom, and she's a fucking trip—not that I don't love her."

"And the army's been better?"

"Yeah, loads better. People there, they're actually hurt. They don't show up with fake back injuries demanding Percocets, or eat themselves into obesity and all the nasty medical shit you get from that. They get hurt risking their lives. They're people I *want* to help... Not that everybody in the hospital I started at was a hypochondriac or a pill-popper or like, totally at fault for their own health problems. But enough of them were."

"Maybe you should work at a VA hospital, if you're so set on helping patients who deserve it or whatever. Someplace where you won't get yourself killed."

"I probably will, once I finish in the service. I definitely won't go back to any place with decent funding."

She nudged his knee with hers and took a long drink. "You're sort of ruining the whole rich-doctor-with-a-BMW illusion. Still, it must be gruesome, being a medic." Mac grimaced, picturing blown-off limbs and third-degree burns, charred flesh like barbecued chicken.

"It is, but I'm not affected by the gore, really. When it's my job...I dunno, I can just do what I have to. Like I know what my role is and I just switch on medic-mode and I feel, like, calm. Not happy, not empty...just calm."

"Wow." Mac nodded slowly, took a couple sips of her beer. "I feel a bit useless now. It's easy to forget—when you're not close to the shit that's going down—that it's out there, happening."

"Yeah, tell me about it."

"My second-oldest brother joined, in '03. He got shipped back with a head injury after his first deployment, but nothing that fucked him up. Not mentally, I mean. I was really glad that he didn't have to go back again. He was too, I think, but he'd never admit it."

"You *should* be glad," Pike said. "War's..."

"Yeah," Mac said, knowing what he meant even without a fitting adjective.

"Anyhow. You've got some moves, Mac."

"You too, Pike. That's your last name, right?"

"Yeah. What about 'Mac'? Is that short for something?"

She nodded. "Machiniak."

He laughed. "You'd fit right in in Detroit with a name like that."

"More than you know—my father grew up in Flint. My grandpa worked for GM. He had loads of shady stories about the UAW."

"No shit." Pike gave her a long, reconsidering look over his can as he drank.

"Are you from an auto family? Which of your parents is Korean?"

"My mom. She's worked at a drycleaners my whole life. My dad's white. He worked for Ford for a thousand years, then he got laid off in the eighties and now he doesn't do much of anything."

"Are they married?"

Pike laughed. "Oh God, no. There is *so* much wrong with that idea. I honestly have no clue how they stayed in a room together long enough for me to even exist. I mean, if the language and culture barriers weren't bad enough, my dad's about fifteen years older than my mom. And anyhow, she can do way better than him. My dad's sort of... No, not sort of. My dad's a real shithead."

"Bummer."

"Yeah, he's never given me much reason to look up to him. Which is weird since he's like six-foot-three."

"Are you guys *anything* alike?"

He laughed, staring down at his hands. "God, I hope not. Same first name," he offered with a shrug. "Same hometown. Same cheery disposition. That's about it."

"What about your manly voice? Is that his?"

"Nah. I don't know where that came from."

Mac smiled at him, quiet for a few moments. She leaned in and bit her lip, then ran a hand over the short crest of Pike's overgrown mohawk. "They let you have that haircut in the army?"

He smirked, the kind of grin that might've accompanied a blush if his complexion had one to offer. "One of the other medics did that, actually. We get bored a lot."

"I like it. It suits you."

Pike cleared his throat, staring off over the yard toward the woods. "Looks like it might rain later."

Mac scanned the expanse of flat gray sneaking in from the east. "Maybe."

"Think maybe I should try and take a nap, before we start the death march."

She pouted at him. "When you could spend the afternoon drinking beers and teaching me some of your secret b-boy moves? You can sleep when you're dead, Pike. After I've won, I'll buy you one of those foam-o-pedic space-age Brookstone pillows with my prize money."

Pike escaped her eye contact, smiling tightly down at his can. "Fine. You're not winning though, hate to break it to you."

"Well, *you're* not winning, so get used to the idea. But I'll give you ten bucks if you teach me how to do that thing that looks like a Russian folk dance on acid."

Pike tapped his can against hers. "Whatever you want, Mac."

DAISEY

BY THE TIME EIGHT O'CLOCK rolled around, Daisey was feeling a couple hours past hungry and the sky had turned a dark shade of gray to match his mood. He didn't fare well with boredom and today had been nothing but.

Rory and Leah had spent the afternoon surgically attached at the face, Mac and Pike lost in some hours-long dance lesson that erupted with Mac's laughter every couple of minutes and got on Daisey's nerves. Chloe had passed much of the day napping in the sun, or wandering around the grounds like a woman itching from a rash burning up the patience-center of her brain. She'd ducked most of Daisey's attempts to get next to her, so smoothly it was as if a summer breeze had carried her off.

That left Ian for company, and even Daisey wasn't *that* hard up for entertainment. In the end he'd spent a few hours in the woods, doing target practice with his knife. Discovering the crew wasn't going to show up with dinner made him wish he'd done a little actual hunting. Even squirrel had to beat going into a challenge on an empty stomach.

The group had their things gathered by seven thirty and shot the shit for a while, then Chloe took out the map she'd commandeered and they started the hike.

The humidity had the mosquitoes out and ready to party and they made Daisey a little homesick for Mississippi. He missed the rig more though, which was fucked—being homesick for a place that kept you away from your actual home. But he missed the sea air, missed being the biggest jerk in the joint, having work to do that was so punishing and near-thankless that he slept like a corpse each and every night. No dreams, no tossing and turning, just perfect, thoughtless exhaustion.

"You're awful quiet for once," Chloe said. They'd been leading the pack for over an hour, Chloe because she had the map and Daisey because he liked being near her.

"I'm grumpy. Wish they'd given us dinner."

"Boredom, hunger, trek through the bug-infested woods, some Objective that doesn't start 'til midnight." She raised her shapely eyebrows. "Coincidence?"

"Think the fuckers behind the cameras are about to go all psychological on us?"

She nodded.

"Bet you're right. You bring any food with you? I know some of us packed granola bars and shit."

"I did. I had a fine supply of staples then they all went mysteriously missing during the Meat Locker."

"You don't think another player stole your stuff? Greg or that annoying redhead or somebody who went out early?"

She shook her pretty blonde head. "No, I do not."

"Hmm. Interestin'."

The sound of singing reached them from behind. Not singing, rapping. He couldn't fucking stand rap, even with somebody as clinically adorable as Mac belting it out. She and Pike were bestest buddies now, bonded together by their capacity to annoy Daisey. And sure, some of that had to do with the fact that he didn't *entirely* mind being the one Mac normally salivated all over. Not that she was being like that with Pike. Still, Daisey didn't share well with others.

"You two," Daisey said, turning to glare at them. "You guys wasted all afternoon dancin' your asses off when you coulda been resting. Now we're probably off on some midnight dodge ball death challenge and you're fucked. Good thing we're all on our own or your teammates'd be pissed."

"It was worth it," Mac said, jogging to flank him, nestling him in a not-unpleasant sandwich between her and Chloe. Pike stayed behind.

"Worth it to not think about mosquitoes and competition for a few hours." Mac shot Daisey an evil grin. "Plus you're just jealous your old joints couldn't keep up, grandpa."

He narrowed his eyes, curled his lips into a sneer. "Very cute, Miss Mac."

"I try."

"You keep that up and I won't let you give me any more sponge baths."

Pike made a theatrical shuddering noise behind them and Mac laughed.

Daisey felt the first cold drop of rain hit his scalp, and he actually hoped the sky might open clear up and drive the bugs away. It was probably nearing nine thirty but behind the cloud cover, the sun thought it was midafternoon. "Fucking Alaska."

Ahead of them, the woods broke. They hiked through the last of the tangled forest and out onto a crumbled old road, half reclaimed by grass and tree roots. With the canopy gone, Daisey was soaked in under a minute.

"Take a right," Chloe said, pointing.

The road was as bad as the woods for walking, maybe worse. The ancient pavement was split up like an ice flow, cracked into a zillion pieces. Daisey stuck to the overgrown shoulder, Chloe doing the same on the other side.

"Look," Pike said behind them.

"Oh yeah," Mac said.

Daisey craned his neck. "What?"

Pike pointed. "There's railroad track under the paving."

Daisey looked at the rusty line cutting a seam through the hunks of road. He remembered the tracks that bisected his hometown, how they'd seemed like the route to Someplace Better when he'd been a teenager, someplace better than his parents could offer.

He forgot his empty stomach, his achy knees and his bug bites. He remembered the reason he was here, and when the rain picked up he didn't even feel it.

CAMERAS 3356, 3357, 3358, 3359

AT A QUARTER TO MIDNIGHT, just as the sun is deciding whether or not to set, seven tired, hungry, punchy competitors emerge from their soggy trek to find an ancient factory by a long-disused stretch of lonely road, two lanes of skeletal, cracked asphalt. The space has the ambiance of a moldy concrete cathedral, stained glass in the most literal sense; broken too, high windows letting in the wind and noise and damp from the rushing storm outside.

On one side of the vast space, an old furnace glows orange, leaking heat that doesn't quite reach the seven metal folding chairs arranged in a small circle in the center of the floor. A staffer greets the group as they file in, handing out Styrofoam cups full of black coffee strong enough to strip paint. He invites everyone to find a seat. Above each chair hangs a hooded, high-wattage light bulb, seven simultaneous police interrogations in the making.

Everyone looks dire under the harsh bulbs save Ian. With his hat brim blocking the glare, he's a picture of sinister confidence, ready to face the music. Chloe's blonde hair glows bright white beneath her lamp, deceptively angelic. Daisey's so tall the bulb glances his buzzed hair and he scrapes his chair six inches to the left, dramatic staging be damned.

The heavy side door creaks open and Lenora enters, letting it squeal shut behind her. Her lips part in a Miss America smile. "Good evening, queens and drones. How is The Ant Farm this beautiful evening?" As if on cue, thunder rumbles outside the warehouse's broken windows, a flash momentarily bleaching the crumbling gray concrete walls white.

"We're getting to be a real cozy group now. I think it's time we all got to know each other a little better." Lenora strolls around the circle, hands behind her back. "Everyone who applied to take part in this experiment underwent some testing in the weeks leading up to selection. Background check, psychological profiling, personal history and a lie detector. I don't believe we've got any lawyers in our midst, as no one seemed to have read their waiver close enough to realize that all of the information is fair game for exploitation."

Murmurs cut through the ring of seven.

"That, or you're all just such open books that you don't mind a little airing of your dirty laundry. Now, pay close attention to the rules. This Objective's a little different. No physical danger, so no buttons."

Rory's gaze snaps to Leah's face.

"We're calling this Objective Twenty-One Questions. There will be three rounds, and at the start of the game, you'll each be issued five tokens. For each round, we have a personal question regarding each of you—in some cases a *very* personal question—which will be drawn randomly by a member of the group. You must read the question aloud, and then make a guess at whose life it refers to. It could be your own. If you guess correctly, you'll receive a token from that person. If you guess incorrectly, the wrongly accused receives one from you. You draw your own question, you'll have a choice of either outing yourself and keeping your token, or offering someone else up, losing your token for a wrong answer but saving face. Your call. You may not, however, falsely claim yourself to be the answer to another person's question. Understood?

"The person—or people, if there's a tie—with the fewest tokens by the end is out of the game. The person or people with the most tokens will win an advantage in the next round. Questions?"

No one speaks, the silence heavy with tension.

"We'll get started in just a few minutes. Enjoy your coffee. It's going to be a late night."

The crowd breaks into murmurs as Lenora exits, everyone escaping the blinding lamps to mill around in the shadows.

Ian sidles over to Mac, flashing her a tight, smug grin.

"Hello, Ian. Welcome to yet another evening in our little Orwellian wet dream. Deep, dark secrets edition."

He grins.

"What?"

"You a betting woman?" he asks.

"Maybe. You want to bet on the winner?"

"Nae, on the loser." He scans the group, lingering on Rory and Leah. "Who knows what those two know about each other now. I cannae wait tae see if one of them fecks the other over."

"No way," Mac says. "They're sticking together 'til one of them goes out. You wouldn't understand it, but it's called loyalty."

"So who then?"

She gives her competitors a good sweep. "What are we betting?"

Ian grins deeper and licks his lips. "I'll go down on you."

Mac snorts, doubling over for a second with shocked amusement. "No thanks. That's not my idea of a prize, Kilpatrick."

"Nae, it's *mine*."

She meets his eyes. "What? You win, you give me head?"

He nods. "Ten minutes or 'til you come, whichever's fairst."

She offers her most contemptuous look. "I won't come."

"Does'nae matter tae me."

"You're creepy…" She nods slowly. "But you're on. You won't win, anyway."

"So what about you? What's your wager?"

She stares up at the ceiling as she thinks, meeting Ian's eyes after half a minute. "I win, you give me all your cigarettes and pills. I want to see you fall on your face when all your crutches are suddenly gone."

He puts out his hand and Mac shakes it quickly, as if it were coated in slime.

"So who's going to lose?" she asks.

Ian looks around. "Darkest secrets, eh? Comes down tae who's the most predictable. I'll go with Daisey."

"I bet you'd love that. Well, I'll say…you."

"That's daft. I lose, I'm gone, and you won'nae be able tae collect on your winnin's."

"Thanks for your concern, but trust me, it'll be more than satisfying."

He shakes his head. "It's nae fun if there's nothing at stake. Pick someone else."

"Fine." She casts her eyes around, seeming to choose randomly. "Chloe."

"Very good." He smiles at her, pure evil, and wanders off, making notes on a little spiral pad.

Daisey watches him stroll by and turns to Chloe. She changed out of her wet clothes when Lenora departed, dressed now for comfort and performance in yoga pants and a fitted thermal top.

"They're placing bets on the loser," he says. "You want in?"

"Between you and me?"

"Sure."

She thinks for a moment. "Anything but my camera and you're on."

"I was thinking something a bit more interesting." His gaze roams her body.

"Ah, of course." She rolls her eyes. "Pigtails not satisfying your appetite anymore?"

"I win the bet," Daisey says, "and we fuck how I want. You win, we fuck the way *you* want."

"Sounds like you win either way."

He steps closer, giving her a chance to ponder what his body is capable of. "C'mon, Chloe. What are you afraid of?"

"I must admit, I do like a spot of gambling. You tell me who you've got your money on, then I'll decide."

He weighs his choices. "Leah. No secrets worth hiding there."

Chloe stares at the girl in question a long moment. "Fine then. I've got my money on you, cowboy."

He snorts. "You think I'm going down?"

"I think you're about as subtle as a brick. And trust me, when you lose, it will be exactly how I want to fuck you. Meaning not at all."

"You're breaking my heart, darlin'."

"Here's to hoping you never get a chance to touch me." She gives him a snotty look and slaps his cheek twice as she saunters past to stand by the furnace.

RORY

Lenora beamed her smile around as the seven competitors took their seats. "I know we're all eager to get to know each other a little better, so let's get started!"

A crew guy set a metal box on a stool in the center of the circle then dumped a bunch of folded index cards inside.

"The order of the first round of questions will be determined by age," Lenora explained. "Youngest to oldest. Obviously, the later your turn comes, the bigger the advantage in guessing. The order will be Leah, Mac, Rory, Pike, Ian, Chloe, Daisey. The topic of this round will be your greatest fears."

Rory turned to his left, to where Ian sat poised with a spiral pad. Rory raised his eyebrows at him. "What's that about?"

"It's like one of those logic puzzles," Ian said. "I'll be up all night, making meself a wee game of it. Folding everyone's dirty washing and hiding it away in my cupboard." He tapped a finger to his temple.

"Yeah, brilliant."

"So, Leah," Lenora said. "You're starting us off. Would you please reach into the box and pull out the first question?"

Leah caught Rory's eyes for an apprehensive second then stood. She stepped forward and reached into the box, coming out with a card. She unfolded it, eyes scanning as she sat back down.

"Read it to the group," Lenora said. "Nice and loud."

Leah cleared her throat. "Who in this group is most frightened of..." She swallowed. "Their own temper?"

A lead weight dropped into Rory's stomach.

"And now please tell the group who you think is the owner of that answer," Lenora said smoothly.

Leah's eyes moved all around the circle, landing on everybody but Rory. "Chloe," she finally said.

"Was that you, Chloe?" Lenora asked.

"Fuck no."

"All right then. Leah, you lose a token for an incorrect guess; Chloe, you gain one for being wrongly fingered."

Daisey snorted, clearly liking the idea of fingering Chloe, wrongly or otherwise. Leah leaned over Pike and handed a yellow chip to Chloe.

Rory shot Leah a savage look as she sat back in her seat. As Mac stepped forward to grab the next question, he whispered, "What was that about? You knew that was me."

Leah made her face stony, her meaning plain.

Mac read, "Who in this group is terrified of dogs?" Her lips pursed and her eyes roamed her six competitors. "Pike?"

Pike nodded solemnly and Rory took fresh note of that nasty scar on his neck. Pike passed a token to Mac.

"Rory," Lenora said, "you're next."

His legs felt unsteady as he went forward to reach into the box. He unfolded the card as he sat down. "Who in this group is terrified of rats? Leah," he concluded without deliberation, eyes still glued to the paper, not wanting to see her face.

"Is that correct?" Lenora asked her.

"No," she said quietly, and accepted the token Rory pressed into her palm. He caught her yellowy eyes for a second and they were full of anger.

"You knock that the fuck off," she whispered.

"What?"

"You fucking know."

He'd never seen her so pissed, and as much as that unfamiliar look made him wince, it made him want to kiss her ten times worse. "Try and stop me."

"Pike," Lenora said in her satiny voice. "If you would, please."

Pike grabbed a paper and read it standing up. "Who in this group is terrified of guns?" He looked around, gaze lingering on Leah then Mac, mouth opening and closing. Then he looked to the other member of the group who'd spent time in a war zone. "Daisey," he said slowly.

Daisey laughed. "Yeah, right. You wish."

Pike's shoulders slumped and he tossed a chip across the circle to Daisey. He took his seat with the flustered sigh of a man quickly running out of tokens.

Ian got up and fetched a paper, plopping back down and crossing his legs primly. "Who in this group," he read, "is afraid of ghosts?"

Ian's unearthly eyes scanned the crowd, skipping over the already-outed Pike. They stopped on Rory, and Ian's smirk told him the tense exchange between Rory and Leah hadn't been lost on him. His tongue flirted with the corner of his lips a moment then he spoke.

"Daisey."

Daisey's eyebrows rose, slow and disbelieving. He reached into his pocket and flung a token at Ian as though aiming to take an eye out.

Ian caught it with a tiny flinch. "Cheers."

Chloe aimed a shit-eating grin at Daisey from across the circle that Rory couldn't begin to comprehend.

"I believe I'm next," she said, and rose to grab a slip of paper. "Who in this group is terrified of small spaces?" She turned from one end of the circle to the other, reading poker faces. "Not Daisey, not Pike. Not Ian, since he did just fine in the Meat Locker. Rory?" she guessed.

Rory shook his head and caught the token Chloe grudgingly tossed to him.

"And finally, Mr. Daisey. You're up," Lenora said.

Daisey took the final paper from the box. "Who in this group is frightened of driving?" He laughed softly.

Rory glanced at Leah, scared of the way she was staring at Daisey, jaw set, lips pursed, practically begging him to pick her. Rory knew goddamn well she was the right answer too.

"Leah," Daisey said, apparently not quite dumb enough to miss the world's intentionally worst poker face.

She stood to hand him a token, down to four now, only Pike below her in the count. Rory glared at her again.

"So at the end of round one, Mac, Ian and Daisey are all tied for the lead with six tokens. Well done," Lenora said. Her flunky dropped a fresh handful of folded cards into the box and rattled them around.

"The next round is all about your sex lives," Lenora announced with a wide grin. "Specifically, your long-lost virginities. The order will be determined by how far you each traveled to be here for the experiment, shortest distance to farthest. That would be Mac, Daisey, Pike, Leah, Chloe, Rory and Ian."

Mac stood and drew the first question. "Heh. Okay…who in this group lost their virginity in an abandoned building?" She looked around, smirking at Pike. "No offense to Detroit, but the odds seem pretty good it's you."

Pike smirked back. "Sorry."

"Shit." She handed him a chip, her face full of fake vitriol.

"Daisey's next," Lenora said.

His huge hand fumbled in the box. "Right. Oh holy fuck. Who in this group lost their virginity in the back of a hearse?" He laughed, shaking his head at the question. "Well, I like Mac's reasoning, and I bet Detroit's got more spare vehicles and casualties than it knows what to do with."

"Fuck you," Pike said.

"Pike," Daisey said with finality.

Pike sneered and shook his head.

"Damn." Daisey flung a token at him and sat down with an angry squint. Rory glanced around, deciding he'd probably have guessed Ian if only because of his morbid complexion.

"Pike, you're up," Lenora said. "And it looks as though you're getting some of those lost tokens back. Let's see if you can earn yourself another."

Pike unfolded his card and read, "Who in this group lost their virginity to their tenth grade English teacher? Good God." He made a distastefully amused face and looked around. "Mac?"

"Oh thanks a lot!" she said, laughing. "No way. *So* not me." She took the chip he offered with a false glower, bordering on flirtation.

Leah got up next, sending Rory's pounding heart into high gear.

"Who in this group lost their virginity on their parents' bed?" she read.

On her parents' water bed while listening to a Dave Matthews album, the summer after she graduated high school, Rory amended. She'd told him that story just six hours ago when they'd been snogging the afternoon away. His heart sank.

"Rory," she said, already sliding a token out of her small stack.

He shook his head dismally and accepted the chip.

Chloe cast them each a leery glance as she went to grab her question. "Ooh, juicy. Who in this group lost their innocence to a member of the same sex? Hmmm… Mac?"

"Nope," Mac said, grin deepening as Chloe slapped a token in her palm.

"You're up," Leah mumbled to Rory.

He gave her another angry, helpless squint and stood. He unfolded the paper, already knowing what his answer would be, no matter the question. "Whose best friend took their virginity at the age of nineteen as a favor?" *Ouch.* "Leah," he said, not even pretending to mull it over.

She narrowed her eyes at him. "No." She took his chip as if he were handing her a snotty tissue.

"And finally, Ian," Lenora said smoothly.

Ian picked out the final card. "Who in this group lost their virginity on prom night, but nae tae their date?"

No one had guessed correctly yet, which left a lot of choices. Ian's eyes slipped from one face to the next as his brain went through its creepy machinations. "Mac."

She huffed out a supremely annoyed breath. "Yeah, here." She flicked the plastic chip at him.

"Right," Lenora said. "That leaves Ian in the lead, and Pike, Chloe and Leah tied for last place with four tokens apiece. Staying with our scandalous theme, the final round will go in order of how many sexual partners you've all had, fewest to most. The order will be Leah, Pike, Rory, Mac, Daisey," Daisey shot up rod-straight in his chair as though someone had shocked him, "Chloe, then Ian."

Chloe snorted at Daisey's murderous glare. "Get over it, redneck. There's no prize for being the hugest slut."

A staff member dumped more papers in the box and disappeared into the shadows. Lenora acted oblivious to Chloe and Daisey's exchange. "Leah, please start us off. The topic of this round of questions will be your darkest secrets."

The atmosphere between the seven competitors went instantly cold. The only thing Rory wanted more than to hide his own murky past was to keep Leah next to him. He wanted to grab her around the waist, hold her back so she couldn't take her turn. He watched her stand and walk to the box, grab a card and read it on her way back to her chair. "Who in this group was charged with involuntary manslaughter at age eighteen?"

Rory's heart thumped as he thought for a second that it was him. But no. He hadn't succeeded, and if he had it would've been one-hundred-percent voluntary.

"Rory," Leah said.

He felt both flattered and guilty that she assumed it *couldn't* be him. "No," he said, taking yet another of her tokens without meeting her eyes.

"Next is Pike."

Pike stood and fetched a slip. "Who in this group has cheated on every significant other they've ever had? Oh classy, kids. Christ..." He searched the faces. "Ian."

Ian smiled and shook his head.

"Oh, my bad." Pike tossed a chip to him. "I forgot no one in their right mind would ever get into a relationship with you."

"People in their right minds dun'nae do much for me anyway," Ian countered.

Rory sighed and went up for his question. "Who in this group killed their...their grandmother," he finished, eyes wide. "Crikey." He had to take a deep breath to bring himself to attach Leah's good name to that one. "Leah," he managed to say, already handing her a chip.

She didn't take it.

Rory's mouth fell open and he couldn't seem to close it.

Chloe muttered, "Oh, fuck me," followed swiftly by Daisey's tactless, "Will do."

Rory took his hand back and sat beside Leah, heart frozen. Her shoulders trembled in his periphery.

After a few seconds she leaned in and spoke in a raspy, desperate whisper. "She was really, really sick. She told me it was medicine. I was seven."

He put out a hand to touch her arm but she pulled it away. "I didn't know—"

"It's fine. I'm going home now. It's what I want."

"Next is Mac," Lenora said, mercifully drawing everyone's eyes off their hushed argument.

Mac grabbed her card. "Who in this group was sent to a detention center at age fourteen for arson? Jeez, we all had some troubled-ass childhoods, huh? How about...Daisey?"

"Sorry, darlin'."

Mac shrugged and handed him a token, still holding a healthy handful. He accepted it with a smile and stood, heading to the box and shooting Chloe a look. "Seriously? You've slept with more people than me? Am I the only motherfucker on the face of the earth you *haven't* nailed?"

Her smirk dripped with satisfaction.

Daisey nodded in what looked like Leah's direction then addressed Chloe. "Hope you're prepared to rectify that."

"Read your stupid question, Daisey," Mac said.

He unfolded the paper and cleared his throat, scanning the words. "Goddamn. Who tried to kill their stepfather with a shovel when they were twenty-two?" He gave each person a long stare. "Quietest man's the one who'll surprise you the most," Daisey said slowly, eyes sliding to Pike. He looked him up and down for what felt like a full minute before his gaze snapped two seats down. "Rory."

The blood drained out of Rory's face but his body didn't have a reaction to offer. "Yeah," he said dully. "That's me."

Mac and Chloe and Pike all stared at him with wide eyes. Ian scribbled something on his notepad. Rory flung a token at Daisey, wishing he could give him all of them, enough to put him in last place and force Leah to make good on the promise she'd made after they'd survived the Meat Locker together. Before they'd even properly kissed.

Chloe's voice cut through the haze. "Oh my... Who in this group slept with their best friend's fiancé—with an extra e in parentheses, I should say—the night before the wedding? Hoo. I've slept with just about anybody who'd lie still for it, but a friend's fiancé is where I draw the line. I'd say Ian, except I very much doubt he's got a friend to start with—"

"Oh, cheers."

"And that leaves Daisey."

Daisey rolled his eyes and huffed out a gruff sigh, holding out a token. He jerked it away from Chloe's hand a few times before she managed to pry it from between his fingers.

Pike turned to Ian. "You're up, man-whore."

Ian stood and strolled to the box, picking out the final question. "Who in this group watched both their parents die at gunpoint when they were seven years old?"

"Oh my God!" Mac said. Then added, "Oops," realizing she'd taken herself out of the running.

Ian smiled down at the card, blinking for a few seconds before he made his decision. "It may please you all tae know, that was me."

Daisey let out a low whistle.

Ian sat back down, no tokens lost or gained.

"Well," Lenora said, taking a spot in the center of the circle. "We've certainly learned a lot about one another, haven't we?"

Pike muttered, "Yes, teacher."

"And at the end of that final round, we do of course have to say goodbye to someone. Leah," she said, swiveling to face her. "You'll have to leave us now. I'm very sorry."

"I'm not," Leah said.

"The staff will escort you out once you have your bags in order."

"I don't have any bags."

Lenora's toothpaste-ad smile beamed so bright it was inhuman. "Okay then. If you'll just follow Josh...?" She waved a gracious hand at her sidekick.

Rory stood and grabbed Leah's arm, pulling her into a hug that was probably against the rules. "I'll miss you."

"You too."

"I hope this is really what you want."

Her limp arms finally rose and locked around his neck. She pressed her forehead to his cheek. "It is. I promise. Now you have to win, okay?"

He nodded. The staffer came over and tugged at Leah's shoulder. Rory let her go, resisting the urge to break down and cry for the first time in years, in front of a warehouse full of his worst enemies. Leah turned as she got to the door and gave him a small wave and a weak smile, offering a halfhearted *call me* phone mime with her hand.

He raised his own hand and mouthed, "Bye."

CHLOE

FOR A HALF HOUR following Leah's departure, the remaining competitors milled uneasily and shot the shit in the gloomy warehouse, unable to settle. Chloe dodged Daisey's initial attempts to wrangle some details from her regarding when and where he might cash in his chips from their wager.

He sidled up to her as she was arranging her sleeping bag. "Second we got tents again," he murmured.

She shook her head, still undecided about whether or not to honor that stupid bet.

"Don't pretend you ain't intrigued," he said, watching her tidying her pack.

She sighed. "Bet you're just as lousy at sex as you are at grammar."

"Another wager you'd lose." Daisey grabbed her arm and coaxed her upright to face him.

She slapped his hand away and narrowed her eyes. Plenty of women might've reveled in the sensation of a big man's strong grip bossing them around, but not Chloe. "Don't touch me."

"Strange words, comin' from the woman who agreed to do way worse just an hour ago."

She kept her voice low, out of Rory's earshot. "Should have guessed the little bitch would slit her own throat."

"So how about it? Next time we got tents?"

She bit her tongue, deciding to keep the door open. Stringing Daisey along with the promise of sex might just keep her ass safe, should things come down to a vote in a future challenge. "We'll see." With that she wandered away, in dire need of a distraction. An outlet.

Ian had gone missing just after Leah was taken away. Chloe pulled open the warehouse door and found him lighting a cigarette a few yards farther along the wall. After her talk with Daisey, Ian looked like a very convenient palate cleanser. Or perhaps a loophole that might just get that redneck off her ass.

It was finally dark and eerily cool, the air electric, threatening more rain. She hugged her chest against the chill and wandered over.

"Congratulations."

"On being an orphan?" Ian asked, squinting through the smoke at her.

"No, on the game, jackass. I'm being serious."

"Oh aye? Well, I took notes, and you're the only one I dun'nae know anything about for definite. You the arsonist or the manslaughter case?"

Chloe smiled at the ground before answering. "I'm the one who's cheated on every boyfriend she's ever had."

His eyebrows rose. He took a deep drag before replying. "You telling me that because you pity me for what I shared?"

"No, Ian."

"Good. Money's worth more than my pride, darlin'. I cashed in a sad old tale so I could get ahead. If I'd thrown that answer I'd be sharin' the advantage with Daisey. So if you think I've done something noble or genuine, you think again."

She smirked, wondering if that was defensiveness edging his voice. "I'm just being straight, one manipulative asshole to another. Plus I'm relieved there's one person here who's a bigger slut than me." She smiled at him and bit her lip. Unfolding her arms, she pointed to his cigarette. "Gimme a taste of that."

He held her eyes, taking a deep drag before handing the cigarette over.

Chloe sucked in the smoke and felt a long-missed lover warm her lungs, stir her blood. She flicked it to the sopping ground, half-finished.

"Oi, woman—that's good tobacco you're wasting."

She touched her fingertips to his throat then pulled him down by the collar until their faces were level. She caught his eyes flick between hers, the first shred of hesitance she'd ever seen the man relinquish. She angled her head, coaxed his lips apart with a slide of her tongue and blew the smoke into his mouth. He sucked in a breath but didn't cough.

He blinked at her. "You jest here tae steal a fag? Or did you come tae torture something out of me?"

She shook her head. "I came here with a different filthy habit that needs satisfying."

"I know he's about as subtle as a battering ram when it comes tae his affections, but I think you may find G.I. Redneck's more than willing."

"He's not my type."

"Flattered, darlin', but I'm nae your type either."

"Can you keep it up?"

He nodded. "Aye."

"Can you follow orders?"

"I 'spect so."

"Then you'll do. That's all I want out of a good-looking man." Chloe narrowed her eyes, attention fully focused on that gorgeous face.

"An' I'm nae really intae blondes."

"That's fine. I'm not really blonde."

Ian didn't move, didn't utter a word as she unbuttoned his tweed blazer and ran her palms up and down the front of his shirt. His gaze merely followed her hands.

He felt good, far firmer than she'd expected. She slipped each button of his rumpled, unwashed dress shirt free from its hole and spread it open. Damn. "Where'd you get this body?" she demanded, taking in his toned chest and long, lean abdomen.

"Does'nae matter. Looks like it's yours now."

"You're goddamned right," she breathed, and raked her fingernails down his skin, leaving a faint pink trail. "You got any other surprises for me?"

He reached out and took her jaw in his hands. She pulled away as he tried to kiss her.

He smirked. "You taste like an ashtray, same as me."

"I just don't care about kissing all that much."

He took her in his hands again, rougher. "That's dead romantic, but you want my cock, you're gonnae have tae kiss me. I'm quite old-fashioned." There was a lie somewhere in this exchange, but Chloe couldn't pinpoint its coordinates.

"Fine."

He grinned and freed a hand to remove his fedora. Chloe examined his wavy hair, black as his stubble and lungs and soul. She let him lean down and brush his lips over hers. The contact made her shiver. The tiniest breath of a laugh escaped from his nose.

Ian didn't kiss as she'd expected him to; he didn't kiss as if he were *getting away* with something. He kissed like a man who'd just taken a woman on a very expensive date. Slow and deliberate, as if he'd earned it.

His tongue traced the seam of her lips and she parted them, curiosity replacing mere tolerance. He caught them with his, suckling the lower one a moment. Then his tongue teased her, wanting in, and she tilted her head and let him penetrate. He did taste of cigarettes, but it wasn't a flavor she disliked. In fact, she missed it so badly it felt like bone-deep grief. The only habit she'd quit before the smoking was kissing men like she meant it. Oh well. If she was going to relapse, she might as well do it with a binge.

Sliding her hands farther inside his shirt, she ran her palms over his ribs and shoulder blades. His tongue drove deeper, slipping against hers, obscene as fucking. Forbidden. She heard a faint noise—his hat hitting the ground—then his fingers tangled in her hair. He kissed her so deep and aggressive she could already feel a climax mounting. Sounds escaped Ian's throat, little grunts and breaths and strangled moans.

A raindrop hit the crown of her head. "I need to fuck you," she said, breaking her mouth from his. "Now."

His eyes opened halfway. "Right. Where?"

She looked toward the near-black woods. The only light was the glow leaking from the high windows of the warehouse. She grabbed his hand and led him around the corner, to a wall with no doors. She pushed his blazer off his shoulders and yanked the sleeves from his arms as rain began to pelt.

"Get on your knees," she said.

His eerie eyes searched hers in the near-darkness then he sank down before her, awaiting further instructions.

Chloe kicked her shoes off and pushed her yoga pants down. Ian watched, and only the twitch of his throat as he swallowed ruined the stoicism he was affecting. Dirt and wet leaves plastered her shins as she knelt. She unbuckled his belt and opened his fly, pulled his pants down enough to reveal his black shorts. He was hard, tenting the cotton, erection curving off to one side. Not bad at all.

"Show me," she commanded.

Ian pushed his briefs down and eased himself out. His cock looked heavy and ready, the ultimate betrayal of his calm, calculating face.

"Not bad," she said, measuring him with her eyes. "Is that as hard as you get?"

He reached down to stroke himself, making his cock a little thicker for her.

"Even better."

He gave her a wicked, tight-lipped smile, then grabbed his jacket and dug in a pocket for a condom. Chloe watched him rip it open and slide it down his length.

She scooted forward and wrapped her bare legs around his waist as Ian spread his knees wider.

"You dun'nae want tae take your knickers off?" he asked, grasping her hips.

"In case you haven't caught on, I like it messy and frantic. And I'm in charge, so keep your mouth shut unless it's panting my name."

"As you wish—"

She silenced him with a hard, wet slap across the face that jerked his head to one side. He blinked, dazed.

She pulled the crotch of her panties aside and he took the hint, angling himself. He rubbed his warm, sheathed head up and down her eager lips, taunting.

"Chloe," he murmured.

"Fuck me."

He slid inside her with the raising of his hips, sinking deep. Nice and thick.

"Good." She began to ride him, taking him deeper, rocking in his lap until she had every last inch buried in her hungry cunt. Ian moaned, finally coming apart. His hands grasped her hips, punctuating each of her motions with a matching thrust of his own. The pleasure mounted inside her, tightening her pussy, making her dizzy. The rain turned heavy, soaking them through, but nowhere near as wet as her sex felt against his cock.

He moaned her name. She grasped his hair and held his pretty face against her throat. "Make me come," she ordered.

He groaned as she rode him harder and dirtier, drawing herself along his shaft at a sharp angle, milking him.

"It feels so bloody good—"

She leaned back and slapped him again, so hard it stung her palm and split his lip. He reeled.

"You're just a hard dick to me. Keep your mouth shut."

Ian recovered enough to moan, "You're so wet."

She slapped him again, wondering if that was what he wanted.

The rain hammered. Ian stared skyward a moment then laughed.

Chloe balked. "You laugh like that again—"

He rocked her onto her back in a flash, catching the back of her head and her shoulder with his hands, knocking the breath from her momentarily.

"Get off me!"

He fucked her, hard and deep. His hips forced her thighs wide and his cock surged in and out, in and out, dominating.

"So tell me, sweetheart—who are you cheating on right now?"

"Fuck you."

"Come for me," Ian said, breath short, words shallow.

"Get—off—of—me," she spat between blows, trying to push him away with a barrage of useless shoves to his sides. This was all wrong. Against her rules. But *fuck* if it didn't feel amazing.

"You better beat me tae it fast, darlin'," he choked out. "I'm gonnae shoot right inside you, it feels so good—"

"Don't you dare!"

"Kiss me an' I'll let you back on top," he said, still pounding her, fast and rough.

"Fuck! Fine!" She pulled his face down to hers and slid her tongue between his lips. His hips slowed, the thrusts deep and explicit as he kissed back. Not dirty, suddenly. Textbook romantic missionary lovemaking. Horrifying. He drew back, sucking on her lower lip and releasing it with a snap. His hips stilled.

He grinned. "I dun'nae usually go all the way on a fairst date. I hope you won't think any less of me."

"Jesus, shut up, Ian!"

"Love when you say my name."

She groaned her disgust and he let her roll them over onto his back. Chloe could feel mud in her hair and all down the back of her shirt. She resolved to turn this encounter into a punishment. She sat up and rode him, fucking his hard dick with rough, mean pulls. The pleasure grew, mixed with the animosity. It redoubled at the sight of him, at looking down at that pale skin glowing in the dim light, tight body shining wet from the rain and splattered with mud and grass.

Her climax rose, building from deep inside as she took him at all the right angles, caressing that gorgeous spot inside her pussy. Her body tightened around him, so desperate.

"Good," he said.

"Shut up." She closed her eyes and reduced him to a hard, thick piece of meat so she could finish. The shocks started, hot little spasms bucking her greedy body against him.

"Come on me," he breathed.

"Shut. The fuck. UP, IAN!" The most beautiful tremor racked her as the name escaped her lips.

His panting sounds told her he was joining her. His hands grasped her hips, kept them still as he pumped her fast from below. He pushed deep and held himself there, lost in moans and grunts. Pleasure rocked her, ripped through her, quieted all the screaming

160

voices in her head for a few glorious moments as her body fluttered and twitched around his.

Reality returned, ushered by an awareness of the raindrops pelting their bodies. Chloe opened her eyes and stared down at him.

He stared back, then grinned. "Was it good for you?"

She took control of her limbs and stood, braced her muddy foot against Ian's bare chest as he tried to stand up. She pushed him back down against the ground with a wet thump.

"Keep your mouth shut about this if you value alliances."

She saw him swallow. Taking her foot away, she fumbled into her wet pants and yanked them up her still-trembling legs. She slipped her shoes on as Ian buckled his belt and draped his filthy jacket over his arm.

"Button your shirt," Chloe said, running her eyes up and down his body, ready to start forgetting him.

He grinned and headed toward the front of the warehouse, dripping shirt hanging open. She followed.

"Just button your damn shirt, Ian."

He grabbed his fedora off the ground and turned. "Why? What else do you think they're going tae assume we've been up tae? Bird watching? And what do you care, anyway?"

"I don't."

"Fine, then." He strode to the heavy door and pushed it in. She followed, skin crawling.

Ian paused at the threshold, leaving her blocked and standing in the pouring rain. He turned to gaze over his shoulder at her. "Oi. You owe me a new shirt, a fag, a condom and my innocence."

She pushed him bodily into the warehouse.

Ian strolled across the dirty concrete floor, leaving a trail of tiny puddles.

Leah's absence was startlingly obvious with the group now down to just six. Rory was lying off to one side on top of his sleeping bag, hands clasped at his waist, attention aimed at the high ceiling. Daisey looked up from a card game with Mac and Pike. His eyes darted from Chloe's dirty hair to Ian's bare chest and slap-pinkened face and bleeding mouth.

Chloe held her breath, waiting for Ian to humiliate her. It'd serve her right. Hell, maybe it would serve her well. She met Daisey's scrutiny squarely.

"Where you two been?" he asked, voice stiffly conversational.

Chloe caught Mac's lips tighten, Pike's eyebrows rise.

"Out for a smoke," Chloe said.

Ian tossed his blazer over a chair with a wet slap. "Hell of a storm out there."

"Looks it," Daisey said. He stared at Chloe, tongue tracing his lower lip. She answered with a roll of her eyes.

"Best keep the things you care about inside on a night like this," Ian said casually. His gaze darted to Daisey. "Lest they get ruined—"

Daisey shot to his feet and toppled his metal folding chair with a clatter.

"Knock it off," Chloe said, staring him dead in the eye. She gave Ian the same look and shook her head, weary. "This night's been drama enough for all our lifetimes. Give it a rest, you two."

She found Rory watching her from his spot on the floor. She wandered over, plunking her wet butt down beside him.

"Sorry about Leah," she said, voice low.

He nodded as best he could with his head against the ground. "Cheers. Sorry for whatever it is Ian just did to you. Or tried to." He made a face as if he were consoling a recent loss.

"He didn't," she mumbled. "I did it to him."

Rory closed his eyes, looking nauseous. "Wow. So not what I wanted or expected to hear."

"Sorry."

"Guess I won't be the only one who leaves a sex tape behind for the shrinks to analyze." He reached out and patted her knee limply in commiseration.

"I guess not."

"Well, mine was worth it. I hope yours was too."

"It wasn't," she lied. She glanced around the gloomy space. Ian was standing by the glowing furnace in his wet clothes, his back to her. Daisey was playing cards again. His eyes darted up from his hand in time to catch hers and he swallowed.

Chloe looked back to Rory. "It was sweet, what you tried to do for her."

His nostrils flared with an irritable inhalation. "That's what Mac said. Sweet old Rory, that's me."

"Sweet Rory, nothing. We all know your secret now, shovel-boy."

He sighed. "Yeah. The last thing she'll remember about me is my failed attempt at patricide. Brilliant." He shut his eyes and took another deep breath. "I'm sort of glad my plan failed tonight, after all that. She's too kindhearted for this. She was right to try and get out. This game's as fucked as she said it was."

"I sure as hell wish you'd succeeded. I lost a bet with Daisey and now he thinks I'm going to sleep with him."

Rory's eyes widened. "You made a sex wager about the game?"

"On who'd lose, yeah. Daisey had his chips on Leah. If I'd known she was planning that, I never would have taken those odds."

He shook his head, looking more exhausted than exasperated. "Why would you even *make* that bet?"

She shrugged. "Sex isn't sacred to me. Competition is."

"Jesus. Are you some kind of compulsive gambler?"

She stared at her muddy feet. "More like an adrenaline junkie."

"Well, take up bungee jumping, for heaven's sake. Or Russian roulette. Anything but chancing having to rut *Daisey*."

"Fair point... So how do you feel about the competition now? You going to roll over and give up?"

"Like I'd tell you," Rory mumbled, shrugging into a flimsy suit of armor.

"I *am* sorry she went out. Especially the way she did."

"I'm sure you are." His sarcasm sounded like hard work for an unpracticed man. "Which were you, anyhow? The cheater or the fire starter...?"

She pursed her lips. "Cheater."

Rory made a face—a martyred, judgmental grimace.

"It was only two boyfriends," she offered.

"Two for two's still a hundred percent."

"Don't act so holy. I'm not the one who tried to bludgeon someone to death. Anyway, I was young. I think I just did it so they couldn't fuck me over first."

Rory's brow bunched, softening his glare.

She went on, not knowing if she was even doing it to keep him sympathetic or not. "I hate losing. I wanted to make sure I wouldn't be the loser."

"You don't get to call it winning if you cheat, Chloe."

"Maybe not. But you don't lose."

Rory's eyes darted over her face and for a second she thought she'd gained some sympathy. But it was far worse than that—pity. The ugliest look there was.

"I don't think I could bloody stand it, living that way."

She picked at the mud caked to her pants. "It beats getting walked all over."

"You make everything sound so...zero-sum."

"Maybe it is. You can't have a winner without a loser."

"What about a tie?" Rory asked.

"I don't believe in ties."

Rory pushed a sigh through his nose and closed his eyes, as though he'd heard everything from her he cared to. Chloe gave his knee a clap then used it to brace herself and stand. "Anyhow, just trying to commiserate about your little girlfriend."

"Don't need your pity, thanks."

"Better watch that temper, Rory. And you might want to try frowning a bit less, if you're not looking for pity."

He opened his eyes enough to give her a distinctly withering look. "I'll be smiling the day they ship you home and you have to go into therapy, knowing you failed worse than a misery-guts like me."

"In your dreams."

He shut his eyes tight and linked his fingers atop his chest, faking serenity. "I'll get back to you on that."

PIKE

A NUDGE TO HIS SHOULDER drew Pike out of a state of half-sleep. He'd been idly trying to guess what Mac might look like with her clothes off, and opening his eyes to find her next to him, fully dressed, was perplexing to his sleep-deprived brain.

"Hey," he said.

Way-too-early morning light leaked through the high windows. Mac scooted her folding chair right up beside his, speaking quietly to not wake the lucky people who'd managed to nod off. "You weren't asleep were you?"

His stomach gurgled, angry and empty. "Nah. Too punchy."

"Me too. I should have passed on the coffee." She yawned broadly and cast her eyes around the room.

Pike did the same. Chloe had unrolled her sleeping bag near the furnace and appeared to have drifted off. Ian was sitting in a chair, scribbling on his spiral pad, not too far from where Rory lay. Daisey was slumped in a chair across the way, snoring with a hand cupped idly over his crotch.

Pike's groggy, hormone-clouded mind wandered again as he stared at Mac. He tried to imagine what she'd be like, going down on him… He bet she'd smile a lot and make eye contact. Maybe she'd pause now and again to mumble his name. *Pike*. He stared at her hands, small and slender with nice, neat, short nails. *Pike*.

Pike.

"Pike." Mac snapped her fingers in front of his face.

He shook his head. "Sorry. What?"

"I said I miss Leah."

"Oh, right."

"It sucks she went home."

"What?" Pike asked, hoping maybe she'd fall for it and lean in closer. She did.

"I'm bummed Leah went home."

He shrugged. "Don't be. It's what she wanted."

"I know. Well, I feel bad for Rory, anyhow."

Even with her stale coffee breath and sweaty, dirty clothes, Mac smelled perfect. Pike lowered his voice and mustered some majorly hypocritical wisdom. "It's stupid to fall for anybody here."

Mac smirked and her eyes jumped to Daisey. "Good way to pass the time though."

He felt a familiar psychic arrow sink into his heart with a *thwack*. "Good way to drive yourself bat-shit," he said, speaking from experience.

"You wanna come outside with me a minute?" Mac's eyebrows bobbed up in a conspiracy Pike couldn't pinpoint. Still, no way he'd tell the girl no when she looked *that* eager.

"Okay."

Mac grinned and stood. She headed for her frame pack, emerging from the shadows with an umbrella and a small leather bag. Stopping to crouch beside Rory, she nudged him awake and made a gesture with her fingers and mouth. Rory shook his head and shut his eyes.

Pike followed her out the front door, still clueless. She popped the umbrella open and led him twenty muddy paces away from the warehouse. The sky was gray, rain coming in lazy, heavy drops.

"Hold this."

Pike took the umbrella, watching as Mac dug a pipe and a bag of pot from her bag. He laughed. "How did you get that through airport security?"

"I didn't fly. I hitched a ride to Calgary with this horse breeder my brother knows, then I took a couple buses to Fairbanks."

"Damn."

She shrugged. "It took like five days, but I hate planes. And the ride was beautiful." She packed the bowl and stashed the weed bag under the strap of her bra. She fished out a lighter and took a hit.

Pike swapped her the umbrella for the pipe and tried to not notice that their lips had now shared a common surface.

He blew the smoke to the side and they swapped again. "Hoo, thanks." He half stifled a cough. "That's pretty good."

"Good 'til we remember exactly how hungry we are, but yeah."

"Damn, this is what I could have used in the Meat Locker," Pike said. "Instead of Ian's stupid Ecstasy."

She snorted. "Ian brought E? Did you take any?"

Pike shook his head. "He and Chloe did though."

She made a face, nodding with a mix of skepticism and grudging respect. "Well, they did outlast us all."

"You don't think it's cheating?"

"Only if it's also cheating that Daisey gets to use his hunting knife or you get to use your medical stuff, or that I get to smoke a bowl right now. There wasn't anything in the rules about drugs being off-limits. Or anything else, really."

"I guess."

"I mean, did you read all those waivers? I think we practically gave them permission to harvest our organs while we sleep."

"For half a million bucks, they can take whatever won't kill me."

"Plus the Ecstasy only *seems* like cheating because Ian's so creepy," Mac said.

They traded the pipe back and forth again and Pike felt that warm, calm contentedness melt his nerves away. The rain sounded crisper, the air smelled better. Mac's eyes looked brighter, even in the dim light and the umbrella's shadow.

She held the pipe out and he shook his head. "That's plenty. I'm out of practice..." Pike laughed. "What was that all about anyhow, your prom-night-virginity thing?"

She laughed. "Oh God, what a ridiculous night. My date ran off with this skank a friend of mine brought as a date. Me and him ended up drinking a bottle of peppermint schnapps and having sex in his parents' basement."

"Wow, romantic."

"Oh, yeah. Nothing sexier than getting it on for the first time on a pile of some guy's grandma's old afghans. What about you? Which one of those was your dirty little secret?"

Pike giggled, a sound he hadn't made in ages, not since the last time he'd smoked, probably. "I'm so not telling you."

She took hold of his shoulders and jostled them, probably something she did all the time with her many brothers back home. She grabbed his wrist with both hands and tugged at him. "Come onnnn..."

It was hard for Pike to deny Mac anything. If he'd liked her *before* they'd spent four hours dancing like morons the previous afternoon, before he'd found out she was the kind of girl who hitched rides with horse breeders and happily shared her superior stash... He was about ready to propose to her now. It didn't hurt that she was cute and nice and smart or that she understood a little bit about where he was from, didn't hurt that she was short enough to make Pike feel tall for a change.

Only one thing about it *did* hurt, and the pain was what Pike imagined it'd feel like to have a man roughly Daisey's size stomp on his windpipe.

"Fine," he said. "Gimme another hit and I'll tell you."

She held the pipe out and waited, eyes on his face until he exhaled. "Spill it."

"I was the one who lost it to their best friend, as a favor."

"Ah ha. Well, that's not so bad."

He shrugged. "Nah, not really. I still thank her for that."

"You guys are still friends?"

"Yup."

"And you never tried being more than that?"

Pike shook his head. "She annoys the living crap out of me. And not in a cute, romantic comedy way. More like an 'area man gets fifty-to-life for brutal murder' kind of way."

"Gotcha."

Pike took a deep breath of wet, earthy Alaska air, cracked his neck and tried to remember what he'd been so irked about twenty minutes ago.

"We better head in, in case they announce what's next or something," Mac said. "You want to roll around in the mud and make everybody think we stole Ian and Chloe's idea?"

He laughed.

"That's probably what everyone thinks anyhow. Since we spent the whole afternoon together."

Pike kept his lips and eyebrows in check, trying to cover up how much pleasure the idea gave him. "You think?"

"Maybe. Although if that's true then now they'll think I tried to invite Rory along to our tryst."

"I'm pretty sure the smell will give away our actual scandal."

Mac stowed her pipe again and they headed back to the warehouse. Pike collapsed her umbrella and shook it out on the concrete floor, hating how dark it felt inside, how moldy it smelled after standing in the rain with Mac. His mood took a nosedive in spite of the chemicals still floating around in his head.

He followed her back to their chairs and they sat in silence for a few minutes, most of the bond they'd just established feeling lost, as far as Pike could tell. Or maybe the weed was making him paranoid.

Pike had gotten used to looking after everyone else's ass first, and it was a tough habit to break. For half a million bucks though, he'd screw his head on straight. He needed a mantra to keep him focused on what his priorities ought to be, here in this fucked alternate reality... *You're here for yourself.* Not the weak ones, not his teammates, definitely not Mac.

He drummed his fingers on his thighs, staring into the furnace's glowing orange jaws. "I wish they'd tell us what's next, already. I'm getting—"

As if scripted, Lenora's magnified voice cut him off. "May I have everyone's attention?"

Rory jerked awake and sat up, looking as though he had no clue where he was. Pike watched his face and spotted the exact moment when he remembered Leah was gone.

"It's time to announce the teams for the next challenge," Lenora said brightly. She strode to stand beside Daisey's chair and face the group. "Members will be chosen at random, and one of you will have an advantage. Ian, because you ended the last Objective with the most tokens, you'll have the option to swap any two competitors, including yourself."

Ian nodded coolly.

"All right." Lenora clapped and turned as one of her cabana boys walked up holding the same box from the Twenty-One Questions challenge. "The first team will be..." She rummaged and pulled out three slips of paper, unfolding them in turn. "Rory... Ian. And Daisey."

Pike's chest swelled with idiotic hope.

Daisey glanced at Rory, face full of skepticism or disappointment. Ian's eerie-ass blue eyes snapped between Pike and Mac.

"And so the other team will be Chloe, Mac and Pike. Ian, do you want to swap any of those teammates?"

Ian looked Pike dead in the eyes as he spoke. "Aye. I'll switch with the good doctor."

"And so you shall," Lenora concurred.

A rain cloud gathered over Pike's mood. He sensed Mac staring at him in his periphery and did his best to block her out. *Doesn't matter. You're here for yourself, retard.*

Lenora went on. "So in the next Objective it will be Ian, Mac and Chloe against Daisey, Rory and Pike. And with that, I bid you all a good night. Or perhaps more accurately, a good morning."

Mac was the only one who returned the sentiment. Chloe climbed out of her sleeping bag and strolled over to Ian. Pike still wasn't entirely sure whether they'd been fighting or fucking before they came in dripping with mud and weird energy earlier.

"You know something we don't about tomorrow's challenge?" Chloe asked Ian.

He cocked a brow. "How's that?"

Daisey piped up. "You passed up a chance to stick with me, or at least swap and work with Pike. I ain't got nothing against the girls—"

"Better not," Mac said.

"But I mean, what do you weigh, Mac, like a hundred pounds with your shoes on?" Daisey turned back to Ian. "If tomorrow's a physical challenge you know you're making your life way harder. And tonight's thing was completely mental—"

"Agreed," Ian said.

"We're just saying," Rory cut in from across the floor, "the whole 'Ian's harem' approach doesn't really make sense."

Ian shrugged. "Dun'nae see why *you're* whingeing, Kiwi. Gave you the muscles and the medic."

Rory sighed. "I don't get you."

"Bet that pleases you."

"It *is* weird, Ian," Mac said.

"I have my reasons."

Pike watched Mac's dark eyes roll. "No doubt," she mumbled.

Ian gave Mac a calculating look that tightened Pike's chest. "Plus, you and me have some unfinished business."

"No, we don't. Neither of us won that bet."

"Perhaps nae, but I have another arrangement in mind."

Mac sighed and rubbed the balls of her hands into her eyes. She turned to Pike, speaking softly. "Man, for a second I thought you and I were finally going to be on the same team for a change."

"Maybe Ian and Chloe have some kind of deal worked out."

"Fine with me. They can stab each other in the back 'til the cows come home for all I care."

"Do you think people have alliances going? The teams keep changing."

She shrugged. "It'd be a hard thing to orchestrate when we don't know how the eliminations work from day to day. Not that I'd put it past anybody."

Pike swallowed then asked her quietly, "What did that mean, what Ian said to you? About your unfinished business? Are you two planning something against Chloe?"

"What? Oh God, no. Nothing like that." She laughed. "Thanks for thinking I'm capable of it though. No, it's just a stupid bet we made." She kicked the corroding concrete floor with the heel of her shoe, smile fading.

"What sort of bet?"

"Nothing to do with game-play, I swear. I'm already five-one. I don't need to stoop to anything." She bumped his shoulder with hers.

Pike mustered a limp syllable. "Yeah."

"Plus, how much you want to bet the perv-o doctors behind all these cameras don't have a pool of their own going, back in the laboratory's break room or wherever? About who's going to win?"

Pike frowned as he considered it, wondering what odds he might've earned.

"Anyhow, I better at least *try* to get some sleep, seeing as how the sun's coming up."

"Yeah," Pike repeated.

"Lenora sort of killed my buzz." Mac stood and looked to Ian. "You got any booze on you?"

Ian dug inside his bag then tossed a flask to her.

"You don't surprise me." Mac unscrewed it and put it to her nose. "Whew, that'll do." She downed two swallows and threw it back.

Ian took a sip and screwed it shut, fixing Mac with a grin that set invisible insects crawling all over Pike's skin.

"Cheers," Ian said and replaced the flask.

Pike heard Mac murmur to Ian, "Let's hope that's the last time I come to you needing a stiff drink, Kilpatrick."

"Won'nae be the last time you come for me, full stop."

"Fuck you too, pretty boy."

Pike clamped his eyes shut, knowing he wouldn't be sleeping anytime soon. On the plus side, he wasn't in the least bit hungry now.

OBJECTIVE FOUR

CAPTURE THE FLAG

IAN

HE WOKE FIRST. Not an astounding feat, considering his sleep consisted of nodding off in his chair in front of the furnace in ten-minute intervals.

Ian checked his watch and decided this would pass for dawn in Alaska. Standing and stretching his stiff body, he glanced to where Mac had set up with her sleeping bag. He wondered if she'd go for his deal. Might be a long shot, but no harm in trying. Then his gaze drifted to Chloe's sleeping form, phantom fingernails raking heat down his back.

Ian wandered to the warehouse's heavy front door and pulled it open, the air outside wet and lush and altogether too wholesome. Strolling to the spot where Chloe had set upon him the night before, he slid his cigarette case out. He lit up and breathed it in—sweet, artificial calm.

He turned his team over in his mind...Mac and Chloe. Both determined. One annoyingly ethical, the other possibly even smarter than Ian was. Interesting mix. No use overthinking it, since he had no clue what the next challenge would be. Could be a game of human chess, could be a triathlon.

He tapped his foot, sucked in a deep hit of fleeting solace. As he lit another cigarette, his brain twitched with theories.

Physical inventory. Himself—strong but exhausted, soon to be a touch crippled if Mac took him up on his offer to trade sex for nicotine. Both women were strong too. Maybe not Daisey-strong, but they'd do just fine.

Chloe wouldn't shock him a bit if she had some scheme going with someone else. Then again, she didn't seem the type to trust anyone else with her place in the game.

Pike was a worry... Fit, sharp, too holy to form any alliances. Well, except perhaps with one person. Though if Ian got his way, he'd soon ruin Mac for Pike, just as he hoped he'd wrecked Chloe for Daisey.

Behind him, the door to the warehouse squeaked open. Rory missed a step as he caught sight of Ian then aimed himself toward the woods.

Ian blew a jet of smoke to the side. "Rory, in the parlor, with the shovel."

"Piss off."

He put his hands up defensively. "Tetchy. Best get your head in the game, mate." For the briefest moment he caught a little glimmer of a man capable of attempted murder in those unremarkable eyes.

The spark faded, leaving only pale brown emptiness. Rory disappeared into the trees, returning a minute later to walk past Ian without acknowledgment.

Ian finished off another cigarette then went inside in search of a less depressing target for his company. He found Mac lacing up her shoes, and crouched beside her. He felt a little jolt, surely the only thing he and Pike had in common aside from black hair.

She smiled sweetly at him. "Morning, douchebag."

"Good mornin' tae you too. You sleep all right?"

"You acting friendly is really creepy, Ian. What do you want?"

"I wanted tae talk about our wager."

Her brows rose. "Nobody won. Unless you're here to wow me with some brilliant semantic loophole you slipped in without my knowing? Did I sign some kind of contract without realizing it?"

He shook his head. "Jest thought I'd offer you a trade. My proposed prize for yours."

Her eyes settled on his chin or his split lip, and she wrinkled her nose. "I'll be honest with you, Ian..."

"Aye?"

"You're good. I don't want your mouth on me but I don't want to compete against you either. How addicted to nicotine are you?"

"Very."

"Fine then."

He blinked, frankly shocked.

"You do what you like—biting and other painful things aside—in exchange for *all* your cigarettes, and any nicotine gum or patches or other things you might have. You let me go through all your clothes and your bag and the hollow compartments you've probably got in your stupid shiny shoes, and let me destroy all your precious chemical aids. Then you get ten minutes on me. Deal?"

"You have tae do that fairst?"

Her gaze leveled him. "We both know which one of us is trustworthy, Kilpatrick. What do *you* think?"

He put a hand out and she shook it.

"I just hope your mouth can do more than make my skin crawl."

He tightened his grip. "Oh, it'll make you do all sorts of things. Jest practice saying my name."

She smirked at him, eyes narrowing to cruel slits. "If I can stop retching long enough, there's only one name I'll be saying and you know damn well whose it'll be."

Ian laughed to cover up the hateful little finger of jealousy jabbing its way up his sternum. He released her hand and they stood. "It'll be a pleasure. When?"

"As soon as we find the opportunity. I won't weasel out. The sooner we do it, the sooner it's over and the quicker you go into withdrawal."

"Cheers. Got one other question for you."

She finger-combed her hair back and snapped an elastic around it. "What?"

"Who was it?" he asked.

"Who was what?"

"Who'd you kill?"

Mac flinched.

"Arson's way too coldhearted for you. And that leaves accidental manslaughter. So who was it?"

She crossed her arms over her chest. "Well, I didn't kill anyone...and I was acquitted."

"Who?"

"A guest on one of my company's climbing excursions fell and died when I was leading the group. It was awful, but it wasn't my fault. He didn't follow the safety procedures."

Ian studied her face, wondering if the rock-solid confidence in her voice—that genuine absence of guilt or baggage—had been drilled into her head by years of post-trauma therapy, or if she really was exactly what she seemed. Immune to the shittiness and inequity and senselessness of an ugly world.

"You're staring, Ian."

He lowered his voice to a whisper. "You fascinate me."

Her brown eyes narrowed. "Like the scene of a car crash, no doubt."

Like a diamond left behind after a steamroller pulverized a mile of rock to fine, gray dust. Something shiny amid the rubble, unbreakable. Venom on that tongue, but a smile just behind those lips. The question of what she might taste like triggered an ache deep in his belly.

Mac turned away and Ian let her go without another word. He watched her disappear out the door, into the light where she belonged. A mythical creature to a man who'd never imagined humanity as anything other than a bleak marriage of the violent and the victimized. Fucking fascinating.

PIKE

PIKE WOKE TO A KICK IN THE THIGH. He sat up in a flash, fist forming, but it was Mac who'd dealt it. She was standing beside him, eyes on the two staff members who'd just come through the door. Pike looked at his watch. Five-forty. Unfuckingbelievable. He wrestled his way out of his sleeping bag and got to his feet, finding he'd managed to doze later than anyone else.

"Morning," the young staff guy named Josh said.

"Morning!" Mac was alone in her cheerfulness.

"Lenora's asked us to lead both the teams to where today's Objective will be taking place. Rory, Mr. Daisey and Dr. Pike, please get your things and follow me. Ian, Chloe and Mac, you'll be following my colleague here." He nodded curtly at the other man and Pike sighed to himself. Way too frigging early for this nonsense.

Still, he got his boots on and his pack assembled and joined Daisey and Rory by their appointed guide. He waved goodbye to Mac but she didn't catch it.

Another day, another death march. Their staffer shared no details about the upcoming challenge, just led them through the dripping, muddy forest for a full hour before any of the men spoke.

Finally, Daisey turned to Pike. "What d'you think we're in for?"

"Beats the fuck out of me. But Chloe's not on our team, so maybe you'll actually be of some use."

A snort. "You're just sore about Mac."

"What about her?"

"Anybody can see you're hot for her. Well, except maybe Mac."

Pike shook his head, irritated. His boots and socks were damp, not a great forecast for blisters. He missed the Middle East with a fresh pang. "It's not always about sex with everybody. I just *like* Mac. She's cool. She can do way better than you."

"Then don't worry your pretty head, Doc. I ain't done nothin' to her."

Pike dismissed the hope blowing bubbles in his chest and shot Daisey a skeptical look.

"Mac's a cute little bunny who follows you around, waiting to get shot between her pretty brown eyes," Daisey said.

"Excuse me?"

"That ain't a good hunt, in my book."

Pike's fist tightened around the handle of his case, plastic biting skin. "And what's Chloe then? A tiger?"

He shrugged. "I like when they put up a good fight."

"Well, I hope she rips your throat out." Pike worked hard to keep actual anger from eclipsing the sarcasm in his voice. "You're a frigging pig."

"All real men are."

Pike shook his head. "If you say so."

Daisey shouted back to Rory, lagging a few paces behind them. "How about you, Crocodile Dundee? You a pig?"

"I'm a Kiwi, dickhead."

"Jesus, you kids are fucking uptight."

Mercifully, a structure in the distance appeared to drive Pike's angst to the back of his head. "Hey, look."

"That can't be part of it," Daisey said. "What the fuck would they expect us to do in that?"

True, the building was barely bigger than a tool shed—a moldering old shack set at the edge of a clearing. As they walked into an open field, Pike spotted a similar building at the far end, perhaps fifty yards off, and halfway between them stood an old-school outhouse complete with crescent-moon window.

"You can wait here," the staffer said, heading for the far end of the clearing.

Daisey dropped his pack from his shoulders and looked around, stretching his arms.

Pike wandered to the nearby shack, its side coated in moss. "Wow, cue the dueling banjoes. This make you homesick, Daisey?"

"Ah ha ha ha." Daisey passed him to peer into a cloudy window. "This can't be it though. This is just some creepy Unabomber setup. What the fuck could they make us do here?"

"Habitat for Humanity."

Across the way, the other team emerged from the woods. Pike's heart—idiot that it was—leaped at the sight of Mac's red vest. He swallowed. "I think this may be it, after all."

From a third spot on the clearing's perimeter, Lenora strode from the woods. A team of her khaki minions followed, carrying a folding table and chairs, the now-predictable carafes of coffee. Lenora beckoned with sweeping arms and the competitors from both sides headed for the center of the grass.

Rory murmured to Pike, "Why'd they bother making us come separately?"

Lenora flashed her unnatural smile. "Good morning! I trust you all enjoyed that lovely hike."

Again, Mac was the lone ambassador for friendliness, nodding amicably. Pike wiggled his toes in his squelching boots and rolled his eyes.

"Your Objective won't begin until noon, so you've got all morning to dry off and enjoy some breakfast. Coffee will be ready in a moment, food to follow shortly. This challenge could take twenty minutes or twenty hours, so I advise you all to load up. You're free to do whatever you like in the meantime, but please report back here at eleven thirty for further instructions." Lenora gave the group a salute and disappeared into the woods.

Breakfast—thank God. Pike looked to Mac, hoping to secure her company, but she looked firmly sequestered between Ian and Chloe. Both had their arms crossed over their chests and their eyes narrowed, scheming machinery whirring. If Pike wasn't nearly positive they'd fucked last night, he'd have wondered if maybe they were fraternal twins born with identical conniving minds.

Daisey marched in to disrupt their silent huddle, handing Chloe a cup of coffee. For once Pike had to admire the guy—he didn't waste any time playing it cool. Thinking it was as good a strategy as any, Pike filled two Styrofoam cups from the spigot, emptying two creamers and a packet of sugar into Mac's. Pathetic that he knew how she took her coffee but didn't even know her first name.

He walked over to her and held the cup out.

She smiled but put her hand up. "Too early, but thanks."

He shrugged then nearly burned off the roof of his mouth gulping his own coffee in an attempt to look blasé. "Oh, fuck me, that's hot."

She laughed, a sound that heartened Pike more than the thought of food. "Very smooth," she teased.

"Yeah, you know me. So we've got over four hours before we get our instructions. What are you going to do? Try to sleep?"

Ian cut in. "Mac and I have a bit of unfinished business to attend to this morning."

Another icy shiver like he'd felt last night trickled down Pike's spine.

"After breakfast," she said to Ian. "Don't need you wrecking my appetite before I get some carbs in. Plus, shouldn't you get to work chain-smoking? Clock's ticking, Ian."

"Fair point. I'll see you in an hour or two."

She fixed him with an exceptionally unimpressed face until he wandered off, popping his cigarette case open.

"What was that about?" Pike asked.

"That thing I said last night—my and Ian's little deal. Like I said, it has nothing to do with the competition."

Pike shrugged. "May as well be. You guys are on the same team today."

"Yeah, sadly. Man, you and me were so close to finally working together... And I still don't follow his logic."

"What would you have done, if you'd been in Ian's shoes?"

She frowned, thinking. "Well, I'd probably have kept Daisey and swapped Rory for you. Or maybe Chloe. Tough call. No offense to Rory, but you know..."

"Yeah, he's a wreck."

"It's almost like he already won, but now his prize is on a plane headed to New York. I'd be a little worried that the fight's going out of him."

Pike nodded.

"Good thing you've got Daisey on your team though."

Pike thought about it. "Not really. I mean, if it's one of those cases where the losing team votes a player out, he'll vote to keep Rory here, don't you think?"

"Yeah. He'd want you gone. But if you *all* had a vote, clearly you and Rory would both vote to get rid of Daisey."

"True." The idea perked him up. "And you...both your teammates are cutthroats, so they probably want each other gone, so you're probably safe too. I mean really, if it worked out that way, you could decide who goes, Ian or Chloe."

"Heh. That's interesting. But who knows how it'll go down? No point getting our hopes up."

Pike turned at the sound of metal clanking—the staff was setting up trays and serving spoons. The scent of bacon reached his nose and his mood floated higher still. He and Mac wandered to the table and Pike ditched both cups of coffee.

"Today will be interesting for you," he said to her. "I mean, Ian and Chloe are probably ages ahead of us in figuring out the vote, if that's how it's going to happen. I bet they'll both be trying to kiss your ass or talk you into bargains all day."

She laughed, peeling a paper plate off the stack. "I'm sure it'll pain them both greatly to pander to a Girl Scout like me." She dumped eggs on her plate and Pike followed suit.

"Who would you get rid of, though, if it did work out that way?"

She craned her neck to scan for her teammates, one enveloped by smoke, the other by Daisey and his cloud of testosterone. "Couldn't tell you yet. I have my suspicions that Ian may not be the man you know and love in just a few hours' time."

"You ever going to tell me what you mean by that?"

She scraped butter over half a bagel and made a shuddering noise. "Trust me, you don't want to know how, but I'm going to destroy that man."

Pike smiled at her evil expression. "And here I thought you were above all the backstabbing and mind games."

"You can start picking out my thank-you gift whenever you like. I prefer my chocolates in heart-shaped satin boxes."

MAC

AFTER BREAKFAST and a failed attempt at napping, Mac spotted Ian caucusing with Chloe by the edge of the woods. Chloe was stretching as though a marathon could commence at any moment, Ian smoking. Their matching neutral expressions implied a casual conversation about the weather, but Mac bet they were plotting to take somebody down. The other team, or Mac herself, each other... Didn't matter to her. Years of river rafting and climbing had taught her that it was far better to take the dips and dangers as they came than waste energy trying to guess what they might be.

She waited until Ian snubbed his latest cigarette then walked over, smiling. "Who're you two scheming to destroy? Not me, I hope."

"Wait and see," Chloe said.

"You keeping our appointment?" Ian asked, tongue tracing his lip.

Mac shivered. "Yup. Let's get this over with." It was with a glimmer of rare, mean satisfaction that she watched Chloe's brow furrow. The woman clearly wasn't used to being on the outside of a conspiracy.

"Woods?" Ian asked.

"It'll have to be. First things first, take me to your stash."

He led her to the spot where he'd set his bag and opened it for her.

"Your jacket." Mac put a hand out.

Ian handed her his blazer. "Mind the switchblade."

She found his flask and cigarette case and tossed them on the grass, starting a pile. She left his weapon where it was.

"Feel free to frisk me."

"That won't be necessary." Mac dropped to her knees to rifle through his duffel. She uncovered a grab-bag of assorted vices. Mysterious pills, two fifth bottles of whiskey—one full, the other nearly so—two more knives in addition to the one in his coat.

Mac unfolded a four-inch blade from its wooden handle. "What do you need so many knives for?"

"Force of cultural habit. Lot of us Glaswegians have adopted a stab-or-get-stabbed mentality of late. Think of it as my security blanket."

Mac honored their agreement, taking only Ian's chemical aids. She gathered up the haul and carried it to her own pack. She grabbed her canteen and drank, hoping to wash away the taste of dread rising from her throat.

She heard Ian whistle and turned back to find him holding the two bottles of whiskey. "You forget something?"

"How very honorable of you, Ian. But you can get as drunk and sloppy as you like for all I care."

"Understood. You ready then?"

"As I'll ever be." Mac shoved Ian's paraphernalia deep in her bag and walked back to him, arms locked over her chest. "Where?"

He looked to the woods. "A ways. Want this tae be nice and private."

"Private with mics and possibly cameras."

"Aye, possibly. Grab your bedroll."

Mac went back for her sleeping bag as Ian did the same then she followed him into the woods. "Why do I feel so suddenly like Little Red Riding Hood?"

Ian shot a way-too-handsome evil grin over his shoulder and ran his tongue over his pronounced canines.

"Freak."

"That's right—dun'nae hold back with the dirty talk."

They walked for a good five minutes, until there was no sight or sound left of the camp. Ian stopped in a small clearing, hands on his hips.

"I 'spect this'll do." He turned to her.

She was a little surprised to see that predatory quality gone from his eyes, replaced by something softer, something that glittered in a way that made her nervous but not nauseous.

He took a couple of steps closer, close enough for Mac to smell the oddly nostalgic scent of his tobacco, a faint and not unpleasant hint of his sweat.

"I'm so looking forward tae this."

She rolled her eyes. "Let's get it over with."

He licked his lips, gaze electric as Mac unfurled her sleeping bag and toed her shoes off, slid her pants down her legs. He looked so eager she wanted to slap him. Or better yet...

She clasped her hands and shut her eyes, faking ecstasy. "Oh Daisey, Daisey, Daisey."

Ian laughed, a glorified sigh. "Man like him's never pleasured a woman in his life."

"Yeah, right."

"Nae properly. You want a door opened, you can break it down or you can pick the lock."

"Or you can use a key," Mac countered.

"Aye, like Rory and Leah. But you need trust for that, and nae many of us left in this group are handing out our keys."

"You gonna pick my lock, Kilpatrick, or just metaphor me to death all morning?"

He grinned at her, eyes narrowing. "Get on your back."

She stepped out of her pants and sat on her sleeping bag. Ian tossed her his own rolled-up one.

"Pop that under your head. You'll be wanting a good view."

"Only of the movie in my mind." She pushed her underwear down in a brisk, no-nonsense, seduction-free movement and lay down.

Ian grinned, taking in the scene. He removed his hat and set it aside, dropped his blazer from his shoulders. He sank to his forearms between her legs.

"Your ten minutes start now," she said, consulting her watch. "Any time you waste on foreplay is your loss."

"Nae a waste," he murmured, distracted.

With a fresh shiver, Mac felt the rough skin of his split lip trace a path up her thigh, a cruel device that made him far harder to recast when she closed her eyes.

"Christ, you smell fecking amazing."

Mac sucked in a breath as his tongue grazed her. He taunted with the faintest strokes, then firmer ones, insistent enough to part her lips. His moan vibrated through her skin, making her clit ache for his attention. Against her better judgment, Mac opened her eyes.

With his smirking mouth preoccupied, it was impossible to ignore how handsome Ian was. Pale skin, black hair and brows, those crazy eyes free of evil schemes and half-closed with excitement. His tongue delved deeper and Mac hummed her approval without meaning to.

"That's right," he whispered.

"Fuck off, Ian."

"Good. Say my name," he teased, then focused his mouth on her pleasure.

And it *was* about Mac's pleasure. His slippery strokes conveyed none of the smug triumph she'd expected, his hunger seeming directly correlated to Mac's enjoyment. And damn if he wasn't good. Goddamn if he wasn't fucking *amazing* at this. His lips finally closed around her pounding clit and she felt the tip of his tongue flicker there.

"Fuck."

Before she knew what she was doing, she had Ian's matted, wavy hair clenched in her fingers. His moan hummed against her pussy, and as hard as she tried to conjure filthy movies of Daisey's powerful body in her mind, it seemed she could only muster the memory of a single far too handsome face. She fisted his hair tighter, thinking he ought to get used to being at her mercy. All this was nothing compared to the withdrawal he had coming to him.

Images of Ian from their shared shower flashed across her mind, the unexpected hardness of his body. She pictured far too much— the electric green of the canopy, Ian's pale body against her tanned one, two sets of knees and hands covered in dirt. For the tiniest moment she even craved his mouth on hers, a sample of tobacco and whiskey and whatever else that dirty accent must taste of.

Her legs twitched against his shoulders and Ian moaned.

"Shush." A false directive—Mac could admit to herself that voice was sexy. Still, she tightened her fist, no longer caring if what she did turned his crank. Let him suffer.

He moved. He kept his weight on his arms, one hand clamped tight to Mac's hip. He freed the other and brought it to her pussy, two cool fingertips tracing her folds.

Tell him no. That wasn't the deal and you don't know where those fingers have been.

Fat chance. She bit her lip to keep from groaning as he slid two digits inside. More images from the shower. Ian's cock. She hadn't seen him hard, but she could imagine such a thing, framed in hair as dark as his skin was fair. Those arms locked around her ribs, hips hammering. No, not hammering. Slow and deliberate and masterful, like his damnable mouth.

Against Ian's head, her hand began to shake, always a dead giveaway. Fuck, how long had it been? Four minutes? *Daisey. Think about Daisey.*

"Harder," Mac said.

Ian's fingers slid in and out quicker, but nowhere near rough enough to make swapping Daisey into Mac's mental porno believable. Goddamn asshole was right—he could pick a lock. Fuck it.

She went with the sensations, hips moving in time with Ian's hand and the rhythm of his body in her head. Her motions seemed to hit him like a crop and he freed his mouth to mutter, "Yeah."

Mac dragged her nails across his scalp and held his head as possessively as she'd hold his hip or ass had they been screwing.

"Come for me."

She tried to tell him to fuck off, but it left her lips as a gasp.

Fingers still working, Ian put his thumb to her clit. Just that miniscule sensation, the contrast of his wet tongue and the pad of his thumb...

"Oh, God."

He kept up the tease and those two different caresses felt perfectly obscene, like having two men, almost. Finally she could picture Daisey. Daisey above her, Ian to the side. Daisey's cock owning her, Ian's fingers playing her clit like a violin.

The fantasy pushed her headlong into orgasm and the pleasure hit its violent peak against Ian's thumb and tongue, his fingers pushing deep. The dirty movie dissolved and she stared at his face, those eyes. That was the color of orgasm, she thought idly. Blue as the deep end of a pool. Mac toyed with drowning for a moment then came up for air, feeling the pleasure ebb as reality returned. The woods rustled and hummed and the air smelled clean and wet in the wake of her haze. She gave Ian's shoulder a push with her foot and he sat back.

She made it to standing, head still swimming. Ian brushed the dirt from his slacks as she got her underwear on.

He replaced his hat and tipped its brim. "Thank you kindly."

Mac buttoned her pants. "Whatever. You're good at that, I have to hand it to you. But try to wipe that cocky smirk off before we get back to camp."

"Won'nae be 'we'. You go on. I'm gonnae fecking explode if I dun'nae have a wank."

Mac snorted. "You get classier by the day, Ian."

"Aye, laugh it up. But you say my name a few times more and I'll come right here and ruin a perfectly good pair of trousers."

Mac bit back a grin, twisted it into a smirk. She couldn't deny the pleasure that having the upper hand over Ian gave her. She took a few steps until she was a foot in front of him, made her voice low and throaty. "Ian…"

He groaned and shut his eyes, leaning against the tree behind him.

"You really like eating pussy, don't you?"

He swallowed. "Depends on whose it is."

"You like mine," she whispered.

Ian's lips parted but no words came just yet. His hands went to his belt and freed the buckle. "Fecking loved yours, Mac."

"Bet you can still smell me, can't you?"

He moaned, working the button and clasp of his pants open. Mac peeked at the bulge in his open fly, shrouded in black cotton. He licked his lower lip.

Too short to reach his ear, Mac addressed the base of Ian's throat, opening his collar and bringing her mouth close enough that her words steamed his skin. "I bet you can still taste me, can't you, Ian?"

She felt him fumbling with his pants, his arms tensing rhythmically as he began to stroke himself.

"Tell me how it felt, Ian, making me come all over your face."

He groaned, sounding pained, and his hand sped. "Thought I was going tae fecking lose my mind. You taste so sweet…wanted tae drown in it when you came."

Mac looked between them. She'd seen Ian's cock, but not like this. It was flushed dark in his tight fist, framed in that soft-looking black hair and the strip of pale skin behind his dress shirt, just as she'd fantasized. Mac reached between them and undid his buttons, spreading his shirt open for a closer look at the lean cut of his stomach.

"You like to fuck, Ian?"

"Christ, yes." His strokes turned rough, hand pumping hard.

"You ever wish you could fuck me?"

"Aye."

"How would you do it?" Mac asked, voice light and cruel.

"Any fecking way you told me tae."

"You like taking orders, huh?"

"I like giving a woman pleasure," he moaned. "God, feck. I'm gonnae come."

Mac opened his shirt wider and ran her small hand over his hard belly. "Right here, Ian. Come right here and let me watch."

His eyes were wild, flying between Mac's face and fingers as his fist worked, his other hand shoved deep in his underwear, fondling his balls. He moaned as his arm began to shake, followed by his shoulders. "Yeah, yeah, yeah."

"Come on, Ian."

"Feck. Say it again."

"Ian."

"Yeah. Oh Christ, Mac—" His moan was choked off by an invisible fist as he came, thrusting his hips forward as two long spurts of come lashed his stomach.

"Nice." Mac fixed him with a mean grin. She gave his cheek a couple patronizing slaps, feeling powerful and triumphant.

Ian looked helpless, chest heaving with deep, gulping breaths. In time he calmed, blood leaving his flushed face once more, eyes losing their glassiness. Digging in a pocket for a handkerchief, he cleaned himself up with an impressive show of dignity. He buttoned his pants and shirt, buckled his belt and donned his blazer.

They gathered their things and walked back toward camp without speaking, and the silence wasn't so much awkward as it was ambiguous.

As Mac tromped through the undergrowth, she abandoned the temptation to regret what had happened. It'd been hot, she'd banked Ian's chemical crutches, and she'd even managed to make him powerless for a glorious minute or two. All that added up to success in her book and she settled into an unexpected cheerful mood.

"So tell me, Kilpatrick…the virginity questions. You guessed mine. Which were you?"

"Which do you think?"

"I gave you your ten minutes and then some. Just tell me."

He smirked. "I lost it tae a bloke."

Mac made a face, trying to decide if she was surprised. "Huh… I guess it explains your dress sense."

"I'm nae bi."

"Banging a guy's *pretty* bi, Ian."

"Mebbe if it was consensual, sure…though I was too drunk tae remember all the romantic details."

Mac's blood ran cold as ice. "Oh. I'm sorry." She searched Ian with a sideways glance, finding his eyes focused coolly forward, face blank. "That's awful."

He shrugged. "Cannae say I've been able tae enjoy vodka since then."

"How old were you?"

"Lucky thairteen."

Mac felt another chill and hugged her sleeping bag to her chest as they walked, goose bumps rising on her arms. It was too much intimacy on top of the sex, too many adjustments to make to her opinions of Ian. And too much of a leap to blindly believe him. She took a deep breath of good-smelling air and freed a hand to smooth her tangled hair.

"Well, I'm really sorry, anyhow. I mean, if you're being honest." She added the last bit to make it clear she hadn't changed her mind about him completely. Ian was still Ian.

He met her eyes and blinked. Something in his expression was dead, as though a shield had gone up, one even Ian couldn't camouflage with cavalier airs. "Even a shite like me would'nae lie about kiddie rape. Nae even if I was after your pity, sweetheart. Which I'm nae."

"You wouldn't get it, anyway. You're still a colossal asshole."

He laughed. "You watch it with those sweet nothings." He kept his gaze glued on his feet as they neared camp.

"So you had a pretty shitty childhood, huh?" she asked.

"Aye, prolly."

"Did you know the person who did it?"

"Aye. He was my uncle's mate, drunk old fecker who worked at the bookie's."

"Did you tell anybody? Did he get put away?"

"I told my uncle. He told me that's what came tae pretty-boys like me. Then he broke my nose and knocked out three teeth, gave me a black eye, said he was doin' me a favor. He hit me so hard I could'nae hear out of my right ear for almost a year."

Ian's answers were coming freely but without emotion, and Mac was torn between curiosity and tact.

"Oh... Did you...did you know whoever it was who... The person who killed your parents?"

"Does'nae matter. He's dead."

"Did you know—"

"I said he's dead." Ian caught her eyes and held them. "Does'nae matter who he was."

Mac chewed her lip. "My parents died when I was little too."

"Oh, aye? Let's start us a wee support group then. I'll meet you by the campfire with a hot dish at eight."

Mac rolled her eyes. "Well, fuck you too."

"Jest 'cause I answered your questions does'nae mean I'm looking tae bond with a good weep over our dead mammies' graves."

As much as he was pissing her off, Mac had never felt quite so warmly toward Ian. It was a relief to discover he was capable of being driven to bitchy self-preservation.

"Fine. Thanks for the orgasm."

That brought his head up and his gaze to hers. "Cheers."

CAMERA 5883

AT ELEVEN THIRTY PRECISELY, Lenora returns to the clearing, a smile on her face and two staff members at her sides. The competitors abandon their anxious milling to wander to the center, just a few paces from the ancient outhouse.

"Thank you all for being so punctual," Lenora says, no mike necessary now with the group whittled to six. "This Objective is fairly simple. Two teams of three in a game of capture the flag."

Daisey seems to perk up at the prospect of a physical challenge. Pike looks around the clearing, a military man taking stock of the battlefield.

"Each team will be given a flag and assigned a base. You will choose where to hide your flag in your base, but it cannot be obscured from sight—so no burying it or hiding it behind opaque objects. All your team needs to do to win is be the first to get the other team's flag without being tagged. Being tagged means getting hit with one of these." She holds up what looks like a blue paintball. "No guns. This is hand-to-hand combat, as it were. These aren't as tough as standard paintballs, and if you slap one of these hard enough against your opponent, it will burst and they will be out of the game. I would advise you all to consider avoiding one another's faces if at all possible.

"Once you're out, you can't attempt to tag your opponent, take their flag or otherwise interfere with their actions. Instead you must return here and sit out the rest of the game. You may, however, speak to your teammates as much as you like." She smiles as though announcing the promise of a make-your-own-sundae bar. "Ian, your team will be blue."

A staff member comes forward and hands Ian, Mac and Chloe three blue paintballs apiece, a blue fabric triangle and the usual emergency alert buttons.

"Daisey, Pike and Rory, you'll be yellow."

Daisey accepts the yellow flag and ammo.

"The Blue Team will make their base there." Lenora points to the shack on the north end of the clearing and noises stir among the competitors—a groan, muttered curses, a laugh. "Yellow Team, your base is there." She points to the shack on the south end.

Daisey murmurs, "Bloodbath," to Ian.

Ian looks unfazed. "We'll see."

"Two girls and a chain-smoker? You're fucked."

"Hey," Mac cuts in. "Girls can run."

Daisey smiles. "Yeah, like girls."

"Neanderthal."

"You love it."

Pike and Chloe sigh in tandem and Lenora interrupts the exchange.

"Does everyone understand the rules? Good. You have," she consults her watch, "twenty-three minutes to strategize and hide your flags, then a horn will sound at twelve-hundred hours to signal the start of the competition. Both teams must start the game inside their bases. Understood?"

Assorted affirmative noises answer her.

"Excellent. I'll see you back here for the elimination once a winning team has been determined. Good luck to you all."

PIKE

"FUCKING CAKEWALK," Daisey said as he and Pike and Rory headed for their appointed shack. "This is just backyard war games, and two-thirds of our team has served."

Pike raised an eyebrow at him. "When exactly did you complete basic training?"

"Those instincts never leave you."

"Sure." Pike gave one of his paintballs a squeeze and decided they were sturdy enough to keep in his pants pocket. "This is going to be the worst game of capture the flag ever. Broad daylight, exactly three things to hide behind…"

"We've got the woods too," Daisey said.

"Yeah, true."

Predictably, Rory said nothing. He'd been a zombie since the previous night's elimination and what Mac had said echoed in Pike's head; Rory's prize was probably a hundred miles away now, winging back to Manhattan along with his drive. Fuck of a place to fall in love.

"Hey." Pike nudged him. "I know you're bummed and everything, but can you give this challenge an effort, at least? Even if you don't care anymore, we do." He flicked a finger between himself and Daisey. "I mean, Lance Corporal Hillbilly here sucks, obviously—"

"Hey."

"But I have big plans for the money, so please don't throw this for us, even if you couldn't give a shit about winning."

Rory shook his head and raised his eyes to stare at the sky. "I won't. I could use the distraction, actually."

"Good." Pike nodded. "I mean, I get why you're...you know." He imagined Mac suddenly being gone and what a mopey little bitch it'd doubtlessly make him. And Pike hadn't even kissed the girl.

"Don't worry about it," Rory said. "This whole scene's just been way more of a head trip than I'd expected. But I guess compared to people's body parts flying off around you, it must seem pretty tame out here to you. Sorry, that sounded glib."

"Nah, it's cool. I know what you mean." Pike gave Rory a slap on the back to punctuate the end of the conversation. They were teetering on the verge of bro-dom and Pike wasn't sure he was ready for that. Not this sober, anyhow, and not with Daisey eavesdropping.

Daisey pushed in the door to their assigned shithole. Eight feet by ten, tops. It was dim inside, one of the two windows obscured by moss and weeds. At one point someone must have lived here. It had a tiny woodstove and moldy shelves, a table and a rotting wooden chest. Pike entertained a story in his head—two feuding hermit brothers sharing the same miserable patch of property and rickety outhouse back when Alaska had still been a frontier territory.

He glanced to the flag in Daisey's hand, wondering how on earth they were going to hide something bright yellow in this miniscule space. The three men began scouting, searching for the best spot.

"Know what's spooky?" Daisey asked.

Pike couldn't resist a chance to exploit that little nugget from Twenty-One Questions. He took a step closer to Daisey and wiggled his fingers, letting rip a spirited, ghostly, "Whoo-ooo-ooo."

"Fuck you, Doc. What's weird is that this wood stove ain't ever been used."

Pike frowned and looked at it. Daisey was right. Behind the grate was a stack of ancient, mossy wood, but the walls were suspiciously soot-free. No time to play detective though. He glanced at the flag in Daisey's hand and inspiration struck.

"Hey. I have an idea."

Pike dumped his pack on the floor in the corner and opened his case on the table, finding one of several fat Sharpies he always carried. He took the flag from Daisey and went to work coloring it in, streaky black.

Behind him, Rory laughed. "Not bad."

Pike grinned, relieved to hear his friend coming back to life. "I listened pretty carefully to what she said, and I don't think this is cheating."

Daisey seemed to concur. "Good one."

"Now we just need a good place to stick it. Maybe on the ceiling? If we can find something to use for tacks."

While Pike scribbled, Daisey and Rory ditched their bags and further inventoried the space.

"Maybe on the back of the door," Rory said. "If it's black and they're looking for yellow, they might just open it, glance around in the shadows then leave it open while they search the rest of the place."

"I like it." Pike finished with the marker and capped it. "Whew. They'll be able to smell it, anyhow. What have we got for hanging it?"

"You have bandages?" Daisey asked.

"Yeah, but those'll give it away for sure. I've got duct tape though." He rummaged for the roll, made a loop of tape and stuck the flag to the back upper corner of the door, near the top hinge. They opened and closed the door a few times.

"What do you guys think?" Pike asked.

"I think we better hope they aren't watching us dick around with the door," Daisey said. "But yeah, not bad. Not that they're getting anywhere close to it."

"We should talk about roles." Pike tested the old table then leaned on it, crossing his arms. He liked roles. In particular, he liked knowing his own. "I'm guessing we need one to be the guard, last line of defense in here. One to be the aggressive one going after their flag and one in the middle, maybe going after the flag or acting as a distraction for the other, ready to run back and play defense if they have to."

"You're overthinking it, General Tso."

Pike sighed. "Again, Korean."

"Seriously, we're in a shack. They're in a shack. We got fifty yards and a shit closet between us. One guy stays here, two rush them. We can take down two girls and an asshole in a stupid hat."

"Whoa."

Pike looked to Rory, squatting by the wooden chest with its lid raised. "What?"

"Just...whoa. Check this out. This is bloody weird."

Pike and Daisey went to stand by him and Rory pushed the lid all the way back. Inside was a mess of wooden and metal panels, wires and buttons. A dish that looked like a prop from a fifties sci-fi film was tucked against one side.

"Shit. That some kind of radio or something?" Daisey asked.

"Or something." Pike read the little plaque on the upper corner of one panel. "Property of the United States Government."

Another "Whoa" from Rory.

Pike crouched beside him, taking in the rusty dials. "Definitely for radio signals. Maybe telegraphs? Why the fuck is it out here though?"

Competition forgotten, they poked at the discovery for a minute or two, Pike confused but spellbound.

"This is fascinating and all, but they're gonna start the game in ten minutes," Daisey said. "What's our plan?"

Pike noticed something additionally odd then—a distinctly cold breeze chilling his left leg. He looked to the wooden floor planks beneath the table, realization dawning. He yanked his pack out of the way and tossed it to Daisey.

"Hey."

"Shut up." Pike put his palms to the floor, cool air leaking through the cracks. He saw them then—hinges set into the wood. "Holy shit." Getting to his feet, he turned the table on its side and pushed it against the wall. He dropped back down and found the seam—so obvious now that he was looking for it.

"Daisey—gimme your knife."

"Why?"

"Just do it, asshole."

The handle appeared at Pike's side and he took it, sliding the long blade into the crack to lever it up, nothing short of a trapdoor rising from the floor.

Daisey laughed. "Fuckin' A."

Pike pushed it wide open, revealing a square concrete chute and a set of tubular metal rungs descending into darkness. Or near-darkness. "There's light down there."

"Crikey."

"You think this is part of the game?" Daisey asked.

Pike turned to offer him his knife and the most patronizing look he could muster. "No, genius. It's just a fantastic coincidence."

CHLOE

"HOLY MOLY."

"Fuck me," Chloe said, echoing Mac's sentiment as Ian pushed the moldy old trapdoor all the way open.

He grinned, a seeming byproduct of the suspiciously good mood he'd been in all morning. Chloe hated to think all that self-satisfaction came from imagining he'd gotten the better of her last night.

"Well, I'll hand it tae them—I did'nae see that coming."

"This sort of wrecks our plan," Mac said.

Chloe laughed, enjoying this little turn of events. "Guess it's not just a silly game of tag after all. You think they have a secret passage in their shack too?"

"Mebbe."

"Well, I call flag-guarding duty," Mac said. "I am *not* going in there."

"Guess we just figured out who's scared of enclosed spaces." Chloe leaned over for a better look. "There's light down there. They definitely mean for us to use this. Whatever it is. I bet you anything they have one too, and we can get into their base this way."

"I bet they don't know about this," Mac said.

Chloe frowned. "Well, we need to know for sure, otherwise the three of them could turn up, take Mac out and steal our flag, and it won't matter that we know about it. How long until the game starts?"

Ian checked his pocket watch. "Eight minutes."

"That's plenty of time. Mac, go over and peek in their window."

She hesitated, looking torn between annoyance at being bossed around and her own eager, go-getter tendencies. "Fine." She headed out into the sunshine.

"This raises a very interestin' question," Ian said, staring at the rungs leading down into the unknown.

"Just the one?"

"Where d'you reckon our 'base' begins and ends? Does our flag stay here, or is that mystery pit down there part of our base as well?"

"That *is* a good question."

"All she did was point and say, 'Blue Team, your base is there'. Does that include its top-secret basement?"

"I'm not losing this on a technicality," Chloe said. "If hiding our flag in a secret tunnel counts as obscuring it, I don't want to take that chance."

"Well, we won'nae know anything for sure 'less we get down there and take a gander."

"Agreed. How long have we got?"

He checked his watch again. "Seven minutes."

Chloe didn't intend to waste a second more. She jumped and grabbed their flag from where they'd pinned it to the ceiling just as Mac returned, pink in the face and panting.

"They have a tunnel too. And Rory totally caught me spying on them."

Chloe nodded, pleased to know where everyone stood. "I'm going down there."

Mac's cheeks went pale. "Better you than me."

"I'll be back before the game starts. We need to try to figure out whether or not our base includes whatever's down there." She headed for the passage, swinging her legs inside and finding the rungs with her feet. Spiders were fine, just no rats. *Please, no rats.*

She descended into the cool, musty, damp air and felt a sprinkling of grit hit her knuckles—Ian was following. She wouldn't say no to the company just now. After fifteen or so rungs she entered a concrete chamber, lit by sickly bluish bulbs in wire cages. There was a closed door to one side and she waited for Ian.

He smiled as he reached the landing. "Cozy." He'd left his hat behind.

"Look." She pointed to the stencil on the door. Base B, North Entrance. "*Base* B. I'll take that as an answer to our question. And I'd say our options for hiding places just got a whole lot broader."

Ian grinned and held his hand out. "Ladies fairst."

She grabbed the handle and twisted it, finding the door unlocked. It squealed inward to reveal more concrete—a platform overlooking a vast open room lined in drab, painted cinder block, lit by more industrial bulbs.

"Door's its own alarm system." Ian swung it on its hinge to showcase the rusty wail. "Cannae miss anyone coming through that." He followed Chloe down a set of steps into the long room, a half dozen more doors on either side and a vast table in the center. She went to the nearest door and found it unlocked as well. Inside were ancient lockers and bunks, not unlike the room she and Ian had shared during the Meat Locker challenge.

"Takes you back," he murmured.

They tried the next room, a mess of outdated electrical equipment. The next one looked like an office, sparsely furnished and void of any papers. A brittle silk fern sat on the corner of the ancient metal desk, both sporting a fine layer of dust. Beneath a predictably modern-looking video camera, a faded calendar hung on the wall.

"September 1964. Damn." Chloe squinted up at the camera and shook her head at their unseen directors. She ushered Ian out to the main room and closed the door. "What the fuck *is* this place?"

"Looks like an operations deal," Ian said, glancing all around. "For spying on the Soviets? Espionage or infiltration or something. Dead mad. Oi, look." He pointed to a large picture frame hanging by the door they'd entered through. As Chloe got closer, she saw what had him so excited. They jogged back up the steps.

"A floor plan." She wiped away the dust and squinted at the outlines of walls and the red dot telling them where they stood in Base B, Map Room. "Shit, it's huge. And look, that must be their side." She traced a path from their base through a long, skinny corridor, flanked by other pathways of faint dashed lines. The other team's side was labeled Base A, Operations, and seemed to have a near-identical setup.

"What d'you reckon those dotted lines are?" Ian asked.

"Maybe more corridors, a level down?" There were no stairways on the map, though, and no time to theorize. "We better find a place to stick the flag and get back upstairs."

Ian grinned. "No need. All she said was we have tae be in our bases when the game starts. We are."

"Mac needs to know what's going on down here."

"Does she?"

Chloe licked her lips, intrigued by the back-stabbing implicit in Ian's tone but not willing to follow anybody's lead. "Yeah, she does. So you hide it and I'll go back up there, maybe try to get a handle on what the other team's up to."

Ian nodded and Chloe headed for the ladder. She heard an air horn blast in the distance as she climbed into the shack. Mac was waiting for her, looking anxious, a blue paintball ready in her hand.

"What's down there?"

"Jesus, I don't even know. Some kind of military base or something. And I do mean 'base'—this shithole's just the tip of the iceberg as far as what we're working with. Ian's hiding the flag." As she said it he appeared behind her. "That was way too fast. Where'd you put it?"

"Darkest place I know of that we've got." He nodded to the tunnel. "On the wall, opposite the ladder. Anyone who goes up or down's got their back to it."

She nodded. "Not bad."

"Bloody brilliant, I think you'll find."

"Yeah, we'll see."

DAISEY

"SHIT." Daisey shook his head as the hoot of the air horn faded away. Two team members eliminated and they'd barely begun the challenge.

Pike emerged from the trapdoor and dusted himself off.

"Great fucking job," Daisey said. "Neither of you was back here when the challenge started—thirty seconds ago. Now you're probably disqualified. Lucky thing I can carry this team—"

"Chill. This up here? This isn't our base. Not all of it."

Daisey crossed his arms. "How d'you know?"

"Because there's a door down there labeled 'Base A'. This stupid shack's just the mud room."

"What's down there?"

"Dude, I don't even know. It's like some top-secret anti-Commie spy headquarters or some shit. It's fucking *weird*."

"Where's the Kiwi?"

"He's scoping things out," Pike said.

"Well, he needs to get up here so we can formulate a new plan. This ain't no simple game of tag anymore."

Pike tucked his hands in his pockets. "Obviously we need somebody up here, guarding the flag. And I think we should let Rory stay down below. It's good for him. Like he came back to life or something."

"Listen, Doc, you and me both know who the weak link is on this team. That boy's fit for guard duty, and that's about it."

"You don't know that."

"It should be you and me down there. The smart one and the strong one."

Pike's eyebrow rose. "You're actually admitting I'm smarter than you?"

"Sure. But I can still kick your ass."

"Let's take turns then. Rory's already down there checking things out, so let him keep going. You take the first watch duty. The setup down there...this challenge could take hours. It's immense. I'll come back and take over guarding the flag in," he checked his watch, "thirty minutes. Twelve thirty..." He frowned. "Then again, isn't it sort of a giveaway, leaving somebody guarding the shack? Doesn't that scream to those guys that we hid our flag in here? If we left it unguarded..."

Daisey nodded. "Yeah, that's a good point. She said what? We can hide the flag anywhere in our base?"

"Yeah."

"So as far as the others think, we'd be retarded *not* to hide it down there, if it's so much bigger."

"That's my thinking," Pike said. "And they know *we know* about the real bases. So if they're giving us any credit at all, they'll assume that's what we did."

"Instead of being idiots and not even thinking to hide it down below," Daisey said.

Pike rolled his eyes, nodding. "But if they're like us, they only had a few minutes to get down there, realize the playing field went way beyond the shacks, come back up and grab the flag to re-hide it. That doesn't leave much time to find a new place to put it. We saw a map down there, a layout of the whole place. It's big, but I bet the rooms where the flags could've been hidden in that window of time are pretty limited."

"How does their base stack up to ours?" Daisey asked.

"They look sort of like mirror images, only not. Same setup, but the rooms are labeled different things."

"But there's only one entrance to each." Daisey nodded at the trapdoor.

"No, dude, they're connected down there. There's a corridor, at least one."

"Shit. So where's the bottleneck?"

Pike puffed his cheeks out with a breath, and Daisey felt a swell of satisfaction. He had Pike outwitted.

"I'm goin' down there," he said, brushing past Pike. "One quick sweep of this shack and they won't find our flag, and they'll figure it's got to be down there. No use in any of us stayin' up here." He shimmied his legs into the trapdoor and found the rungs. Tight fit.

As Daisey descended, Pike's voice drifted down like an echo. "We can't *all* be on offense."

"Sure we can. Let 'em play chess all day long. We'll play massacre."

He emerged from the dark hole into a cramped little cinderblock landing. The door to his right was already open, revealing a room vast enough to scramble Daisey's perception of reality.

"Holy shit."

Pike's voice echoed above him. "I told you."

"You ain't told me shit, son." He stepped onto the platform beyond the door, another landing that overlooked what smacked distinctly of a disused control center. Looked like something out of an old war or spy flick, the sort of place where generals barked orders and radars blooped, buttons got pushed and enemies got vaporized.

He jogged down the steps and headed for the nearest in a long line of lifeless consoles. It had an old-fashioned glass monitor, panels of buttons that reminded Daisey of the 1960s Hollywood vision of what the future would look like. He heard Pike behind him, every soft footfall magnified in this concrete cave.

He turned to find the man looking alert but unmistakably anxious, eyes jumping all over the room.

"You know you can't take me out with my own color, right?" Daisey asked, nodding to the paintball in Pike's fidgeting hand.

He looked down then up at Daisey and they made eye contact, like electricity zapping between two conductors. Pike knew what Daisey did—if this challenge came down to a vote, Daisey was cooked.

Pike broke the stare and walked to another console, pushing buttons. "Of course I know that. And I want to win, anyhow. I'm not playing double agent. I'm just trying to stay ready."

"You wanna win so you maybe get to pick teams for the next game," Daisey said, feeling him out. "Maybe make sure you and Miss Mac end up together?"

Pike shot him a killing look then jerked around at the sound of a creak. Rory emerged from a side room.

"We're all down here now?" he asked.

Pike shrugged. "Daisey had a point—if they're giving us any credit at all, they'll assume we were smart enough to hide our flag down here. And if they check the shack and don't spot it, we'll send them on a wild goose chase."

Rory's lips narrowed to a tight line but he nodded.

"Whatcha find?" Daisey asked.

Rory shook his head. "Couldn't even tell you what half these rooms are. Lockers, some of them, others are like this place, full of barmy old controls and screens. Found one interesting thing though." He waved an arm and Daisey and Pike followed him back toward the exit steps, to a framed map posted on the wall.

"We're here," Rory said to Daisey, palm circling the left-hand side of the schematic. "They own this half. This is a proper hallway." He tapped a long connecting corridor strung dead center between the two halves. But these…" His fingertips traced two long, thin rectangles that also connected the bases, grayed out with hash marks. "I found what I think one of these is. A ventilation shaft, I reckon. I couldn't see inside, but I found the grate on our end."

"How big?" Pike asked.

"Big enough." His eyes jumped to Daisey. "Well, big enough for one of us," he added to Pike. "Big around as…as one of those mini-fridges. Crawl-able."

"Right." Pike's eyes narrowed. "Where?"

Rory headed for the far end of the room and the other men followed. A short hall jogged around a corner, and to the right was a door to what had to be the real corridor. As they passed, Daisey peered through the small window in its thick door. The passage itself was dark, but at the far end he could make out a tiny point of light— the window at the other end. "Must be fifty yards," he muttered.

"Half a football field." Pike crouched by the grate Rory had described.

Daisey joined them. It was maybe two feet by three, bolted to the wall by four screws. Too small for Daisey, borderline for Rory.

"We could do this," Pike said.

"You *could*," Daisey said, "then you crawl your ass through fifty yards of dust and rat carcasses only to realize the other side's bolted from the outside."

"Shit."

"He's right," Rory said.

Daisey grinned his satisfaction at yet another mental victory and crossed his arms.

Pike stood, face in its constipated, gears-turning expression. After a moment of frowning, his brows rose. "I have an idea."

CHLOE

AT THE SOUND OF A WHOOP, Chloe abandoned her study of the facility map and jogged to follow the noise. She found Ian seated in a chair in one of the many side rooms, grinning ear-to-ear before a panel of black-and-white monitors, all of them lit and displaying a different image.

"Oh my God, are those surveillance cameras?"

"Too right. And look." Eyes still glued to the screens, he passed her a numbered list typed on a sheet of card stock—about thirty rooms in total. She looked to the monitors, each with a channel number displayed in its corner.

"Map's on the back," Ian said.

She flipped it over. "Whoa. Where are we? Maybe this is Surveillance B. Can you switch one of those to channel…" She scanned the key. "Twenty-one?"

Ian dicked around with a dial on a monitor and suddenly they were watching themselves from behind and above in grainy black and white. He swiveled beside her as well as on screen, and waved to the camera. "Brilliant."

For a short but potent moment, Chloe imagined the two of them on that screen, ripping at each other's clothes and fucking in the squeaky old desk chair where Ian currently sat. She stared at his black hair, matted from his absent hat, and a strong urge to clench it in her fingers stole her focus from the matter at hand.

Banishing the thought, she cleared her throat and consulted the list. "Don't get cocky—there's a Security A on this roster too. They might be watching us."

"What's the channel?"

"Ten."

Ian dialed another monitor to reveal a room just like their own, only empty. The screen didn't reveal any monitors, only the edge of a panel covered in switches and shapes too fuzzy to identify.

"Interesting," Chloe said.

"An' useless. Who knows what the other side of the room's got? Mebbe screens, same as ours."

"Any controls in here for adjusting the camera angles?"

Ian shook his head. "None I've found."

"Still, what a boon. Now all we need is a handy little map of all the fuses so we can pull the plug on *their* security equipment."

"Check the map."

She did, but the room labeled A-B Electrical was dead center between the two bases, off the narrow connecting corridor. "Tricky. But maybe worth it."

"Let's see if we can find them." Ian took the listing and flipped through all the channels for Base A, finally scoring. "Ha!" He tapped the screen showing Pike in a room lined with filing cabinets.

Chloe spotted something equally intriguing just beside Ian's elbow on the desk—a loudspeaker-style microphone with a similar dial as those on the TVs. "What channel is he on?"

"Four."

She twisted the knob until a zero and a four showed behind a tiny glass window. "You do it. He hates you."

"Oh, ta very much." Ian pulled the mike close and pressed the TALK button. He cleared his throat and on screen, Pike whirled around.

"Hope you're nae about tae commit any thoughtcrimes, Dr. Pike."

Pike spotted the camera and glared up at it.

"That's right. Big Brother is watching you."

Pike flipped them off then headed toward his case. Chloe and Ian watched him pull out a roll of duct tape, rip a measure off with his teeth and jump to slap it over the camera lens.

Chloe groaned. "Shit, we should have seen that coming."

"He's got the right idea. What have we got tae cover our own cameras with?"

She considered it. "Do we want to though? We might end up on that side, wondering what's happening here in the B rooms."

Ian nodded. "Knocks your fuse box plan on the head too."

"Keep checking the channels. Let's at least figure out where they are now."

Ian clicked through the rooms. "What we need are walkie-talkies. One of us in here as the eyes, telling the ears where's safe tae go."

"I have my phone in my pack but it doesn't get a signal outside, let alone in this freaky spy bunker."

"How ballsy d'you reckon their team is? Think they'd invade our end fairst?"

She mulled it over then Rory appeared on a screen Ian was perusing. She checked the list. "It's their version of our Map Room. Operations." She squinted at the screen and could make out banks of dark monitors and chairs set before equipment. Rory disappeared into a side room and Chloe oriented herself with the map. "Try channel seven."

Sure enough, there was Rory, looking around what appeared to be a galley kitchen.

"I'm gonnae feck with him."

"Be my guest."

Ian switched the mike's channel and engaged the TALK button. It must have made a speaker buzz or crackle, as Rory jumped.

"Would'nae say no tae a cuppa, if you're putting the kettle on," Ian said. He let the button go and cracked up alongside Chloe as Rory's eyes went wide, scanning the room. Pike appeared and spoke to him. He pointed to the camera. Both men turned to face the lens, hands on hips, mouths trading muted words.

"They trying to talk to us?" Chloe asked.

Ian shrugged.

Pike suddenly gave Rory a punch in the upper arm, the kind of hit that accompanied an idea. He began speaking to Rory and gesturing.

Chloe frowned. After a few seconds Ian held down the TALK button again. "Dun'nae bother. We can hear you."

After he released the button, Chloe clapped. "Genius. I hope they fell for it."

Pike glanced up at the camera a final time then jerked his head toward the exit. Rory followed him out. Ian flipped back to the Operations Room and they watched both men head right to a door at the end that Chloe had been dreading.

"Shit, they're going into the connecting corridor."

"So we ambush them when they pop out the other side." Ian was distracted, checking the list and tuning the TVs. "And anyhow, you're wrong." He stopped at a channel showing the length of a long, narrow cinderblock hall, dark but unmistakably empty.

"Huh…" She took the sheet and turned the map this way and that. "I thought for sure that was the way to our side. But maybe it's their exit and I've gotten it all turned around."

"Or maybe," Ian said, "they've already figured out what those dotted lines on the floor plan are."

The thought intrigued and unnerved her equally. "Well, we can't just sit here all day, waiting to play defense."

He shook his head. "What's your plan?"

She took another regrettable and distracting glance at Ian's gorgeous, scheming face then cleared her mind.

"We figure out what they seem to already know. What those dotted lines are. Can't be hard. Just head for the main corridor and look to either side. If they're accessible on this floor, we can't miss them, right?"

"Works for me."

Chloe kept the map as they left the security room, double-checking the layout. They each got a paintball ready as they passed through the long map room. Every step Ian took, his hard-soled dress shoes clacked against the concrete floor.

"Your stupid shoes are so noisy. We're splitting up as soon as possible."

"Pity. I thought we made such a bonnie couple."

"Shut up."

At the end of the room, a hallway jogged around a corner and Ian peered into it. "Clear."

The hall was perhaps twenty feet long with a single door on one side, a heavy-looking one with a small window. Chloe peeked through it, finding the long stretch of dark hallway the camera had promised. She tested the handle, finding it unlocked. Just a short sprint and they'd be infinitely closer to the other team's flag...

But no. Better to be Ian than Daisey in this challenge. Weasel over rhinoceros.

A creepy sound pulled Chloe from her thoughts—the sound of Ian chuckling to her right.

"What?"

"Think I just found their flag," he said.

She hurried over to where he was crouched by a vent.

"Also figured out what those other 'corridors' are on the map," Ian added.

Chloe squatted and peered through the grate. There was indeed a point of light at the other end and a glimmer of yellow. "They can't do that...that's obscuring."

He shrugged. "Mebbe it's attached on the other side, not inside the shaft."

"Maybe."

"Either way, pouting about it won'nae move the fecker."

Chloe left him to sprint through the map room to where she'd left her pack, grabbing her camera and its zoom lens. She screwed it on as she jogged back. Kneeling, she aimed the lens down the shaft to the light at the other end and focused it. There was indeed a yellow triangle with a dark square of tape sticking it to the grate. "I can't tell for sure, but the bits of grate around it look crisper than the ones behind it. I wonder if they attached it to the inside then bolted it back in place. Cheaters."

"Mebbe it's nae obscured if you hide it behind something with holes in it. And if it was cheating, you'd think the game would've been called by now. Those cameras dun'nae miss many tricks."

"Yeah, true. So, only one thing to do."

"Dun'nae let me stop you," Ian said, standing.

Chloe shuddered, imagining the bristle of rats brushing past her in the dark. "I'm not going in there."

"I won'nae fit," Ian said. "Or mebbe I'll fit enough to make it to the end, but it's bloody impossible crawling backward out of a tight space, and their end's got tae be bolted shut from the outside, same as ours."

Chloe stood and brushed the dust from her knees. She looked Ian square in the eye. "Mac."

"She could'nae even make it down the hatch. How d'you think you'll ever get her in that wee chute?"

"I won't. You will."

MAC

TORN BETWEEN PARANOIA and boredom, Mac leapt up from her post as footsteps echoed from the creepy trapdoor. Paintball at the ready, she approached the opening.

"Who is it?"

"'S'me," Ian said, just as his head emerged at the tunnel opening.

"What's going on?"

He looked strained as he climbed out. "Bad news. Chloe's out."

"Seriously? Fuck."

"There's worse news than that though." He got to his feet, dusting off his sleeves. "I jest found their flag."

She frowned. "Why's that bad?"

"'Cause it's at the end of a long ventilation shaft, and I'm too big tae get tae it."

Mac's heart pumped ice water for a moment before freezing over completely. "Oh."

"You guessed it, sweetheart. Need you tae man up and go in there."

"I can't. I'll literally hyperventilate and pass out. The crew will have to throw a grappling hook in after me and drag me out."

Ian stepped close—close enough for his proximity to fill her body with conflicting instincts. He put a hand to her shoulder, the same hand she'd watched stroking his cock mere hours earlier.

"I need you tae do this."

She pushed his hand away. "That little heartfelt Hallmark move doesn't work when it comes from you. And like I said, I seriously can't. There's nothing else aside from this in the world I'd ever say that about, but I can't."

"You're a tiny wee thing," Ian said, pinching two fingers close together. "It won't seem that tight tae you, I promise."

"A subway tunnel would feel tight to me."

He mimed a large rectangle for her. "Like that. Please? We'll lose if you cannae do it, and we'll win if you do. And if we lose, I cannae imagine meself or Chloe are going tae be particularly fond of you, should this come down tae a vote."

She blinked at him, tempted to slap him across his infuriating face. "I see."

"So, mebbe think about it. Is facing your fear worth a chance at that half-million dollars, d'you reckon? Ten minutes' bravery tae keep yourself in the running?"

Anger bubbled from her gut up through her chest to her cheeks and she glared daggers at him. Searching his expression for signs of nicotine withdrawal, she was disappointed to not find any yet.

"Fine," she spat. "Show me where."

Ian grinned and clapped her on the shoulder. "Knew you had it in you. Never pegged you for a quitter." He turned back to the trapdoor and disappeared into the dark. Mac pocketed her paintball and followed, moving too quickly for her brain to realize what she was doing. Half a breath, then into the deep end of a frigid psychological pool. Her focus fuzzed out as she found the rungs with her feet and descended into a surreal space of damp, cool air and darkness punctuated by tiny blips of light. Not a good sign. Little spots always danced in her vision when she was flirting with a good faint.

After what felt like two hundred rungs, her feet hit solid ground. She followed Ian through a door and onto a platform overlooking the weirdest damn sight she'd ever seen. "What the *fuck...?*"

"I know. Dead mad." Ian practically danced down the steps to the floor and she followed, overwhelmed by adrenaline and shock at the hugeness of this place. He led her into a room off to the left lit by a dozen or more monitors, each displaying a different view. Ian consulted a list and twisted a dial, bringing up the image of a short hall with a door on the left. "See that?" He tapped the screen and circled a fingertip around a rectangle at the far end.

"Yeah."

"That's their side of the shaft. Flag's taped tae the inside, so you need tae shimmy through and grab it, right?"

"And how long is this shaft?"

Ian shrugged and she took that to mean miles.

"And you're *positive* it's in there?"

"You think I'd feck around with your greatest fear jest for a laugh?"

Mac made a face that said yes, yes she did.

"Well I'm nae. Chloe zoomed in from our end with her camera. It's there, plain as day. Have tae hand it tae them...bloody brilliant hiding spot if it's nae cheating."

"If it's not cheating?"

"Tough tae say. They hid it behind something, but something full of holes. Nae sure where that lands on the continuum of 'obscuring'. But surely the good doctors have been watching, and there's been nae messages about the game being called on a technicality. Does'nae seem very sportsmanlike, though, I'll give you that."

"Like you've ever cared about fair play before in your rotten life. Wait, so... Is that stupid shaft the only way to get between the two bases? Surely they'll be watching it."

"Nae. There's a proper corridor."

"What? Well why do I have to shimmy through some horrible ventilation system? Why can't we just head to their side and open the stupid thing?"

"'Cause there's two of us and three of them. And look." He twisted another knob until a monochrome Pike appeared on one of the monitors, stalking through a large room and peering into a side door. He messed with another until Daisey and Rory appeared, talking in front of a nondescript stretch of wall. Ian checked the sheet again then pulled an ancient microphone close, fiddling with its setting and holding down a button.

"Aye, brilliant plan," he said into the mic, and Daisey jumped on screen. "Excellent. Go with it." Ian released the TALK button, grinning.

Rory frowned up at the camera. He disappeared from view for a moment while Daisey glared at the lens. Rory returned, scribbling on a piece of paper against his palm. He finished and held it for the camera.

WE KNOW YOU CAN'T HEAR US, ARSEHOLE.

Ian sighed. "Well, that was fun while it lasted."

Rory disappeared again.

"Can they watch us too?" Mac asked, eyes darting to take in all the different rooms.

"I thought mebbe, but then I noticed that according tae the map, this is the only 'surveillance' room. Lucky us."

On the monitor, Daisey glared at the camera and grabbed his crotch in a rude manner. When Rory returned he had a roll of duct tape in his hand. He ripped off a strip and jumped, covering most of the lens.

"Darn."

"Aye. They've been doing that."

"Well, stop annoying them. They might cover up the camera that watches their end of the shaft-thing." Her gaze jumped nervously to the view in question. "We should come up with some code. Like, for you to let me know if they've spotted me."

"No need tae be subtle. I'll jest yell 'abort'."

"Yeah, I guess that's true. Okay. Just yell it loud, so I can hear it over my heart attack. So where's our end of the shaft?"

Ian stood and she tailed him back into the vast control room. She skirted the immense table in its center and ran her hand over the film of dust on one corner. "Whoa. Don't tell Rory, but it looks like New Zealand's still under British rule. I wonder when this place was last used."

"September 1964," Ian said. "We found a calendar."

Mac reached the far end of the map table, where someone had scrawled *TURN AROUND* in large letters in the dust. "Turn around? Who wrote that?"

"Me."

She followed him around a corner. "Why?"

"Jest tae feck with them."

Mac shook her head. "Psycho."

Ian led her down a short stretch of hall. "Here we are. Their flag's on their end of this shaft." He gave it a gentle kick with the toe of his shoe.

It wasn't as big as Ian had mimed. "Oh God, oh God!"

"Breathe, sweetheart." Ian pulled his knife from his pocket and crouched. He angled the blade and loosened a screw. Mac prayed the next one would be rusted tight, but it wasn't. Neither were the remaining two, and far too quickly, Ian was setting the grate to one side.

"For the love of all things holy, be as quiet as you can in there," he said. "Must echo something terrible. Looks like there's a bloody great clump of wires along the edge, as well. If it looks like any…you know, *wildlife* has chewed them…"

"What? Don't zap myself to death? Like a game of human Operation?" She dropped to her knees and peered down the shaft at a far too tiny point of light. "I want Chloe's camera. I want to see this thing for myself before I go in there."

"She took all her things when they ushered her out."

"Ushered her out where?"

Ian paused. "Could'nae tell you. Mebbe jest tae a side room, 'til this Objective's over."

"Did you see her go?"

He shook his head. "Some staffer announced it on the P.A. system."

She nodded. "Okay." The fear was filling her with adrenaline, and not the sort she knew how to exploit. If she were clinging to the side of a cliff or rushing down a nasty set of rapids, she'd be smiling right now. Anything but small spaces. Anything but this and she'd enjoy the high.

"Nae time like the present."

She inhaled deeply, breath dry and raspy as she sucked it in.

Ian smiled at her, licking his lips. "If we had the time, I know a brilliant way tae calm you down." The smile deepened and Mac shuddered.

"Thanks, Ian. This horrible death-shaft is suddenly seeming more and more appealing."

"Ha-bloody-ha. You say that, but I've tasted it when you—"

"Seriously," she said, putting her palms inside the opening. "Keep flirting. It's a great motivator to get the hell away from you."

"Careful when you talk in there, eh?"

Right. She shut her mouth and the amputation of her voice felt like the shedding of a safety harness. She might've been able to get through this if she'd been allowed to talk to herself.

Getting her knees inside, she found that mercifully the metal-lined tunnel didn't buckle or move under her weight. She pushed at the wall to her left, the side not lined by a bundle of cables. It moved as she'd expected, thin metal giving way then bouncing back with the clatter of a dropped cookie sheet. *Great. Don't touch the sides.* Way too fucking much like Operation now. She checked her breath, finding it still coming in shallow but steady gulps. Arching her back, she found there were about two inches of clearance above her. Not comforting, but this was possible. Possible would have to do. She set off.

"Watch your hands," she mouthed. "Watch your hands. Watch your hands and don't think about how much harder this will be on the way back. Think about five hundred thousand dollars. Think about how maybe the person who actually captures the flag gets immunity, so Ian and Chloe can't stab you in the back if this stupid contest comes down to a vote. Half a million dollars, Machiniak. That's an education and a nice vacation or two. That's new fencing for the ranch and a couple of decent trucks, and some damn good weed to celebrate when you get home."

Her hands were picking up a thick layer of grit and dust, which felt disgusting, though not nearly as disgusting as the rat bones or insect casings she'd feared. Dust was nice. Dust was lovely. Lovely if she could keep from sneezing, anyhow.

Breaking her promise to keep her eyes on her hands, Mac looked ahead. The light at the other end was stronger and brighter. She could indeed make out a splash of yellow. These assurances weren't comforting, however. This was merely proof that she had perhaps twice as difficult a journey to get back once she'd snatched her prize. What if she did make it all the way back, only to the find the grate screwed closed at her feet? Locked in by a rival player, or by Ian, for some reason too evil and complex to decipher?

No no no. Don't think about that.

"Watch your hands. Watch your hands." It wasn't working anymore. "Think about your safety button," she mouthed. "Lovely, safe, safety button. Unless it doesn't work in here, in this metal tube of subterranean death. Shut up shut up shut up! Watch your hands…"

Her throat was tight, eyes watery from the dust. The air was thin, or felt that way. She could suffocate. For a moment she froze, struggling to hit the mental PLAY button in the back of her head and get her brother's Zenned-out voice cued up.

You're not dying, you're just scared. You're not suffocating, it only feels that way. You've got as much air now as you did before, but you need to relax your throat.

For all his pot-induced eccentricities and space-cadet airs, Tim could do calming-voice-of-reason exceedingly well. She conjured all those mantras he'd cooed at her when she'd first discovered her claustrophobia, on perhaps the least opportune occasion possible— spelunking. *You feel like you're going to die, but it's only a feeling. Feelings can't hurt you.*

She took a deep breath, and it felt like inhaling the wad of cotton from a bottle of aspirin. She took another and it came a bit easier. After a dozen breaths, she felt assured that there was indeed oxygen in the tunnel, and she was indeed in control of her body.

She recommenced the long, shuffling journey, one knee at a time, palm over dusty, itchy palm, toward the flag.

Intermittently she let herself glance forward. The light grew closer. The yellow triangle became clearer. *Get it. Get it. Get it and pray that means you earn some kind of advantage. Get it and stay in the game. Get it and, for the love of God, fuck Daisey tonight.*

Ooh, good prize. Better distraction. Mac couldn't muster a proper debauched fantasy at such a supremely unsexy moment, but she tried nonetheless. *Underestimate me a touch too much, Daisey? Well, I just won the challenge. Impressed? I thought so. You know, I can think of at least one way to get me on your side...* Tacky, sure. Ian-esque...perhaps. But fuck it, she'd gamble her karma for a half-hour's go on that huge body.

Soon enough Mac was squinting, and not merely from the dust. From the light, stronger now, all but blinding after who knew how many yards of near-darkness. Yellow, just twenty feet from her grasp. No warnings from Ian. No shadows moving beyond the grate to tell her the enemy was lying in wait. Most miraculously of all, no invisible hands squeezing her windpipe.

Heart pounding, sweaty palms making a nasty paste with the scuzz plastered to her hands, breath short...but this was simple fear, not panic.

She felt it then, her adrenaline-processing machinery switching modes. From flight to fight. From the terror of small spaces to the exhilaration of a free climb or the thrill of the romantic chase in the colorful shadows of some strobing, bass-throbbing club.

"Grab it," she mouthed, mere feet from the flag. "Grab it and you get to fuck the living daylights out of Dai—"

Her fingers made contact with their goal and it took several seconds for her brain to slip into gear and process just how wrong this was.

The yellow triangle was stiff against her fingertips, bendy and smooth.

Paper.

She grabbed it and pulled, the loop of tape detaching from the grate. A dummy. Just a scrap of yellow file folder.

Fifty yards of torture and another fifty backward—and for nothing.

Her brain glazed over and her lungs sped. Light spread beyond the squares of the grate, blobs of it growing and bursting in her periphery and the sound of disembodied gasping filling her ears.

The sound of rushing, like the world's longest wave, poured into her skull as grayness descended.

PIKE

"IT'S NOT AS GOOD AS CAMERAS," Rory said.

He and Pike leaned closer to the speaker, straining for the sound of Ian's voice.

"Oi, look at this." Rory picked up a sheet of cardstock from the desk and blew the dust away. "Explains these numbers." He tapped the tiny window in the speaker base, under which a one and a nine were showing. "Nineteen... That's 'Map Room, North Corner'."

Pike grabbed the list and scanned it. "Try twenty-one. That's their surveillance room."

Rory fiddled with the speaker dials until it displayed a two and a one.

"*If she has'nae hyperventilated,*" Ian was saying. "*If she has, you know who gets tae go in after her.*"

Chloe's voice followed. "*Fuck that. I'm not going in there. Even if I did, there's no way I'd be able to drag her dead weight back all that way. We'll have to grab it from their side. You go check on her. I'll scan these and see what they're up to.*"

Pike glanced at the camera in the corner of the room. "Shit. Where's the tape?"

Rory left the chair and jogged out into the gigantic main room, returning with the dwindling roll. He ripped off a strip and slapped it over their lens.

Chloe's voice murmured, *"Come on, assholes. Where are you?"*

"Assholes?" Rory caught Pike's eye and they shared to sets of raised eyebrows before cracking up.

"I bet they think we're the stupid ones," Pike said. "But if they hadn't wasted their advantage harassing us on the loudspeakers, half their precious cameras wouldn't be blacked out now."

"Too right."

"What do you think they mean about Mac?" Pike asked. "Hyperventilating?"

"No idea. But 'our side'? They must be just about ready to make a move."

"Nice to be ahead of them." As soon as Rory and Pike had figured out they had the advantage of audio and realized all three of the other team's members were underground, they'd sent Daisey outside to infiltrate via the enemy's shack.

After another minute of silence on the other end, Rory said, "They must have moved on." He flipped the numbers, slow and methodical, eventually finding something—a weird noise like an animal suffering.

"What the...?" Pike stared at the speaker, taking in the shrill, gasping sounds it broadcast.

"It's coming from..." Rory consulted the list. "Bugger me, it's coming from our side. 'Connector Alcove'." He flipped the key over. "That's the hall with the vents and the main corridor."

"Fuck, they're in."

"Sounds like they're shagging."

"You stay here. Shout if you get any indication that they've spotted me."

"Right."

Pike got a paintball ready and left the room, walking as quickly and quietly as possible past the many banks of consoles to the little hall at the end. He searched the wall for changes in light and shadows and saw none. He could hear it now though—those creepy wheezing noises. He flashed a hand around the corner but nothing happened. Peeking his head around, he found the space empty. He tiptoed to the door to the main corridor, and a glance revealed that it too was empty. Then his ears told him the sound was coming from below, from the grate to his left.

"Holy shit." He went over and crouched before it, able to see little aside from a small hand wrapped limply around a scrap of yellow paper. "Mac?"

More gasping answered him.

"Fuck. Mac? Can you hear me? Are you hurt?"

He didn't wait for a reply, and none came anyway. He shoved his paintball back into his pocket and fished out his utility knife, prying the screwdriver arm from its gritty slot. He got the grate off in seconds flat, heart pounding. He grabbed Mac's forearm and tugged. The hundred pounds she must weigh felt like a ton, but eventually she tumbled onto the concrete floor. Pike rolled her onto her back and assessed her rigid frame, her racing breath and strained features. He tugged the bandanna from her hair, making a cup from the fabric and holding it over her mouth and nose.

"Breathe slow, Mac. You'll be fine." His attention jumped all over her face and Pike couldn't help himself—he put his free palm to her pale cheek.

Scuffing sounded from the main room and Pike held his breath until Rory appeared.

"Bloody hell. What's wrong with her?"

"She's hyperventilating. She'll be okay in a couple minutes."

Rory chewed his lip. "It's really bad form to whack somebody with a paintball when they can't breathe, right?"

Pike nodded.

"Maybe we could like, slit it open and gently smear—"

"Not now," Pike said. It was the first surge of anger he'd ever felt toward Rory, but for a brief moment he was ready to deck the guy. Irrational. But right now all he wanted to do was protect Mac. Professional reaction. Deeply engrained. Definitely not because he was stupid for her. Definitely not.

"Just go and keep monitoring them," Pike said. "I'll take care of this."

"Bugger that—we've got a clear route to their end if their grate's open on that side."

Pike felt Mac's breaths slowing inside the bandanna and he struggled to keep his attention on his teammate. "Yeah, fine. Go for it."

Rory nodded. "Ask her where their flag is, before she gets her sense back, eh?"

With a concerted effort Pike managed to hold back a hostile reply. Seeming content without one, Rory dropped to his knees and got his shoulders inside the chute. *Better you than me*, Pike decided. As Rory's feet disappeared, Pike looked back to his patient.

"Mac?"

Her eyes were open, their glassiness seeming to clear.

"Mac?"

She blinked and Pike removed the handkerchief. "Nice, slow breaths. Not too deep."

"Pike." The syllable came out as a long, ugly rasp.

"Yeah."

"Hey."

"Hey, Mac."

For a minute or more she gulped then swallowed, seeming to regain control of herself. "Which side am I on?"

"Ian and Chloe's." *Sadly.*

"No, I mean, which side of the base?"

"Oh right. You're on my side now. And you captured our fake flag. Good job. Very ambitious."

"God."

"You feel okay? Want to try standing up?" Pike backed off and got to his feet, giving Mac room to test her limbs.

She took his hand in her dirty one, some strength returning to her grip. He helped her to her knees then hoisted her onto wobbly legs.

"Feel like you're going to faint?"

She shook her head. "Nah. Little dizzy, but I'm cool." Her gaze flashed from her feet to the yellow paper flag on the floor to Pike's face.

His hand went to his pocket without him willing it to, fingers closing around the paintball. Mac's hand went to her hip then stopped there. She dropped her arm.

"Go ahead. Just not in the face, please." She shut her eyes and clenched her fists, waiting.

Pike hesitated.

One of her eyes opened. "Go on. Not only did I fall for your trick, but you treated my anxiety attack. You win. Seriously."

Pike took the ball out and squeezed it gently in his fist. He could do it. It was the point of the whole game. One harmless slap on her shoulder and he'd do good by his team. He brought his hand up, gaze stuck on Mac's wincing face.

Fuck it.

"How about this…"

Mac opened her eyes.

"I'll do a deal with you."

"What sort of deal? And why? You could just take me down now."

"I could," Pike lied. "But the toughest part of this game is finding the flag, right? And you and me are the only two honest people playing it."

"And maybe Rory."

Pike nodded tightly, still a bit pissed at his friend. "But let's do this. I'll let you stay in the game if you tell me where your flag is hidden."

She crossed her arms over her chest, the old Mac seeming to return in a flash. "No way. I'd rather go out. I'll only tell you if you tell me the same."

Pike's shoulders slumped and he gave her a don't-bullshit-me look, holding up the paintball. "I'm still the one at an advantage here, you know. I'm not doing an equal exchange."

Mac's hand shot to her pocket in a flash, a blue paintball clutched in her upheld hand. For a second they just stared at one another, wide-eyed. Mac took a step forward, and Pike took one to the side. They circled each other in a slow rotation.

"This is stupid," Pike said. "I've got longer arms than you."

"Bet I'm quicker."

"You said a minute ago I had you, fair and square."

Mac shrugged then smiled, distinctly evil. Distinctly adorable. "You had your chance."

"Fine. But how about a ceasefire? I'll trade you a clue for a clue, about where our flags are."

Mac very slowly lowered her hand and Pike mirrored her until both had replaced their ammo in their pockets.

"Okay," she said. "But it should be fair. Not so one of us can give the other a lame clue and the other gets a good one."

"Right… How about this? We each get to ask the other a question about where our flags are, and we both have to answer honestly. So if we ask shitty questions, it's our own faults."

"Yes or no questions," Mac said. "No 'what room is your flag in?' questions."

"Sure."

Mac wiped her palms on her pants, face set with concentration. She extended her hand and Pike gave it a firm shake.

He immediately began concocting his question. After a full minute's deliberation he chose what he thought was a good one. "You first," he said, just in case Mac's was better.

"Fine. Is your flag down here, as opposed to up in the shack?"

Fucking hell. Of course she had to ask that one. Pike struggled for a few breaths for a way to make it into a trick answer. Failing to find any, he replied in a purposefully unconvincing tone, praying she'd think him capable of lying to her. "No."

Mac's eyes narrowed. "Great. Now you. What's your question?"

Pike cleared his throat, hoping perhaps stealing her question would prove the other team had been slow on the uptake in re-hiding their flag as well. "Same question. Is your flag in your shack or down here?"

Mac's mouth opened but she didn't reply for a moment. "Yes or no question," she said.

"You know what I mean. Which is it in?"

"Yes or no question."

Pike sighed. "Fine. Is your flag in your shack?"

She relaxed. "No."

"Fuck."

Mac smiled, and Pike was torn between wanting to kiss her and wanting to wring her charming neck.

"So now what?" she asked.

"We go our separate ways. Ceasefire for, what? Say five minutes? Then game-on the next time we see each other."

She nodded.

Shitty deal, Pike decided. She was already on his side of the base, and Rory and Daisey were both on the other. Nothing between Mac and their shack but Pike, and he'd given his word he wouldn't eliminate her. Five minutes was more than enough time.

"Right. Well, good luck." Mac began to pass by him and Pike grabbed her. They wrestled for a few sloppy moments and he got her hands pinned behind her back. Rummaging in her pocket, he found all three blue paintballs.

"Pike!"

Still grappling with her, he staggered toward the vast operations room and tossed her ammo across the floor.

"Hey!"

"You can get them back later."

"Let go of me!"

Both hands now free, Pike got a better grip on her, pinning her arms at her sides in a bear hug. She kicked at him but he managed to steer her back to the alcove. He got the door to the main corridor open and flung it wide with his foot, pushing Mac inside. With her paintballs gone she was less of a threat, and Pike released her long enough to maneuver her over his shoulder. Her fists pummeled his back, flailing feet kicking dangerously close to his face and crotch.

"Pike!"

"I carry dudes twice your size for my job," he said, intentionally, annoyingly casual, as if her fists weren't making his breath hitch. "Do your worst."

He nearly lost his balance as she gave a mighty thrash and Pike picked up his pace, jogging toward the other end.

"I'll let you go, I promise. Soon. Pretty soon." He wondered if Rory had made it out of the shaft by now. Probably. If Daisey had made it as well that gave them a fair fight on the right end of the war zone.

Mac got him with a good heel to the nose and Pike blinked the spots from his vision. He felt wetness trickle down his lips. "Jesus, dude. Don't break my nose. It's just a game."

Mac's body went rigid against his. "Sorry."

Pike frowned and hurried onward. Then he felt something unexpected—a trembling in Mac's thighs and stomach.

"Dude, are you laughing?"

A gasp and snort sounded behind his back.

"Yeah, awesome. My nose is bleeding and you're laughing."

She laughed harder and Pike smiled to himself, unseen.

"Oh yeah, keep that up. The longer you laugh, the longer I'm hauling you around with me." Well, that was yet to be seen—Mac was light, but a hundred pounds was a hundred pounds.

Her happy convulsions continued until Pike reached the end of the hall. He set Mac on her feet, finding her face red from the inversion or the laughter. Keeping a firm grip on her arm, he got a paintball in hand, turned the door handle and pushed it open. He marched Mac out in front, a runny-nosed, streaming-eyed human shield.

"Enough," she said, breath short for reasons preferable to those from ten minutes' earlier.

"Nearly." Pike toyed with barricading her someplace, but that was too mean. He'd haul her around with him a bit longer, until he spotted their flag or at least narrowed down the possible rooms where it might be hiding.

The Blue Team's main room was huge, dominated by a giant map table out of some Bond villain's lair. Their base seemed to house just as many side rooms as the Yellow Team's.

"Shit. You know what this is like?" Pike asked the back of her head. "This is like we're playing Clue, and on your very first turn you accidentally figure out which room it happened in. And I drew one room card out of the whole pack."

Mac laughed. "One sad little card…the shack. Well, you won't be peeking at my hand again."

He nodded. Wanting more mobility, he slid his hand to her wrist, dragging her behind him as he scanned the room. She paused, making Pike to pull her arm harder than he meant to.

He looked over his shoulder to where her gaze was aimed but found nothing. He turned to study her face. "What?"

Mac bit her lip, looking distinctly nervous. "Nothing."

"What did you just see?"

She sighed. "I didn't see anything. I just had a thought, but never mind. It doesn't matter."

Pike searched her expression, trying to place it. Her dark eyes were snapping from side to side, unable to settle on either of his. Her lips parted.

"Thanks for saving me back there." Mac swallowed. Her voice was soft. "You could have just tagged me out and you didn't."

"Yeah, well. First do no harm." Suddenly self-conscious, he rubbed his wrist under his bloody nose.

"Any of the others would have."

"Yeah, but I'm not them. Thank God."

Her eyes dipped unmistakably to his mouth. All at once Pike's tee felt like a dress shirt, buttoned to the Adam's apple and a size too small.

"You're the nicest person still in this game," Mac said, attention still glued to his lips.

Words failed him. His palm felt sweaty on Mac's wrist and he had to be cross-eyed, staring at her this close up. His lips twitched, waiting for his brain to supply some words for them to utter.

"You think I'm okay, right, Pike?"

He nodded slowly. "Sure. I think you're okay." Far better than okay.

Her gaze jumped up and down from his eyes to his mouth, the iris-only equivalent of a vigorous *go ahead* instructional nod. As Pike leaned in, for the first time in his life five-foot-seven felt like six-four. He shoved his paintball back in his pocket so he could grab her other arm, the hold utterly different than it had felt a minute earlier. Before they touched, his lips hovered millimeters from hers, close enough to feel the heat of her breath and smell coffee and cherry ChapStick. A tiny noise escaped her throat.

Then, her mouth. Small, like the rest of her, small enough to make Pike feel big. Her skin was imperfect, faintly chapped, and Pike memorized the detail as he pressed his lips to hers.

Hands slid up his front to his neck, surprising calluses reminding him how physical this woman was. As he parted his lips, her palms held his jaw. Pike shut his eyes, blocking out everything else on the planet. He let the tip of his tongue tease the crease between her lips and they answered his question, opening. She tilted her head just as he did and Pike pushed inside. He'd guiltily fantasized about far more explicit ways in which he'd die to penetrate Mac, but at this instant the kiss felt like sex, raw and needy and goddamn perfect.

His cock roused as his tongue slid against hers and Pike felt his hips urging him, begging him to coax her back three paces and press her into the ugly gray wall behind them. Her small hands covered his ears, ushering in a sound like the false sea inside a shell. Images blipped and flashed, ones involving sand and salt water and rolling around with Mac on some unpopulated beach in—

Smack!

A strike to his back knocked Pike's breath into Mac's mouth and conked their foreheads together, clicked their teeth. He whipped around to find Chloe standing behind him, outstretched palm slathered in the same shade of blue now surely streaking his tee.

"Fuck me."

Chloe was grinning, laughing without making a sound. Pike whirled around to stare at Mac. She was smiling as well, though there was something tight in the gesture, something that told him she felt poorly to have tricked him.

In an instant, Pike rearranged his face and reordered his relationship with Mac.

Friends. *You're friends, dumbass. Always were just friends. Friends and enemies.*

"Seriously?" he asked, every muscle in his face aching with the discipline it took to appear pissed instead of utterly destroyed.

Mac smiled deeper, a taste of relief softening her eyes. "Sorry." It came out as three syllables, hitched by a laugh.

"Yeah, I'm sure."

"No, really—I'm sorry. But think of that as revenge. You took advantage of my easy portability; I took advantage of your simple male predictability."

"Yeah." Male predictability, yes. That's what had happened. He'd fallen for that because he'd been male. Not because he was half in love with her and prepared to launch himself off a cliff toward the tiniest sign of a mutual attraction.

"Hey." Mac turned to Chloe. "You're out, aren't you?"

Chloe smirked and shook her head.

Mac's expression soured. "Oh, thanks. You were both in on that? Thanks a ton, teammate—I hyperventilated in that stupid shaft, I'll have you know—"

An unseen P.A. system fizzled to life all around them then boomed with Lenora's echoing voice. *"Dr. Pike, please leave the base immediately via the nearest exit and report to the appointed area for eliminated players. Thank you."*

In a way it was a relief. For the first time since laying eyes on her, Pike wanted to be away from Mac. Then, as he stepped toward the exit, he remembered a caveat they'd been told at the outset.

He cupped his hands over his mouth and bellowed, "Chloe and Mac are in the map room! Mac's unarmed! Their flag is in their base, not the shack!"

He continued toward the exit slowly, waiting to see if his distress call had been of any use. It had.

Footsteps scuffed to his left and Daisey burst out of a side room, surprising the heck out of him. "Whoa. That was quick."

"Shit," Mac said. "Their flag's in their shack!" she shouted to Chloe, then ran. She bolted past Pike, making a beeline for Daisey.

Pike laughed as Mac threw herself bodily against Daisey, knocking him back a few paces with a pair of mismatched grunts. More footsteps, then Rory entered from the other side at a cautious jog, paintball in hand.

As Pike reached the stairs, Chloe blew past him and bolted up the steps to the exit.

Rory shouted, "Shit!" and Pike slowed to leave the stairs clear for him to chase after her.

Ian appeared from the last place Pike expected—beneath the hulking map table. He ran faster than Pike knew a chain-smoking pretty-boy could and caught Rory as his legs were about to disappear up the rungs after Chloe, whacking a paintball against his calf.

"Fuck!"

A laugh colored Ian's voice as he shouted up the chute, "Bad luck, mate!"

"Rory, please make your way to the appointed eliminated player area via the nearest exit."

Mac screamed and Pike looked to where Daisey had her straddled, pinned to the ground by her hips, a yellow stripe smeared across her chest.

"Mac, please make your way to the appointed eliminated player area via the nearest exit."

"Oh, shut up." She whapped Daisey's arm and he stood. He helped her up and she put her hands to her breasts then kicked his shin.

"Ow!"

"You're lucky it's not your balls! You ever been slapped in the tits? Asshole."

Pike would've laughed if he weren't so thoroughly gutted by everything that had just happened. As if to place the rancid maraschino cherry on the peak of his shit sundae, the speakers crackled back to life.

"All players, please report to the yard. This Objective is now complete."

CHLOE

In what felt like no time at all, the players were making their way to the outhouse in the center of the field. The first to report, Chloe looked at her sweaty fingers smudged with Sharpie ink, then took inventory of the others as they exited the Blue Team's shack. Only three had gotten tagged. Checking her watch, she figured they'd spent an hour and a half skulking around, exploring and strategizing, the game then over in one chaotic minute. She squinted at Mac as she strode to the center of the yard, yellow smeared across her front.

"Hey," Chloe said as she neared. "How'd you know where their flag was? And if it wasn't in the ventilation shaft, what *was* that?"

Mac shook her head, looking for once to have been overtaken by a less-than-chipper mood. "No comment."

"You manage to seduce some useful info out of Pike before I got there?"

Mac exhaled, long and sullen. "More like a stroke of good luck. We had a ceasefire deal going, after you and Ian tricked me into confronting my worst fear and giving me a heart attack in that horrible metal death hole."

"It all worked out for the best."

"Yeah, *you* can say that." Mac huffed another angsty breath. "You weren't the one who got suckered into—" She stopped as Pike neared.

Chloe lowered her voice. "Excellent work, by the way." She gave Mac a look she didn't offer many people very often—a respectful smirk. "Good to know the ethical doctor's got an Achilles' heel. Or an Achilles' crotch, at any rate."

Mac pursed her lips, eyes cast down.

"Don't look so tortured," Chloe said. "All's fair in love and war and all that bull. You and I get an extra bit of ammunition in this battle. You won't catch me pouting about using it."

She shrugged. "He let me stay in the game when he didn't have to. I feel like a shit, tricking him like that."

Chloe rolled her eyes. "Save the sportsmanship for your Brownie badge."

The rest of the players arrived and Chloe eyed them, wondering who she might be paired up with for the next challenge. Or not. If only one person was kicked out now, they'd be down to an uneven five. Fine with her. If not...

Her eyes jumped from face to face. Mac was susceptible to a bit of bullying, so she wouldn't be the worst teammate ever. Daisey could likely be bought with a few more vague promises to make good on what she'd wagered. She and Ian would probably eat each other alive, but not before they won the next round. Rory looked like a shell of a man, and not in an easy-to-mold way. He and Pike would be the worst choices. Dead weight and annoyingly incorruptible.

Ian strolled over, his hat back on his head, a swagger in his step. But something was off about him as well.

He stood beside her, facing the same direction. "All right?"

"Just lovely. Well played, teammate."

"I dun'nae suppose you still smoke?"

She shook her head. "Not in years."

"Bugger."

"Why? You run out?"

"Nae exactly. I might've traded all my fags and pills for something else."

"Oh? What?"

Ian shrugged. "Something well worth it...but fecking Christ, I need a smoke."

"I think you're on your own. Sorry." Chloe gave him a good, long sideways study and Ian turned to fix her with his unnatural eyes. They were etched at the corners with tiny lines, his five o'clock shadow making him look like the personification of Chloe's favorite male quality—desperation.

"You think I'm jest a jackal with its leg in a trap now," he said.

She nodded.

He turned back toward the others. "Aye. You may be right there."

At long last Lenora appeared, flanked by two of her all-American minions. "Greetings, players!"

"Hey," Mac said flatly.

"Well done, everyone. I'm sure you're all anxious to know how this next elimination is going to work, so I won't keep you in suspense."

Chloe snapped to attention.

"Now, the elimination will work a little differently than you may have expected."

Rory muttered, "Shocker."

"This challenge was about teamwork and strategy, and how well you all collaborate to achieve a common goal." Lenora clapped as one might when attempting to get a group of kindergarteners juiced for a singalong. Chloe sighed.

"The losing team is going to be voting amongst themselves and eliminating one member."

Several people nodded, unsurprised.

"And the winning team will be doing the same."

Chloe's cocky bubble burst. She waited for Lenora to explain how the player who'd actually, *physically* captured the flag was off-limits in this vote, but that caveat didn't arrive.

She looked to Ian and Mac, no clue what Ian's game would be. Mac though—easy. Nobody made her skin crawl like Ian, and he was a threat to boot. Didn't matter if Mac's decision was personal or strategic. Ian was gone, as long as Chloe voted for him as well. Shame, though. Withdrawal or not, she'd almost been looking forward to working with him again.

Behind her, Pike and Rory were muttering to one another. "I could give a shit," she heard Pike say. "I'm just so fucking glad Daisey's going to be gone."

She heard Rory clear his throat then Lenora went on as a staffer approached with the usual voting slips and box.

"Here we are. Thank you, Josh. Everyone, please take a pen and a card—yellow if you were on the Yellow Team, and likewise with the blue ones—and clearly print the teammate's name whom you believe deserves to go home. Then fold your vote and place it in the box. In the event of a tie, the opposing team will earn a chance to vote out a member of the other team."

Interesting, but no matter. Chloe accepted a blue card and pen and wasted no time writing down the three easy letters that would leave her and Pike in a tight race for the smartest remaining competitor. Well, not so tight a race when Mac was anywhere near Pike, shaving twenty points off his IQ.

Chloe folded her card and tossed it into the box.

DAISEY

"HOW LONG DOES IT TAKE to tally the results from six motherfucking votes?" Daisey asked no one in particular.

His soon-to-be-former teammates were sitting on the grass close by, the two groups having separated themselves during the vote. Daisey's stomach was knotted tight. End of the line. He'd envisioned himself at least being one of the final two or three people in this game, not some poor dipshit who got the boot with three whole challenges still to come. But that's how it'd be. Pike hated Daisey for multiple reasons, and he liked Rory. Rory didn't look as though he liked anything anymore, but surely Daisey still had to rank among the truly hate-inspiring entities in the world. Not much room for surprises in this decision.

Daisey had voted for Rory on the off-off-off chance Pike might secretly feel for Daisey what Daisey did for him—grudging respect. Or that Dr. Idealistic had some moral hang-up about teammates who didn't put in their hundred-and-ten percent, maybe fed up with Rory's moping and half-assery. When Pike spoke, Daisey gave him his full attention, straining for some clue to his motives.

"How you doing?" Pike asked.

Rory took a deep, ragged breath, looking far older than thirty or whatever his age was. "I'm a box of birds, mate."

Pike raised an eyebrow.

"I'm peachy," Rory clarified.

"Right…"

"Don't worry about it."

Pike sighed, sounding annoyed. Hope stirred in Daisey's gut.

Mac walked over. "Hey." She said it mainly to Daisey, he thought, though the other two raised limp hands in greeting.

"Wow, you guys are chipper."

Needing the distraction and indeed one last chance to piss Pike off, should his minutes be numbered, Daisey crossed his arms over his chest and gave Mac a long, slow smile, just to short-circuit her pussy.

"How you doin', Miss Mac?"

Predictable as a puppy, she perked up at the attention. "Okay. I think I'm safe. I figure I'm the smallest threat on my team. Unless those two have some sleazy alliance." She nodded over her shoulder at Ian and Chloe. "But whatever. Nothing I can do about it now. You?"

"Forecast ain't lookin' quite so sunny for me, I'm afraid." He gave Pike and Rory each a pointed look. "Guess you were right all along, makin' friends with everyone."

She nodded.

"Shame I probably won't get a chance to fuck that innocent look right off your pretty face."

Pike made a throaty noise and got swiftly to his feet to wander away.

Mac shook her head at Daisey, looking annoyed but also pleased. "Yeah. Shame." She pinched the hem of her ruined shirt to showcase the paint. "I was so looking forward to that, after I let you get to second base on me with your stupid paintball."

Daisey held up his hand and wiggled his yellow-stained fingers at her.

She rolled her eyes. "I hope they stop you in airport security for that."

Lenora appeared then, yellow slips in one hand, blue in the other. "Thank you all for your patience. I have the results of the vote."

"'Bout goddamn time," Daisey muttered and Mac punched his arm.

"There will be no need for a second vote, as both teams submitted the ballots necessary for a definitive decision."

Daisey nodded. That'd be him. No clue what the other team had decided. Probably Ian. Daisey hoped that wouldn't mean he'd get stuck sitting next to the shithead on his flight out of Fairbanks.

"After I announce the results," Lenora said, "I'll ask the two eliminated players to please gather their things and follow the crew members. And without further ado, those two people are..." She consulted the fan of cards in her left hand. "From the Yellow Team... Rory."

Daisey started. He jerked his head to the right, where Rory stood nodding his solemn agreement. Daisey looked to Pike next, raising his eyebrows and nodding, a facial thumbs-up for Pike making the right choice in the end. But the guy's mouth was wide open, eyes uncharacteristically round as he stared at their ousted teammate. The look on his face confused the holy hell out of Daisey.

"Seriously?" Pike blurted, the word sharp with anger.

Rory met his stare, looking poised to reply, but suddenly Pike lunged through the crowd toward him, sending a collective intake of breath shushing through the group. He nearly got a swing in but Ian grabbed him as he passed, snagging his wrist and twisting it up behind his back as naturally as another man might shake hands. Ian held him there, seeming none too bothered by Pike's thrashing.

"You fucking pussy!" Pike shouted.

Rory stepped back a couple feet, eyes wide.

Mac recovered from her shock. "Jesus, Pike. What the hell?"

Chloe hadn't moved. She just crossed her long arms over her ribs and watched Pike struggling with a face full of dark amusement.

Lenora stepped between Rory and Pike, seeming not to have noticed the ruckus that had just gone down. She turned her attention to the cards in her right hand, as if she didn't already know the answer. "And the departing player from the Blue Team will be...Chloe."

Chloe's smug grin dissolved, mouth and arms dropping as she turned to stare Mac dead in the face. "Ian? Over me? You are *fucking* joking."

Mac shrugged.

For a second Chloe's eyes met Daisey's, then they snapped back to Mac. "You. Horny. Little. *Bitch.*"

Mac's chin came up an inch but she kept her expression cool.

Chloe's icy glare flashed between them one last time. "I hope he leaves you with a limp."

Mac smiled sweetly. "So do I."

Daisey glanced to Ian, wondering what had made him vote Chloe out as well. Then he decided trying to figure out what passed for logic in that fucker's skull wasn't worth the headache.

Rory cut the tense silence, turning to Lenora. "Are we done here then? I'm ready to leave this whole bloody head trip behind me."

"Yes. Why don't you and Chloe gather your things?"

Rory left without a wave or any parting words, didn't even give Mac a chance to snag him in a hug.

Chloe beamed each and every remaining player a liquid-nitrogen look, freezing all the blood on the premises before she mustered dignity and followed after Rory and the crew men, her blonde hair flapping with each livid step.

Ian released Pike's pinned arm. Pike rolled his shoulders then glared at Ian and moved to the opposite side of the dwindling group.

Daisey heard Mac hiss, "What the fuck was that about?"

Pike shrugged, unfocused eyes staring somewhere in the middle distance. His hand went to the scar on his neck, rubbing idly.

"Well, then," Lenora said. "We're down to just four competitors. And because we want to reward good teamwork as much as punishing the bad, the two players who did not receive any elimination votes from their teammates have earned themselves a bonus. We were going to give this bonus to the player who did the actual flag acquisition, but Chloe has sadly left us. So instead, for the next challenge, Mac and Pike—you're going to be deciding who is paired with whom."

They exchanged a tense look.

"The catch is that you won't know what the next challenge is, or how the next person or people to be eliminated will be determined. You have five minutes to decide, starting now." She nodded to the open clearing and Pike and Mac headed off to caucus in private. Lenora departed in the direction of the crew, leaving Daisey and Ian alone.

Ian took a couple steps closer. "All right, mate?" His tone was pure put-on sympathy with a side of douchebag. "You and Chloe would never have worked. Would've been like those fighting fish you have tae keep in separate bowls or else they tear the shite out of each other."

"Sounds good to me."

Ian's eyes roamed the field. "You know we're the two biggest arseholes left."

"Always were."

"You think they'll stick us together an' hope one of us wakes up strangled?"

Daisey shrugged. "If they each take one of us and the winning team gets a vote, one of us is guaranteed to go home. They leave us together, we'd probably win and one of them's heading home."

Ian made an impressed face, clearly not having expected much in the way of strategizing from Daisey. "Mebbe."

"But who knows how the elimination's going down. Could be the whole losing team."

Ian shook his head. "Only one's going home. Otherwise there's nae enough players tae finish the final two challenges. From here on out, we lose one player per game."

Daisey nodded, pretending to have realized this himself. "Yeah. But at any rate, you and me are in one camp, those two in the other, and we're the fuckers in the black Stetsons. If they're smart they'll each take one of us and hedge their bets. Even on separate teams they'll stick together, those two. They're like bestest buddies."

"Mac did'nae look too impressed with the good doctor jest now."

"Yeah, but she's a softie. She'll be all kittens and rainbows again by the time they're back."

"Aye, we'll see. She's still itchin' tae get in your pants. If you get the chance, I suggest you take Pike out of this competition."

"Duh." He wasn't stupid. Daisey wanted Pike out as bad as Mac wanted his dick in her pretty little mouth. And Mac would keep him around over Ian if she had the chance. Only way he was fucked was if Pike and Ian were solely in charge of a vote, or if he lost the next Objective outright, which wasn't an option as far as Daisey was concerned.

He raised a cocky eyebrow at Ian. "'Less somethin' real crazy happens, you'll probably want to be keepin' your bags packed."

Ian shrugged. "I've got as good a chance as you."

"You think Pike would keep *you* over me?"

Ian nodded.

Daisey laughed, shook his head. "You keep thinkin' that."

"He's sweet on Mac. He'll want you gone."

Daisey tossed the idea around then shook his head. "He's too much of a pro. He wants the cash. He wouldn't let somethin' dumb like that sway his decision."

Ian made an are-you-sure face and took out his cigarette case. He stopped in the middle of the reflex and frowned, replaced it and chewed his lip, fingers drumming the top of his hat.

Daisey laughed, clapping his hands with satisfaction. "Enjoy that withdrawal, motherfucker. I been there. You're gonna be a fuckin' nightmare to be around tomorrow."

"Dun'nae you worry yourself about me. Worry about the next vote."

"What bet did you lose that Mac got to swipe all your smokes?"

Ian stared off toward the woods with a weird, faint smile on his lips. "Was'nae a bet. More like a trade."

"I hope whatever you got was worth the days of pure hell you got comin' before you can get your ass to a gas station."

Ian grinned, eyes focusing to lock on Daisey's. "Oh yessiree." He put on a spaghetti-western cowboy accent, thumbs jammed in his pockets. "I'd say it's a dang good consolation prize...'cept I know I'll be the one walkin' out of these woods five hundred thousand bucks richer."

"We'll see."

Ian's voice went back to normal. "Two of us'll see. The rest of you will be back home, one week older with nothing tae show for it. You find yourself in England sometime and I'll take you out for a sympathy pint, how about that?"

"How 'bout you swing by Biloxi after *I* win and I'll let you buy your own fucking drink?"

"I'm gettin' all misty jest thinking about it. You an' me, reminiscing about the old days up in Alaska."

"This whole thing is so cracked. Especially now, after all that." Daisey nodded to one of the shacks. "Retrofitting some ancient bunker or whatever, all the time and money it must've taken to fix the closed-circuit wiring, plus to set up all those other cameras?"

Ian nodded.

"Thousands of dollars it must have cost, just for that. So some kinky doctors can watch us play tag for a couple hours. Must be frigging Howard Hughes behind those lenses, some rich, bat-shit motherfucker with more money than sense."

Ian's jaw clenched and unclenched, eyes narrowing.

"What?"

He frowned then shrugged. "Mebbe it's not jest for us. Who says we're the only group who signed on for this bloody Ant Farm?"

Daisey let that thought tumble around in his head for a minute before letting it go. He was sick of tripping over questions he'd never get answers to. "What d'you want the prize money for, anyhow?" he asked Ian.

"Nae too bothered about it, actually."

"Yeah, right."

"What about you?"

Daisey shifted from foot to foot, wishing he hadn't brought it up. "Got my reasons."

"You gettin' too old for the world's most dangerous profession, eh?" Ian's grin was slow and mean and begging for a fist.

"Laugh it up, Oliver Twist. You're—" Daisey stopped as Lenora appeared from the woods, making a beeline for Mac and Pike. They spoke at length.

"Christ," Ian muttered. "I need a fecking fag."

"I'll bet."

"You know what's funny?" Ian asked. "We're over here, worrying about Mac and Pike and the alliance they'd be wise tae get going. But you an' me, we aren't bothering tae form one ourselves."

"Yeah, like you'd keep me in the game if you had a choice. Our alliance would last about as long as it took for one of us to get our knife out and stab the other in the back."

"Aye, that's true."

Daisey nodded, almost liking Ian for an instant. When a man was dishonest enough, it made him nearly as predictable as one who only told the truth.

Ian sighed. "So, I've got a question for you. Why'd you vote for Rory, eh? Why nae keep the weakest one in the game?"

"I thought about it… But the way I figured it'd go, both of them would vote for me, no contest. They're all buddy-buddy, plus I'm the biggest threat in this whole group."

Ian smirked.

"So I just figured, fuck it. I voted for the one of them who was pissing me off worse. Thought maybe I had a chance in hell that Pike was fed up with Rory too. Not the way I thought it'd go down, but I ain't complainin'."

"Indeed."

"Lucky too that Chloe got the boot. Good job, you and Mac."

"Thought you had your heart set on fecking her."

Daisey shrugged. "Icing on the cake. But the cake's what's important."

"Sure it's not because I got tae her fairst?"

He turned to face Ian and remind him just how many pounds and inches Daisey had him beat by. "Don't bother wastin' that jealousy head trip on me, cocksucker. Save that shit for Pike."

Ian licked his lips. "Will do."

OBJECTIVE FIVE

BRIDGE BUILDING

CAMERA 6505

LENORA HALTS in front of Ian and Daisey. Mac and Pike stand beside her. Their faces are set, agreement implicit and the brief animosity from earlier seemingly gone.

"Mac and Pike have made their decision," Lenora says brightly. "The teams for the next Objective will be…" Her gaze hops back and forth like a drum roll between the two self-proclaimed assholes, as if she's about to announce who won the sweepstakes. "Mac and Daisey, and Pike and Ian."

For a second, no one reacts. Daisey's nostrils flare with a long exhalation and Ian blinks stoically. Mac moves to stand next to Daisey but Pike stays where he is, looking like the dictionary entry for *exhausted*.

"What's going to happen now is that you've got the evening off, and tomorrow morning the next challenge will begin. This Objective is called Bridge Building, but that's all I'll say about it. The crew will bring out your dinner in a short while, then the two teams will be retiring to separate campsites. Wake-up call tomorrow will be at oh five hundred hours, so I suggest you get some rest. The next Objective will be a grueling one.

"Okay. Everybody relax, grab some water. I'll see you bright and early with your marching orders." Lenora flashes her five-hundred-thousand-dollar smile and turns with the precision of a cadet, marching off into the woods a final time.

Ian runs his tongue over his lips, studying Pike. Pike's got his eyes on the ground, posture locked into an imitation of cool professionalism.

Daisey looks between Mac and Pike a few times. "Interestin'."

PIKE

AN ENTIRE FUCKING NIGHT with Ian for company... Surely this ought to count as extra credit toward the next day's Objective.

Dinner had been buffet-style yet again, though it was hard to ignore how few trays of food were needed now that the survivors had dwindled to four. Down from twelve in just four days. Those days seemed far longer—a couple of weeks, at least. Pike couldn't even remember the faces of all the original players.

After the last beers had been drunk and paper plates tossed, the teams had been led in opposite directions, Pike and Ian marched two miles through the woods and over a river until they were told to make camp by its bank. Ian had dropped his bag and promptly wandered off, leaving Pike alone with his fatigue.

He sighed and leaned against a tree trunk, wishing the sky were dark. It felt like about four in the morning to him, and the three helpings of lasagna he'd eaten that afternoon had spiked his blood sugar then crashed him, hard. The ten p.m. sun shined like midafternoon and Pike just wanted to sleep. He couldn't though. His body was exhausted but his brain was revving hard enough to overheat, plus the pink glow of the sun through his closed eyelids felt unnerving.

Thoughts of what the next challenge might be jockeyed for his attention alongside the memory of Mac kissing him. Shit, that stung. Now she was off with Daisey, alone. Not even that far away either. He'd heard Daisey's voice not long ago, the annoying bass rumble carrying from what sounded like the other side of the river.

Craving a task, Pike got up and spent a half-hour constructing a meticulous fire for when the sun would eventually disappear. He watched the orange flames against the blue river behind them, wishing they'd hypnotize him and let him be free of his gnawing thoughts for a little while. Normally they would. He liked fire, always had. Liked it a bit less than he used to though, thank God.

Ian wandered over with his pack. His hair was wet from a dunk in the river. Not the worst idea. Pike probably had a nice crust of blue paint dried to his back.

Digging a hand towel from his duffel, Ian rubbed it over his head with a glance at Pike. "Oi, don't look so down, teammate. You're with the man who has'nae yet been on the losing side of a single challenge."

Pondering that, Pike was surprised to realize it was true. "Huh." *Teammate*, his head echoed. Worse still, with both of them comparably smart and strong and roughly the same age, there was no clear rank or seniority to be gleaned, which made them *partners*.

Ian tossed his towel back in his bag and sorted through the other contents. He came out with a bottle—a fifth of whiskey—and tossed it to Pike.

"Mac let you keep your booze, huh?"

Ian nodded. "Seems she's keen for me tae impair meself."

Pike uncapped the bottle and took a sip. He normally only drank beer, and the heat of the liquor tingled up through his sinuses and stung his eyes. He passed it back.

Ian said, "Cheers," and downed a swig.

Pike accepted it again and held it between his palms for a long time, enjoying the weight of it, the thickness of the glass. He imagined hurling it at the rocks by the river's edge and watching it shatter, wondering what the fire might do when sprayed with the liquor. A rainbow of flame as the liquid arched and fell.

He pushed the thought away and listened to the insects and the breeze in the leaves, the pop of the branches in the fire. He and Ian passed the bottle back and forth for twenty minutes or more without speaking, and Pike let the alcohol trick him into relaxing, even feeling content. At long last, the sun dipped below the tree line.

"So," Ian said. "Rory voted himself out then?"

Pike flinched to remember. "Yeah, he must have. I sure as hell didn't put his name down."

"Surprised Daisey did'nae try tae vote *you* off."

"Me too. Guess he thinks even less of me than I thought."

"Bit thick, he is. Bet he jest voted off the next tallest bloke."

Pike looked up at the sound of Ian's lighter clicking open, the snick of his thumb toying with the wheel, the clink of him flipping the lid closed. He imagined borrowing it and burning the entire forest down, leveling all the foliage to make whatever Mac and Daisey were up to impossible, all that privacy disintegrated to ash. Fuck, he was going loopy.

Ian's voice pulled him back into the twistedness of reality. "I cannae help but wonder how these teams are really set up."

Pike held his tongue.

"You and me, Mac and Daisey. But nae really, right? You and Mac against the two of us, individually."

Pike stretched his neck from side to side. "You'd do the same."

"Aye, no doubt. You cannae predict how the elimination will work though."

"No, so I'm not bothering to obsess about it."

"How d'you know she won'nae keep him around, over you?"

Pike exhaled, long and weary. "Nothing I can do about it if she does. Think I'll leave the speculation and conniving to you. Now that Chloe's gone, you're the sole evil genius. Congratulations."

Ian smiled and took another drink. "Cheers tae that."

They traded the bottle a few more times and Pike felt his muscles go slack along with his brain. Just seven hours until the head games started up again, and he decided to luxuriate in the evening, despite the shit company. Who knew? A bit more whiskey and even a turd might blur enough to pass for a truffle.

Pike cleared his throat. "So. Let's bond. What d'you do, Ian? Surely 'sociopath' doesn't pay well enough to exclude you from a day job."

"Funny you should word it like that."

Pike stared at Ian out of the corner of his eye as he took another drink. "Seriously. What do you do?"

He grinned broadly. "I'm a nairse."

"A what?"

Ian cleared his throat and spoke slowly with a patronizingly neutral accent. "A nurse."

Pike was silent for a handful of seconds then laughed. "No, you're not."

"I am."

Pike passed the bottle back. "Who on *earth* would hire you to look after a patient's best interest?"

"Place called Broadmoor Hospital, in Berkshire, England."

Pike succumbed to a bout of drunken giggling, the sound surprising even himself. "Oh. My. God. That is *twisted.*"

"Aye, laugh it up. I thought you of all people would respect the occupation."

"I'm not laughing at the job, I'm laughing that someone hired *you* to care for and comfort sick people."

"Very sick people," Ian said, nodding. He took the bottle back.

"What, emergency? Trauma unit?"

"Nae. Broadmoor's a lunatic asylum."

Amusement drained from Pike like rainwater. "You're a *psych* nurse?"

"Aye. All male patients. Personality disorders, mainly."

"Jesus... It must be catching." At any rate, it explained Ian's physique. Pike remembered that hold he'd been trapped in when he'd tried to belt Rory, and for the first time ever he chose to believe the jerk. "They don't really still call it that, though, do they? An asylum?"

"Nae. But a pretty name does'nae change what goes on in there."

"What made you go into that?"

"Same reason I'm here. Fascination." Ian tapped his temple with a finger. "With people's brains. I fancy being in groups, seeing how people get on. Personally, I'd rather be on the other side, watching the tapes." He took a sip. "Dun'nae really care if I win. Jest want tae be here tae see what happens."

"What do you care what's going on in other people's heads?"

"Beats the feck out of pottering around in my own," Ian said. "My garden's a big mess of weeds and rubbish. You'd go out visitin' all the bloody time if you lived there, too."

Pike stared at his hands. "You know, Mac said once that you're Iago. Maybe she was wrong. Maybe... Maybe you're fucking Shakespeare." He started laughing again, feeling like a candidate for commitment himself just then.

"What about you? Why are you here?"

"The money," Pike said.

"That's it? That's your entire answer?"

He nodded.

"Why nae be a regular old civilian doctor then, mate? Why a medic if you're so keen on the dosh?"

"I was going to be a regular doctor." A caricature of his mother's long-suffering face flashed across Pike's mind. "But it wasn't for me."

"Nae enough bombs exploding around your feet? Or you some kind of idealist?"

"I dunno. I just couldn't take the system. All the paperwork and litigation… I'd rather sew up a guy who took shrapnel on the job than kiss some patient's ass so they won't sue me for emotional distress because I wasn't sympathetic enough about their hangnails or whatever."

"You lacking a wee bit on the bedside manner then?"

"It's just not worth the paycheck, coddling hypochondriacs and jerks who're just after a Vicodin scrip."

Ian looked off into the woods and smiled. "I follow. Still, you coming here for the money? That's dead mad."

"Well, you're the only one in the whole group claiming a different motivation, so I hate to break it to you, but you're probably the crazy one."

Ian shook his head. "Nae. I'm jest outnumbered by the nutters. As usual."

Mac's distant laughter rang out across the water and Pike sobered by a degree or two. He cleared his throat.

Ian clicked his lighter open and closed, open and closed. "I 'spect she'll finally be gettin' her way tonight."

"God, I would've pegged her as having better taste in men," Pike said, eyes rolling.

"I'm sure you'd peg her most any way you could. Nae accounting for taste, I s'pose. Guess she jest likes 'em primitive. She's been after him from day one."

"He's more than a decade older than her and a *fraction* as bright."

"Aye, and he's going tae have her and you aren't, so get over it." Ian laughed. "Bet you reckoned you'd hit the lottery, down in that map room. Finally you get your chance with the lass and she's jest in it for the game for a change."

"I'm in it for the game too," Pike said, largely to remind himself of that fact.

"Oh, aye, you keep telling yourself that, Doctor."

"Give me that." Pike snatched the whiskey back.

"Mebbe we ought to head over tae their camp. Rattle some chains, put on a good ghost show, scare the living shite out of him."

Pike had to laugh at that. After a deep drink he said, "I'm only going to ask this because I'm hammered."

"Shoot."

He tapped his fingers against the bottle. "What was Chloe like? That night you two went missing outside the warehouse? And how did you manage to talk your way into her pants?"

"Talk my way, nothin'. She practically date-raped me."

"No way."

Ian placed a hand over his heart. "On my honor, for what it's worth. I dun'nae know exactly what her game was, but she's prolly never lost, the way she plays. She's a very persuasive woman. An' downright certifiable." He smiled deeply and took the booze back. "An' beddin' her—that was like a snake and a mongoose. Feck or be fecked. Still dun'nae know which I was."

"Why'd you do it?"

"Why does any free man do it? I was hard. Plus I could'nae pass on a chance tae piss Daisey off."

"Why?"

Ian shrugged. "I have my reasons."

"Well, it's your funeral, getting on that dude's bad side."

"Way I see it," Ian said, "after this round's over, if there's a vote, he and I are through competin'. They win, I'm out, guaranteed—you and her are top mates, and like you said, I already dug my own grave. We win, he's out. I say that because he's the last one I want tae face in another physical competition, and you won't be able tae stand the sight of him after Mac gets her jollies tonight. But either way, you and her, you're not finished yet. Be thankful for that."

"I know who I'd prefer to see go tomorrow." He looked over at Ian, shocked that he'd actually be hoping for the guy to stick around for another challenge, if only to see the back of Daisey.

"So you think. But who said I dun'nae want her meself?"

Pike narrowed his eyes. *"You* want Mac?"

"Want her?" He took a deep, deep drink and tossed the empty bottle over his shoulder. "Hell, I'm bloody in love with her."

DAISEY

DAISEY ROLLED HIS JEANS up to his knees and stretched his legs out, digging his bare feet into the coarse, wet sand at the edge of the river. "Oh fuck me, that feels good."

Across the water he could see Pike and Ian sitting by the woods, a fire blazing on their beach. Not a bad idea.

Mac returned from a trip downriver, screwing the cap onto the canteen she'd filled. "I like your thinking." She unlaced her hiking boots and toed off her socks, sitting beside him.

Daisey watched their massively mismatched feet flexing in the current, unnerved by the tininess of hers.

"You don't smoke, do you, Daisey? Weed, I mean?"

He laughed. "Wow. Didn't see that question comin'. And no, not since I was your age. Never really my thing. Made me too lazy to get up to no good. Gimme alcohol, any day."

She nodded.

"Go ahead though. Don't let me stop you."

"Nah. It's no fun if it's only me."

"Guess we just got each other for entertainment then." Daisey left the remark open for Mac to find whatever innuendo she felt like in it. He wasn't an honorable man. He'd be deluded to pretend he wouldn't give in to whatever she decided to tempt him with tonight.

"What a weird elimination." Her voice sounded spacey, eyes looking glazed as she stared across the river—exhaustion. Made her sound stoned without the weed.

"I did *not* see that coming," she went on. "Rory going home."

Daisey nodded. "Why'd Pike try and take a swing at him, anyhow? He tell you?"

Mac smirked. "I think it's pretty obvious."

"Enlighten me."

"Well, because he assumed Rory would vote you out. I think Pike was really looking forward to you being gone. You've been baiting him every chance you got from the moment this game started."

Daisey smiled to himself. The girl was really that oblivious to the real reason Pike couldn't stand the sight of him? Probably. She seemed to take everyone at face value. That worked just fine for Daisey, since his surface was probably the only thing she'd like about him if she bothered to do the slightest bit of digging.

He shook his head. "Still, didn't see that little outburst coming from Pike. Mr. Over-It."

"No. I've never seen him lose his cool before. Not that we've known each other that long, of course. But still."

"Feels like a long time though, don't it?"

"Yeah. Feels like a month ago that Leah left. Like we must have started this game in June, not four days ago."

Daisey stared at her, not caring if she saw. As if she'd care. As if she weren't staring at *him* most anytime he took an inventory of her eyes.

She was so unlike the women Daisey went for, she was nearly another species. He tried picturing her, plunked down in his hometown amongst its other twenty-five-year-old females, most of them already with a kid or two under their belt, a shelf full of dusty old pageant crowns. Mac rolling a joint at the table while her contemporaries drank instant coffee and gossiped about whoever wasn't in the room. Mac with that tiny, strong body, circled by women the same age but who looked a decade older. Small towns aged people before their time.

Not that Daisey had any right to judge those women for their unextraordinary lives, lives not unlike his momma's. As if going off to the army then making a career on an oil rig was anything so worldly, where he came from.

He cleared his throat. "So tell me, Miss Mac…"

"Hmmm?"

"You enjoyin' yourself on this trip?"

She laughed. "Yeah. I am. Are you?"

He shrugged. "I dunno. If I win, sure."

"Well, I'm having a great time, mostly. I never leave New Mexico unless it's to pick something up for my family's business, so this is like vacation for me. Maybe a vacation with a huge check for a souvenir."

"Maybe." He thought about it. Could Mac win all this? She was well positioned, as Pike liked her, Ian seemed amused and unintimidated by her, and Daisey would rather see either of those guys gone *long* before her. He imagined it was the two of them in the final challenge, tallest and the shortest, the near-oldest and one of the youngest of the original group. The sweetest versus a strong contender for the title of Supreme Shithead. It could happen. Pretty likely, really.

"What do you think Lenora meant by 'bridge building'?" Mac asked. "Do you think that's literal?"

"Maybe. Why else would we be camped by a river?"

She stared across the water and waved. Daisey looked in time to see Pike raise a hand in return.

"Maybe we'll have to storm their camp before they can storm ours," she said.

"Maybe."

She sighed, long and mournful, and craned her neck from side to side. "Am I *ever* going to trick you into sleeping with me?"

Daisey laughed at her tactlessness. "I figured that'd be inevitable tonight."

Her eyebrows rose. "Oh?"

He glanced across the river to Pike then back at Mac. "I'm not a particularly honorable man, and you don't seem likely to take 'no' for an answer."

She made a face, pursing her lips as though trying to downplay a grin.

Having already decided for sure he'd go there with her, Daisey felt his body warming. Wasn't as good as the thrill of getting a disinterested woman to change her mind—he preferred being the chaser, not the chased. But he thought of another way to make this go the way he liked. Fuck Mac, fuck with Pike's head. Ruining Mac for the doctor was enough of a bonus to take the edge off Daisey's misgivings about nailing the girl. And pissing off a rival male was nearly as good as coercing a challenging woman.

"Let's wait until the sun's down," Daisey said. "Should only be a half-hour or so. Then we'll sleep like babies after."

Her grin broke through and Daisey had to laugh.

"You always this subtle when you got it bad for some guy?" he asked.

"Sorry. No, I don't think I'm this bad usually. But I'm coming off a dry spell and you look like a steak to me, like in one of those cartoons about two starving people on a deserted island."

He laughed again. "Your brothers spend much time sitting on the roof with their shotguns trained on any men who try to approach?"

"Nah. I just live really out there. And men like you don't usually show up looking for a river-rafting excursion."

"Men like me?"

She nodded.

"Like you know what kind of man I am."

She shrugged. "I have a few guesses."

"Hope I don't disappoint you, whatever idea you got built up in your head about me."

"Certain evidence was already tendered in the hot tub."

Daisey shook his head. "Jesus, you're shameless. Bet you gave your poor father a few sleepless nights when you were a teenager."

Mac's smile tightened. "My parents both died when I was young."

"Oh."

"Don't worry—I've had seventeen years to get over it."

Daisey shifted, feeling uncomfortable in his own body. Both his parents were still alive, still married, pretty happy. Seemed unfair Mac could have grown up so well adjusted without her folks, when Daisey had gotten a complete and enviable set of them and turned out an asshole in spite of their best church-going efforts. He wondered what became of kids with a mix of those options, kids with deadbeats for parents. Was that better or worse than losing them outright? Disappointing instead of disappeared?

"Think I'll take a swim while I wait for the stupid sun to go down," Mac said.

Daisey nodded, still lost in his head, not really listening.

"You wanna come?"

He looked up at Mac, stripping to her jog bra and undies. He glanced across the water just in time to see Pike stand and disappear into the woods. *Not what you think, Doc.* But it could be. And why the fuck not? Bit of messing around might get Daisey out of his annoying thoughts for a while.

"Yeah, sure. Could use a good scrub, anyhow." He stood and stretched, pulled the tiny microphone clipped to his collar close to his lips to tell it, "Trust me, you don't wanna hear what's about to go down." He unbuttoned his flannel shirt and tossed it aside, along with the mic. He caught Mac's eyes on his bare arms, that starved-animal quality she was such a pro at.

"You bring any soap?" Daisey asked.

"Yeah."

"Grab it."

She headed for her pack and Daisey went to the water's edge. He stripped away his undershirt and unbuckled his belt, kicked away his jeans. It all felt just like that first night in the luxury cabin, until Daisey stuck a foot in the cool river. He made it up to his knees by the time Mac arrived with a bar of soap in hand.

"Not as toasty as that Jacuzzi," he warned.

"That's all right." She waded out to her butt, no hesitation. The cotton of her light blue panties turned translucent and Daisey's misgivings faded to a dull buzz and hid behind his withered conscience.

"Over there," he said, and pointed to a boulder a little ways downriver.

Mac dunked and came up swimming and Daisey trudged behind her. He glanced to the opposite shore, to where Ian stood on the bank, pale face turned in their direction. A wholly innate part of Daisey wanted to protect Mac from the creepy fucker's eyes. "Over here." He waved to the side of the boulder facing their shore, where the worst of what they might get up to would be blocked from the other men's view. Ian's and Pike's views, anyhow. Who knew where the cameras were and what show the doctors might be in for.

Mac settled against the boulder. The river wasn't deep. It came up to her navel and Daisey's crotch. She turned the soap around in her hands, eyes perusing Daisey's body like a menu of her favorite foods.

"Can't say I ever met a girl so happy to get caught starin'." Daisey stepped closer, until he was just out of her reach. Weird to be the one doing the teasing. Weird and satisfying.

"I'm pretty lousy at playing coy," she said.

"And I'm pretty lousy at sayin' no, so have at it. Whatever you want."

Her smile deepened and she curled a finger to invite him closer. He gave her what she asked for, coming near enough to remind them both that she only came up to his chest.

"Wow." Her voice was so hushed he barely heard her over the din of the river. For a few seconds longer, the soap turned around and around in her hand, blobs of suds dropping into the current.

Spotting a chance to be the instigator for a change, he took her wrist and moved one soapy palm to his ribs. Her hesitation evaporated. She handed him the soap and her small hands began their explorations in earnest. He kept his own hands at his sides and let her do what she liked. Slippery palms roamed and assessed his chest and stomach and sides and biceps as her eyes did the same.

"Why me?" Daisey asked.

With what looked like a major effort, she peeled her gaze off his body and moved it to his face. "Because you're…well, you're huge. It's very sexy."

He laughed. Dipping the soap in the water, he lathered the bar in his hands and returned the objectification. "You're tiny." He ran his hands over her shoulders, her breasts, her waist where it met the river. Behind him the sun was finally setting, the sky turning the color of a new bruise.

"Lose this." Daisey plucked at the thick straps of her yellow-splattered athletic bra. He stepped back so she could peel it off and set it on the boulder, revealing breasts as small and perky as their owner. To a man who lived on a rig and usually had to get his T and A fix from porn, Mac was fascinating. A mix of different tan lines, scrapes and scars, tiny breasts, no makeup. Frankly she could stand to shave her pits, but lost in the exoticness of studying a real woman, Daisey decided even that was sexy.

And damn, the size of her. It made Daisey feel huge, got all those aggressive, possessive chemicals pumping through his veins. The fact that this petite woman might stand between him and half a million bucks compounded the heat, sent all his blood racing to his cock. Mac watched as he adjusted his growing erection behind his shorts with a soapy hand.

"You look hungry, girl."

Her gaze jumped up to meet his. "I've been waiting very patiently for this…as everybody in the whole stupid competition knows by now."

"Well, before you get yourself too excited, I oughta point out, we ain't got no condoms."

Mac chewed her lip. "That's fine. There's plenty of other stuff we can do."

"You can start by takin' those off." He nodded to her panties, hidden by the current.

Not wasting a second, she reached down and her legs jerked this way and that, and she whipped her panties high over her shoulder, wet cotton slapping against the boulder and sticking there.

Daisey lost himself to a deep, body-quaking laugh. When he straightened up again he found her smiling, brown eyes twinkling in the lingering glow of the lazy northern sun.

"You're just a tiny bit crazy, aren't you?"

Mac curtsied with an invisible skirt and Daisey laughed again, shaking his head.

"You're a weird girl, Miss Mac."

"Thank you."

He turned toward the shore and flung the soap there, done flirting. Ready to get down to business. Looking back to Mac, he stepped close again, near enough that his hidden erection brushed her belly. He reached down and found her legs in the water. With a hand behind each knee, he lifted her up, slowly so as to not scrape her back, and pinned them together against the rock, crotch to crotch.

"Whoa." Mac's face changed to one Daisey knew well—that *oh shit, what did I just sign up for?* look he often inspired in women. He let her feel his weight and strength as he ground against her, done being the seduced and coerced, ready to be the aggressor.

"This what you been wantin'?"

She nodded.

Digging his fingers harder into her thighs, he moved his hips, rubbing his shrouded cock back and forth against her pussy.

"Daisey."

He nearly corrected her, nearly told her to call him Brian... But nah. This was good. It kept him feeling like the boss, the one dishing out the orders. Enough with the eager Girl Scout shtick. She'd get him the way he was, no woman's fantasy, many a woman's guilty regret. He pulled away from the rock and her legs locked around his waist. He grabbed her bra and carried her to shore, where the growing darkness would keep this private enough. Dropping to his knees, he laid her down in the coarse sand then stood.

"On your knees."

She obeyed, looking up at him expectantly.

He stood before her and stroked his cock through his wet underwear, eyes glued to hers. If she wanted him, she'd get him—the way he liked, whether she was prepared for it or not. They were competitors and she'd been making him nuts for days, leaving him half-annoyed and half-aching to come from her constant advances.

xx

She'd also gotten Chloe kicked out of the game, and Daisey would give Mac everything he'd been reserving for that infuriating goddess.

He stepped closer and Mac took the hint, taking over the stroking. Daisey shut his eyes and groaned, cock going stiff and thick as her small hands squeezed him.

"Good." He cupped the back of her head. Creeped out by her pigtails, he slid the elastics from them and messed up her wet hair with his fingers.

He shoved his waistband down and she gripped his dick. Groaning deeper, he thrust his hips in time with her pulls and coaxed her face closer with his cupping hand. He watched her lips tease his head, just the faintest graze of her skin across his.

"Taste me."

The tiniest lick taunted his tip, making his hips buck. She tongued his slit then closed her mouth over his crown.

"Fuck, yeah. Suck that cock."

He wanted to slam himself down Mac's throat, but as riled as she sometimes got him, Daisey wasn't *that* determined to punish the girl. With gentle motions of his hips, he asked for more and she gave what she could.

Daisey was used to a different breed of blowjob—the kind his normal type of woman was an expert at, those sloppy, porn-quality ones. Mac's style was something else entirely, something less about performance and more about hunger. She sucked cock as if it was the only thing on the planet she wanted to be doing, and graceless or not, it got Daisey so hot he was nearing the edge already, way too soon.

"Slow down, slow down." He eased himself from her mouth. "Get on your hands and knees."

Mac did as she was told and he knelt behind her. He used his shorts to dust the sand off his hand and reached between her legs—far wetter than he'd dared hope. He wished she didn't sigh quite the way she did. Her voice drove their age difference home but Daisey shoved it to the back of his mind. Twenty-five was plenty legal, and plenty old enough for the girl to know better, if she chose to know better. And Daisey was plenty horny enough to forget all about his recent resolutions to be a better man.

He lined up his cock between her thighs, thrusting until he was soaked in her, until they were both moaning. With a hand on each of her hips, he pushed until Mac brought her thighs tight together, trapping his slick cock. He locked his knees outside her legs and began to pump, the length of his dick sliding between her ass cheeks, her lips, his head glancing her belly as he drove deep.

"Yeah. Take me."

"Daisey."

She wanted him, and he'd give her more than she'd surely bargained for. He hammered her hard enough for the slap of wet skin on wet skin to ring out in the darkening dusk, hard enough to drive her knees deeper into the sand and force her bracing arms forward. He wished they did have a goddamn condom. He'd fuck her deep enough to prove what a perfectly terrible idea all of this was, how utterly wrong the two of them were.

"Jesus."

Just that word, the quality in her voice that told him she was wondering what in the fuck she'd gotten herself into… Shit, that got him hot. Fucked-up fetish, needing to think a woman just might regret her decision to sleep with him, but goddamn if it didn't make his body race with pleasure. He didn't want to be Mac's stupid fantasy—he wanted to be her mistake.

He waited for her to ask him to go slower, take it easy. And he would. But he wanted that proof that he was too much. Spurred by the thought, his hips drilled her hard and fast.

A huff of a laugh. "Slow down."

He did, but even as the friction eased, his body got sucked deeper into arousal. He moaned as he felt his limbs losing some control, his grip on her waist feeling heavy and clumsy. The blood had long left his head to pound in his cock and a pleasurable cloud engulfed his mind. Heat and pressure grew in his belly, streaking up his cock with each thrust, given voice by Mac's punctuating gasps.

The orgasm arrived like a punch, a blinding sensation in his cock that rang out through his arms and calves and fingers and toes and spilled from his throat in an almighty groan. "God, fuck!"

Through the pounding of his pulse in his ears he heard his name in her voice. Shit, that voice. Too high. Too goddamn young. He gathered his wits in the haze of fading pleasure. Shuffling back on his knees, he looked at her, wishing it was dark enough to obscure the details of her body. Too small. Way too small.

Daisey stood and bent over for his shorts and pulled them up his legs, wetness and sand be damned. "Thanks. I needed that."

Mac flipped over, kneeling. He could make out her expression in the dusk light, dark eyebrows raised in surprise. "Wait, seriously?"

"Sorry girl, I'm done." He shivered at his own choice of words.

"Well, I'm not."

"Like I said, sorry. But that's what you're gettin'. Exactly what you wanted—a man like me."

She stood and put her hands to her hips, seeming just as at home in nudity as in hiking clothes. It intimidated Daisey just a bit, a woman so comfortable with her body and her wants.

"A man, yeah—that's what I wanted. And a *man* cares whether or not the woman he's with gets off."

"Not in the mood to debate you on the semantics, Miss Mac. I gotta build us a fire now. How's that for manliness?"

"You're actually serious?"

"I gave you a hell of a fair warning not to get with me," Daisey said.

"Haven't you got any pride?" He couldn't make out her expression.

"Nope, can't say I do."

"That is so tacky." She stared skyward, blinking, her frustration plain.

"That's me." He turned his attention to the beach, eyes straining for his jeans and shirts, for branches to build them a bonfire.

"Well. I guess you come exactly as advertised then," Mac said.

"Yup."

"Yeah, lovely. I hope you had a great time."

Daisey let his silence mark the end of the conversation. As always, the release of orgasm didn't feel like that—a release. Felt like a soulless victory, like taking the pot in a game he'd cheated at. He liked that feeling though. Felt like how he guessed it might feel to give Pike a good punch in his sainted face while he lay sleeping.

Ian's voice broke through Daisey's smug, cold triumph—the voice of game play. *Prolly feels jest exactly like shooting yourself in the foot, mate.*

He glanced in Mac's direction. Yeah, probably. But it also felt like the only thing he valued—winning. And Daisey never felt as though he'd won until somebody else lost.

PIKE

DAWN ARRIVED AROUND THREE A.M. Alongside the light came several other unwanted intruders—the realization of where Pike was, the band saw gnawing at his hungover skull, and the memory of his last glance at Mac the previous evening, off for a good old skinny-dip with her perfect specimen of maleness.

He opened his eyes to stare into the brightening sky, the ground cold and lumpy beneath his achy back. In this moment, right now, he knew he wasn't in love with her.

People who truly loved other people wanted them to be happy, no matter if that happiness came at their own expense. Pike didn't want her to be happy if it meant Daisey got to fuck her. So he wasn't in love with her. In fact, he was over her, finally.

That thought was nearly enough to cheer him. Nearly.

It was enough to inspire him to sit up though, but the good vibes ended there. His brain sloshed to the front of his head like a water balloon. He knew what hell tasted like, now. Tasted like whiskey aged four hours in his unwashed mouth.

"Fuck me." He made it to standing and the world spun. Bridge Building. That's what today was. Pike could barely lift his own body and he had to spend the day doing manual labor. *Just let this one go*, he thought. Just show up for marching orders then sleep the day away on the beach.

Lose this challenge, and who gets the vote? Maybe just Daisey and Mac. They'd keep him in the game over Ian. If he and Ian had a say as well... Well, he'd vote to get Ian out too. But no, because Ian would probably vote for Daisey.

Ian would—

The blood drained out of Pike's body, leaving him a hollow wire mesh of nerves.

I'm bloody in love with her.

Pike hadn't pursued that conversation. He hadn't known what to say or what to make of it in his drunken confusion, so he'd shut off. Then Mac and Daisey had started up across the river and Pike had left to make camp at the edge of the woods, praying neither was a passionate vocalizer. He'd passed out more than he'd actually fallen asleep, and probably just in time.

Fuck it. Pike wasn't in love with her.

Neither was Ian. How could he love anybody? It had only been four days, plus he was *Ian*.

Nobody was in love with Mac and it didn't matter if they were, anyway. It was all a stupid game. A stupid game that would continue on without Pike if he didn't get his priorities straight.

Maybe there was no vote. Maybe the elimination would be based on performance. If so, he had to de-pickle his brain and get his shit together. Get his head screwed on about why he was here. Five hundred grand. Not revenge, not puppy love, but for a decade's salary in one lump sum. Shit, he'd have put up with all this for less.

He staggered to the river and scooped cool water into his mouth, what felt like a gallon of it. If he didn't he'd be pissing turpentine, probably stay drunk until high noon.

Hydration, done. What else was good for a hangover? In high school he'd been told the hangover cure was two pints of water and four Advils before you go to bed, and med school hadn't offered a better idea. Still, too late for that. Only way he'd found to get over a hangover was to work—flush it out and get your mind and body focused on other stuff. He ditched his shirt and socks and shoes and stepped into the current. Cold but not frigid. Couldn't possibly make his body feel any worse than it already did anyhow.

He must have swum for an hour. By the time Pike convinced himself he was sober and struggled his way back upstream, Ian was awake, standing on the beach. Pike ignored him, passing by in search of his pack.

"Oi, mornin' tae you too."

As surely as he felt it himself, Pike could hear Ian's strain. Behind the pithy snark lurked a rasp born from an orgy of alcohol and a dearth of nicotine.

Once he was dressed, Pike returned to the beach to face his teammate. "What time you got?" Pike studied the dark circles under Ian's eyes as he scanned the face of his watch.

"Twenty minutes 'til kickoff."

"They better give us breakfast," Pike said. "Think I'm still loaded."

"You're welcome."

"I won't complain. You must feel ten times worse than me."

Ian shrugged. "I feel like shite most all the time." Again, his words were betrayed by his voice. There was a watery edge to each syllable, as though Ian's entire body was vibrating. Or maybe that was another byproduct of Pike's hangover. Maybe *he* was the one who was shaking.

At precisely five a.m., a staffer appeared from the woods and bade Pike and Ian to follow him. They marched a good mile to where the river ran narrower and faster and crossed over the old foot bridge they'd used to reach their camp the night before. Another mile and they arrived at the enemy's side. Pike's nerves buzzed, overshadowing his headache. Daisey was already standing on the beach. Mac appeared from the woods a moment later, zipping up her vest against the morning chill. She offered Ian and Pike a weak smile and locked her arms over her chest, loitering in a loose circle with the rest of them. She seemed to stand as far from Daisey as possible, which puzzled Pike.

Her body stiffened suddenly and she whipped around to face the river. Pike glanced in the direction Mac had, to the big boulder ten yards into the current, something pale blue stuck to its side.

Ian must have noticed as well. "Nice knickers."

Lenora appeared then, saving them from whatever conversation might have followed Ian's comment.

"Morning, campers! I trust you're all well rested."

Pike glanced around, deciding everyone but Daisey looked like the walking dead.

"As I said yesterday, today's Objective is called Bridge Building. It'll take a bit of ingenuity, and plenty of stamina and strength. I'm going to explain it and then you'll have an hour to eat breakfast and confer with your teammates, as there are important decisions to be made at the outset.

"As I'm sure you've all guessed, this river is the location of the challenge. All you need to do is engineer a structure that will get you across that water, dry from the ankles up. You may get as wet as you like during the construction, but to win, both members of your team must cross the river, either simultaneously or in direct succession, and set both feet on the other team's bank. No time limit."

Her eyes traveled from face to face, pausing to smile at each person as the announcement sank in. "Here's some basic information—the river is one hundred feet across at the point directly between your two beaches. At its deepest, it's five and a half feet. The current is a gentle half-knot, as I believe a few of you discovered for yourselves last night."

Pike looked reflexively to Mac and Daisey, neither of whom offered the other the faintest flirty, conspiring acknowledgment.

"You'll be needing tools, of course. But *which* tools will be up to you to decide. We'll be providing a selection from which each player may choose one. Pick wisely. In addition to the provided tools, you may also use any items you packed and of course the natural materials of the landscape. That is to say, trees, leaves, rocks..."

The group nodded its comprehension.

"Excellent. Follow Josh and you'll find breakfast waiting for you."

Pike's mind was already rousing with buds of ideas, hangover fading to a annoying hum in the rear of his skull. Mac and Daisey led the group and Ian fell back to flank Pike.

"You know much about engineering?" Ian asked.

"Probably as much as you do. But the simpler the better, I figure."

"Cross your fingers there's a chainsaw on the menu."

"We'll want rope," Pike guessed. "And yeah, something to take down a tree."

"Plenty of wee boulders 'round here," Ian said. "Sturdy. Simple."

"That might work for the first ten feet, then the water gets deep, and how're stepping stones supposed to help us?"

They wandered into a small clearing set with the usual table of food. Pike piled a plate with eggs and bacon and a couple of bagels and he and Ian set up a pair of folding chairs. Ian had a cup of coffee in each hand, no food in sight.

Mac and Daisey settled at the other end of the clearing, heads together, planning. Pike couldn't get a read on them this morning, but if Mac's body language was any indication, they hadn't had much of a honeymoon. The idea warmed him like a mug of cocoa.

Though he was definitely over her, nevertheless. Definitely.

"What about just two big trees, chopped down and dropped across the river from either bank?" Ian asked, dragging Pike's head back into the game. "She said it's what? A hundred feet across? That's two tall trees. Mebbe a thaird in the middle for where the fairst two thin out on top?"

Pike looked into the canopy above them, evergreens mainly. "It'll be a hell of a job to walk across those, if we can even down them. Branches sticking out every which way…"

"That's why we pray for an axe," Ian said. "Hack away any obstructions."

"Maybe. Or what about a cable bridge? All we'd need is maybe three hundred feet of rope. One line for our feet and one to hold onto, tied to a tree on either side. She said we can get as wet as we want while we build it. Just swim across, attach the end, swim back, maybe figure out some way to, like, twist a thick branch to make them super tight, like a tourniquet?"

"Simple," Ian said, nodding. "Mebbe. Or mebbe they give us exactly enough rope tae hang ourselves, nae enough for a bridge."

"Well, if there's enough, I say we go for that idea."

"You know, she has'nae said anything about whether we're allowed tae feck with the other team's bridge yet."

A fair point, though if that were within the rules, this challenge could go on for days, an endless cycle of sabotage and rebuilding.

Pike sighed, exhausted at the thought. "What kind of fucked-up competition is this, where you have to wait for explicit instructions about whether or not it's cool to cheat?"

He focused on his food, going back for seconds and thirds, not knowing when or if lunch would arrive. He shoved six bagels in his pack as an insurance policy. By the time the crew disassembled the buffet, neither he nor Ian had come up with any ideas better than a two-cable bridge or simply knocking trees down.

Lenora appeared, a pair of young henchmen behind her, each pushing a large, shiny red wheelbarrow laden with supplies.

"Gather around and see what tools you get to choose from." Lenora beckoned the pairs forward with a sweep of her arm. "Same options for each team. Rope, two axes, two handsaws, a tarp, a sledgehammer, a shovel and the wheelbarrows themselves."

Pike eyed the coil of rope, thinking the thickness was just about right for their plan. "How long is that rope?"

"Fifty yards," Lenora said brightly.

He did some mental math. "Shit. And there's only one rope available to each team?"

She nodded.

Damn. Probably only half of what they needed to cross the river and the banks *and* attach to the trees. Pike leaned over to whisper to Ian, "Do you think it'd hold us if we unwound it into two lengths?"

"No way in hell."

Pike had to agree. "Two axes then?"

"That'd be fastest, if it's speed you fancy."

"Or if one went dull." Pike didn't have the first idea how long an axe stayed sharp, and he suspected he'd likely slice a finger off if he attempted to sharpen one with a rock. Two axes seemed wisest.

"Sounds like a plan," Ian said. "Mebbe nae a good one, but a plan."

Pike nodded and straightened. Mac and Daisey had finished whispering as well but neither team wanted to choose first and risk giving away its strategy. Finally, Mac stepped forward and lifted an axe from her team's wheelbarrow. Pike did the same.

Daisey and Ian stepped up simultaneously, Ian taking a second axe, Daisey the rope.

Lenora spoke. "Those are your final choices?" When no one protested she smiled grandly. "Excellent. Good luck to both teams. Oh and incidentally, any team caught interfering with the other team will be penalized two hours per member, during which time they will not be allowed to work on their own structure. Understood?"

Pike nodded along with the others, intrigued. So foul play was allowed, but it came at a price. He heard Ian's voice in his head. *Interestin'.*

"If Pike and Ian would please follow the crew back to their camp, this challenge will begin at oh-seven-hundred hours, at the sound of the air horn. Happy building!"

The fact that Mac offered no cheerful reply cast a shadow on the group, as though a rain cloud had rolled in.

As he and Ian hiked back to their side, Pike wondered what could have turned her so uncharacteristically mopey. Daisey had turned her down. The sex had been awful. The sex had been great then Daisey had broken her heart somehow. Pike laughed at a thought too delightful to be true.

"What?" Ian asked.

He hesitated a moment then thought, fuck it—Ian knew about his stupid crush. *Former* stupid crush. "I was just wondering why Mac seemed so bummed. I thought maybe old Daisey had some trouble getting it up last night."

Ian laughed too. "Mebbe he said the wrong name."

Pike grinned.

"Mebbe their wee tryst got interrupted by a bear."

"So what you said last night..."

"Aye?"

"You said you like her too."

Ian's gaze stayed glued to the trail in front of them. "I said more than that."

"Right. So that was true?" He knew he wouldn't be able to concentrate on the game until he got his head around it.

"Aye."

"Why, though? What do you see in Mac?"

"Same things as you do, I reckon."

"As I *did*, past tense. I'm over that now."

"Course you are. How silly of me."

Pike ignored the remark. "But I would've guessed you'd be into somebody like... Well, like Chloe. As evil as you."

"As if you'd know the fairst thing about my taste in women, Dr. Pike."

"Maybe I don't know," he said as they stepped back onto their sunny stretch of beach. "But you having feelings— Shit, you having feelings full-stop is weird."

"Cheers."

"But you having feelings for Mac is just creepy. That's like a spider saying it's got feelings for a butterfly or something. I don't buy it."

Ian stared into the sun for a long moment, those eerie eyes lit up like blue cough lozenges.

"Mac's everything good in a world otherwise filled wi' shite. And she does'nae pretend there's nae piles of it everywhere, either. She jest goes about her merry business, focused on the spaces between the shite piles, lets everybody else do the shoveling and flinging."

Pike frowned, angling his axe to watch the sun glint off its brand-new blade. If pressed to describe his own erstwhile feelings for Mac, he'd have employed a metaphor less riddled with shit piles. But the sentiment felt about right.

"I hope I never say this to you again, Ian, but I agree with you on that one."

Ian nodded. For once, Pike wasn't the one who changed the subject. "Which tree, d'you reckon?"

Pike scanned the edge of their woods. "Well, we need one from our side, one from theirs." He peered across the water. Both sides were well stocked with tall spruces, no worries about inventory. "How about that one?" He nodded to one right at the edge of the woods. "Bonus if it lands and wrecks whatever it is they're working on."

Ian's lips twitched. "Now you say that, she never did mention if *accidentally* destroying their bridge counted as sabotage."

"I think the fact that we just had this conversation, on tape, probably complicates the semantics of the word 'accidentally'."

Ian nodded.

Pike looked across the river, to where Daisey and Mac were standing. Daisey had taken possession of the axe and was aiming it this way and that, pointing to trees. Mac mimed a shape with her arms, a gigantic rectangle, Pike thought. Then another thought dawned on him. "Oh crap."

Ian raised an eyebrow.

"I bet we didn't even need more than the one rope," Pike said. "String one length across, high enough, and just go hand-over-hand."

"Aye, nae a bad idea. Too late though, eh? 'Less you're keen on making a deal with those two."

He shook his head. "We'll stick to the original plan."

"You're the boss."

Through the peace blasted an air horn, marking the start of the challenge. Pike looked to Ian and they both marched to the appointed tree. This could really go quite easily.

"So if we want it to fall that way," Pike said, pointing to Mac and Daisey's camp, "we chop this side." He tapped the side of the trunk facing the river.

"Easy enough."

"Take turns?"

"You right-handed?"

Pike nodded.

"Me too. I dun'nae trust you swinging an axe left-handed in my direction any more than you fancy the same, so I say switching off is'nae the most comforting plan ever. Plus, if one of us heads back tae that side tae start on the other tree, we can spy on them."

Pike considered the points, both valid. And no, he didn't really want a hungover, cigarette-fiending psych nurse with no axe skills wielding a heavy blade anywhere near him. "Fine with me. Who goes where?"

Ian's smile was slow and sticky. "Know you're dying tae spy on the honeymooners. You go on. I'll take this side."

Reflexively, Pike searched for sinister reasons why Ian might want to stay on this bank, but he couldn't find any worth stressing over. "Cool. Sounds like a plan."

For what felt like the millionth time, Pike made the hike through the woods to the other side, carrying the axe and a bag with his canteen and the bagels. For reasons unclear to him, he suddenly wanted to win this challenge, badly. Not just get by and make it to another round. He wanted to *win*. He wanted to beat Daisey.

Weirdly, he also wanted to beat Mac. Beat her and draw a definitive line under all the time he'd wasted seeing her as anything more than friendly competition.

His strides had grown brisk and resolute by the time he reached their beach, but then some of his resolve deflated, fair play hijacking his bloodlust.

"Hey!" he shouted.

They both turned.

"Bit early in the game for sabotagin'," Daisey said, moving in a pointless attempt to block what they were doing—piling branches, it looked like.

"I'm not sabotaging," Pike said. "Not right now, anyway. Just thought I'd give you fair warning that I'm here." He left it at that and wandered to the water's edge, trying to decide which tree was most directly opposite the one Ian was busy attacking with his axe.

"Jesus." Mac shielded her eyes and stared across the river. "Are you guys chopping down whole trees?"

"Seemed like the fastest strategy," Pike said. No point pretending their noisy, outlandish plan could be kept secret.

"You have any idea how hard it is to fell a tree?" she asked.

"I'm sure it takes a while," Pike admitted, cockiness fading.

She laughed and Daisey locked his arms over his chest. They looked unified in their joyful skepticism and Pike frowned.

"Good luck," Mac said, turning back to her own arrangements. "You'll need it."

Whatever. As if river guides from New Mexico routinely chopped down trees. She was just psyching him out. Pike picked a tree, one he guessed was maybe sixty feet high, two feet thick at the base. He looked behind him, figuring out which direction would land it straight across. *Pretend it's tall enough to squash Ian*, he told himself. Always helpful to have a solid motivation.

Pike took the first whack. It rattled his wrists and the blade struck at a funny angle. He adjusted his swing and the next one was better. Not as deep as he'd envisioned, but that was okay. They had time. He glanced to Daisey and Mac again. Daisey carried the rope to a nearby tree and held one end up against the trunk. Pike frowned, no clue what he was up to. With an effortless whack, Daisey chopped the end of the rope off then did the same to the other end. He marched back to Mac and handed it over. She went to work separating the individual cords as Daisey headed back to the woods.

Whatever they had planned, it looked intricate. Well, they could build their bridge out of toothpicks for all Pike cared—he and Ian would be done in a fraction of the time, even if their design wasn't destined to win any engineering awards.

Another dozen whacks and Pike's hands were blistering, the axe blade tacky with sap. He tugged his tee shirt off, unclipping his mike and attaching it to his belt. He wrapped the shirt around the handle, promptly flinging the axe into the undergrowth with the next spirited swing.

"Watch it!" Daisey shouted.

Pike blanched and rooted around in the bushes, recovering the projectile and picking thorns from his pants. The next time he swung, he kept a death grip on it.

After what felt like an hour, he had a nice, pulpy groove gnawed into the trunk, perhaps a third of the way through. Not an attractive effort, but it looked nearly ready to fall. Was he supposed to push it?

Daisey was nowhere to be seen, but Mac had taken an interest in Pike's progress. She wandered toward him, checking over her shoulder for her teammate.

"Hey," she said quietly, standing beside Pike.

"Hey."

They both studied the tree for a minute.

"Does it just fall when it's ready?" he asked.

"Well, you're supposed to chop a notch into it. Like a vee." She made a Pac-Man shape with her hands. "You just chopped straight through, so it's got nowhere to tip. That'll take a lot longer."

"Oh right."

"You can still fix it though."

She shared some shifty eye contact with him. "And when you're starting out, you can cut a bit of a notch into the opposite side as well, a bit higher than the vee. It creates a hinge, so the tree's more likely to fall the way you want it to. Not too deep though."

"Right."

"I better get back. Good luck."

"Yeah. You too. Thanks." Pike watched her walk away, surprised and yet not surprised. Mac had some conniving in her too—he'd learned that when she'd kissed him. She knew as well as he did that she was safe even if her team lost, if it came down to any type of vote.

He knew something else now—she really *was* his friend. She might *want* Daisey, but she liked Pike. That, coupled with the fact that she and Daisey seemed chilly toward each other this morning, was enough to buoy Pike's spirits considerably.

"Timber!" Ian's voice carried across the water, and on its heels came an alarming creaking noise. Pike jogged to the shore in time to see the canopy rustling and catch Ian sprinting down the beach, away from his tree. It took a long time for the actual falling to happen, but once the tree began its descent it came down fast, with an almighty splash and rush of limbs and needles.

It also came down at a forty-five degree angle to the river's banks, totally useless.

"Oh fuck." Pike and Ian stared across the water at each other for a long moment. Ian shrugged.

Daisey came crashing out from the woods with an armload of branches and began laughing. "Holy shit, that's awesome."

Pike shook his head. "Shut up."

"How about yours?" Daisey asked. "When do we get to see yours fall? Twenty bucks says it goes backward."

"Fuck you."

Daisey crowed over the felling incident for some time, and all the while Pike kept chopping away, doing as Mac had said and creating a notch. By the time he heard the first ominous creak, his hands were raw and red, torso and pants soaked in sweat.

"Oh fuck. Timber!" He ran to the side, not trusting his own handiwork. The tree *did* fall toward the river, in nearly the perfect complement to Ian's. Two perfectly, uselessly parallel trees jutting out like twin bridges to nowhere.

"Fuck."

Mac caught Pike's eye and offered a sympathetic grin before going back to her work, lining up branches.

"Looks like it's time for a Plan B, Doc," Daisey said.

"Yeah, like that suspension bridge or whatever you're making is a better idea." Pike pointed to their project. "You'll be out of rope a quarter of the way across and you'll die of old age before you even get *that* far."

Daisey grinned. "Maybe we'll make good use of those trees you left out there for us."

Pike decided to block him out. He ate a bagel and went back to work, not caring if his finger bones were showing by the time he was done, so long as he succeeded. Half an hour later, his second tree fell. He'd lined it up perfectly, but then the wind took it, landing it at a nearly equally useless twenty-degree angle. Ian dropped one next, barely any better than his first. Four trees lay across the current and all of them utter shit. Simple plan Pike's ass.

His hangover returned with a vengeance as the sun and the temperature rose. His head pounded and his stomach went sour. But after a good puke and restorative dunk in the river, he was ready for a final try at chopping. He timed it. Twenty-six minutes it took, and every whack felt like a cheese grater against his palms. He called out as the tree creaked, held his breath as it fell. "Please please please…"

It sped toward the ground with a mighty rush and struck the river in a great sprucey belly-flop. Not perfect, but—

"Wow, nice one." Mac offered Pike a thumbs-up, red in the face from whatever she was up to at the water's edge.

"Thanks." Pike stared across the river to where Ian stood with the axe dangling from one hand. He raised the other, something shiny glinting in the sun. His flask. He toasted to Pike's adequacy and Pike thought then that a beer had never sounded so delicious. Hangover? What hangover?

He dropped his axe and walked to his third fallen tree. The branches started just at the water's edge, leaving an awful mess of limbs and needles to fight through to reach the halfway point of the river. By then the trunk would surely be thin and floppy, the last ten or even twenty feet of the tree useless for crossing the deepest point in the river. But add a successful tree from Ian's side, maybe pile up a bunch of extra wood in the middle to fill it out…this was possible. They could actually win this thing.

Pike considered getting to work chopping away some of the bigger branches, then thought better of it. Not a great place to stand while trees were falling, plus who knew—Ian might land one even better than this. He decided the best thing to do would be to head back to their side and share Mac's wisdom with Ian.

He grabbed his axe and saluted her as he left for the trail, hopefully for the last time. When he next crossed over to this side, he prayed he'd do so on their bridge.

The euphoria was fairly short-lived, however. Ian had already shredded his leather driving gloves, and progress slowed greatly due to their savaged hands and aching shoulders, axe blades dulled with gluey sap. An hour later Pike determined his earlier success was a fluke as, between them, he and Ian dropped another two trees, neither of them any use.

"This is getting absurd." Pike stared out across the river, now littered with the huge green corpses of their many epic failures.

Ian nodded, his breathing heavy and labored. He'd ditched his shirt a while ago. Pike stared at him. Pale as a corpse and built like nobody would guess if they looked at him with his clothes on— slender with stark muscles, that tight, desperate, fatless physique Pike usually associated with meth addicts and mean, hungry dogs.

"Hey," Pike said. Ian looked up and Pike tapped the mike he'd clipped to his belt loop. "Don't forget we have to wear these things all but two hours a day." If he didn't need Ian's help to win this challenge so badly, Pike would've been tempted to withhold that reminder.

Ian nodded and jogged to where he'd left his bag, coming back with his mike and attaching it to his pants pocket. "Doctors must love this. Hours and hours of *whack whack whack* and the soothing rustle of crotches."

He knelt to grab his axe and Pike glanced at the bold, black gothic letters inked between his shoulder blades. It took a couple seconds for the joke to register. Pike set his axe head on the ground, leaning on the handle as he laughed harder than he had since he and Mac had danced that afternoon before Twenty-One Questions.

Ian looked over his shoulder, brows raised. "What?"

"Your tattoo. That is so fucked."

Ian grinned wearily and walked to his bag, pulling out a water bottle. "You would'nae laugh at a man wi' a Bible verse tattooed across his back."

"That's no Bible, dude."

"Is tae me."

Pike shook his head. "Fine, whatever. That edition's outdated, anyway. You need a touch-up."

Ian shrugged, a flexing of the knotted muscles of his shoulders. He tossed his bottle in his bag and looked to Pike. "Break now, or one more down before we give it a wee rest? I dun'nae know about you, but I cannae keep going like this."

Pike nodded. "This is all feeling a bit too *Bridge on the River Kwai* for my comfort."

"You Japanese?"

He sighed, wanting to scream. "No, I'm half-*Korean*. Do I need to tattoo it across my fucking forehead? And that's not what I meant, anyhow. Just, you know…futile. All this work, and we're not getting anywhere."

"Dun'nae give up jest yet. One more lucky tree and we're nearly there. Plus, like I said, you're nae going home."

Pike shook his sore head, fed up. He looked across the water to where Daisey and Mac had still progressed no farther than the beach. "At least they seem to be failing as miserably as us at bridge building. They've got like ten feet built, and they must need about twelve times that." There was a lot of rope being tossed back and forth, branches arranged in stacks by size, it looked like. "They're making it way too complicated. It's not an engineering contest."

Ian stared across the river, then back at Pike. "You have'nae guessed yet, have you?"

Pike frowned. "Guessed what?"

"Thought *we* were the smart team meself, but they've got the right idea…"

"What idea?"

Ian stared over the river with his freaky eyes and smiled. "They're nae building a bridge. They're building a raft."

MAC

MAC FLEXED HER SAVAGED FINGERS, blistered and splintered with a thousand tiny flecks of coarse rope fibers. Turning to where Daisey was sorting their wood supply, she called, "Can you cut me two long, really thick logs? Like as big as you can carry? I think we're nearly ready for the pontoony bits. All this is looking really good."

She patted the base of what would be their raft, really quite handsome considering they'd made it from spruce boughs and dissected rope in only a few short hours.

Daisey did her bidding, lugging the first log over a half-hour later.

"Wow. Thank you." She eyed his work gloves with envy.

"Can't believe my luck, gettin' the riverboat captain for a partner... Shit, I never would have thought of this." Daisey smiled at her, way warmer than he needed to be. Way warmer than was convincing. He'd been making lame efforts to get back in Mac's good graces since breakfast. *Nice try.*

She held her tongue, still pissed about last night. Disappointed in him, in herself, annoyed her fantasy had fallen so disastrously flat.

Mac had good karma. She didn't tend to attract or pursue assholes, but for the first time in a long while she'd picked a loser. All the signs had been there. Funny how easy it could be to not notice those signs with a body like Daisey's distracting the eye. Plus when this competition had started, she'd mistaken his unapologetic swagger for refreshing honesty. Next to conniving players like Chloe and Ian, Daisey had seemed oddly pure. An open book, if a crass one. What an annoying moral. *If it walks like a jerk and talks like a jerk...probably fucks like a jerk.* Oh well. Lesson learned.

She eyed the work she'd done today. If Ian and Pike kept fucking up on their end, she and Daisey would win this, easily. Why build a bridge when a raft was just as surely a structure, and one requiring a mere fraction of the materials and labor? She'd never done this before, but she knew how.

And she knew how to make it float—as surely as she knew how to make it sink.

A few strategic weak spots, a surreptitious slice from a pocketknife halfway across the river and bingo, down they went, along with Daisey's reign in this ridiculous competition.

She was surprised to find the deception didn't sting her conscience. What *did* sting was not doing her best. Everyone was right—she was a total Girl Scout. But if this merit badge were for winning the greater competition, not for raft-building, she was certainly aiming to do the best damn job anybody ever saw.

"Timber!"

It was Pike's voice. Mac stood and edged toward the woods, nervous despite the fact that no tree was tall enough to come anywhere close to landing on her. She spotted the tree in question, its top shaking, then tilting, falling directly toward her side. Spot on. A bit of wind and its course was tweaked, just the angle to land on Pike's first successful fell—nearly a perfect overlap of the top dozen feet of each.

Whoops carried across the water and Mac had to smile. Hell, if the enemy won quick enough, she might not even *need* to cheat.

Behind her, wood scraped against gravel. She turned to find Daisey dragging her second pontoon from the woods' edge.

"Shit," he said, eyes locked on the other two. "They actually fucking did it?"

"Yeah. And only clear-cut half the forest in the process."

"Shit," Daisey repeated.

Yesterday his crassness would have charmed her, but right now Mac couldn't think of anyone she'd rather be away from. Not even Ian. Hell, especially not Ian. The man who'd demeaned himself for a chance to get her off, and didn't ask for a thing in return. She sighed, bewildered to find herself waxing wistful about Ian's chivalry.

"How you holdin' up?" Daisey asked.

She offered a withering look, one that said what they both knew. She was perfectly fine doing this challenge, and he was giving away his own guilt about the previous evening, pretending to coddle her.

"What d'you need next?" he asked.

Mac bit her tongue then thought, *fuck it.* "Oh. *Now* you're worried about what I need. How very convenient for you."

He sighed. "Not the time or place, Miss Mac."

"I'm not going to make a *thing* of it," she said snottily. "I just think it's funny that you're so eager to give me what I ask for now that there's something in it for you."

"I ain't gonna turn this into some kind of couples' counseling session," Daisey said, all the sugar gone from his voice. "You wanted me and you got me. That's what happened."

"Yeah, I know. I was there. Or was I? I'm not sure you realized I was, now that I think about it—"

"Enough."

She shook her head. "Not *nearly* enough. But whatever. Let's just get this thing done."

"Yeah, let's. So what do you need?"

To watch you go down. Hard. "I need you to build some paddles. Something long with something flat lashed to the end. Two of them."

"Right." Clearly pleased for an excuse to escape her, Daisey headed back to the woods.

Mac stood, examining the craft. Nice. She'd be sad to watch it capsize. Once the pontoons were attached, she looped a length of rope around the closest one. She dragged the raft to the beach and into the water, inch by laborious inch, pleased by how nicely it floated. She hopped on and it barely dipped at all. Adding Daisey's weight would be another matter, but very nice indeed. Maybe she ought to suggest this to her brothers—adding a survival skills retreat to their tourism repertoire.

Before the raft could carry her down river and crash her into Pike and Ian's log jam, she hopped off and hauled it back to the sand.

She'd earned a break, so she grabbed her canteen and stood at the water's edge, watching the other team struggle. She could just spot Pike between the boughs of the far tree, walking along the trunk, balance-beam style, axe in hand. Each time he hit a troublesome branch, he went to work hacking it away then tossed it behind him. Looked like a hell of a lot of work. Ian disappeared and emerged from the woods every few minutes, lugging more branches. His bare shoulders and chest looked pink, from exertion or sunburn, Mac wasn't sure.

She turned at a splash, in time to watch Pike struggle his way out of the water and a tangle of tree branches and back onto the trunk. With his shirt off, balancing on a tree, he looked like a training scene from a Kung Fu movie. He caught her eye and offered a little self-effacing bow, nearly falling over again.

Mac dissolved into giggles. "Don't make me pee my pants," she shouted.

"That's not the Objective?" he returned.

"Ha!" She gave the raft a little kick. "So. You boys figure out our genius plan yet?"

Pike nodded and wiped his wet face. "Yeah, Ian called it ages ago. I gotta hand it to you, it's pretty smart."

"My idea," she called cockily.

"Yeah, no doubt."

She smiled at that. She'd be stuck with those two for the next day's challenge, all things going as planned. Her ego could use the boost of being around Ian, knowing she could make him beg to please her again if she wanted. Which she didn't. But still, nice to know.

And Pike, well, he was just good company. Either man would be tough competition when it came to one-on-one time in the home stretch, but she knew which she'd rather be stuck with.

She cleared her throat and dredged her memory for lyrics, ones she knew in her brother Tim's voice as well as the one from the original tape he'd worn out when she'd been little. She cupped her mouth and shouted to Pike. "Casualties of war as I approach the barricade!"

He looked up from his chopping. He wiped his brow again then screamed back, "Where's the enemy?"

Mac joined him for, "Who do I invade?"

She laughed and Pike kept going, trading her a line, hacking at a branch, over and over until they'd belted out the entire song.

Mac clapped. Nice to feel like she had a proper teammate in this competition, even though they seemed destined to always wind up on opposite sides.

"Okay," Pike said, then whacked another limb away. "Let's see if you remember this one." He shouted out the first line to another Rakim track and she joined him.

Halfway through the chorus, Ian shouted, "Jesus Christ, shut the feck up!"

Mac laughed. "Knew that withdrawal had to hit you sooner or later, Kilpatrick!"

Pike ignored his real teammate and kept Mac company from sixty feet away, Ian's curses punctuating the lyrics like a beatbox. As she swapped lines, Mac set about tying a few strategic knots in the rope that held the raft together. Rip cords, she thought. A couple of covert yanks and she and Daisey were waterlogged.

After another hour's work, Mac's voice was scratchy from the spirited shouting and the competition had tightened. Pike had one of their trees fairly well cleared of its worst roughage and he and Ian had an assembly line going, thick limbs passed from man to man, piled to bolster the middle of their bridge so it resembled a beaver dam. Daisey returned then, bearing two not particularly impressive paddles—nice-size branches but lashed with spruce boughs. Better brooms than oars, but Mac let him think otherwise.

"Perfect. Well, I tested it, and I think we're ready."

Daisey nodded. "Good. Those two look like their homely-ass bridge might actually work, so let's get a move on."

"Current's tricky," she said. "It'll plow us right into their stupid fail-trees if we don't paddle fast." Far better to set off on the other side of the dam, but Mac chose to withhold that observation.

"Why paddle? River's only like six feet deep, Lenora said. Can't we just push ourselves with poles or something?"

She frowned. Fair point. "Okay. Well, these'll do anyhow." She waved her oar.

"Let's win this motherfucker."

Mac nodded, mostly sure he was referring to the challenge as "motherfucker" and not her. "Let's start upstream a bit, so we don't immediately drift into their trees."

They hauled the raft up the beach a dozen yards and Daisey dragged it to the water's edge.

"Ready?"

She nodded. It felt as though they ought to do something to announce the official start of their first attempt. She spoke to her mike. "Um, we're going to cross now. Thanks."

They pushed the raft into the river and Mac hopped on first. She eyed the corner she'd set up for sabotage and took her spot there.

Daisey stepped aboard and his end of the raft immediately sank into the sand.

"Hmmm..."

"Better get out a bit farther." He jumped off and pushed Mac and the raft out another yard.

"You can't get wet higher than your feet," she reminded him.

"Get ready for a jolt then." Daisey backed up a few steps and made a run for it, jumping onto the edge. Mac was immediately launched off her side like a teeter-totter, whacking her arm on the edge of the raft as she landed in a foot of cold water.

"Ow! Jesus." She stood, rubbing where the ends of the branches had scraped bloody lines down her forearm.

"Hey!"

She turned to find Pike staring.

"You okay?"

She stooped to rinse her skin and decided the bleeding was minor. "Yeah, I'm okay. Thanks!"

She thought she could make out Pike's frown before he turned back to his work.

"Probably dying for an excuse to examine you," Daisey said.

"Shut up. And get back on the beach." They both stood at the water's edge for a moment and Mac decided that counted as an official restart for the purposes of their first crossing attempt. She might be planning on failing, but she'd at least adhere to the correct procedure.

"Okay. Clearly, you have to get on first," she said.

Daisey stepped aboard and they used their paddles to push the raft out far enough that it was floating. Mac took several paces back and made a run. She landed on the edge neatly with both feet, her weight offering Daisey little more than a wobble to cope with.

She took her position in the Corner of Deceit. "Right. Let's win this thing." *For the other team.*

They each jammed the ends of their oars into the sand and pushed. Another foot into the current and the raft began drifting.

"Uh oh. Push hard this way." Mac made a slicing motion with her hand, forward and upstream.

Daisey took this directive to heart, proving exactly how much stronger he was than her. With a mighty shove of his oar to the river bottom, he spun the raft halfway around, nearly throwing Mac off again.

"Whoa, watch it. Again, on three, but less violent."

"Right."

She counted them down and they pushed together the next time, heading in the generally right direction. She heard Pike swear from forty feet away. *Save your breath for victory cheers.*

"Fucking genius," Daisey said.

She nodded.

"Maybe uh…maybe tonight I'll thank you for saving my ass in this competition," he added.

Mac took a deep breath through her nose, rolling her eyes behind his back.

"You know—"

"Oh yes, I know what you're so delicately implying. You've really got my motor running, offering to let me earn my orgasm. Very benevolent. Check me swooning."

Daisey sighed, more of a grunt given the exertion.

"Let's just finish this stupid challenge." As Mac said it, her eyes jumped to the knots by her feet. When they hit the halfway mark of the river, she swore.

"What?" Daisey craned his neck to face her.

"I think we've got a technical problem." She tossed her oar at Daisey's chest to distract him. Dropping to her knees and hunching over to block her handiwork, she grabbed the closest slipknot and tugged. The pontoon log shifted beneath the branches. Not enough. She tugged at another trick knot and it did the job. Forced by the current, a half dozen branches fanned out and detached at her end.

"Oh fuck!" Mac launched into a frantic charade, pretending to try to retie the ropes.

"Shit." Daisey moved closer, raft tipping.

Mac held back a warning for him to stay put. All at once the raft collided with the nearest of Pike and Ian's felled trees.

It wasn't an almighty impact, but enough to dislodge half the branches and knock Mac into the river. As she surfaced, she watched Daisey topple in seeming slow motion—a thrash to one side then the other, a waving of arms, an impressive *slap* as his back hit the water. She held in a whoop, a fist pump, a hissing *yessss*. Pike and Ian's collective laughter would have to be celebration enough.

Daisey treaded water until the river carried him to the fallen spruce and its jungle of branches. If Mac's conscience weren't so fraught she'd have laughed at his comical flailing.

"Fucking fuck!"

"It's okay," she said. "We can rebuild it."

He swam away from the tree and used the raft to dock himself. "How the fuck did that happen? Thought we did a perfect job."

Mac shrugged as much as one could while swimming.

"Shit…" After a half a minute of swear-riddled pouting, Daisey grabbed one end of the raft and began the laborious trip back to their shore. Mac had lost track of the oars, identical to the mess of boughs they'd gotten swept into. Screw it. Any of the branches still piled on their bank would do. She set off after Daisey, the swim harder than she'd anticipated while wearing hiking boots and a regular vest, not her usual safety getup. The struggle felt good though—harder the work, slower the recovery. Sabotaging their efforts a second time would be a bitch to camouflage.

She beat Daisey to shore and helped him lug the raft back onto the sand. Behind the sap and spruce needles he'd been tarred and feathered by, he was a different Daisey than the one she'd been paired with only ten minutes earlier. Mac had never seen this man truly frustrated before. A mix of feelings fought for primacy— triumph to be the cause of this normally unflappable asshole's flared nostrils and slumped posture, a strange breed of shame at realizing she could ruin him this way. Ruin what she'd until recently found so attractive.

As they set to work rebuilding the ruined half of the raft, Daisey's energy stayed off. Confidence had been swapped for something more desperate, more frantic. Guilt grew in Mac's stomach like a sour snowball, sprouting spikes when she glanced to the other team. Ian was hacking away at the most troublesome branches on the near tree, Pike jumping up and down on the dam they'd bolstered the middle with.

"Shit," she said, suddenly meaning it. "They're really close."

Daisey looked up, set features turning even stonier. He went back to work.

It was no use. Even if they got their raft in the water in the next five minutes, it was hopeless. She didn't need to cheat again. It would take an answer to Daisey's prayers for Ian and Pike to lose.

And in what felt like no time at all, it became clear that Daisey wasn't due any favors from the man upstairs.

Pike and Ian fumbled back to their beach, ready to make their first attempt, no doubt. Both Mac and Daisey quit their frantic activity as Pike edged onto the far trunk, Ian close behind him.

"Fall," she heard him mutter. "Fall, cocksucker."

Funny how she'd been mentally chanting a similar mantra just seconds before Daisey had toppled from their ill-fated craft.

Still crouching over their raft, Mac studied Daisey as the other team slowly made their way across. He looked utterly and completely beaten, and pissed at the man or not, it ripped a hunk of her guts out.

Ian reached the halfway point, their beaver dam looking solid.

Daisey sighed. "I'm officially fucked."

"We don't know how the elimination's going to work," Mac offered, trying hard to not sound overly patronizing. "It could be me going home."

"Not if there's a vote."

"No, probably not. But you never know."

Daisey dropped the rope he'd been holding, sounding a hundred years old. "What d'you want the prize money for, anyhow?"

"School, mostly, and repairs to fix up my family's business."

He nodded.

"What about you?"

"School too."

Mac blinked. "For yourself?"

He cleared his throat. "Nah, for my daughter."

Mac felt her eyes go round as beach balls. "You have a daughter? You're not married, right?"

His gaze fell to meet hers, supremely weary. "Course not."

"How old is she?"

"Fourteen."

Fourteen. "Damn... You must not get to see her much with your schedule."

"I seen her about ten times in her whole life."

"Oh." She watched Ian and Pike edging their way along the closest tree.

"I'm a bit of a deadbeat. Though to be fair, I didn't even know about her until she was six. Still, I've been a pretty shitty father."

"And you wanted the money to start kicking in your share, or...?"

He nodded. "Want to pay for her to go to a better high school than her hometown can offer. And for her college someday."

"Why'd you decide to start ponying up now?"

Daisey pushed a breath through his nose, not quite a snort, not quite a laugh. "Her mom's gettin' married next year. I know I been a pretty awful dad, but my balls just about fell off when I heard that. When her mom called me up and pretty much said, 'I know you never cared to begin with, and now that I met somebody decent let's just cut all ties. Keep your damn child support checks', that sort of deal. I'm a lousy role model, but I gotta say, that tore me up. Knowin' my daughter's out there callin' somebody else 'daddy'."

"Ouch."

He shrugged. "My own fault. Just thought maybe I could make a whatever it's called... A grand gesture."

"You should just start with spending time with her."

He sighed. "Listen, Miss Mac. I don't really want to talk about this with you. If you wanna know why I kept you and your advances at arm's length this whole competition, it's because before I know it my daughter'll be twenty-five, chasin' after dudes my age 'cause she didn't have no decent male role model when she was little."

"Hey! I didn't go after you because I've got daddy issues."

"You ain't got a father though, right?"

"I've got a brother who's more than close enough. And I went after you because you're fucking hot. I'd have done the same if you were twenty-three, I promise." Bit of a lie—Mac did tend to relate better to guys closer to her brothers' ages. She stood and huffed out an exasperated sigh.

"Anyhow, that's what I wanted the money for."

"Well, that's very noble. But I'm sure you could find other ways to make things up to her. Maybe your ex would—"

"Listen. You're cute as a button and everything but if you keep spouting this happy-ass rainbow bull at me, I swear I'll wring your neck."

Mac blinked at him. She shook her head and busied herself picking spruce needles out of her damp hair. "I can't imagine how it is you're single, Daisey."

He cleared his throat. "I know you're pissed about last night, and maybe this'll only make me seem like more of a creep to you. But the second I was done… Shit. I just look at you sometimes and you're so fucking young. I know twenty-five ain't fourteen but Jesus, it weirds me out. I'm forty next month and that officially makes me some nasty old man. Sort of man I'd punch if he looked at my kid wrong, you know?"

Mac shook her head, not wanting any part of Daisey's midlife crisis. As she looked up to check on Ian and Pike's progress, it seemed that once again, Daisey's wishes were doomed to go ungranted. Pike and Ian wended through the last stretch of branches and sappy stumps and made it to the enemy shore, incontestably successful.

Mac slow-clapped. Daisey swore. An air horn blasted through the relative peace and a flock of birds exploded into the sky.

Pike came back to life, overtaken by a brief bout of celebratory prancing in the sand. Ian just grinned, mean squint aimed right at Daisey. If it came down to a vote, he was right to gloat—all four of them knew this had just been a contest to see which cutthroat got sent home.

"Well done!" Their perky emcee appeared from the trees behind them. Mac wondered idly where the crew slept. Lenora always looked so unnaturally well rested. Maybe she was twins, working in shifts. Or a cyborg.

"Very well done indeed, Pike and Ian. You have completed this challenge. Mac and Daisey, I'm afraid you were not successful." Her eyes lingered on Mac in what felt like a protracted stare. It gave Mac the willies and drove away the last of her tainted triumph.

"No doubt you're all eager to hear how the elimination will go. Once again there will be a vote, all four of you voting to send someone home. You may vote for your own teammate, if you wish. Ian and Pike, you will get two votes apiece, and you may split them between different opponents or use both toward the same person. Mac and Daisey, you will each get a single vote."

Beside Mac, Daisey mumbled, "Well, I'm fucked."

She nodded.

"Please follow me back to the clearing and we'll hand out the ballots."

It was a quiet process, a formality whose result surprised no one.

Lenora returned to face the group after a brief consultation with the khaki minion on duty. She held the index cards in her hands in a fan. "Well, the vote was highly definitive. Mr. Daisey, please gather your belongings and follow my assistant."

He nodded once, expression blank. Mac's body twitched, for the briefest second poised to hug him—purely reflexive. She averted her eyes to stare at Ian's shoes as Daisey passed them to grab his stuff.

"See ya, shitheads."

Pike alone returned the sentiment, waving cheerfully. "Suck it, asshole."

Daisey disappeared into the woods with his middle fingers raised.

Mac sighed, releasing a breath of utter exhaustion. The sound drew Pike's attention and he walked over, hands in his pockets.

"Don't look so down. No offense, but he's a total dick."

"It's not that. I'm just feeling really beat today. I'm ready for this whole thing to be done with."

He nodded. "I really thought you guys had that one. Bummer about your raft."

She mustered a shrug. Pike looked away and Mac studied his bare upper half with absentminded interest. After her prolonged fascination with Daisey, Pike seemed like a different animal entirely, a tidy machine to Daisey's excessive physique. Trim and practical to Daisey's physical *vulgarity*. Her eyes drifted to Ian then, also still stripped to the waist. It struck her suddenly she was the only woman left, as she had been the entire day. She'd outlasted a few impressive competitors, left now with both the most and least honorable players for company.

"Just me and you and Ian now," Pike said, reading her mind.

She nodded.

"I don't know what Ian plans to bribe you with to get you into some alliance," he went on, "but I've got five dirty, stale bagels in my pack. I can cut you in for, like, three of them."

She smirked, shaking her head.

"Morphine?"

Mac laughed. "Intriguing, but no thanks."

"Mad beats? Free dance lessons?"

She nodded again. "Better."

"I'm not Ian?" Pike ventured.

"Ooh, ding ding ding. You win." Mac mustered a tired smile and Pike returned it. "Hard to top 'not being Ian' out here when it comes to desirability."

"Oi, I haird that."

She shot Ian a mean look. "How's that withdrawal coming along?"

His voice rose to a high and wistful singsong. "Nae as nice as the heartache you're surely suffering, now your beloved's left us."

Mac caught Pike biting back a laugh or smile. If she'd had more energy she'd have run with the game, traded insults 'til the crew showed up with supper.

Instead she took a seat on one of the folding chairs, pushed off her boots and peeled away her wet socks. She flexed her wrinkly feet on the grass as the rhythmic beat of a helicopter grew fast and insistent in the distance. She watched along with the men as it rose above the woods a mile or more upriver. As it passed above them, carrying Daisey out of the game and into her memories, she saluted him with a single finger, and mentally wished him luck.

OBJECTIVE SIX

TREADING WATER

CAMERA 6712

At oh-eight-hundred hours, Lenora saunters through the trees and onto the beach. Only three competitors to go, and despite the relatively late wake-up call, none of them look pleased as they drag themselves from the pup tents.

"Good morning, campers!"

Mac exchanges a look with Pike then grumbles a greeting to their hostess. Ian is a living statue, gray and brittle.

"Yesterday's challenge was quite a bit of work, I'm sure you'll all agree, so I hope you enjoyed sleeping in. Food is on its way, as well as coffee. You'll be wanting your strength yet again, so eat up.

"If it's any consolation, you won't be hiking miles to a new destination for today's Objective. It's going to take place nearby, just a short walk downriver."

Three pairs of eyes shift to the water, still littered with fallen trees and bits of raft.

"Like the Meat Locker, this Objective will be all about endurance. It's called Treading Water, and the rules are so simple I suspect you can all guess the gist. After breakfast I'll outline the official details for you, of course. But for now, please get dressed and report to the clearing for food and socializing."

Mac shoots Pike another look at "socializing". Pike flashes her a grin so ludicrously cheerful it belongs on a psychopath. Ian's expression stays blank, mood as dark as the bags under his eyes. The final players shuffle like zombies to their tents, bodies stiff from the cold, hands rubbed raw, energy tapped.

Overhead, the first clouds roll in, gunmetal gray and heavy with foreboding.

PIKE

PIKE SAT WITH A HUFF and pulled his socks on, hurting all over. His head hurt from too much sun and the remains of the previous day's hangover. His back and arms hurt from chopping, his hands destroyed. Worst of all was the ache in his chest.

This should have been a morning to revel in—Daisey finally gone, and Ian reduced to an irritable, dragging husk, finally seeming the most likely candidate to go home. That left Pike and Mac in the final challenge, if he could just get through this one day.

Still, the old thrill was gone. Mac's spark was gone too, and it couldn't be a coincidence that it had departed in tandem with Daisey. Pike wondered if maybe she'd mustered all that energy and enthusiasm *because* of Daisey. Lust could be a stronger drug than nicotine. Maybe Ian wasn't the only one in withdrawal.

He finished dressing and zipped his tent closed just as Mac appeared from hers.

"How'd you sleep?" she asked, walking over.

His mood shifted tangibly, just from hearing her voice. "Can't even tell you. I was so exhausted I was out like a light. But now..."

"I know. I don't feel like I got any rest at all."

They walked through the woods to the clearing, and Pike perked at the smell of coffee and food. Making a bee-line for the cups and caffeine alongside Mac, he hoped the rest of the competition might feel this way. A little warm glow of happiness amid all the exhaustion. Mac might be a tired wreck, but damn, she still did that to him. Hopeless.

"How's your arm?" he asked.

She set her cup down and pulled up her sleeve, revealing three nasty scrapes.

"Ouch."

She poked one of the red stripes. "It looks worse than it is. Thanks for asking though."

Pike cleared his throat and watched Mac gingerly roll her sleeve back down. "So, there's only three of us," he said, more to himself than her.

"I know. Weird." She picked up her cup.

"Are you in combat mode? Do you mind if I eat with you?"

She laughed and her face instantly changed, lit up once again. It faded after a moment but Pike was buoyed just to know she still had that in her.

"Sure, you can eat with me. It's the cheerleader table though, so try to act cool."

Pike followed her to the folding chairs and they set their coffees down before heading back for food. As he took a seat with his eggs, Pike studied her, not caring if she saw. Her blessed obliviousness to his hopeless crush seemed as tenacious as the crush itself.

After a few bites, she met his gaze. "Have I got something on my face, or you just have a thing for girls who look like they've been run over by buses?"

"Just wondering how you're doing. You do look a bit rough, no offense."

"You don't look like the poster boy for rest and relaxation yourself."

He shook his head. "I'm beat. Doing better than Ian though. Wherever he is."

"Probably rooting through my bags for his cigarettes."

"Did you keep them?"

"Nah. I tossed all that down the outhouse crapper before we left the crazy soviet spy bunker place."

"Good idea...though he looks so wrecked, I wouldn't put it past him to go down there after them. So, um, you just tired? Or are you upset that Daisey's gone, or...?"

She shrugged, no longer meeting his eyes. "I'm glad he's gone. I don't want to compete against him, obviously. I just..."

"What?"

Pike's brain supplied her reply. *I'm just so in love with him.*

"The way the last challenge went down..." she trailed off. "The way he went out, I guess. I feel kind of shitty about it."

"Why?"

"I feel guilty."

Pike frowned. "It wasn't only your vote that kicked him out. If you even voted for him."

She stretched her shoulders, looking uncomfortable, as if she'd said more than she wished she had. "Never mind. It's just that I learned something about why he was here last night. I dunno. He sort of went from two dimensions to three for me. Made sending him home sting."

"But you didn't send him home yourself. He got four votes between me and Ian. That's all he needed."

She nodded absently.

A crunch of branches announced Ian's approach. He looked more like himself, or more like the man he'd been when he'd first arrived. His face was still tired and lifeless, but he'd put on his blazer and hat against the cold, a costume that distracted the eye from his frayed mental edges. He filled a cup from the coffee spigot and wandered over to join them, against Pike's silent wishes.

"Morning," Mac said.

"Aye. So it is."

"Ready for some swimming?"

Ian shrugged. "Stroke of luck, really." He held his free palm up, as savaged as Pike's. "We'd all be buggered if today's challenge had been a pat-a-cake competition."

Pike flexed his own fingers, ruing what a difficult part of the body it was to effectively bandage. All the ibuprofen he'd popped before bed and upon waking didn't seem to be helping a jot.

The group fell silent, perhaps all of them contemplating what Pike was—how uninviting a dip in a cold river sounded. Well, not that they should get their hopes up that it really was so literal or as predictable as Lenora had suggested.

"I'm going to win today," Mac announced, apropos of nothing.

Pike looked at the smug glow on her face and smiled, pleased for another sign she hadn't left him with just a Mac-shaped shell for company. "Well, don't we sound cocky this morning?"

"Can either of you claim that your job description covers today's exact challenge? I can't tell you how often I get pitched into freezing rivers."

"Cannae be that easy," Ian said. "We know from yesterday, that river's only as deep as Pike's tall. Bet you anything they'll tie our ankles, or make us carry weights in each hand, dump a lorry-load of sharks intae the water."

Pike nodded.

"Well, whatever happens, I'll bet either of you I still win." Mac stood to stretch.

"Bet my fags back an' you're on."

She shook her head. "Your smokes have gone to a better place. Same place one of you'll be going by the time I win this challenge." Mac made an epic throw-down gesture with her arms, all urban bravado.

Pike sucked in a breath. "Oooh, burn."

"Still, I'll pony up," she said. "Whoever wins today can take whatever they want from me."

Pike glanced at Ian, knowing they shared a similar wish-list, and wondering what Ian might select if given the chance...panties, prolonged examination of her naked body, hand in marriage.

"I'll take your weed," Pike said.

Ian's black eyebrows rose. "You been holding out on me?"

"It's good stuff," she said. "And sure. I'll put up my stash. But not my pipe—my brother made that."

Pike thought a moment. "I've got a battery-operated razor. I'll put that up."

"Ooh, I could use that." She hiked up a pant leg, examining leg hair Pike couldn't make out.

"What have you got left worth putting up, Ian? How about your watch?" Pike asked.

"No fecking chance. That's an heirloom."

"How about your notes, from the Twenty-One Questions challenge?" Mac asked.

Ian smiled at her, slow and mean. "You keen for a bit of insight on all your competitors, eh? Fair enough. I'll wager those."

Mac stepped forward and crossed her arms, offering each man a hand to shake. They did then Pike reluctantly shook with Ian. Ian gave a mean squeeze, setting Pike's savaged palm screaming. He squeezed right back until it devolved into a thrashing, anarchic thumb-war. They stood and the coffee formerly tucked between Pike's knees got pitched, sloshing down Mac's leg.

"Watch it!"

Pike managed to wrench his hand free, clasping it protectively with the other. "Sorry."

"Toddlers." She rolled her eyes at the pair of them and stalked off, presumably to change her pants or search for a towel.

Pike turned to find Ian also massaging his hand. "Jackass."

Ian grinned, seeming more his usual self by the minute. Pike, on the other hand, felt his mood darkening alongside the now-overcast sky. He grabbed a fresh cup of coffee and returned to his seat, but with Ian for company all he tasted now was bitterness.

Furiously, he prayed Mac was right—that she would win. The final challenge after this one was bound to be epic. He couldn't stand the thought of facing it with Ian, undiluted by the others.

"You look like your puppy jest got put down," Ian said. He was leaning forward, elbows on his thighs, hands clasped between his knees. Conniving.

"My puppy's just fine. Worry about yourself."

"You've got a hint of textbook chronic depressiveness about you," Ian said.

It hit a nerve, a raw one. Pike's dad had something like that—whatever a man came down with after he got chewed up in his prime by Vietnam and shit out into the grind of endless manual labor.

"Don't diagnose me," Pike warned. He drained his cup and set it aside.

"You've got a wee whiff of defeatist on you. Competition finally gettin' tae you, is it? Or is this because of Mac?"

Pike stood, done with this conversation.

"Evasive, eh? Exhibits an unwillingness tae hear criticism. Classic signs of denial."

"Shut up."

Ian stood and stooped to pick up his coffee. "Does'nae matter where she's been, mate. We'd all be fecked if we were judged by what we did in the past. Who cares if she and Daisey—"

Pike held a hand up and shot Ian a killing look. "Fuck you. Your little mind games don't work on me."

"Oh, no? Well then, you won'nae mind knowing I'm making it my primary objective to send you home after this next challenge," Ian said with a grin. "Then she's all mine for the final stretch. Could be an overnight. Wonder how well she holds her liquor..."

Pike shook his head in a warning, fisting his hands to keep them from shaking.

"Never cared about the money, meself," Ian added. "Wonder if mebbe Mac might be interested in a bargain. Promise her my go at the prize in exchange for a night or two of playing house in one of those wee tents."

"Fuck you."

"Playing *doctor*," Ian amended. "Funny how you never managed it yourself, eh? Must be jest like a brother tae her. Good for a dance and laugh but never a feck?"

Pike ignored him.

"You reckon mebbe if it did come down tae you and her... How bad d'you want that prize, eh? Mebbe nae bad enough tae find out if Mac might jest be your whore for half a million dollars?"

Pike lunged a step and shoved Ian in the chest, hard enough to send him staggering and land him on his ass, coffee whipping the air in a graceful arc.

"Shut up, dude. Seriously."

Ian got to his knees on the ground, lips parted. He blinked at Pike a couple of times before he stood and spoke. "I ate her out."

Pike felt the blood drain from his face, ice water trickling in to replace it. "That's a lie."

Ian dusted his hands off on his slacks, eyes on the task. "Nae, it's true. And I'll tell you, when she came it was like the fecking sweetest pear you ever tasted—"

Seconds went missing from the time Pike was still standing to the moment he hit the ground on top of Ian. The next thing he was aware of was pain in his knuckles as his fist collided with Ian's jaw, a skin-muffled, sickening crack meeting his ears amid another sound— his own voice, bellowing.

Reality rushed back as quickly as it had left and Pike found himself straddling Ian's chest, a dark ribbon of blood strung from Ian's nostril to his ear, something fundamentally wrong with the symmetry of his face.

Pike scrambled to his feet and stepped back as he heard footfalls rushing through the woods to the clearing.

He took one look at Mac's eyes and something harder than the fist he'd just broken Ian's jaw with seemed to belt him in the guts.

She halted over Ian's unconscious body. "Oh my God, Pike. What the fuck did you do?"

He stared at the slits of Ian's blank blue eyes, pale face, crimson blood. "I think I just made you five hundred thousand dollars richer."

OBJECTIVE SEVEN

THE FINAL STRETCH

CAMERA 6720

IT'S JUST PAST ONE in the afternoon, two hours after Ian's unconscious body was removed by the crew, along with the buffet tables. The helicopter had returned then disappeared back into the grayness.

The two remaining competitors sit in silence on a log on the beach of Mac and Daisey's former camp. Pike recovered Ian's lighter from the ground after the fight, and he flicks it open and closed, open and closed, watching the flame as though it might hold answers to whatever questions are swirling behind that stony face. Mac is staring into the woods beyond the river, her stillness interrupted every minute or two by a broad yawn.

A crunching noise from the woods disrupts the silence and both competitors turn, Pike getting to his feet.

Lenora appears from the trees, a paper bag in one hand. "Greetings again!"

"Hey," Mac says, looking surprised.

"I trust our final two got enough breakfast before that unfortunate little incident interrupted the morning's pleasantries."

Pike's brow furrows as Mac stands and dusts her butt off.

"*Are* we the final two?" Pike asks.

"Of course. You're here, aren't you? As you probably guessed, it's been determined that Ian must be sent home due to a serious injury."

"Yeaaah," Pike drawled.

"He'll be just fine in a few weeks, though his jaw's been wired shut, I'm sad to announce. He's confirmed for us in writing that it was an accident."

Pike's mouth drops open as Mac's eyebrows rise.

"How very unfortunate. And how very surprising, given what the surveillance footage suggested. Funny how unreliable cameras can be." A look passes over Lenora's face, one that could've easily belonged to the newly absent player. "So, that leaves you two, spared actually finishing the penultimate Objective. Shame—it would have been a good one." Lenora manages to pout and smile at the same time. "Oh and Ian said he took this from you, Dr. Pike."

Lenora hands him the paper bag. He opens it the tiniest bit and peers in, frowning.

"So today has been redesignated the eve of what will be the two-day, seventh and final Objective," Lenora announces brightly.

Mac crosses her arms over her small chest, looking intrigued. "Two days?"

"Two days, if you both tackle it as capably as the doctors expect. And like the first Objective, this one will be a race. Very straightforward."

"Right," Pike says, still looking punch-drunk.

"I'll bet you two can just about feel that grand prize in your hands now," Lenora goes on, a slow smile curling her lips.

Both players hold their tongues.

"Tell me...what are the two of you planning to do with the winnings?" Lenora asks with a gracious, toothy grin. "How about you, Dr. Pike? What are your great ambitions for five hundred thousand dollars?"

He pauses before answering, gaze darting between the two women. "I was planning on using about a hundred and fifty grand to pay off my mother's mortgage. And I could use a new car." He thinks a moment. "I don't really need the rest... I'll probably put some in the bank and maybe give the rest to my old school or the V.A. hospital in Detroit."

Lenora smiles. "Very noble." She shifts her attention to Mac, expectant.

Mac gives Pike a sarcastic smile and nudges him with her elbow. "Did you say that so I'd look like a total bitch if I don't let you win?"

Pike's mouth falls open. "No, I was—"

"Just messing with you." She turns to Lenora. "When *I* win, the money will go to improvements to my family's business, plus a bunch socked away for emergencies. That's about four hundred grand."

"You've given this some thought," Lenora says.

"Then about ninety-five for future tuition for myself, and the last five thousand I'll probably use for a blow-out vacation to go climbing in Asia and Indonesia." Mac bites her lip, eyes snapping to Pike again. "Actually, ninety for school, ten grand for the trip. I'll bring Pike with me. You like climbing, Pike?"

His black eyes widen. "I—"

"Lovely!" Lenora claps her hands officiously and looks between them. "What wonderful ideas. Keep those in mind as you tackle the next two days' challenges. For now, you have a half-hour to pack up your belongings, and then the crew will be transporting you to the start line for the final Objective."

The remaining players exchange a tense look, questions posed but not answered. Lenora turns with a final pageant-queen grin and marches into the shadows.

PIKE

IT HAD BEEN A DAY AND A HALF since the whiskey binge, but Pike suddenly felt hungover again. With the shock of discovering he hadn't shot himself in the foot and been disqualified now fading, a throbbing headache took up residence in his skull once more.

He and Mac gathered their gear in silence. This was what he'd wanted—the two of them in it to the end—and as a bonus, they were being spared an entire challenge.

Still, Pike couldn't find it in himself to rejoice. He hated himself for losing his cool that badly, so like his dad. He hated the universe a bit for rewarding him for it. In fact, the only thing he didn't hate just now was Mac. He didn't feel for her the way he had a couple of days ago, but as he watched her stuffing her sleeping bag back into its sack, his chest loosened. His final opponent was also the one he most trusted. Pike was over the kissing deception. That was nothing compared to ousting a rival by breaking their frigging face.

She caught him watching her and smiled. "Weird, huh?"

He nodded. "Very weird."

"I'm not complaining though." She stared at Pike a long time then wrapped her hand around the mike clipped to her lapel and nodded to indicate Pike should do the same. "Really, getting punched in his smug face is just about the most poetic way for Ian to go out. Plus wherever he's headed, there'll be cigarettes. Well, if he can smoke through his gritted teeth, that is."

Pike succumbed to a dark pleasure at that visual. "He'll manage. I guess you're right. You don't think that was massively uncool? That I hit him? Like, should I even get to be here still?"

"I'd like to think I know you, Pike. And I know Ian, as much as a stranger can. And I am *one-hundred* percent sure that whatever he did, he earned what he got. So..." she added, seeming to buck herself up. "Just you and me now." She uncovered her mike and Pike followed suit.

"Just us," he echoed.

"Exactly how I'd hoped it'd be."

He blinked. "Really?"

"Sure. Ever since the afternoon before Twenty-One Questions. You and me in an epic dance-off to the end. Best possible scenario."

Pike felt his stupid crush bubbling back to the surface but shoved it down, determined to smother it for good. *You're here for yourself.* Plus he couldn't begin to process what Ian had told him, or what it made him feel aside from confused and acutely nauseous.

She stooped to haul her frame pack out of her tent then scanned the gray sky. "A swimming challenge is still sounding good to me. Looks like we're getting wet, either way." She hoisted the pack onto her shoulders.

In the distance, a buzzing grew loud enough to drown out the birds and breeze and humming mosquitoes.

"Plane," Pike muttered.

She nodded and swallowed, face suddenly white.

"Forgot you don't like planes."

Mac nodded again. "It's cool. It's worth it. I've done plenty of things I'd normally avoid to get this far."

It was Pike's turn to nod, and to wonder again if that thing Ian had claimed he and Mac had done was true. If it was, did it rank among Mac's compromises?

While they waited, Pike stared at his and Ian's bridge. What he felt, it wasn't quite guilt. Guilt required sympathy, and he didn't have that for Ian. It felt more like shame or paranoia. Self-hateful regret for nearly losing the game to a stupid flare of his temper. Bad enough Ian had spotted that weakness in him, far worse to have taken the bait. He'd worked so hard the past ten years to not turn into his dad. Now here he was with his knuckles bruised, an aching reminder that he still had that in him, like a tumor. Never cured, merely dormant.

A staff member arrived and bade them to follow. After a quarter-mile walk through the woods, Mac punched Pike's shoulder.

He looked at her. "What?"

She kept her voice low and murmured, "Look," nodding to the left.

Pike peered through the trees to the river. "Whoa." In the distance he could make out three large cylindrical tanks, perhaps ten feet high and made of what looked like Plexiglas. Clear with metal seams and pipes, the type of contraption that might incubate an alien or mutant in a sci-fi movie.

"Treading Water," Mac whispered.

"Simple my ass." The tanks disappeared from view as they continued the walk and Pike shivered, no longer feeling at all relieved he'd managed to spare them whatever water torture those had been outfitted for. No relief, just dread. That dread had been rising since the Meat Locker, spiking during Twenty-One Questions, warping further down in the bunker-base, then easing during the relative normality of Bridge Building.

Pike glanced at Mac, her face reflecting his own anxiety perfectly.

After a ten-minute trek they arrived at a wide point in the river, a Cessna waiting for them at a modern aluminum dock. Lenora stood beside its entrance, arm cocked like a spokesmodel.

Pike waved his hand and Mac preceded him into the back of the plane. They dumped their gear and exchanged limp niceties with the two staff guys occupying a pair of the half-dozen seats. Even as Mac mustered a brave smile, her eyes darted violently around the cramped cabin.

"Best of luck!" Lenora said just before a staffer slid the door closed.

Pike looked to Mac and they strapped themselves in. "Does that mean she won't be giving us instructions, do you think?"

Mac shrugged, gaze still ricocheting around the cabin. Pike doubted she'd even heard his question. Her eyes shut as the propellers started up, fingers dug white-knuckled into the armrests. For a moment Pike's heart beat as hard as hers must be. He tapped her hand then slid his beneath it. She laced her small fingers between his without even opening her eyes. Pike gave her hand a squeeze that he hoped said something comforting. His savaged palm screamed in protest, but he barely heard it. The gesture felt earnest...too earnest, nearly. He cleared his throat, trying to think up a good diversion as the plane began to move.

"What are you going to eat first when we get back to civilization?" he asked.

Mac's pursed lips parted, brow furrowing with thought. "Cheese."

"Any crackers with that?"

"Just cheese. Thick slices, dipped in brown mustard straight from the jar."

Pike laughed. "No sausage?"

"Yeah, okay. Like that summer sausage. The really salty kind with the wax-papery wrapper."

"We got a Christmas basket with that in it one year when I was little," Pike said, just as the plane lifted off. "I didn't know you were supposed to peel that off, so I ate like half the fake casing."

Mac laughed, eyes still shut tight. "The first time I convinced my brother to buy me Fruit Roll-Ups for school, I didn't know there was that layer of plastic on them. I got maybe three bites into one and thought they were really overrated."

Pike started laughing so hard his arm shook, setting Mac off. In seconds she was wheezing, tears streaming from her closed eyes, so not for the reasons Pike had feared when they'd boarded.

"You like, chewed and swallowed the plastic sheet?" he asked through his convulsions.

Mac nodded, mouth open in silent laughter.

"Oh my God…"

Mac gave his hand a couple of admonishing thumps against the armrest.

"When I was about fourteen," Pike said, voice hitching, "my cousin came up to me with this eye-dropper full of, like, lemon juice maybe, and he told me it was LSD. He put two drops on a little scrap of paper and I set it on my tongue…"

Mac already looked close to peeing her pants.

"And dude, I seriously saw things. I totally placeboed myself into seeing rainbows and goblins and crazy melting stuff, stuff I probably got from a movie or something. I wandered around my aunt's living room going, 'Whoa dude, I'm so high. I'm totally tripping. This is *good shit*.'"

Mac's voice returned, a series of squeaky gasps overtaking her.

"It went on for like a half-hour, I bet. He still brings it up when I see him back home." Pike let a fresh series of giggles overtake him, feeling high just then. As Mac's sobbing laughs slowed, he gave her sweaty palm another squeeze. For perhaps five minutes they sat in silence, fingers intertwined, bodies vibrating to the pitch of the plane.

Mac's hand grew restless, clutching Pike's in tiny, subconscious pulses.

One of the crew members unbuckled his seat belt and stood, crossing the aisle to address Pike and Mac. "Hey, guys?"

Mac's eyes opened and she slid her hand from Pike's.

"You'll be disembarking soon. We need you to gather your stuff and bring it to the door."

Pike's body cooled. "Sure." He went to the back and hauled his case and bag to where the crew guy pointed. Mac followed suit, tossing her pack over one shoulder and edging slowly toward the door, as though crossing a skating rink.

"Go ahead and leave your bag right here," the guy said.

Mac dropped her pack beside Pike's. "Oh God, are we parachuting?"

"Not exactly."

The other staff guy left his seat to stand by their bags, and without further ado the first one slid the cabin door open.

The plane dipped low, but they were still twenty feet or more above the water.

Pike turned to find one of the staffers looking at him expectantly.

Pike laughed. "You can't be serious."

The guy's face was stony. "Jump or get pushed. Jump and stand a chance of hitting the water feet first. Jump soon, or risk us running out of lake to land in."

Panic set in. Pike looked to Mac, finding her eyes as wide as his own felt.

"Go, Pike."

Jump or get pushed. Jump or we'll be more than happy to break your neck for you. Pike chose *jump.*

After a second's freefall he hit the water hard, not quite upright—a graceless landing that knocked his breath out and submerged him for a terrifying moment before he got his wits together and ordered his body to swim. He surfaced and found himself treading water as reality returned, Mac doing the same about twenty yards to his left.

"Oh, fuck me." Pike choked the words out then launched into a coughing fit, bringing up water. "You okay?"

Mac paddled toward him. "Yeah, I'm fine. Better, actually. You?"

"Yeah…motherfuckers. No bags? Seriously?"

"No, they threw our stuff too, right before I jumped." She jerked her head in the direction of her pack and Pike's case floating a ways off. Mac's green sleeping bag had come detached, bobbing nearby. "I think your pack sank… I wonder how deep it is."

"Well, we'll find out, I guess." Pike reached down, floundering as he got one boot off, then the other. He struggled to float and tie the laces together then made his way to Mac, draping them over her shoulder. "Hold those. Where did you see it go down?"

"There-ish," Mac said, pointing to her left.

Pike took a deep breath and went under. He hadn't swam much since his junior high days at the YMCA, and as clear as this lake was, it was damn dark even ten feet down. His wet clothes made it feel as though he were digging through pudding. Grabbing blindly in the shadows, he felt only creepy weeds and slimy branches for the first four or five dives. The next time he went down, however, his hand found canvas, the strap of his pack. He hauled it up with a mighty effort, lungs burning as he broke the surface.

"Nice work!" Mac clapped, sinking a moment.

With one glance at her smile, Pike's anger mellowed to irritation. "I'm surprised yours didn't sink—it's big enough."

"Mine's designed to float. Getting thrown out of rafts is like a daily occurrence for me." She swam in a circle, looking all around at the shore. "Shit. Which way should we go?"

"I dunno. I don't even know if we're supposed to be looking for something, or if the next instructions'll come to us later…"

"Yeah."

"Let's head over there," Pike said, nodding to the closest strip of beach. "I have no clue which direction's which with all this cloud cover, but let's get out of the water. Start a fire, get dried off."

"Good plan."

Pike took his boots back and swam to his floating case, tossing Mac her semi-waterlogged sleeping bag. They floundered their way to shore, perhaps a quarter-mile swim that took a seeming eternity. The beach was pebbly, a good spot for building a fire and hopefully for sleeping, in case no clues about the Objective presented themselves.

"It'll take hours for us to get everything dried off," Pike said. "You want to just make camp here for the rest of the day? If we're missing something, challenge-wise, at least we're being idiots together."

"Deal." She unzipped her pack and began tossing wet things into a pile.

Pike did the same, flinching as his hand found the spongy bagels he'd hoarded. "Oh gross." He flung them toward the water. "Food'll be interesting."

"Yeah. I brought snacks but they all went missing way back at the oil-operation place."

"Mine too."

"Can you hunt? If they don't turn up with craft services like usual?"

Pike shrugged. "I've got a knife, some stuff I could try and make into snares. Not sure it'd be worth the energy."

Mac nodded, lips pursed into a damn-cute frown. "I *technically* know how to do that stuff, but I've never actually had to. I'm more practiced at rustling up boil-in-a-bag rice and canned beans."

Right on cue, Pike's stomach cursed a blue streak. He shifted his attention to other concerns. "We should get dry before we both die of pneumonia."

They argued for ten minutes about the best way to construct a bonfire before Pike acquiesced, and Mac's method proved perfectly adequate. They strung a length of her climbing rope between two trees and hung their things up to dry. Mac was the first to strip off, and Pike did what he thought was a decent job of keeping his eyes off her lower half. His periphery told him there were wet—possibly translucent—yellow panties involved, but he corralled his curious gaze strictly onto her neck and wet hair, the water beading on her shoulders beside her bra straps.

He cleared his throat to make sure his voice wouldn't come out an octave higher than normal. "Figures we'd get another overcast day."

Mac laughed. "Are you always this glum, Pike?"

He peeled his socks off and set his boots by the fire. Holding his pants before the flames, he pondered her question. "Yeah. Pretty much. But we did just get tossed out of a plane with no warning."

"Nothing about this trip surprises me anymore. Plus I've been told my whole life I'm insufferably optimistic, so I give you about four hours before you snap and strangle me."

Pike cringed. She meant it as a joke but without a doubt, Mac was the last person he'd wanted knowing he was capable of violently flipping out.

"Poor, broody Pike," she teased, wringing out a dripping pair of pants and tossing them over the line. She stepped closer, holding her thermal shirt up to the flames and bumping his shoulder with hers. "Poor Charlie Brown."

The gesture drove away some of his guilt. "I guess it's because of my work. I'm trained to plan for the worst. I think it makes me notice when things go wrong more, like I'm looking for proof."

"Jeez. They should train you to be positive. It can't be good to have a mopey medic around critically injured people."

"Well, I'm not that bad around patients. But it's still the army. It's not the most happy-Hallmark-huggy place. There's a reason the optimistic soldiers always get snuffed in the movies."

"I guess. For me, all of the nonsense this week is an adventure. For you, I guess it's more like a battle."

He nodded for a long time, struck by how true that was, how simply but perfectly it summed up the differences in their dispositions.

"But anyhow, I'll tone my glitter and unicorns down if you promise to fake a smile once an hour."

"Deal," Pike said. "Oh and thanks a fucking lot—giving me a stake in your vacation if you win."

"Just getting you back for how guilty I'll feel if I deprive the poor V.A. hospital of your much-needed thousands." She offered Pike that snarky smile that always made blood rush to undignified places.

He took a deep breath, adjusting to the idea that he and Mac were trapped together in the woods, *alone* together, for the next two days. *If* they stayed together, that was.

"Well," he said, cheering somewhat, "if I win, I'll drive you around in my new car."

"What kind of car?"

"It'll be for when I'm in Michigan, so I'll get lynched if it's not American. And the winters suck, so definitely not a convertible. And it can't be super-nice, since somebody will just steal it."

"Classy."

"Maybe I'll get some sweet old seventies boat. If I sign up for another tour, I probably won't be home that much so the gas-guzzling won't be too bad. I could get my uncle to help me fix it up. He's into all that hot rod stuff."

"That your mom's brother or your dad's?"

"My dad's."

"And your dad's white, right?"

Pike nodded.

"Where is he? Is he around?"

"He's around. Well, he's in prison."

Her face fell and Pike wanted to hug her.

"I'm sorry," she said.

"Don't be. It's not a new development."

"Well, better in prison than dead." She rolled her eyes in a fake woe-is-me gesture.

"Oh," Pike said. "For how long?"

"Since I was little, like eight. Both my parents. Don't worry, it doesn't hurt to talk about."

He nodded. They finished hanging things up to dry and Pike helped Mac erect her pup tent, partly impressed but mainly perplexed she'd packed it.

"Why'd you bring a tent? The instruction letter said they'd provide them."

"I figured if I lost early on, I'd still want to enjoy Alaska. I've barely ever been out of my hometown. Plus Alaska's supposed to be overflowing with rugged, jacked men who are hard up for pussy. Jackpot. This is like my Bangkok."

Pike's eyes must have gone wide because Mac laughed at him. "I'm kidding."

"Oh. Right."

She slid the collapsible tubing through the tent's seams and Pike noted with some disappointment how opaque her jog bra was.

She glanced up and Pike swiftly moved his eyes to her face. "You're welcome to share tonight, you know. If we end up having to spend the night here."

Pike caught "share" and "spend the night" and lost the ability to reply for a few seconds. "It's not a very big tent."

"Well, we're not very big people. And I don't have any cooties."

Words fell out of Pike's mouth before he could stop them. "Unless you caught some of Daisey's."

Luckily Mac merely laughed. "I think you're safe there."

What about Ian?

"I snore though," she said.

"And I bunk with a dozen soldiers with their noses all clogged up with desert dust. I'm sure I'll be fine. But you know, if it's not crazy-cold and the rain stays away, I'll just camp in my bag by the fire."

"Yeah, and wake up with your face swollen into one massive bug bite. Remember for a second who we've been traveling with for the last week," she said, "and quit with the gentleman act. Sleeping with you will be a huge step back toward civilization."

Pike found himself extraordinarily preoccupied with the tent's nylon shell for a minute.

"Oh." Mac stood and dusted her hands off. "I meant to ask, what did Ian take from you? That bag Lenora gave you?"

He looked to the woods, trying to shrug off the lingering creeps Ian gave him. "Nothing. It doesn't matter."

She shot him a skeptical look.

He'd dropped that in the crew's trash before they left the river...his so-called stolen property. Ian's whiskey and condoms. Even if neither had been tampered with, every other possible sentiment attached to the gifts made Pike's skin crawl. Even if they'd been offered with the kindest and least likely possible intention—to help Pike get what Ian assumed he was after—Pike would rather slam his dick in a door than accept seduction aids from that toxic prick.

"So, about you and me," Mac said.

Pike met her gaze, nervous.

"Pitted against each other?" she clarified.

"Right."

"I say we stick together. Then when the finish line's in sight, it's a footrace to the death."

Pike thought a moment and nodded. "To the wealth."

"Footrace to the wealth," she agreed.

"Okay, you're on. I mean, if the rules make that possible."

Mac began wandering around the immediate area, gathering branches and sticks for the fire. Pike busied himself doing the same, if only to keep from staring at her butt.

"I mean, maybe we'll hate each other an hour into the challenge and change our minds," Mac went on. "And I know this is probably the totally wrong attitude to have, given the circumstances... But I just want this to be fun, you know? Like, all the fuckwits are finally gone. Ian and Chloe and Daisey and Marissa. Let's just enjoy this. Like a vacation. Then in a couple days, when the finish line's in sight, it's game on."

Pike straightened up with two fistfuls of kindling. "You thought Daisey was a fuckwit?"

She snorted, still scavenging. "Yeah. Didn't you?"

"Well, yeah. But you know, everybody said you were trying to get with him."

"Does Alaska have a law against wanting to sleep with fuckwits?"

"No."

"Good. So anyhow. You and me stick together, at least for day one. Deal?" Mac stood up straight and they both shifted their sticks to free a hand.

Pike grinned as they shook. "Deal. Man, what a boring turn of events for the sad sacks who have to watch the hidden-camera footage."

Mac looked around them, waving at random trees. "I keep forgetting we have an audience. I guess that's just what they want."

"So..." Pike trailed off.

"So what?"

"Did you ever get what you wanted? You know, from Daisey."

She nodded, blasé. "More or less."

Hate punched Pike dead in the solar plexus. "Good."

She shrugged. "I think I set myself up for disappointment."

"That's too bad." Pike's eyes flitted all over the ground as a cautious tide of relief seeped in to dilute the nausea.

Mac flapped her elbows in a shrug. "I'm over it."

Unsure if he wanted details or not, Pike kept his mouth shut.

She spoke after a long pause. "I'll say this... You can get yourself worked up over the most gorgeous pair of shoes ever made, but if you buy them and they don't fit, you just end up with blisters and a huge credit card bill."

Pike laughed. "Daisey gave you blisters?"

"Only on my soul. Never mind though. I saved my receipt."

Another ugly question darkened his mood, one he wasn't about to come out and demand answers to. Not directly, anyhow. "Did you know, um... did you know Ian had feelings for you?"

She stopped in her tracks, staring at him for a long moment. She dumped her wood by the bonfire. "What?"

"Ian told me—well, he could have been lying. But he said he was in love with you. He said so during the Bridge Building Objective. Maybe he was just trying to fuck with me."

"Why would that be fucking with you?"

Pike felt his cheeks burn and was thankful for his uncondemning complexion. "Oh, I dunno. 'Cause he's Ian. Who knows with that guy? He's a psych nurse, I found out," Pike said, steering them away from more dangerous topics.

"No *way*."

Pike tossed his sticks onto Mac's pile. "I believe him, actually. Someplace in England. Men with personality disorders."

"Oh my God... Nurse Kilpatrick. That's hilarious. You sure he didn't say he was an escapee?"

Pike laughed. "Wouldn't shock me, either. But it definitely explains the tattoo."

"The Roman numerals? Do you know what those mean?"

"There's no Roman numeral S," Pike pointed out. "Or T or R."

Mac blinked. "Oh right. So what's it supposed to mean?"

"The *DSM-IV-TR* is like, *the* encyclopedia of mental and behavioral disorders. Ian said it's like his Bible or something."

"Oh Lord... You know, hearing he's a nut-house nurse actually makes a fuck of a lot of sense." Mac put her hands to her hips, drawing Pike's eyes undiplomatically to her crotch. "Still, why would he say he's in love with me?"

"Beats me. Maybe he was." *Why wouldn't he be?*

"I was never anything but bitchy to him." She shrugged again. "Maybe that's what he's into."

"He um, he said you two...did stuff."

Mac made a distasteful face. "No comment."

"Well, anyhow. He can pine for you while he drinks his meals out of a straw for the next few weeks." Pike wondered if his tone gave away too much of his actual bitterness.

"He knows how to box. You must have caught him with a hell of a punch."

"I don't really remember much of it actually happening."

"Weird how he exonerated you," Mac said.

"I guess...but I'm giving up on trying to decipher that asshole's rotten brain."

She looked thoughtful, gaze frozen on the dark lake.

"Whatcha thinkin' about, Mac?"

"About Ian."

"Oh."

"I bet he's spent practically his entire life trying to make sense of massively sick men. Mentally sick. And to try and like, get control over them. I think...I think he may be the most emotionally shut-off person I've ever met. I wonder if he feels happy ever."

"He sure smiles a fucking lot."

"That's not the same as being happy."

"Well, I wouldn't waste my time worrying about it," Pike said. "It's Ian. It's strange to think he never did lose a challenge. I wonder if he would have won if…you know." An unsettling emotion, some inbred cousin of guilt, gurgled in Pike's middle.

Mac chewed her lip then seemed to let her thoughts go. She faced Pike, her brown eyes uncharacteristically melancholy. "When we started all this, did you have a guess about who would win?"

Pike batted the question around in his head as they watched the fire. "Not really. Once in a while, during the challenges, I'd look at Daisey or Chloe and think, 'Shit, they're gonna win'. But I didn't have my money on anybody."

"Did you think you'd get this far?"

He shook his head. "No. Not when I saw how bad other people wanted it, during that race at the very start. Not after Daisey and Ian tricked me and I realized how cutthroat some of those freaks were."

"Before she threw herself under the bus, Leah told me Rory had said he hoped it'd be you or me to win," Mac said. "He said we were the only ones who wanted it bad but weren't stabbing people in the back to make it happen."

"Or punching them in the face?"

Mac smirked and shook her head. "Let it go, Pike."

"I wonder if these so-called doctors are planning on letting everyone know who wins it in the end," he said, dutifully changing the subject.

"You know what scares me?"

Pike met her eyes. "What?"

"I'm scared we're going to get to the end of this thing, one of us will win, and there'll be a catch. Some twist or something, and there won't be a prize. Like the psychological cherry on the top of this whole experiment, watching one of us crumble to brain dust with disappointment after everything we've put up with."

"God, that'd be sick."

CARA McKENNA

"Yeah. I've had a couple dreams about it."

He cleared his throat. "I had a similar thought, actually."

"Oh?"

"Yeah… You ever read a book by Stephen King called *The Long Walk*?"

She shook her head.

"Well, anyway…I'm pretty sure they're not shooting the losers in the head after they exit stage left, but this whole thing's been trippy. I've entertained some downer theories in the last week."

Mac fake-gasped. "You? Never."

He smiled tightly. "Do you think I'm…you know…miserable? Do you think I'm a mopey prick?"

She swatted his arm. "Oh, God no. I think anybody who wasn't reduced to a bitchy wreck, hanging out with some of the people we have for the last few days, he'd have to be a saint."

"That's you."

She shrugged. "It's in my job description to be trapped with strangers for days at a time in the wilderness. And believe me, we get our fair share of assholes. Usually of the fussy, whiny variety. I am an *ace* at faking cheerful good humor."

"I'll bet."

They stood before the fire in silence for a while, eventually turning toward the woods to warm their backs. That unfamiliar earnestness grew in Pike's chest again. He took a chance he normally wouldn't have and opened an emotional release valve.

"I have to say, if I lose this stupid competition, I'll go home a little bit happy knowing you won."

Mac made an adorable, disgusted face at him. "Don't say that. That makes it sound like you won't be trying as hard as you might if this was Daisey or somebody."

"No. I still want the money just as bad."

346

"Yeah, but you don't want to squash me as a bonus. Gimme some bloodlust, soldier."

"If the final two had been you and Daisey, would you have stuck together?"

She laughed. "Fuck no."

"No?"

Her head shook passionately. "My libido might've convinced me to a couple days ago, but not now. He'd just exploit my orienteering training then conk me on the head a hundred yards from the finish line."

"Daisey's not bright enough to exploit anybody," Pike said.

"I think he's smarter than you give him credit for. But in any case, I bet being a douche is instinctual with him. Like a defense mechanism."

"It's an art form to Ian."

She nodded.

"And you wouldn't have conked Daisey on the head a hundred yards from the end?" he asked.

Her mouth opened and closed and she shook her head, looking uncertain. Pike had never seen Mac go quiet that way, as if she were uncomfortable, and it clammed him up for a few minutes too.

They tested their clothes and each found enough dry items to get dressed then returned to the fire, identically rumpled and barefoot on the cold sand.

"Where do you think you want to go to school?" Pike finally asked.

"No clue. I haven't ever let myself dream too much about it. You know, in case it never panned out. My family runs the business like a co-op—there's just no extra cash lying around. We can't always afford five hundred bucks to fix a truck. Tens of thousands to send one of us to college is out of the question."

Pike caught her gaze. "There's always a way to go to school. Take it from a lifelong scholarship slut."

"I wasn't exactly a stand-out student."

"I got a free ride through med school, and I burned a frigging *house* down when I was in eighth grade," Pike countered.

Mac's brows rose.

"So trust me, you can find a way if you really want to."

"Whose house?" she asked.

"It was abandoned." *By my dad.*

"Jeez. Well, I know what you're saying, Pike, but it's not just tuition. It's covering the costs that would pile up if I wasn't at home, putting in the work. Doing my share."

"Don't your brothers support you, wanting to go to college?"

She chewed on her lip. "Yeah, they do. But it scares the crap out of them too, whether they'll say so to my face or not. Anyhow, if I won this thing, I could pay my way *and* do my financial bit for the business."

"I hear you…"

"But?" she prompted.

"But if you don't win, don't think you can't have whatever you want. You can figure out a way to make things happen for yourself."

Mac laughed. "What have you done with the real Pike?"

"I'm just saying, you'll be fine, even if you don't win."

"I know. I just want to be better than *fine*. I've barely ever been out of New Mexico. I love what my family does, don't get me wrong. It's a blast. I just don't want to wake up in twenty years and never have experienced anything else."

"You should join the Peace Corps. You'd be great at that."

"You think so?"

"God, yeah. You could live in a foreign country and learn new stuff. And you're great with people, and your skills are probably super-desirable. I'd tell you to join the service, but to be honest I wouldn't wish that on anybody."

"Except yourself."

"It's different for me." Pike grabbed a sweater off the line and held it up to the fire. "But anyhow, if I win this thing, apply for the Peace Corps. You'd be perfect for it."

"Maybe. Maybe I could get a gig in Syria or wherever. We could be neighbors."

"If I ever catch you anywhere near where I get posted, I'll kick your ass back to the States faster than you can blink."

"Too bad. That would've been fun. Too bad you don't live in Santa Fe. I'd totally drag you out clubbing after we get back home."

Warmth trickled from Pike's face down through his chest. He swallowed. "Too bad."

"Nobody else will ever be able to fathom what went down on this trip." She looked him dead in the eyes. "I'll miss you when this is over, Pike."

He tried his damnedest to return the sentiment, but he just couldn't find the sac. Too easy for it to snowball into a full-blown proclamation, his feelings returning with a vengeance.

"Well, why don't you and me get a sham marriage, then I'll ditch the service and we'll join the Peace Corps together? You and me masquerading as man and wife, saving the world."

"Oh yeah, we'd be the new Brad and Angelina."

"Bit shorter," Pike said.

"Would the service let you go that easily?"

Pike felt his nerves prickle, shocked she was running with his silly, hypothetical pipe dream. "Probably not…though my two years of active duty are already fulfilled, and then some. Anyhow, I was just fucking around."

"How about this? You win this thing, go home and get crowned Prince of Detroit and have your parade. Then you drive your sweet old boat out West and I'll take you on a rafting trip or something. Then we hit Vegas, get ourselves sham-hitched at an Elvis drive-thru chapel and ship out to Ethiopia or wherever."

"Deal."

Mac put her hand out once again and Pike shook it, fearful of the pleasure that radiated up through his arm.

"But that doesn't mean you get to give up in the final stretch," he said.

Mac offered an uncomfortable smile that turned Pike's warm glow to frost. "Trust me, I won't. And as much as I'd like to sham marry you and run off to save the world, I can't leave my family unless some major money magically appears to replace me. So don't you worry—I'll be bringing my A-game at the end of this race."

"Good."

"What'll you do if you lose?" Mac asked. *"When* you lose," she added, the cocky tease sounding hollow, weary.

"Same old, same old."

"Yeah."

"Well," Pike said, "I gave *you* a Plan B. What's mine?"

"Hoo… You could write a bestselling exposé about this stupid experience."

"Yeah, and get myself sued for violating the terms of the agreement we all signed."

"Oh, right. Well, you could finish your duty and work for your beloved V.A. hospital, moonlight as a plastic surgeon and save up enough to buy your mom her house."

"A lot of folks in Detroit can barely afford electricity these days. I don't think they're looking to get their faces lifted. Plus I think my soul would fall out."

"That leaves one option, then," Mac said.

"Which is?"

"We'll just both have to win."

"Wish we could."

She shrugged. "Well, I'm not losing, so you'll just have to suck it."

"We'll see."

The look in her eye scared Pike a bit, that hard streak of determination that told him he'd been an idiot to think the last challenge was going to be fun just because it was down to Mac and him. It'd be a million times worse, actually. Sending Mac home brokenhearted would hurt almost as much as losing.

Almost.

Pike reevaluated what he'd thought earlier. This wouldn't be a boring twist for the doctors at all. This was two pit bulls chained together, docile until the moment they spotted the steak and started ripping out each other's throats.

If it were Pike watching from behind those cameras, he'd be placing bets and getting the popcorn ready for a good show. He beamed a mental fuck-you to everyone with their money on Mac, anybody who thought he'd lie down and let her win as if this were some Walt Disney wet dream.

He glanced at her, that small, strong body looking like a threat as much as a tease. Adrenaline and something else, something primal and bloodthirsty, lit him up. For the first time since he'd met her, Pike didn't want to kiss Mac. He wanted to fuck her ever-loving brains out.

MAC

MAC CRAWLED INTO THE TENT and zipped the mosquito netting closed. "Bet you're done teasing me about lugging this thing around now, huh?"

"I bow to your superior planning." Pike made some penitent motions with his arms.

Mac settled in on top of her sleeping bag, fingers clasped at her belly. Beside her Pike was twitchy, probably downright itchy if his clothes were as damp as hers. For hours they'd kept the fire burning, but the misty air made everything clammy. Mac was desensitized to uncomfortable sleeping arrangements though.

"You okay over there, Shifty?"

"Yeah, sorry. Just not very sleepy."

"Me neither." It was distracting, lying there with three inches separating her and Pike... She felt a thrilling buzz, an adolescent-type excitement at the physical proximity of a friend of the opposite sex. A big old emotional Mad Lib that read, *"[female name] and [male name] lay in the [adjective] tent. He [verb]ed over and [verb]ed her."*

Pike didn't seem poised to fill in any of those blanks though. And if he did they'd probably be "turned" and "snored on".

Off in the distance, something howled. A wolf maybe, Mac wasn't sure—she only really knew the animal sounds of the land surrounding her home. Beside her, Pike tensed up so tight his body swished against his sleeping bag.

She turned her head. "You okay?"

He swallowed, black eyes on the translucent red ceiling above them. "Fine."

"You really don't like dogs much, do you?"

He laughed, busted. "No. Not big ones, anyhow."

"That's where you got that scar?" She reached over and put her fingertips to the uneven texture marbling one side of Pike's neck.

He swallowed again—a great, labored gulp—then cleared his throat. "Yeah. Got attacked by some douchebag's Rottweiler when I was little. Now I get nervous when a pug passes me on the sidewalk. I was almost sued by some lady when I kicked her Corgi in a park when it jumped on my leg."

Mac laughed.

"If your stupid unleashed dog jumps on me it's gonna get booted," Pike muttered at the invisible woman.

"What about army dogs? Don't they use those for like bomb-sniffing or whatever?"

He shrugged against the ground. "They're more like my coworkers...plus I can put things aside when I'm on duty, sort of get outside myself and override things like that. Still, you won't catch me petting them."

"Gotcha."

"What about you—oh wait. Duh. Small spaces. Like, *any* small spaces?"

She swiped her fingers over the dome above them. "Not all. Only tight spaces where I feel like there's no exit or not enough air."

"So the Meat Locker wasn't your idea of a good time either, I guess?"

"I'm lucky I didn't hyperventilate in there too...but I kept it together all right. Daisey was a welcome distraction."

"Right."

"Greg too, though he dropped out pretty early on."

"About that challenge, when Greg went out... I'm guessing you voted for Greg, he voted for Daisey and Daisey voted for you."

"That's what I figure."

"Were you pissed," Pike asked, "that Daisey tried to vote you out?"

"Nah. A little miffed, sure. But it's a competition. And I decided that probably meant he saw me as some kind of threat. I tried to be flattered by it."

"You cut that dude a lot of slack."

It was Mac's turn to shrug. "I was hot for him. Plus Daisey's not *evil*. Just a bit of a jerk. And jerks are people too."

"Even Ian?"

"Yeah, Ian's human. I'm about ninety-five-percent sure now."

They fell silent and after a minute another howl sounded in the distance.

Pike sighed. "I'm not getting any sleep in tonight."

"Me neither."

"You want to go and smoke a bowl?" he asked. "Shoot the shit by the fire and try to dry out some more?"

"You're on."

PIKE

HE WATCHED HER PACK THE PIPE, enjoying the smell, the look of her smooth face in the firelight. Pike reached in his pocket for Ian's lighter and flicked it open, holding it for her as she took a hit. The flame licked his finger.

"Ow. Fucking Zippos."

Mac exhaled. "Thanks."

Pike took the pipe and just held it at first, already feeling buzzed. "Must be nearly midnight. It's finally getting dark." The clouds had mostly dispersed and he looked up into the navy sky, a hundred white points promising to become billions. "Stars are pretty amazing here."

He took a hit and they traded back and forth, and soon enough Pike felt that familiar shifting of his senses as the weed breathed extra life into everything around him.

Just him and Mac for miles and miles... Pike felt eerily calm. The sensation might pass the next time a wolf bayed, but for now he was adrift in contentedness. The pot didn't hurt. He watched the blaze, spruce needles sending golden threads of light curling up into the darkness. The magic of the fire awed him, just as acutely as the violence of it had hypnotized him as a child.

Mac packed her paraphernalia away and looked into the sky, dark eyes black in the warm, dancing light. Then she looked to Pike, to his bare arms and their innumerable scratches.

"God, you're a mess."

"Oh yeah, you're one to talk." He grabbed her wrist and gently pushed her sleeve up to showcase her own gashes.

"Where's your kit?"

Too content to argue, he got up and fetched the case, setting it by her foot.

Mac flipped the latches and rooted around, setting bandages and alcohol wipes in the empty lid. She laughed then, a sudden, happy sound as bright as the fire.

"What?"

"You've got condoms in here." She squinted at a wrapper. "Unlubricated?"

"Yeah, I've got lots of stuff. And they're not for me, the condoms. I wish. And usually they don't end up getting used for sex, anyhow. They make good rubber ties, like if you need to take a vial of blood. Watertight, sterile baggies. All sorts of things."

She put them back. "God, poor Rory, having to grovel to Ian."

Pike laughed. "I wish I'd known he was in the market."

"What's this?" Mac asked, pulling out a small device with a purple light bulb. "A black light?"

He nodded. "There's a tube of UV epoxy in there someplace, for mending glass. I carry all kinds of weird stuff."

She grinned widely, her heart-shaped face so *fucking* pretty Pike wanted to slap himself for noticing yet again.

"Want to see something top secret?" Mac asked, devious.

"Secret?"

She nodded. "Follow me."

Pike let her lead him into the woods, a couple hundred paces until the fire faded and hiking became difficult in the dark.

She stopped. "Close your eyes."

Pike did. He heard rustling and crunching, Mac moving around.

"Keep them closed."

A small, warm hand, scratchy with climber's calluses, took hold of his wrist and the smooth plastic of the UV light was pushed into his palm.

More rustling then Mac said, "Okay. Open your eyes."

Pike found her facing away from him, stripped to the waist, the pale expanse of her bare back visible in the residual light of the fire and moon.

"Turn it on," she said, craning her neck to look at him over her shoulder. "The light."

Pike took his eyes off her naked skin long enough to flip the bulb on, bathing everything in its shallow range in a dark blue glow. All over Mac's back and shoulders, stars shone—swirling patterns of blue-white dots, an entire night sky's worth.

"Oh my God."

She laughed.

"Are those tattoos?"

"Yeah. What do you think?" she asked.

"Holy shit. I've heard of blacklight tattoos, but I never knew anybody who actually had one. Let alone a galaxy. That's...that's really cool."

"Thanks."

"Is it, like, a real astrological pattern or just made up?"

"It's the night sky from the day I was born," she said. "The sky over Santa Fe, anyhow. Does that sound totally self-important or what?"

"No, it's really cool," he said again. He stepped closer, studying all the glowing points, a hundred constellations he couldn't name.

"I saved up all summer when I was twenty-one and ordered my star chart from a psychic."

"Wow. So, can you see them at all without the backlight?"

"Not since they were new. When I first got them it looked like I had chicken pox back there for a couple weeks."

Pike put his hand out, watching the dark silhouette of his fingers interrupt the patterns. "Wow. That's the coolest tattoo I have *ever* seen."

"Told you I was a club-rat. Cross your fingers the ravers who have them don't all come down with some crazy form of toxic cancer in twenty years."

Pike ignored her comment, too awed to joke. He swallowed then took a deep breath. He fanned his fingers and pressed his palm to her back, cupping her shoulder blade. Her skin was soft and smooth and cool and he half expected the stars he covered to be gone when he pulled his hand away, burned onto his own palm. But they were just where they'd been. Pike wanted to lie her down on a bed in a pitch black room and memorize every last one.

"Wow," he said one last time.

"Thanks." Mac yanked her sports bra and her thermals back over her head and faced him.

Pike switched the light off as Mac started back toward camp. He shook his head, hard, trying to dislodge the strange, foggy awe swirling in his brain. He looked up as they reached the fire, millions more stars surely looming above, only snatches of them visible in the cracks between the banks of clouds.

As they sat back down before the fire, Mac grew silent. She was lost contemplating her own surely pot-framed thoughts, but Pike was lost in her. He watched every little movement—her throat as she swallowed, her nose as she breathed, her hair as the breeze moved it. When she eventually yawned, the universe turned inside out, pulling

Pike out of the space contained solely within her gravity and dropping his ass back on the sand.

He got up and grabbed his jacket off the line, rolling it up as a pillow before lying down a few feet from the bonfire. Lacing his fingers atop his ribs, he stared into the sky. His mind blipped in and out of reality, all those stars above them, holes punched out of the precious, fleeting darkness. Mac's stars, hundreds of secret points of light. He thought about constellations, ancient Greek and Roman wars being fought up in the heavens. He thought of where they were—her adventure, his battle.

He heard shifting at his side then Mac reclined, resting her head on Pike's shoulder. Sobriety enveloped him and he fidgeted.

"Sorry," she said sitting back up. "You just looked so comfy."

"No, it's fine. Go ahead."

She did. She curled up on her side, her cheek resting below Pike's collarbone, her shoulder tucked against his arm. He could smell her hair and skin, feel her breathing.

"I can hear your pulse," she mumbled, spacey. "Buh-bum. Buh-bum." She tapped his knuckles with each beat. "Oh, it just sped up. Buh-bum-buh-bum-buh-bum."

No doubt. He swallowed and deepened his breaths, trying to ignore how freakishly intimate this felt. He tried to make it feel like what it must be to Mac, just two weary, buzzed friends chilling by a campfire.

Suddenly she sat back up, crawling to Pike's medical kit and returning with his stethoscope. She lay on her belly and propped herself on her elbows, sticking the scope's tips in her ears. Nudging Pike's hands away, she pressed the chestpiece to his sternum.

"Oooh."

He laughed. "You're so high."

"I'm not *so* high… Wow, this is crazy." She shifted, moving the cool plastic of the chestpiece to Pike's neck, his scar. The most intimate part of his body, aside from the more obvious ones.

"Swallow," she whispered.

Pike obeyed.

"Oh, weird. Do it again."

He did, suddenly needing to anyhow.

"That's awesome." She moved away, kneeling. She tested her own chest and throat then removed the scope, cleaning the eartips on her shirt. "Too bad I can't put this thing against your temple and hear what you're thinking."

Pike laughed. "I always thought that'd be the worst super power. Who wants to know what people really think of them? I'd way rather fly or turn invisible."

"Flying would be good," she agreed. "No more planes for me." She leaned over and stuck the ends of the stethoscope into Pike's ears and lay the tubing across his torso. "That's so crazy, that you're a doctor. It sounds so grown up."

"It's just a job."

"Now *that's* as close to a superpower as you can get, in the real world. Unless you believe in psychics."

"Bet you can guess the answer to that."

She smiled and leaned forward, placing her warm palm on Pike's forehead and rearranging his brain yet again. She shut her eyes. "You're thinking…"

"Uh huh?"

"You're thinking, *Mac is so awesome*…"

He held his tongue, the marijuana convincing him for the slimmest second that perhaps she *was* psychic.

"Mac is so awesome, and you can't wait to let her win the half-million dollars tomorrow."

Pike laughed and took her wrist, impulsively moving her palm to his chest. Her eyes opened and whatever taunt he'd had ready vaporized. For a long time they stared at each other, her hand on his chest, his on her wrist. The fact that it wasn't an awkward moment scared Pike after half a minute and he let her hand go.

"Freak," he said, sitting up.

"Freak with good weed," she replied through a yawn.

"Yeah, fair enough."

"I'm sleepy," Mac announced, then another yawn overtook her. "We should try to get some rest. Who knows when or if there's a wake-up call tomorrow. Or if we have to wander around all day, looking for the frigging start line."

He nodded.

Mac stood, taking away her comforting proximity. She looked at Pike and laughed. Reaching down, she wiped at his bare arms, at a dozen or more mosquitoes camped out on his skin.

"Oh shit." He got to his feet and slapped them away. He stowed his stethoscope and closed his case before following Mac to the tent.

He wanted to linger and stare up into the sky, wanted to go back to where they'd been a minute or two ago, skin against skin…but the flap was open and the bugs hungry. He kicked off his shoes and climbed inside, zipped them in.

Mac was already folded into her sleeping bag, body curled toward the wall. "Night, Pike. See you at the big game."

"Night, Mac."

MAC

MAC WOKE TO FIND her arm draped across Pike's ribs, her foot slung over where his legs hid behind his sleeping bag.

"Oops." She always did that. She'd tuck—or zip—herself in at bedtime only to discover she'd gone zombie in the night and bucked the covers away, feet seeking cool, fresh air. She'd also been told by a lover or two that she kicked. And snored and mumbled. Probably other things they'd been kind enough to let her think she was too ladylike for. A glance at Pike's nylon-covered shoulder showed it to be mercifully un-drooled-upon.

She rolled over and unzipped the inner tent flap, letting in a burst of brisk, clean air. The cloud cover had returned, and with the sky flat and gray it could be any time…three a.m. or ten. She fumbled for her pants and vest and found her watch. Six-oh-eight. Good enough.

Once outside she tugged her layers on, checked on the clothes strung by the dead campfire only to find them still thoroughly damp. It took some doing but she got the fire going again. Standing by it for a long time, she waited for Pike to wake or a sign to appear from the behind-the-scenes doctors.

She thought about her tentmate. Jeez, she was surrounded by doctors now. Maybe she could become a doctor... If she won this thing, she could become anything. Then again, the money she'd have leftover after the family business gobbled up the lion's share of her winnings probably didn't cover med school these days, plus she didn't really have the stomach to fix people's wounds, physical or mental.

Mac turned around to warm her achy back, then started. A few yards beyond the tent, yellow squares ran down the trunk of a tree, six of them. Her eyesight wasn't fantastic so she jogged up the beach to investigate. Yellow cardboard squares, five inches by five inches, had been pinned to the trunk with old-school arrows.

"Oh yes, very theatrical." She toyed with pulling one of them down but decided her pact with Pike to tackle this Objective together included this as well as the actual journey. Curiosity nipped at her heels every step it took to run back to the tent.

She unzipped the two flaps and stuck her head in. "Pike."

He moaned, sounding like an eight-year-old on Saturday morning.

"Hey, get up. There's a clue." Now *she* sounded like the eight-year-old, nagging a sleepy parent on Christmas.

He turned over, rumpled hair and bleary, squinty eyes, a grumpy Pike-burrito in his sleeping bag. Awful cute, she had to admit.

"What sort of clue?"

"I dunno. I'm waiting for you so we can find out together."

"Fine, fine."

Mac went down to the shore with her canteen and inspected the water, deemed it drinkable. She filled her growling, empty stomach with a couple of pints, hoping it might trick her into feeling full for a little while.

Pike emerged in his hiking pants and a tee shirt, and he looked weirdly exotic in the cold morning light. Adrenaline and atmosphere made the beach feel like a scene from a stylized movie, Pike its stern leading man, surely armed with choreographed killing skills and a thirst for vengeance. Then he yawned and wrecked the mystique and Mac shook herself back to normal.

"Where's this clue?" he called.

Mac pointed and headed for the tree, meeting Pike there.

"Huh."

"I don't know what we do," she said. "Do we pick one, and we're stuck with whatever instructions are on it maybe?"

Pike's hand had risen to the third square up but it froze then. "Oh. That's not a bad guess at all. That sounds like something they'd do."

"Did you, um... Did you still want to stick together?"

He looked down at her, face giving nothing away. "Did you?"

Mac spent ten seconds debating it. Company versus winning versus the good or bad luck that might come from drawing separate marching orders; a shared hike and frantic race to the end versus a lonely trek along God-knew-what route the crew had planned.

"Yeah," she decided aloud. "I still want to stick together."

"Well, if we only get to pick one, lady's choice."

She bit her lip, eyes jumping over the identical squares. She hopped to tap the second one from the top and Pike pulled at its arrow. It didn't seem likely to move, so he bent it until it snapped then slid the square off.

It was sturdy, folded paper, attached at three edges with perforated strips. Pike handed it over. Mac ripped off the edges and pocketed them. She unfolded the card to reveal a long map, detailed with the shadows of hills and woods, marred by the mirrored holes where the arrow had stabbed it. Its little scale told them it represented roughly sixteen miles from the bottom to the top. A route was plotted in red, its bottommost point labeled "You Are Here" and the top, "Day One Base Camp". Along the route were sprinkled black Xs at occasional intervals, five of them in all.

"Uh oh," Pike said.

"What?"

"Those Xs. What if those are checkpoints or prizes or something? Buried treasure, X marks the spot? And if we don't each hit all of them, we can't finish."

Mac's heart sank. "Hm."

They stood side by side for a minute, trading irritable nose-breaths and blinking at the five remaining squares.

"Well," he said finally. "We don't have much choice but to look at another one."

She nodded.

Pike freed the bottom square and unfolded it to reveal the same map, but with a different route. The first square's route had largely followed the edge of the lake, but this one was different, seeming to venture into the woods and hills. It had only three black Xs along the way.

"Maybe they aren't prizes," Mac said. "This coastal route looks way easier, but it's got five. One of them looks like it's in the water… This other one looks like a nastier hike, but it's only got three. Maybe they're obstacles, not prizes. Or maybe they're worth different amounts…of something. God, I dunno."

"Me neither."

They looked at each other with identical uncertainty.

"I think we're going to *have* to split up," Mac said. She watched Pike's face as he studied the maps, searching for glimmers of relief or disappointment. She knew which she felt.

"Maybe we don't," he said.

"No?"

"Not if we hit all these Xs together."

Mac looked between the two routes. Zigzagging back and forth could add an extra five, six, seven miles, easily. "It'll take a lot longer."

"I've got all day," Pike said. "How about you?"

She laughed, far more relieved than she'd let on. This man was still her adversary, after all. Best to maintain some glimmer of a poker face, if only to keep her own head on straight about it all. "Yeah, true. And I bet a twenty-mile hike with someone to talk to will feel a lot shorter than fifteen or sixteen by ourselves."

"Cool. It's decided then."

"Good. If only they'd given us some breakfast." Her eavesdropping stomach growled its agreement.

"Let's just hope one of those Xs is food then." Pike folded both maps and tucked them in his pocket, heading back to the beach.

They brushed their teeth, packed their clothes and supplies and disassembled Mac's tent. Together. Nice. Comforting after a week of ruthless group dynamics.

Pike dug a pen from his case and they carefully plotted one route onto the other's map, then vice versa, each taking one. They picked the closest X to head toward and set off.

Mac's middle grumbled again—anxiety replacing her hunger for a change—as they left the four other yellow squares behind them.

"Shit, I hope we did that right. Picking one apiece."

Pike shrugged. "Logical as any other fucking guess out here."

"Yeah." Mac did some math. Twenty-two miles, she guessed their revised dual route was. Ten-hour hike, *bare* minimum. Probably twelve or more, depending on the terrain.

"So today's only day one," Pike said, eyes on the ground as they skirted between the lake and the edge of the woods.

"Yup."

"Maybe the Xs are advantages, for tomorrow."

"Maybe."

"Maybe," he said, "the Xs are where a staffer pops out from behind a tree and punches you in the face."

She laughed. "Maybe they're trapdoors, like in a cartoon. You step on a hole covered in leaves and *foosh!*"

"Or you trip a wire and a cage falls on you, or a net scoops you up into the treetops."

"Guess we'll find out. After that weird-ass spy bunker and those freaky glass tanks we passed, I won't put anything past them. How far 'til we hit the first one?"

Pike squinted at the map. "Five miles, maybe a little less."

"I've got a nasty caffeine-withdrawal headache coming on."

"I still feel like I've got a hangover from the night before the Bridge Building challenge."

"Do you? Where'd you get booze? Oh—Ian's whiskey."

Pike nodded. "Never drinking that shit again."

"Must have been quite a cozy little bonding session for you two."

"Oh yeah. Bromance abounds."

"I bet we can all find each other after this is over," she said. "Any of us could Google 'Ian Kilpatrick' and track his e-mail down. Weird to imagine Ian with an e-mail address though. Oh my God—what if he's on Facebook?"

"Seems more the type to scrawl his thoughts on a piece of parchment with blood or something creepy."

She laughed. "From an asylum, no less. Like the Marquis de Sade. Did you ever read that book? The hundred and some-odd days of Sodom? I forget the actual title."

Pike snorted. "No."

"Oh. I did."

He looked over at her.

"I read anything I can find," Mac said. "We don't get any TV stations where I am. Anyhow, it's really boring. It's just like hundreds of pages of laundry-list sex positions."

"Huh. I should get that for the infirmary patients."

"Maybe. I guess it's like *Penthouse Letters*, if they were written by an old French guy who hates the Catholics."

Pike laughed. "What do you know about *Penthouse Letters*?"

"Only what you find out from having three older brothers who know nothing about housekeeping or discretion."

"Ah, of course… I found my first porno mags in my dad's garage when I was about nine. Way more interesting than the bike pump I'd been looking for."

"I'll bet."

"That said, I could've used a less-terrifying introduction to sex than a stack of *Hustlers* from the early eighties."

"Oh, gross! God, the stuff we don't need to know about our male role models."

"Yeah. But my mom would never have given me the sex talk," Pike said. "Or if she had, it would have been all about pregnancy and diseases and death. Better I deciphered the basics between Larry Flynt and those older kids who taught me how to break-dance. Hey, let's take a right through here."

The map took them away from the lake and into the shadowy woods, up a gentle slope through the spruce trees.

"My oldest brother's stoner girlfriend of the moment gave me the talk," Mac said. "I must have been about twelve. She did an okay job, I guess, but everything she said, I couldn't help but try to picture her doing it with Tim." She made a shuddering noise. "And even at twelve I wasn't convinced it was as trippy and spiritual as she made it out to be. I think she used the phrase 'soul-merging'."

Pike laughed. "More poetic than what I got, at any rate."

"Yeah, but when it finally happened, that was *not* a soul-merging."

"Peppermint schnapps."

"Yeah."

"I think mine was christened with a bottle of pink Arbor Mist. I tried to make it like some grand seduction, even though my friend had totally already had sex and was doing it as a favor."

"Well, maybe you liked her secretly," Mac teased.

"Dude, she was willing to let me have sex with her. I'd have signed over my kidneys."

"How was it?"

Pike made a thoughtful face.

"Quick?"

"Well, quick to me. Probably felt like ages to her. God knows how awful I must have been."

"I don't even remember mine," Mac said. "But I was really relieved to have it done with. I was seventeen and it was just a big checkmark. Virginity, done. Next up, SATs."

Pike laughed.

"Not like I needed the SATs," she added. "I knew I wasn't going to college."

"Well, you might now."

"Yeah, maybe."

"Fifty-fifty chance."

With that they fell silent, hiking without speaking for an hour or more.

"Whoa," Mac said, peering into the distance at a yellow shape in the trees. She pointed. "Look."

Pike nodded then checked the map. "That must be it. The first X."

"I can't really make it out."

He squinted. "Looks like a box. You any good at climbing trees? It must be thirty feet up."

"Tim calls me Monkey Girl. I can get that, no problem."

"Cool. The next X is the one in the water, not too far," Pike said. "Half a mile maybe."

She nodded.

"How about I try to tackle the one in the lake and you do this tree one, and I meet you back here when I'm done?"

"No, I'll meet you on the beach. I won't take long, and I need to fill my canteen anyhow."

"It's a plan."

Pike took off down the hill toward the water.

Mac dropped her pack, sizing up the climb. The first fifteen feet offered no helpful branches, but the rest looked simple. She unpacked her climbing rope and doubled it up, slinging it around the trunk with an end gripped in each fist. She jerked it up a few inches and pulled hard, jumping to get her legs hugged to the sides of the trunk. She sort of wished Pike was still here. It was one of her more impressive skills, and she wouldn't have minded him seeing. Not that tree-climbing was anywhere near as useful or cool as saving people's lives… Still, she respected him a lot. Earning his admiration for manlier credentials than having a cool tattoo and good weed would've been nice.

With little annoyance other than some scrapes and sap, Mac made it to the branches, draped the rope over one and made the rest of the ascent easily.

The box was made of aluminum, painted yellow, and she knew that shape, that latch, that handle anywhere. "Lunch, bitches. Hallelujah." It made the climb down trickier but once she got back to her rope, she lowered the box gently to the ground before making her own descent. She stowed the rope and jogged down the hill, dodging branches and rocks, the contents of the lunchbox rattling and piquing her curiosity. But she'd wait for Pike, in case it held any exciting surprises aside from the food she was praying for.

Finding him was easier than expected. As soon as she reached the lake she spotted him a few dozen yards down the beach.

"Hey!"

Pike turned and waved, then looked back to the water. He'd stripped to his underwear and as she neared she could see he was wet, hair dripping, arms shivering in the breeze.

"No luck yet, I take it?"

"Well, I found it."

"Oh, that's good!"

Pike looked to the lunchbox. "Is that full of what I hope it is?"

"I haven't looked yet, but I sure hope so."

"Nice work. This other X is a box too, but it must weigh about twenty pounds. It's sitting at the bottom of the lake. You can see it from the surface when you're swimming—it's only about fifteen feet down. But it's too heavy to haul up."

"I've got rope," Mac offered.

"Oh shit, you do, don't you? What about a carabiner? This thing's got a handle I could hook it to."

She dug several of the metal clips from the front pocket of her frame pack. "What color?"

Pike laughed. "Red, I guess."

He took her carabiner and rope and got his setup figured out. Mac watched his trim muscles flexing as he worked, deciding officially that he was a much nicer shape than Daisey. Far less garish, more...accessible. Simply less, overall, but in a good way. Manageable.

We'd fit, she thought. Not in a tab-A into slot-B way, more like if she were a cushion, she'd tuck nicely against Pike, were he a sofa. Cozy. She frowned and shook her head, wondering where that stoner analogy had come from.

"Right. I'm going in," he announced.

"Good luck. Do it quick so we can find out if there's food in here." She shook the lunch box.

"Quit that or the soufflé will fall."

Mac gave him a friendly punch on his damp, bare shoulder and he headed for the water.

Damn, nice ass. Nice everything, really.

He strode into the rippling water and swam out fifty feet or so, then began treading, looking around. He ducked below, gone for nearly a minute, exactly long enough for Mac's heart to speed before his head broke the surface. He whipped the water from his hair and raised a thumb at her.

Mac clapped.

Pike swam to shore and hauled the cargo in hand over hand, until another metal yellow box, this one looking more like a toolbox, was dragged onto the sand. Pike knelt beside it and waved her over.

She crouched at his side. "You open it. You did the work."

Pike nodded and snapped open the latch, pushed the lid up. They peered inside, two sets of shoulders slumping.

"That's a bit underwhelming," Pike said. Just a metal box full of water and cylindrical lead weights. He picked one up and set it in the sand. "I wasn't expecting gold bullion or anything, but jeez."

Mac grabbed a weight. She picked at it, on the incredibly off-chance a layer of paint might chip away to reveal something precious. No such thing happened and she dropped it heavily to the side. They emptied the box of a dozen of them then she spotted it. "Look, there."

Beneath the final weight was a yellow chip, the exact sort they'd been issued at the close of The Ant Farm's first race and during the Twenty-One Questions head trip. "You hold on to it," she said.

Pike carried it to his case and stowed it, then tugged his clothes over his wet body. He nodded to the lunch box. "Now yours."

Mac held her breath as they knelt beside it. She snapped the latch and flipped it open, and laughed. "Wow. Welcome to second grade."

An apple, a tidily bagged sandwich, a packet of chips, a yellow Thermos, napkins.

"No token," Pike said.

"I'll take potato chips over poker chips right now. Plus napkins? Not wiping our asses with leaves will be a treat."

"Yeah, true."

Mac unscrewed the Thermos and sniffed. "Tomato. Don't they know they'll never get the smell out, now? That happened to my Snoopy Thermos. Ruined it for hot cocoa."

Pike laughed. He unwrapped and inspected the sandwich, their sharing implicit. "You like ham and cheese?"

"I was ready to eat pinecones this morning. Ham sounds like ambrosia."

Pike dragged his case over and they used its lid as a tray. Mac split the sandwich in two with her utility knife then did the same with the apple.

"Soup's cold," Pike said, passing her the Thermos.

As she took a drink, something weird clicked against her teeth and she jerked away. "Oh." Peering inside, she saw it—a yellow chip floating on the surface. She tilted the Thermos and coaxed it out with her knife's blade, licked it clean.

Pike laughed. "Okay, I see where this is going. They must intend for us to cash these in when we reach the first night's camp. Eight if we find all of them from both maps."

"Four apiece?" Mac asked.

"Even if one of us does the work to get more than the other, we split them equally."

Mac nodded her agreement and they set about devouring the rest of the food.

"No Fruit Roll-Up for dessert," she lamented as Pike crumpled up the chip bag.

"Yeah, bummer. I totally could have just given you the plastic wrapper and eaten the good part myself."

Mac whapped him on the arm and stood, dusting off her butt. "Well, I feel a zillion times better. Ready to head for the next X?"

PIKE

THE REMAINDER OF THE DAY'S HIKE—hike and a half, really—went smoothly. Eerily smoothly, in Pike's pessimistic opinion. After much trudging, searching, climbing, wading, digging and not nearly enough eating, they'd recovered all eight of the yellow tokens. The sky had even decided to clear.

Pike checked the map, then his watch. "Half-mile to go, I think. I bet we covered over twenty miles in thirteen hours, plus all the time wasted finding the stupid tokens. Not too shabby."

Mac yawned, keeping his steady pace. "Go team. What time is it?"

"Not quite nine."

"Dinnertime."

Pike nodded. "If they feed us."

"Fuck that. We'll eat the crew."

"Mmm, khaki."

Mac's laugh was swallowed by another mighty yawn.

"You sound wiped."

She shrugged. "Nothing dinner wouldn't fix."

"Feet okay?"

"They've been better, but I'm holding up. If tomorrow's more of the same, I'll be all right."

"Hey—look!" Pike aimed his finger at a blessed sight in the distance, the glint of a fire between the shadowy trees.

Mac's face lit up, posture straightening. "Oh, sweet."

They picked up their shared pace, jogging by the time they reached the top of the hill and the tiny clearing where the fire had been built. Beside it were a couple of logs for sitting. Mac dumped her pack beside one and stretched, looking around. Pike set his case down and dropped his bag, praying they were done moving for—

"Greetings!"

Mac yelped and Pike jumped, and Lenora appeared from between the trees, grinning and impeccably laundered.

"What a tremendous coincidence, you two arriving at camp at exactly the same moment," Lenora said silkily.

Neither replied.

"Well, welcome! And congratulations for completing the first day of the final Objective. Have you been wondering what those tokens are for?"

"Yeah," Mac said.

"They're very valuable indeed. Each entitles you to a choice of luxuries this evening. Tell me, how many did you each earn?"

"Four," they said together. Pike felt a chill at Lenora's too-easy smile and shifty eyes.

"Four apiece. Lovely! And how perfectly equitable."

"What are the luxuries?" asked Mac.

"One token will buy you one of any of the following," Lenora said. "A meal, a hot shower, a pup tent, a warm blanket, a six-pack of beer, a bottle of wine or liquor, assorted first aid and pharmaceutical items, a sleeping pad, various toiletries, a new pair of wool hiking socks in your size, or a dosage of legal stimulant in pill form."

Pike exchanged a puzzled look with Mac then his brain began ticking with questions. "Is there any reason we might want to keep any tokens for tomorrow?"

"No, Dr. Pike. The tokens are good only for these luxuries, this evening."

"Right… Hang on." He took Mac by the wrist and pulled her a few paces away. He suspected she felt how he did—that they were together in this decision as surely as they'd pooled the tokens between them.

"You've got the first aid covered," she said.

"I could use a tent," he said carefully.

"Yeah, but if we bunk together in mine again, we can eat more." That answered two of Pike's most primal prayers at once.

"Cool. Thanks."

They conferred for another minute then grabbed the tokens from their packs and returned to Lenora.

"Well, that was rather unorthodox. Are you two combining your resources then?" Her smooth tone contained a touch of venom.

"Yeah," Pike said. "We'd like seven meals and a six-pack of beer. Please."

They each held out their yellow chips.

One of Lenora's perfect eyebrows rose and she turned to summon a minion with a wave. The one named Josh appeared, hurrying forward to take their requests and payment. Pike glared at his back, not having forgotten this was the same man who'd so coolly informed them they'd be pushed from a plane if they didn't jump.

"Sleep well," Lenora said. "I'll see you bright and early tomorrow for the start of the second leg of the race. As you both arrived at precisely the same time, you will both be allowed to commence together as well." She offered them a tight nod, then turned on her heel and strode off in the direction the staffer had come from.

"They must have a trailer or something," Mac muttered. "If they're offering up showers."

"Tempting one," Pike said.

"Not nearly as good as food. I'm so ready to binge."

"Thanks. You know, for sharing your tent again."

"Of course."

Pike held his breath and waited for something dreadful—a clap on the arm and a pronouncement of how like a brother he'd become to her. It didn't arrive and he found himself able to exhale.

In fifteen minutes' time the staffer reappeared with a helper, and they set up a folding card table and stacked it with seven covered aluminum trays, two sets of camp utensils and a six-pack of lousy domestic beer in cans.

"Thanksgiving," Mac murmured.

The staffers disappeared without a word and Mac and Pike stood on either side of the table, neither quite ready to dig in.

She took a noisy, deep breath. "I can smell it. It's actual food."

"What if it's, like…"

"Poisoned?" Mac ventured.

"Or rancid."

"Or wax."

Pike sighed. "Better find out." He grabbed the closest tray and uncrimped its edges to free the lid. He tossed it aside to reveal—

"Oh my God, is that mac and cheese?"

He nodded.

Mac opened another, full of steaming mashed potatoes and gravy and sliced turkey. They opened them all—ziti, chili, barbequed chicken, plus a couple of repeats.

"Oh my God," Mac repeated.

"This is so much better than socks or blankets or showers."

She nodded vigorously.

Before the food could get any cooler, they gorged.

Between courses, Pike entertained a glum thought. The Last Supper. He studied Mac, not thinking she was any more capable of turning Judas than he was. Though time would tell.

After twenty minutes, he collapsed onto a log before the fire, a new and exhausted man. He licked barbeque sauce off his fingers and accepted the can Mac passed him.

"To food," she said, sitting beside him. They tapped cans and chugged the first two beers.

"You know," he said, always the suspicious one, "I don't even care if, like, the challenge starts at one a.m. I can handle anything now."

"Food is just... Shit, food is the best."

He nodded. After another beer, he looked at her, buoyed nearly as much by her smile as by the warm grub. The beer knocked sentimental thoughts from his head. "It's nice to see you looking like the old Mac again."

"I feel like her again."

"I was worried before. After the Bridge Building thing, you seemed so bummed out. I thought at first it was since Daisey went home." He mumbled that bit. "But maybe you were just as tired and grumpy as me."

"No one's as grumpy as you," she teased, bumping him with her elbow.

"Yeah, true."

"And it definitely wasn't because of Daisey leaving."

Pike blinked down at his boots. "No?"

Mac laughed. "God, no. Jeez, you keep bringing that up. Did you think I was in love with him or something?"

"I dunno... Why then?"

She sighed, the sound of a woman three times her age. "I was upset because I cheated in that challenge."

His brows pinched together. "But you lost."

"I know. I sabotaged me and Daisey's raft."

Pike jolted. "What? Why?"

"Because I was pissed at him. And I was hoping if there was a vote to decide who left... Well, I knew you and Ian would want him gone too."

Pike stared at his feet. "Wow."

"Anyhow, I feel shitty about it."

"You shouldn't. That's exactly the kind of underhanded scheme anybody else would've cooked up in your position. If anything, I think you get bonus points for that."

"Maybe," she said. "But I don't want to be that person. I've never been that person. If I'm going to win, I want it to be because I tried the hardest, you know?"

"Well, I think what you did was fully in the spirit of this twisted game."

"I guess."

"Cheer up," Pike said, and nudged her shoulder. "I'm the mopey sad-sack, remember?"

She smiled, shaking her head.

"And all the creeps are gone. You did the right thing, okay? I mean, at least you didn't punch somebody in the face to get ahead."

Mac laughed, a faint, sweet noise barely audible over the crackling of the fire.

Pike unlaced his boots and tossed them aside, flexing his feet. Spurred by the pure intoxication of physical comfort, he tried to word an epic confession in his head. His heart throbbed, then hammered.

He cleared his throat. "Listen, Mac. I think you're... I think you're probably the coolest girl I've ever met."

She looked away, smirking.

"Not like, *cool.* Like you're the nicest, smartest, most positive person. And you don't let people get to you, even though you're way better than them."

Mac put her hand on his arm and she laughed, looking embarrassed by his praise. "God, Pike, enough."

He decided to cut it off there and spare them both the awkwardness of announcing that he had a hopeless crush on her. "I just want you to know that. I think you're pretty amazing. Club-rat or not."

"Well, thanks… I hate to break it to you, but you're way cooler." She took the can from his hand and shook it to confirm its emptiness before fetching and cracking the final two beers. As she passed Pike his can, their fingers brushed. Hers felt warm and rough against the cold, smooth aluminum.

"Thanks."

"You," she went on, "have traveled all over the place, and you save people's lives for a living. In war zones, which is badass. And you're from the city, and you dance better than I do, you're more exotic than me. You read *Hustler* instead of *Penthouse*—"

"Yeah, true."

"You've got *street cred*," she added, throwing down some made-up gang symbols with her hands. "So I hate to break it to you, Pike. But you're cooler."

"I disagree, but keep telling yourself that. Tell everyone that, actually. I won't stop you." As he drank his beer, that urge returned. The urge to tell her how he felt. He drummed the can with his fingertips, eyes on the fire.

"I bet they're done with us for the night," she said. "We should gather up some wood if we want to keep—"

"I like you, Mac."

She turned to face him, expression curious. "I know that."

"No, dummy. I *like* you, like you."

She frowned. "Oh."

Not sensing an impending reply, Pike sighed and drained his can. She grabbed his arm as he stood.

"Sit down. I wasn't done digesting what you said."

He sat. "Oh, right. Sorry. I thought that was an uncomfortable silence."

"No, not at all. Just surprised."

He cleared his throat and joined her in not knowing what to say. After a loaded, quiet minute, he concluded with, "I just wanted you to know, I guess. Since this thing's almost done. I guess it might make sharing a tent kinda weird."

She made a noise in her throat, an unrealized snort. "I'm not that delicate, Pike. In fact I'm flattered you feel that way."

"Oh. Well, good."

Making eye contact for the first time since his announcement, she offered a guilty smile. "You've got to know I'm, like, the camp skank."

"I don't care, Mac."

"And what Ian said, it *is* true—whatever he said happened between me and him."

"I don't care."

Two pairs of eyes went from hesitant to charged. Mac's gaze jumped all over Pike's face, his own attention drawn in a frantic loop between her eyes and lips and throat.

Her brows pinched together and her voice came out a whisper. "So you like me. For how long?"

"God… Since I first saw you. Then way worse after the dancing. You seriously didn't know? Everybody else did."

She shook her head. "You're a tough guy to read. And I'm not one of those people that look for little hidden signals from others. I'm not a subtle person."

Remembering her tactless crush on Daisey, Pike nodded. His feelings were surely as covert as a dog whistle to a girl as forward as Mac.

She bit her lip, gaze retreating to the woods over his shoulder.

Pike felt her go cold then and he pulled back a couple of inches. "Sorry."

"No, shut up." She looked back to his face. "I'm sorry. About what happened at the end of that stupid Capture the Flag challenge. That must have…"

Pike laughed and nodded, busted. "Yeah, that sucked. Well played, though."

"I wouldn't have played you that particular way if I'd known…you know…" Mac began, then trailed off. Pike held his tongue, giving her time to word whatever it was she needed to say to him. She stared at her hands and beer, the bonfire. She sighed heavily and met his stare. "I think you're very sexy."

He blinked, blindsided. "Oh."

Finally, that smile. "Don't look so surprised."

"You know it's me though, right? The short guy with the attitude problem who hasn't showered in a week?"

Mac nodded, leaning in just an inch closer. Pike's heart was pounding in an instant, brain disbelieving that this might actually be about to happen. He swallowed. "And my waist's about as big around as Daisey's neck."

"Shush."

She came even closer and Pike muttered, "I haven't got any Arbor Mist."

"I haven't got any peppermint schnapps."

He leaned in, as thrilled as always by that rare sensation of largeness he felt with her. Any second now, an air horn, an announcement from Lenora… But nothing.

He closed his eyes as it happened. She tasted like cheap beer, same as him. Her lips were cool and rough, breath warm. Pike felt something odd touch his elbow—her can. He slid it away and set it on the grass, nearly moaning aloud as her palm alighted on his arm. Those climbing calluses…way sexier than some silky-smooth, manicured hand. The smell of her skin and hair a million times more seductive than perfume.

When her other hand touched his neck, he groaned against her lips. He let her feel his scar, just as he was reveling in all of her smaller imperfections. She let him deep inside, let him kiss her the way he'd been dying to for days, a kiss that didn't belong to two strangers but to lovers who'd known each other for years. That was how it felt to him. No clicking teeth, no trying one another on. They just knew—every angle and taste and gasp of air.

Pike shoved his fingers inside her vest's arm holes, palming her warm shoulders. Her body was as antsy as his. Hands pawed his arms and back, her knee bumping his as they devoured one another. She turned to straddle the log and he did the same, mourning her mouth for the handful of seconds they were separated. For a beat they stared at one another and he held his breath, fearing her lapse in judgment may be over. But no, their faces came together once more, hungrier than before. He felt the weight of her leg as she swung it over his thigh, and her mouth swallowed Pike's surprised moan. Before he could understand it, her thighs were hugging his waist, their mouths blissfully level. Their chests brushed, surely filling the doctors' tapes with rustling to drown out the panting. His dick was hard and trapped at a funny angle, but fuck it—he'd been in pain from wanting her for a week now.

The kissing transformed, switching from frantic to exploratory. It reminded him to slow down, to savor, to appreciate that this miracle was actually occurring, instead of attacking her as a dog might an unguarded platter of steaks. He recorded the shape of her bottom lip between his, memorized the feel of her jaw in his hands.

As his body slowed, his mind raced. He imagined them in the tent, sleeping bags spread like a slippery nylon imitation of satin sheets. It seemed Mac was lost in similar scenarios—her hips fidgeted against him, beginning to grind.

Pike broke away. "Hang on." He shoved a hand between them to adjust his erection then pulled her back against him. "Sorry."

"Don't be sorry."

She kissed him deeply and braced her forearms on his shoulders. Pike groaned as she moved in his lap, stroking him between far too many layers.

He moaned.

She answered with more glorious friction, hips gyrating and torturing. Pike assumed at first this was for his benefit, then he noticed her breathing, heavy and rough, distracted little strokes of her thumbs against his neck...

Holy fuck, she was into this. She was into *him*. It tossed Pike right over the edge, far from the past few minutes' reverence and back into the greedy kisses from earlier. He fumbled between them, tugging the zipper of her vest down so he could slide his hands around her waist. He felt the muscles of her lower back writhing as she rubbed against him, strong and shameless and sexy, so exactly *her*.

"God, Mac."

"Call me Casey."

His record skipped. "Okay. Call me Ross."

She kissed him again, reminding him with a fresh thrill how easily they fit together. Heat filled him—not comforting, gooey warmth, but fire. And fuck if Pike didn't like fire. It was eating him alive right now, burning up through his spine and boiling his brain, sadly not singeing away their clothes or melting the stupid mikes.

She let him touch her breasts through her shirt and her annoyingly unrevealing bra, let him palm her ass. Everything she was—climber, rafter, dancer—shaped this body. He wouldn't have traded her rough hands or hard arms or short hair for any glamorous, calendar-worthy woman. She was too perfect.

He wanted wondrous and horrible things all at once, to worship and defile and possess her with his own body, everything sweet and dirty and sloppy that sex could be. He would, too. Tonight, in that tent. He could feel it. Ditch the mikes for an hour and just be alone, using each other in the most generous ways imaginable. Alone and equal and utterly separate from what went on inside the glass walls of the stupid Ant Farm. All that bullshit—he wanted it gone, stripped officially from whatever went on tonight.

He pulled away just long enough to form a syllable against her cheek. "Mac."

"Yeah?"

"Sorry, Casey. I just want you to know…whatever's about to happen… I'm not going to let you win tomorrow or anything—"

She stiffened in his arms. "Excuse me?"

"This isn't going to change anything about the competition or—"

She scooted awkwardly from his lap back to the log, eyes dark in the firelight and narrowed in his direction. He knew that look. He'd earned that look any number of times from women and never saw it coming, never knew exactly which foot he'd crammed into his mouth until it was too late.

"Mac—"

She stood before he could continue.

He got to his feet, body struggling to pump the blood back to his brain. "I think you heard something I wasn't trying to say."

She squinted two angry eyes at him. "I think I just heard you call me a whore."

"No, I didn't—"

"'Slut' I can deal with, Pike, even if it's not my idea of pillow talk. But I wasn't messing around with you because I was looking for an easy win tomorrow."

"I know you weren't. That's not what I meant."

She locked her arms across her chest, looking a heck of a lot taller than five-one suddenly. "What *did* you mean, then?"

"I just wanted you to know that whatever was going on there, it's separate from the competition. I wanted it to be just about…us. You and me."

"Then why would you even bring the stupid competition up in the first place?"

Pike just stared at her for a few seconds, terrified whatever he might say next would only dig the hole even deeper.

She shook her head, posture loosening but not by much. "Jesus, you look for the worst in everything. Charming to know that includes me as well." She left him to walk to their pile of supplies. She rummaged for a moment before straightening and marching toward the woods.

"Where are you going?"

She aimed herself between the trees. "For a smoke. I'll see you later."

He sat frozen, unsure if he was supposed to grovel or give her space. But after a few moments of torturous inactivity, he scrambled for his boots and yanked them on, laces ignored. Mac was already gone and he grabbed his entire case, no time to search for his flashlight should he need it.

"Mac!"

Her footsteps replied for her, crunching through the undergrowth. Pike jogged after her. "Mac, wait! Jesus. Let me talk to you." As if his mouth was likely to do him any favors—

Pain flashed through his toes first as he tripped, then his forearms as he hit the ground, his chin as it struck dirt. Worst in his leg, blinding and sharp. "Ow! Fuck." As Pike rose to kneel the pain exploded and he tipped over, shocked into silence.

His hands grasped at his thigh and he felt the dead branch imbedded in his flesh. "Fuck fuck fuck."

Snapping into professional mode, he blocked out the physical sensations and measured the damage. The branch was maybe a centimeter thick. He wiggled it and let a scream burst from his lungs. Yes. Fine. Good. Not very deep. He sat up enough to ease it out with a gasp then collapsed back against the ground.

Mac arrived at a run. "Jesus, Pike!" Her frightened face looked blue in the bright moonlight.

"It's okay. Don't freak. It's only a puncture. No bones sticking out or anything gross, just hurts like a motherfucker."

She nodded frantically, eyes on the blood Pike could feel dampening his pant leg. Suddenly her expression changed as though someone had injected her with instant-onset calming serum. "Tell me what to do."

"Bring my case over." He pointed to where it had landed.

Mac pocketed her pipe and weed and fetched the case, setting it by his side. "What else? Do you want some pot?"

He'd have laughed, if not for the searing pain. He sat up and took things out of the case—gauze and alcohol and swabs, clotting agent, surgical scissors, sutures. "I might need a few stitches. And I'll probably need your hands while I'm sewing them."

He expected her to wince or gasp, but she merely nodded, steely and calm. "Whatever you need. Jesus, I'm sorry. This is my fault."

"No, it's... Well, anyhow, it's going to be gross."

"Just tell me what to do."

"Get a medical qualification so I can shoot myself full of morphine and let you do the dirty work," Pike said.

She smiled her apology.

"Just hold tight." He rummaged for his flashlight and Mac held the beam on his hands as he ripped the tear in his pant leg wide open. The wound was worse than he'd expected—a ragged inch-long gouge. He got the site ready, disinfecting the hell out of it and nearly passing out from the sting. He numbed the area with analgesic spray and tidied the torn skin with the scissors. Mac obediently pinched the wound together as he sutured himself. She swabbed him when he asked, handed him what he needed.

He got the gash sewn up with eight stitches and breathed a sigh of relief, only to realize how much the fucking thing hurt now that his task was complete.

"Good work, Mac."

"Done? Thank God. That was disgusting."

"That was nothing, but thanks for your help." He wrapped his leg and gave it a press, triggering a sharp pain.

She clicked the flashlight off and they sat together in moonlit silence for a minute or more as their collective adrenaline dissipated.

"You can have your morphine now," Mac said. "Or that pot I offered."

"I'm cool, thanks though. Wouldn't turn down another six-pack, that's for fucking sure."

"Me neither."

"Well," Pike said, needing the conversation to keep his attention off his throbbing leg. "If we end up in that footrace to the finish, I think you've got it in the bag. I'm going to be limping something nasty tomorrow."

Mac's eyebrows merged into one judgmental line. "You aren't seriously thinking of finishing?"

"Yeah, of course I am. It didn't hit an artery or anything."

"But there's a hole in your leg! We might have another twenty miles to hike."

"I don't think you know how bad I want that money, Mac." His hackles rose and he spoke before he thought hard enough about it. "Did you think you'd just won?"

"No, I wasn't thinking about that at all."

Pike held his tongue. His cynical self was still grappling with his idealistic one and he didn't know which he truly believed yet.

Mac sighed angrily and let her top half fold over her knees.

"I didn't mean that," Pike said. "I'm sorry."

She raised her chin to stare at him. Her face looked so tired Pike could imagine how she'd look at forty. He liked it.

"I'm sorry, Mac. I know you wouldn't ever think that way."

"Damn straight."

They fell silent, suspended in communal exhaustion while Pike put off the inevitability of standing. Mac spoke five or more minutes later.

"What were you trying to say before? When I got pissed and stomped off into the woods? All that stuff about you and me fooling around not having anything to do with the competition?"

"I was trying to say..." Pike paused. "I wanted you to know the sex, or whatever we were heading toward, that it wasn't about me trying to manipulate you, or use the prize to..."

"To bribe me into fucking you?"

"I dunno. To make you think maybe I was playing some kind of game like that. So yeah, sort of."

"You think I'd even entertain something as sleazy as that?"

"No. I just didn't want you to think I had some kind of agenda about it. I didn't want *you* to think *I* was being a sleaze. Shit, Mac. I was just trying to be romantic."

He caught a shift in her body, her shoulders relaxing, the angry creases in her forehead smoothing.

"Why would I think that?" she asked. "Why would I assume you had an agenda?"

"Because everybody here, or a lot of the people, they were pretty cutthroat. I didn't want you to think I had some scheme in the back of my head, because a lot of those jerk-offs...they would've."

"Why would I think that? Pike, you're the most honest guy in this thing. I was messing around with you *because* I think you're a good guy. And for the record, I didn't do what I did with Daisey to get ahead, either."

"I never said you did—"

"I did it because I thought Daisey'd be the best lay of my life. And what I did with Ian was basically just a dare, to me anyhow."

"I believe you."

Pike watched Mac heave out a gigantic sigh and rub her face with the balls of her hands. Then something she'd said hit him as hard as one of his mother's slaps, knocking his thoughts loose and inflating a balloon of hope in his middle. He kept his mouth shut while Mac rolled her neck from side to side. She sighed, sounding calm again.

"Help me up?" he asked.

She stood and he grabbed her arm and made it to his feet. He put weight on the injured leg and it didn't feel too awful. Then he tried a step and his thigh shrieked in protest. "Oh, fuck me."

"That bad?"

"At one angle, yeah. But it's okay."

Mac closed Pike's case for him. She carried it in one hand and let him lean on her other shoulder.

"So…" Pike began, then chickened out.

She sighed again, so theatrical he knew she'd officially mellowed from this latest drama. "So what?"

He hobbled a few more feet. "So Daisey wasn't the best lay of your life?"

She laughed, the sweetest sound ever. "No. Far from it. I mean, in the moment… Oh, never mind. You probably don't want to hear about it anyhow."

Pike grinned against the pain. "Are you kidding? That's like a birthday present, you saying that."

She laughed again.

"I know you think I'm an honest guy and above all the bullshit that's gone down here, but seriously, you can tell me Daisey was shit in bed all night long and I promise I won't ever rise above the sick joy it gives me."

"Fine… But I think I'll keep the details to myself, all the same. Nice to see you stooping to that, though, Dr. Honorable."

Pike nodded. He concentrated on his steps as the firelight grew close between the trees.

"I'm sorry if I overreacted," she said. "Especially since now you're limping because of it."

"Whatever. Not the first time my sweet nothings have fallen short of the mark with women."

They returned to the log and Pike gingerly lowered himself to sitting. "I'm hoping this means we're good again? That I can still share your tent?"

She smiled. "Yup. All you had to do was hari-kari yourself. I'm a cinch to win over. Sorry it interrupted…you know." She nodded her head from side to side, seeming to mean the two of them, there on the log.

"What? You wanted to dance some more?"

She nudged his shoulder. "You know. Sorry our little hot-and-heavy session had to end the way it did."

"Mac, if it meant I stood a chance of getting my hands up your shirt or down your pants, I'd happily hack my own foot off right now."

She made a face, looking equally amused and grossed out. "I'm not gonna test that resolve. C'mere." She beckoned his face to hers. Kissing him light and lingering, she took his mind off the throbbing pain in his leg for a few perfect seconds.

She mussed his hair, the gesture feeling remarkably familiar. "I'll get the tent set up."

MAC

SHE SLEPT TERRIBLY, weird dreams full of yellow things—boxes, tokens, paper squares and paintballs and flags and bandannas. Every few minutes Pike broke in and woke her, groaning softly in his sleep. The ibuprofen he'd taken clearly hadn't helped much with his leg.

Eventually her eyes opened and stayed open, and judging from the light coming through the tent, the sun was already halfway up the sky. She was as dead-tired as when she'd lay down, perhaps more so, if that was possible. Her head felt heavy, brain slow. This was bound to be an irritable day. More of whatever nonsense the doctors had planned on top of this fatigue, then other stresses when she and Pike became enemies in the final stretch.

Still, whatever. Just one day to get through, then even a plane would be a welcome change, if only for the dry air and a soft-ish seat and a toilet. Laughable that she'd ever imagined she'd want to go camping at the end of this competition.

Autonomous as always, her body had curled around Pike's in the night, her chest to his back and her arm around his side, their hands nearly touching. With her face near his neck, she could smell him. A very nice smell. It reminded her of the way his mouth had tasted last night, behind the beer. Flavors and scents elementally Pike.

It was easy to mesh with him...easy to talk and joke, to dance and kiss and sleep and simply to be. He fit in a way that Daisey never could have, as though custom-built to put her at ease. It was bound to make the final moments of this Objective and this entire trip painful.

On the topic of painfulness, Mac's wrist hurt. She flexed her hand, feeling a funny tweak there. Oh well. A finite number of hours to get through. She could grin and bear anything today. And tonight, tomorrow morning, whenever this challenge wrapped and they were free, she might be a half-million dollars richer.

The thought cooled her body even against the warm comfort of Pike's. Might as well get up and screw her head on straight before the drama began anew.

Confusion struck as Mac rolled over. A fresh pinch at her wrist, a tug, a startled snort from her tentmate as he woke.

"What the—" She stared at her hand, at the metal bracelet cuffing it to Pike's. "Pike."

He too rolled, jerking her hand down. "Whoa."

"Wake up. They handcuffed us."

He sat up and yelped, then rubbed his leg through the sleeping bag. Frowning blearily, he held up his wrist and looked to Mac. "Oh fuck. Seriously?"

"GOOD MORNING!"

Mac screamed and their tent flap dropped, revealing Lenora's smiling face as she stooped to address them.

Pike narrowed his eyes against the sun. "Jesus, dude, turn your mike off. We're right here."

"Don't you two look cozy?" Lenora's gaze jumped between them. "As you've surely now noticed, you've been cuffed."

"Yeah," Mac said, glaring down at their linked hands.

"The doctors decided that since you both seem so keen to stick together, you ought to be bound by the wrist. We trust today's hike will give you plenty of time to reassess your priorities. Now would you please join me outside?"

Mac took a deep breath, not feeling capable of absorbing any more information. Her head felt distinctly funny. Swimmy. Still, she and Pike fumbled to shed their sleeping bags and managed to crawl out of the tent and into the cool morning air. Mac had ditched her dirty pants before going to bed and she shivered, surely looking stupid standing there in her underwear.

"Now, never fear," Lenora said. "Shackled or not, the race is still on. Your cuffs will be removed when you reach the final stretch." Her eyes narrowed for just a second, something unwholesome glinting there. "That's your game, isn't it? Stick together until the last possible moment?"

"How far until the final stretch?" Mac asked.

"About fifteen miles from here."

"Oh, *great*—"

"Or a mere eleven if you can manage to swim across that lake." Lenora waved a hand majestically in the direction of a massive body of water to the west, just visible through the trees. "And no maps today. It's very simple. The final leg of the competition begins at that signal fire." She aimed her finger and Mac squinted at the tiny black line snaking through the sky in the far distance. Shit, that'd be tough to keep track of in the woods.

"Your cuffs will come off when you reach that fire, and you may then turn on each other however you see fit."

Mac glanced nervously at Pike but his eyes were glued to Lenora.

"Also, in light of how *close* the two of you seem to have become, the doctors want to make certain you understand this is still a competition. With that in mind, be assured that this race is not designed with friendly loopholes. If you're entertaining any thoughts of finishing together and splitting the prize, be warned that the doctors have orchestrated the finale not to allow such an outcome."

Mac and Pike glanced at each other, and she bet he was wondering the same thing she was—would they have attempted that? A tie?

"The only way you two will walk away as equals is if neither of you wins the money."

Mac frowned, unable to imagine a circumstance in which a forfeit would be preferable to a fight. Then again, the doctors weren't lacking in creativity.

"That is all," Lenora said, and clapped once with finality.

"Breakfast?" Mac asked.

"Oh, I'm sure you two had plenty to eat last night," Lenora replied smoothly. "Best of luck." Her attention dropped to their hands for a beat before she flashed them each a sunny grin, turned and disappeared into the woods.

"Psycho," Pike muttered.

Mac nodded at the mike clipped to his collar. He took it in his free hand and held it to his mouth. "Psycho," he repeated, louder.

"Do you... Does your head feel funny?" Mac asked. "I feel really dim-witted."

Pike nodded. "You think they drugged us to get these on?" He jingled the chain that connected them.

"I do believe they did."

"Charming. Yet another bit of what-the-fuckery I missed when I read the waiver."

Mac glanced at his torn, bloody pants. "How's your leg feeling?"

Pike shifted from foot to foot. "Tender. Real tender."

"Sorry."

He shrugged. "Well, what do you think? Hike or swim?"

She stared into the distance, calming. Fifteen miles was far, but finite. The end was literally in sight. "With all our stuff and your leg? Hike, probably."

"Yeah. I should probably keep my gash dry."

"Which is too bad. Our bodies are pretty well synchronized." She blushed at her own wording, reliving for a moment the movements of their locked hips. "I mean, because we're both on the small side. And coordinated."

"Yeah."

Mac pondered everything that had gone on in the past twenty-four hours then laughed.

"What?"

"I was just thinking, it's lucky we ended up sleeping with our clothes on. In case we woke up *naked* and cuffed together. I wouldn't have even been able to get a bra on."

Pike laughed, then jerked his arm up and yanked Mac's wrist by mistake. "Sorry."

Mac knew that little mannerism already—Pike touched his scar when he was nervous.

"Shit. Figures they'd cuff my dominant hand. You aren't a lefty, are you?"

She shook her head.

"Well, that's something. You're the alpha in this two-man pack, then."

"I guess we better get going. Get to work training for this modified three-legged race." She jangled their handcuffs.

"Three-legged is right," Pike said. "Sorry my limping's going to slow us down. Going up hills is really going to suck."

They got to work disassembling the tent and managed to not lose any eyes between them, wrestling with the poles.

"This'll make going to the bathroom interesting," Mac said.

"Fuck, I didn't even think of that."

She laughed. "What a sexy date, between the flesh wounds and the handcuffs and the peeing."

"Yeah, very kinky. Fucking pervert doctors. Yeah, *you*," he added to his mike.

After twenty laborious minutes they had their things organized, and Pike checked on his wound, cleaning and re-wrapping it with the cooperation of Mac's hand.

She looked to each of their packs and frowned. "Oh shit."

"What?"

"We can't get our bags onto both shoulders."

Pike concurred. "Oh shit."

"Well, I guess we could each cut one of our straps." Another ten minutes lost as she and Pike dissected their bags and fumbled to re-tie the severed straps.

"Ready?" he asked, picking up his case.

"Here, give me that."

"It's pretty heavy."

"I don't care. You might need that arm for balance."

"Maybe. I probably need a walking stick too." He handed it over.

Pike checked the direction of the signal fire with his compass and they limped down to the water. They brushed their teeth with some effort and filled their canteens, and he found a decent branch to walk with, which helped their progress. Helped their hands too, both clamped to the branch so they didn't jerk each other's wrists with every step. Slowly but surely they found a workable rhythm, skirting the lake. It didn't have a nice, pebbly beach like the other one, and they had to wind through the edge of the woods for much of it.

And slow was okay. Mac's feet ached after a week of this nonsense and she didn't mind taking it easy. As a small comfort, it felt good just having Pike's warm fist butted against hers.

After the first mile, Pike laughed, pulling Mac from her thoughts.

"What?"

He sighed. "Just this whole situation. I can't stop wondering who these assholes are—the 'doctors' in charge. Like, what do they even want to get out of this experiment? Out of punishing us for being decent to each other?"

"I guess cooperation isn't enough of a stress test."

"Everything's been set up to make everyone as uncomfortable and distrustful as possible. It's not shocking or anything, but Jesus. It's fucking exhausting."

"And how many months do your tours of duty last?"

He laughed. "I know. But this is different. This stress is a different kind of mind-fuck. The danger and the bickering, all the drama, it's all because of the money. It's pretty petty."

"Half a million dollars isn't petty to me," Mac said.

"No, I know. Me neither... Shit, I don't even know what I'm saying anymore. I guess it's working. You win," he said to his mike. "I'm officially cracking up."

"Leah would have cracked," Mac said, picturing it. She remembered something Daisey had said that very first day. "Did you read *Lord of the Flies*?"

"Sure."

"Who's who, do you think? You must be Jack. Oh wait, no...he went all power hungry. Maybe that's Daisey. You're Ralph. Or maybe I'm Ralph..."

"You're the nice one, who's kind to everyone and doesn't try to take over everything." Pike said. "I can't remember any of their names."

"Ian would be Roger. He's the sadistic boy who murders Piggy. I wonder who Piggy is..."

"Lenora's the boar-head-on-a-stick," Pike said.

Mac laughed. "Or maybe *she's* Jack. Maybe the boar head is the money, or the doctors."

"Deep, Machiniak."

She nodded. "I always liked that book. I bet I've read it four times. I always wished I might get marooned somewhere exciting on a field trip gone awry. God, that's sad—praying for an adventure so badly I would've settled for *that*."

"Sounds to me like your life was nothing but adventure. Rafting and climbing and camping..."

She shrugged. "I guess. But it was also like that was all just my backyard. Huge, but I knew every tree and rock and stream by the time I was ten. When I'd sleep over at somebody's house who had TV, *that* seemed exciting to me. Anything not like how I lived. Cities with all that glamour and huge, fancy apartments."

"Not all cities."

"Then when I hit my teens and got to experience a little bit of it, meeting new people in high school and trying new things... I realized all that crunchy hippie nature stuff is, like, engrained in me. I tried really hard to enjoy hanging out at the mall, but the novelty wore off fast. I just wanted to be outside. So, any chance to be outdoors—just not in New Mexico—that's exciting."

"Well, you got it."

"I guess I did."

After a few minutes' silence, Mac could make out Pike's breathing, slow and deep and strained, and not merely from his injury.

"I can hear you thinking," she said. "What's on your mind?"

He swallowed, brown eyes trained on the ground, scanning for hazards. "What do you think would happen if we *did* try to tie? If we like, walked across the finish line hand-in-hand or grabbed the final token or whatever, at exactly the same time?"

Mac smiled at him, sadness overtaking her.

"You don't want to split it, do you?"

She sighed. "It's not that, Pike. I'd split it with you in a second. I mean, who really needs five hundred grand all for themselves? But she just said they won't let it end like that. If we tried, I bet we'd get disqualified or something."

His pursed lips told her he found her logic sound.

"Plus didn't they try that in one of the Harry Potter books and it totally backfired?"

Pike shrugged, and offered her a tired grin. "I didn't read them."

"Well, I did. And it totally did backfire. We're going to get to the end of this thing and there'll be a humongous hedge maze." She held out her arm, waving Pike's case. "And one of us will end up magicked to death in a creepy graveyard."

"Jesus, I thought those books were for kids."

She focused on the trail and Pike followed suit. For a half-hour or more there was nothing but the sound of their feet snapping twigs in the undergrowth, the tinny jingle of the cuff chain. Then a thought popped from Mac's lips.

"Do you think Rory and Leah have gotten in touch?"

"I can't imagine anybody could stop them."

"Well, I hope they do. I liked them."

Pike nodded. "Bit of a haul, New York to New Zealand. Or vice-versa."

"Bit of a haul, Santa Fe to Detroit. Or Fallujah or wherever, for that matter. If you and I wanted a little reunion, I mean. Bet you I'm the only Casey Machiniak in New Mexico though. Very easy to look up."

Pike laughed. "Well, if you Google me, don't be put off by the fact that there's a Ross Pike in the state pen."

"Oh right. Are you a junior then?"

"Third, actually."

"Wow, Dr. Ross Pike III. That's so distinguished."

"Oh yeah, quite a legacy."

"Think there'll be a fourth some day?"

Pike frowned. "Jeez, I dunno. I'm pretty neutral on the whole kids issue. It'll only make me sound like more of a gloomy sad-sack, but the world's pretty fucked. I'm not sure how I feel about bringing a kid into all that."

She nodded. "Me neither. Not because of the world being fucked, just because I feel like I haven't done anything yet. I think I'd be okay at it, but it's at least ten years off my radar."

"Yeah. You should travel. Meet some exotic dude who, like, runs a safari in Africa. Start some outdoor adventure conglomerate."

Mac laughed and bit back an earnest thought. Pike was exotic to her. His accent might not be the most poetic and his worldliness more duty than wanderlust, but she liked him. She *liked* him, liked him. She liked him more than she'd ever liked Daisey. Daisey was a school-bus-yellow Hummer, huge and obvious and *too much*. Impossible to ignore, but also rather tacky. That made Pike a mid-nineties sedan, grumpy but reliable. Again, he fit. Very easy to park.

"Whatcha thinking about?" There was an edge to Pike's voice, one that told her his leg must hurt, and badly. She realized then that masculinity didn't have to hit one in the face to be powerful. Pike's was quiet and unselfconscious, and more authentic because of it.

"Nothing," she said. "I could use a break, if you don't mind. Maybe just head down to the lake and fill our canteens."

"Sure." They changed course, struggling down a steep slope to where the woods met the water.

"How far do you think we've gone?" Mac asked.

"Shit...maybe three miles?"

She groaned. The distant smoke seemed as far away as ever. "Bet they're moving that stupid fire, the closer we get," she muttered.

"Heh, you sound like me, grumpy-pants."

They coordinated sitting on a flat expanse of rock by the water's edge. Pike undid Mac's pack strap and she returned the favor, and they dumped their loads to either side. She gave her spine a good twist.

"Can't you just picture it?" she asked. "Lenora pulling the fire farther away in a little red wagon or something..."

"She gives me the creeps."

"Me too. She didn't use to, but since last night… Yeah, I'm with you there."

"She's given me the creeps since Twenty-One Questions," Pike said. "It's that smile, dude. Vanna White with a little sprinkle of Hannibal Lecter, watching us all getting outed for our worst memories."

Mac nodded. Pike had set his stick aside and she felt a little zap, noticing how close their hands rested on the rock, linked but not touching. She let her knuckles brush his, for no other reason but to feel it. Their cuffs clicked.

"How's your wrist?" he asked.

"Getting kinda raw. But whatever. Home stretch."

"Home stretch to the home stretch," he corrected.

"Yeah." A dozen more miles, perhaps a bit farther once the cuffs were removed. Mac considered the man seated to her left. A week ago they hadn't existed for one another, now here they were, shackled together, the final two survivors in this strangest of contests. Friends. Something bordering on lovers. Perhaps most intimate of all, soon-to-be-enemies.

As much as she dreaded the removal of the cuffs, it also got her blood pumping.

Without thinking about it, Mac laced her fingers with Pike's and raised his hand to her lips, kissing his knuckles. Their eyes met as she set their hands down. His gaze was steady and calm, but Mac stared down at their interlaced fingers, suddenly shy.

"I'll miss you when this is all over," she mumbled.

"You too."

"If we did ever hang out someday, it'd be weird, wouldn't it? You and me all clean… I don't even know what you usually dress like," she said as she realized it.

"Same to you."

"This isn't too far off, club nights notwithstanding." She stared at her bare legs, way overdue for a shave. She looked to Pike's face and touched his chin. "You inherit all that stubble from your dad's side?"

He smiled. "Yeah, I guess so. I'd trade beard-making abilities for more height though."

"You're tall to me."

Pike's smile tightened and his eyes drifted toward the water. "You, um… You make me feel tall."

"I'll bet."

"No, like… Never mind. I meant it to sound all poetic. I'm not much good at that, I guess."

She considered that, perplexed that Pike should feel like a small person. "You're a bigger man than Daisey," she offered.

He laughed, looking embarrassed.

"No, really. My turn to be a lousy poet. I think you're very impressive, Ross Pike. And I think you're a good kisser. A very good kisser."

His eyes met hers, brown as stout beer; nearly black, even in the sunshine. If they ever had a kid, Mac thought idly, it'd be short, with dark hair and eyes. Excellent dancer.

When Pike didn't move, she did it for him, craning her neck to press her mouth to his. His hand held hers tighter, body otherwise still as stone. After half a minute he spoke, right against her lips.

"I think I'm probably in love with you."

She didn't have any words to share that would do anything except detract from his perfect ones, so she answered with her body. They kissed deep and slow, jaws angling, free hands seeking faces. God, they fit.

He fussed between their chests and Mac looked down in time to watch him unclip his mike and toss it aside. She followed suit. She looked around them, knowing what was about to happen. "Sleeping bags?"

He nodded. With a graceless joint effort, they got their bags free from their packs and unrolled them, one on top of the other.

"Here." Mac sat and he did the same. "What's comfortable?"

Between their cuffed wrists and Pike's leg, it took some trial and error to find a good position, but soon they settled on their sides, already kissing even as their arms and hands fidgeted for a workable arrangement.

Amid all the clean, cool, fresh air, Pike smelled like sex. He tasted like need. The deep, throaty noises that slipped from his mouth to Mac's sounded like everything a man ought to.

"I love your voice," she murmured against his lips.

"I love your... Shit, I love everything about you."

She pushed his shirt up and held in a laugh, realizing how awkward this entire experience was—Pike injured, both of them filthy and exhausted, possibly being recorded, hard rock beneath them...handcuffed, so they couldn't even get their shirts off. Fuck it. She shoved the hem of his tee up to his armpit and stroked his bare stomach and chest, skin smooth and firm, his entire body warm and responsive. His mouth grew hungrier—dirty and greedy. She thrilled to the feeling of his tongue teasing hers, and the feeling of such a self-possessed man turning so unmistakably frantic.

"What do you want?" she asked.

A sigh answered her, Pike's breath warming her lips as he gathered his thoughts. "I don't even know. I just want *you*. Anything. Whatever you're cool with."

She answered him back with her touch, drawing his cuffed hand right along with hers as she found his belt. He returned the threat, fingers toying with the snap of her shorts. It dissolved into clumsiness, fingers pinched by the chain as they fought to undress one another. Pike's canvas belt had a metal clasp, military-style, and she heard his breath suck in as she disengaged it. He lowered her zipper. The aggression pumping through her body pleaded for an outlet and she took his lip between her teeth. It earned her a deep, rumbling groan that only sharpened the ache pounding between her thighs.

She wiggled her hips, fidgeting until they managed to get her shorts down her calves. She pushed them the rest of the way off with either foot, along with her boots. Next were Pike's ripped and ruined pants, eased down his legs more gently, mindful of the thick bandage wrapped around his thigh. The white cotton stood out against his golden skin. Mac stole a glance at his crotch as he struggled with his boots. Predictably practical gray boxer-briefs tented by the erection she'd ground against the previous evening. Steady, reliable, honest Pike—horny as a teenager despite his wound and the outrageous circumstances.

She felt powerful, having done this to him. Surprised and flattered and grateful. She felt something else, as well—adrenaline.

As her fingers traced the waistband of his shorts, she murmured, "We're going to be rivals again in a few hours." She felt guilty saying it, but it gave her an undeniable high.

Pike nodded, eyes locked between their bodies on her flirting fingers.

"It's sort of sexy," she admitted. "Fucking the enemy. Is that awful of me to say?"

His attention stayed glued to her fingers. "I wasn't really listening. All I heard was 'fucking'."

She laughed. "Good." Ending the torture, she cupped her hand over his cock. "Wow." Hard. Harder than Mac knew a man could get. Pike moaned as she stroked him, the hand linked to hers shaking intensely enough to jingle their chain.

His cuffed hand tugged hers along with it as he pushed his waistband down. She took him in both her small palms, memorizing his smooth, dark, hot skin, his soft hair, the stiffness of his flesh and the slick fluid beading at his head.

He set his hand on hers, joining the strokes without dictating them. "Oh God."

"You feel amazing."

He didn't reply, looking pained as he watched. She squeezed him and his eyes closed, lips parting.

Pike returned the touch with his other hand, the pads of three fingers finding her clit through her panties. Her breath hitched, nerves electrified by the contact.

"Pike."

His caresses were cautious at first, or distracted. Then, just as they had the night before, their bodies clicked. She knew how to stroke him, as sure as he knew how to tease her. As his hand dipped inside her underwear she shut her eyes, held her breath until his fingertips found her.

Pike's hips began to move, small motions that thrust his cock into her pulls. She mirrored him, moving against his fingers. Two bodies remarkably attuned, already telling Mac how good they'd be without all these hands in the way. Pike's fingers slid lower, finding her lips. He moaned and she could feel how wet she was, and how excited it got him.

Impatience eclipsed the cautious explorations. She tugged at his shorts and Pike took the hint. They shed their underwear together in a clumsy rush. Mac grabbed his case by the handle and hauled it closer, flipping the latches and rooting for a condom. His eyes followed everything.

She paused as she got the package open. Oh right—unlubricated. No matter. She had them covered.

As demurely as possible, she spat in her hand. Pike groaned as she slicked her palm down the smooth skin of his cock, a gorgeous, pained noise. He took the rubber from her and slid it down his erection.

As he rolled her onto her back, excitement sizzled through her body. They got their joined hands arranged, Pike's palm braced against the ground, her fingers clutching his wrist beside the cuff. She angled her hips and parted her legs, hugging her calves to his ass. She felt and heard it when he stopped breathing—his body lowering, cock brushing against her lips.

"Pike, your leg."

"I can't even feel it. Trust me."

"You sounded like it hurt."

"It doesn't hurt. That's probably the sound of my head exploding, realizing this is actually happening."

"Oh. Good."

"You ready?"

She stroked his arm with her free hand. "I'm ready."

He nodded, attention trained on the miniscule space between then. Angling his cock, he pushed. He slid inside smooth and easy, as though they'd done this a thousand times before, as if they'd spent the last five years mastering each other's bodies.

After a few slow, testing thrusts, he sank in deep and held there. Mac released her breath and touched his neck and face, marveling. She felt his weight on her and appreciated the differences in their sizes.

Pike eased out and slid back in. He started them out slow and Mac joined him, meeting his hips with hers to punctuate each thrust. He read her mind or her body, picking up his pace, taking her a bit rougher. Rough was good. Rough to match that charming scowl he often wore, rough to match his hometown and his chosen profession.

He cleared his throat, scattering her thoughts. "What should I... What do you like?"

She didn't even care about coming. It wasn't about that, as it had been with Daisey, when it had been about nothing but pleasure and talking her way into his pants and using him. Now she couldn't give a shit. She just wanted to *see* Pike, watch him come apart and know it was *her* he was so worked up over. She wanted to revel in how right they were, how innately her body knew how to move with his.

"I don't care, Pike. I mean Ross... Actually no, I mean Pike." Definitely just Pike. She looked down between their bodies then, finding that his knee had slid off the nylon. "Watch your leg."

"Fuck my leg."

Fair enough. She let it all go and surrendered to whatever he needed.

Pike found his rhythm and the steady, uniform thrusts of his hips reminded her of just what perfect mastery he had over his body.

"You look amazing," she said.

"Please," he mumbled. "Tell me what you need."

Ah, chivalry. "I don't care. I just want this—getting to watch you."

"I wanna make you come," Pike said, sounding close to the edge himself.

"Okay. I'll try." She slid her free hand down her belly to her mound to rub her clit with her middle two fingers. Pike watched, his face full of fascination, the look of a man seeing all this for the first time.

"Here." He braced himself on a single strong arm and nudged her hand out of the way. His hips never missed a thrust. Two fingertips stroked her clit in perfect time. "Like that?"

"A little lighter."

Stroking turned to grazing and Mac melted. "Like that. Exactly like that." Hand free to explore, she surveyed his arm with its sculpted, locked muscle. The hard knot of his shoulder, smooth skin of his side beneath his shirt. The pleasure grew against his fingers, hot and electric. "Faster."

His hips and fingers sped in tandem, giving her precisely what she craved—proof of what he could do. Beyond the fiery touch of his fingers on her clit, she zeroed in on his cock. Smooth, quick, deep thrusts, exactly right. Exactly Pike, she was learning. Head full of grumpy ethics, body full of surprises.

As the pleasure sharpened to a mean, greedy ache against his fingers, she stared at his face, at all those stern features turned so helpless and awed. Mesmerized, she touched his cheek then slid her thumb to his mouth. He parted his lips and took her in, suckling. Hot and hungry and wet…she imagined that mouth on her pussy, those thirsty moans vibrating against her clit.

She fisted his hair as the pleasure mounted and his eyes opened, a further connection with this extraordinary, unexpected man.

"God, Pike."

Her excitement did something to him, like spurs jabbed in his sides. His body owned hers as the orgasm rushed in, fingers meticulous as his thrusts sped. She heard her name on his breath, not even a whisper. Then all her consciousness was sucked straight to where his fingers were teasing and spasms hit, fast and harsh. Her hand slid to his neck, his scar, her fingers clutching at his collar, and she swore and bucked and said who-knew-what, utterly lost.

"Mac." His fingers stilled and his hips slowed, and when she opened her eyes, his were locked to hers like magnets.

"Whoa."

Pike cleared his throat. "Yeah."

She tugged at his back, inviting him to be selfish. Dropping to his elbows, he held her cuffed hand and lowered so their bellies touched. He took her deeply, dark groans and animal grunts replacing the measured breaths and exciting her all over again. All these alternating layers—man, beast, man, beast. It excited her to have uncovered the animal in him again. She wanted to see him lose his mind.

"Fuck me, Pike."

The words seemed to singe him and he closed his eyes. "Mac."

"Fuck me."

He changed again—harder and faster but still perfectly controlled. Color rose in his cheeks and ears.

Mac wanted to gnaw the stupid handcuffs off so she could hold his ass in both hands and feel him working, stroke every inch of his back, rip away his shirt and her bra and feel his bare chest on hers.

"God, Pike."

All at once those measured strokes jumped their tracks. Pike's hips hammered into the home stretch and watching him lose control was just as hot as watching him wield it. Hotter.

"Come for me, Pike."

"Fuck, Mac."

She watched his face, eyes squeezed shut, lips parted with disbelief or shock. Sliding her hand between them, she wrapped her thumb and forefinger around his shaft where it drove into her and gave him a squeeze. He moaned, taking her harder.

"Pike…"

Again his body answered for him, and this time she felt him ripping to pieces above her. Inside her. A dozen rough thrusts and he froze, hips jammed hard to her thighs, as deep as he could go. He pressed his forehead to hers, so close she could feel every rumbling moan in her own chest. She plastered her palm to his ribs to ride their rise and fall, to memorize his slippery skin and blazing heat.

"Wow."

With a final groan, he collapsed beside her. She turned onto her hip and slung an arm across his middle.

"Oh, Pike—your knee." It was scraped and raw from the rock.

He took a look then shrugged against the sleeping bag. "Worth it."

She pressed her cheek to his shoulder and smiled. "Badass."

For ten minutes or more they lay in the open air and warm sunshine, staring at the sky, the water, one another. Pike's breaths slowed beneath her palm and the frantic sex chemicals fled her system to be replaced by glowy, satisfied ones.

Pike broke their lazy silence to remind them both why exactly they were here, what had brought them together in this wild stretch of nowhere.

"So. Just ten hours of hiking to go."

Mac laughed. Right now, she could walk a thousand miles. One-legged, blindfolded, through the tiniest and most airless tunnel ever constructed.

"Bring it on, bitches."

PIKE

PIKE CHECKED HIS WATCH. Ten after five. At long last—bug-bitten, raw-wristed, filthy and exhausted—they staggered into view of the smoke's source. Bitten and filthy and exhausted and, in Pike's case, euphoric.

As much as his body hurt, his head was swimming, floating. And not from whatever the doctors had slipped them the night before. Just good old-fashioned infatuation.

But the closer they got to the fire, the more gravity intruded, pulling him down. End of the line for this honeymoon. His mood sank and all he felt was beat.

They reached the top of the hill, fire a mere twenty paces away. Pike paused, forcing Mac to do the same. Her eyes darted around, seeming to scout for booby traps.

"This is it," he said.

"What?"

"This is where you and I have to quit being friends and…and everything else."

She smiled, expression softening. "I'll still be your friend after these cuffs come off. I can be your friend and still kick your ass."

Pike mustered a laugh, heart not in it. He gave her face a long study and she seemed to read his mind. Her hand rose, dragging his along with it as the walking stick fell to the ground. Metal clicked and jangled in Pike's ear as they touched one another's cheeks, and he lowered his mouth to hers.

He'd never kissed a woman and felt this way before—felt what the movies want you to think kissing should be like. Fuck it, maybe the movies had it right.

Pike wondered if the doctors surely watching *this* video could tell what he was feeling, see the fireworks bursting in his chest, hear the film score rising to mirror his pulse. He didn't really care. He only hoped Mac could feel it.

They broke away after a minute or two, both turning to the fire. Mac saved Pike the pain of stooping for his stick and handed it to him.

"Thanks."

They walked forward together.

"Hello?" Mac shouted. Pike heard the strain in her voice, the same as what he felt in his aching body. Final stretch. The moment when lovers turned back into competitors. And he wasn't fit for a foot race.

Rory might have managed to view love as an adequate prize in exchange for all this torture, but Pike wasn't quite so romantic. The sex had banished the ache from between his thighs, but not his pragmatism.

No staffers appeared to uncuff them or offer instructions so they staggered to the fireside and collapsed downwind from its dark smoke, ditching their packs.

They sat. And sat. And sat. Nearly an hour it must have been, then the flames waned.

"What the fuck?" Mac asked, the first words they'd exchanged since plopping down.

"No clue."

"Are we missing something?"

"Probably…but my brain's totally fried. Even if a clue was right in front of us, I doubt I'd be able to make any sense of it."

She nodded. Then she sat up. Pike watched her eyes go from squinty to round. As she shot forward to her knees, she yanked their wrists.

"Fuck, sorry."

Pike moved to kneel beside her, ignoring a fresh surge of pain. "What is it?"

Mac grabbed his walking stick and angled one end into the dying fire, nudging forward a tiny black shape from among the gray ashes. A key.

"Oh, Christ."

She slipped the bandanna from her hair. Wrapping her hand in it, she grabbed the key and tossed it to the grass. Pike unscrewed his canteen with his free hand and doused it. Mac poked it and deemed it cool enough to handle.

And just like that—a frantic ten seconds following a grueling ten hours—they were free.

Mac flexed her wrist with a sigh, then looked up and gasped. Pike turned to spot the source of her surprise—Lenora materializing once again from the woods.

"I see you two lovebirds have finally separated yourselves," she said sweetly. "About time, too. The doctors were getting very bored observing you. With the exception of a rather fascinating piece of footage in the middle, that is."

Pike's blood heated and churned. They both got to their feet, Mac far quicker than Pike on his aching leg. It felt odd to suddenly not be locked to her. Felt vulnerable, not liberating.

"I'm sure you've both realized this is the end of the road. The final stretch. In a few minutes, one of you will be five hundred thousand dollars richer, and one of you will merely be the last player to lose."

"Where's the finish?" Mac asked curtly, clearly as fed up with the drama as Pike.

"It's not going to be so simple, I'm afraid. You two have failed to get into the spirit of the race so far, plus Dr. Pike is no longer in any shape to put up a good fight."

His heart beat faster, undeniably excited to know he might still have a decent chance at the money.

"So the doctors have devised an alternate end to this competition," Lenora said. "A wonderfully simple one that they doubt even you two will be willing to twist into a draw."

"What?" Pike asked.

Lenora curled a finger and beckoned them to follow her. She strode quickly enough that Pike had to walk faster than was comfortable, but fuck it. It'd be over soon. He could go home. He and Mac could say goodbye to all this bull and maybe stay friends, even separated by vast geography and half a million dollars. Maybe hold hands on the plane ride south. Maybe even share a hotel room on a layover and say goodbye in style, before they returned to their normal lives and set about forgetting all this.

Lenora led them to a little patch of civilization—a small, moldering building with just the base of what must have once been a gigantic antenna mounted beside it. Four crew guys stood nearby, hands behind their backs, bodies rigid with military-esque patience. One of the folding buffet tables was set up. A simple olive green case sat on it, not unlike Pike's medical kit. Lenora clicked open its latches.

She flipped it open and removed two semi-automatic pistols.

Mac squeaked.

Pike narrowed his eyes, too fucking tired to be shocked, too tired to be scared or hesitant or anything but pure *pissed*.

"What? Whichever one of us shoots you first wins?"

Lenora shook her dignified head. "Whichever one of you shoots the other first wins."

Pike went instantly sober, ice cold. "What?"

"Non-fatal, of course."

"You can't make us do that," Mac said, sounding distinctly unsure of herself.

"You must puncture the skin, and you must hit bone. That is to say, no earlobe technicalities, if you follow? You'll both be locked in that building, and the first one to shoot the other wins the grand prize." She smiled, something sharp and predatory in her eyes. She flipped the guns so she held them by the barrels. "Very simple. Any questions?"

"What happens if one of us shoots *you*, right now?" Pike asked.

"You'll go to jail for assault or murder," she said brightly, "and then neither of you will win. Follow the rules and one of you will earn a trip to the nearest hospital, all expenses paid, the other walks away with the half-million dollars. Understood?"

Pike looked to Mac. She just shook her head, her helpless, bewildered expression summing up everything Pike was feeling.

Lenora held the guns out. "Entrance is right over there." She nodded to the little radio outpost. "What a thrill-packed finale this will make, don't you think?"

Pike balked when Mac reached out to accept a gun. She didn't turn it on Lenora, didn't swivel to shoot Pike and end this entire fucked-up game, just took it, held the grip, fingers curled well away from the trigger.

"Come on," she said to Pike. "We both want to go home."

He turned to Lenora. "What happens if we go in that room and neither of us can do it?"

"I'd imagine you'll both get very hungry after a few hours. And in a couple of days' time one of you will die of dehydration. In which case, the survivor wins. Fair?"

Pike gaped. "What?"

"I'm teasing, of course," Lenora said. "If neither of you chooses to follow through, you will both forfeit the prize. And indeed, the last week of your lives, which you've so thoroughly invested in this competition. Such a waste. But if no shots are fired, the door will be unlocked after one hour and you'll be escorted back to Fairbanks."

Mac sighed. "Come on, Pike."

"Are you fucking nuts? Oh, wait, no, you're not. *She* is." He took the gun from Lenora and aimed it right between her eyes. Not the slightest flinch, only a slow, subtle curl of her lips. Pike held it there, just to imagine what it'd be like. His hands were eerily still, the one no longer handcuffed to Mac's feeling strange, disconnected, amputated. Reality was so twisted now, shooting Lenora seemed like the sane thing to do…except the bitch wasn't worth a prison sentence.

He lowered the weapon and turned to Mac. "You seriously even want to discuss this?"

Her face was steely, her unspoken answer affirmative.

Pike turned back to Lenora. "I'm not setting foot in there 'til you tell us exactly what happens if somebody gets shot. Who's going to treat the wound?"

"We have a pair of highly competent medical trauma specialists on hand, and a trailer set up nearby with all the necessary equipment to handle any unpleasant complications."

"Show me."

Lenora's smile was a strange mix of amusement and contempt. "You're very demanding, Doctor. But that's enough stalling, I think. We'll start the clock in one minute, whether you're inside that building or not."

He looked to Mac. She nodded, looking more weary than resolute. Pike grabbed his case and Lenora escorted them to the door, her back turned to them, begging for a bullet. Opening the door, she twirled a gracious hand to invite them in. Pike stepped inside first, the dimly lit box seeming dark after all that unrelenting Alaskan sunshine.

The space was tiny, a padded cell, literally. Not asylum-style, more like sound-proofing. Ricochet-proofing. Maybe eight-by-eight feet, another eight feet tall, lit by a single weak bulb dangling from the ceiling. A camera was mounted not far away.

Way too prepped to have been tossed together at the last minute, a so-called alternate ending.

Pike shot Lenora a killing look. "You were going to do this all along."

"I'll see you if and when a winner has been determined." She shut the door on them, an external deadbolt twisting with a cold snap of finality.

Mac huffed out a breath and set her gun on the ground. "Oh my holy God. What do we do?"

Pike tried to think about it honestly. He wanted that money, but not bad enough to pull a trigger and hurt Mac. He switched on the safety and released the magazine, just in case this was a test. Nope. Fully loaded. Enough rounds to take out the whole fucking crew, he mused. He slid the magazine back into the grip and glanced at Mac's weapon on the floor. "What do you *want* to do?"

"I don't know."

"It can't be worth it—five hundred grand to shoot each other? Right?"

Her gaze darted around the room.

"What are you thinking?" he asked.

"I don't know. I can't do it. I can't do either of the choices," Mac said. "I can't shoot you but I also don't think I can just toss my hands up and have wasted this entire crazy week. My week and yours and everybody else's time who wanted this."

"You're talking about one of us getting shot. Fuck everybody's wasted time."

She shook her head. "I don't know. I have no clue."

They sat in silence for ten minutes. Alarmingly, as the seconds ticked by, Pike began entertaining the idea of seeing this final challenge through with more and more curiosity.

"You said you can't shoot me," Pike murmured.

She shook her head.

"I can't shoot you either."

Mac sighed, actually sounding irritated with him.

His brows rose. "Wait, were you sitting there, like, waiting for me to find the balls to pull my trigger on you?"

"I'd rather get shot than do the shooting."

"Would you rather go home without the money than either of them? Because I'm not shooting you."

She held her tongue.

"But I mean, you could maybe do me," Pike said, thinking aloud. "My leg's already a mess. A chipped bone's not going to make things much worse."

Mac's eyes roamed the room, lips pursed to a bloodless line.

"Really. If one of us is going to win, that's how it has to happen. Otherwise I'm not doing it."

She shook her head. Her arms hugged her chest as though she were cold. "No. You have to do it."

"No way."

"Shooting you isn't worth five hundred grand, Pike. If I messed up and you got really badly injured, I couldn't live with myself."

"That won't happen."

"It could," she said, voice rising an octave. Her shoulders began to tremble and Pike realized where she was—her worst nightmare on top of the other psychological sadism.

"Small breaths," he said. "Sit down before you hyperventilate."

"I can't do it. And I don't know if I can walk away from here without either of us winning and making this whole circus worth it. Do me, Pike. Please. Knock me out or give me morphine, and just do it. You know how to shoot a gun and you'd know what to do with the wound. Who knows who they've got on hand to treat the loser?"

For a minute Pike didn't reply, mind racing with chemicals and far-too-few brilliant solutions to this impossible puzzle. He looked to her hands, his own fist tightening around the pistol's grip. He glanced to where he'd set his case.

"You sure?" he asked finally.

"Yeah. I can handle it. I've broken bones a zillion times." Mac looked confident then, or close to it. Maybe affected, maybe not.

"If that's what you want."

"I want you to win, Pike. The things you had planned for this money, and the fact that you made it this far... It's yours. I want you to have it."

The solution clicked into place, a decision that sat cold and hard in his gut. "That's really what you want?"

"It is."

He nodded slowly. "Okay. Well, if we're going to do this, let's do it right." He sat and flipped his case open, rooting through his supplies. Role defined, decision made. Comforting. He looked up at Mac, hating what he was about to do but not seeing any other choice. "Where? Pick the arm or the leg. They heal the best and we won't risk hitting organs." God, what a fucked conversation to be having.

"Not my arms," she said.

"Femur then."

"Sure, whatever."

420

Pike nodded…couldn't seem to *stop* nodding. "Roll up your hem."

Mac folded one leg of her shorts up, face stony. "This is going to fucking hurt, isn't it?"

He surveyed her leg. "Doesn't have to." He rummaged in his pack and held up a vial and a sealed syringe.

"What is that?"

"Morphine," Pike lied.

She shook her head, smiling grimly. "Doctor, will I ever dance again?"

Pike managed to return her smile, stomach turning. "Yeah, you will." He took a look at her arms and swabbed a likely vein. "What do you weigh?"

"I'm not sure. Usually about one-ten. Probably less, after this week."

Pike nodded. He prepped the syringe and filled it.

"What's the street value of what I'm about to score for free?" Mac asked.

"Quiet. Just try to relax." Pike tamped the needle. "Scoot back and lean against that wall, and hold your arm out for me."

Mac did as she was told, swallowing as Pike knelt beside her.

"I'm sorry, Mac."

"Don't be sorry. Just do what you have to."

Pike nodded. He met Mac's eyes, looked to her leg, back to her face. She didn't make a noise as he eased the needle in and injected its contents.

He set the syringe aside and smoothed a Band-Aid over her puncture, so obscenely tidy and clean compared to what was about to go down. He took a seat at her side, waiting.

"How long before I go loopy?"

"Not long."

Already her eyes were losing their focus, body slumping.

"Sorry I lied to you." He knew she couldn't hear him anymore, but no matter.

Pike grabbed the gun from beside him on the floor. He knelt before Mac's limp form and for a minute he simply studied her, trying to remember her for who she'd been to him this past week.

You're in this for yourself, his brain reminded him. What a fucking crock.

He rolled her cuff back down and propped her more upright against the wall. As he tucked her hair behind her ears, the kiss he stole felt tainted by the deception... But if this was the last time they'd lay eyes on each other, he couldn't go through with this without a final, definitive goodbye.

He reached out and took her hand, sliding the handle of the gun into her palm and threading her index finger through the trigger. He got his own body as far from the barrel as he could and prayed he'd hit bone on the first shot, finish the job that branch had started. He clicked the safety off.

"See you around, Mac. I hope you find what you're looking for at college."

Pike took a deep breath and squeezed her hand. For a split second he was lost in a burst of noise and pain. Then, nothing.

THE FOLLOWING JANUARY

AFTER AN INTERMINABLE WAIT at the luggage carousel, Pike shouldered his duffel and headed for the exit. One flight down, a couple to go, but no more tonight, thank Christ.

He glanced at the landscape beyond the tall windows, everything looking foreign. Desert. Desert meant work, stress, duty...and all the relief that came with those things. But today it meant other unknowns. Exciting ones, but without any guarantees. He glanced at a clock on the arrivals board. His flight had been early by twenty minutes and he wondered if he ought to find something to eat, kill some time before his ride got here. He didn't know how long the drive would be, or how long before he'd get a proper dinner.

"Pike!"

He turned at the voice, a voice that sounded realer than it had these past six months on the phone, as real as it had been in Alaska.

Mac strode toward him, waving, all white teeth and happy excitement. Pike returned her smile with a slightly tighter, slightly nervous one. He hoped his lingering limp wasn't too obvious as he walked to meet her.

The way her body collided with his in a hug said she wasn't concerned for his well-being.

"Oh my God." Her words warmed his neck, strong, slender arms squeezing his shoulders. She pulled back, beaming. "It's so great to see you."

"You too." He wanted to kiss her but figured... No, fuck figuring. Pike leaned in and kissed her mouth, to hell with overthinking it.

When they separated she pursed her lips, ran her tongue over the lower one as if tasting him there. "Well, hey. Glad we got that out of the way."

He nodded.

She led him toward the exit. "How was the flight?"

"Uneventful. There's supposed to be a snowstorm in Michigan tomorrow though. Timing couldn't be sweeter."

"Let's hope the twenty hours it takes to get to the Philippines are equally boring."

Pike nodded again, rendered a bit too stupid for coherent communication, being so close to her again.

"You ready for a couple days' warm-up before Objective Rock Climbing begins? See what sort of freaky place breeds a spaz like me?"

Pike hurried ahead to push the door open and hold it for her. "Yeah. I want to meet this nutty stoner brother of yours who raised you to be the perfect woman."

"He's rather interested in you too," Mac said. "I give you guys a couple good hours of hip-hop-fueled camaraderie before you start arguing about what business the U.S. has being in the Middle East. But yeah, should be interesting." She gave her arms a rub against the

January cold. "I hope you weren't expecting it to be a desert paradise out here."

"With the winter we're having in Detroit, I'll take forties and no ice any day."

Mac led him to a faded red pickup, as big as she was tiny, its bed rigged to haul who-knew-what.

"So I couldn't help but notice," she began then opened her door, climbed in and leaned across to unlock Pike's.

He got inside. "Notice what?"

"Your limp." She frowned and nodded to his leg.

"No way in hell you get to feel bad about that," Pike said, slamming his door. "You mention it again on this trip and I'm going home. Rock climbing's all about upper-body strength anyhow."

"Well, kind of."

Pike nodded. "It better be, because I've been doing chin-ups like they're going out of style."

Mac cranked the engine and drove them out of the parking lot, heater filling the cab with warmth a fraction as comforting as her nearness.

"How about dancing?" she asked. "Can you still dance?"

"Haven't tried, really. But get a few drinks in me when we hit a club in Manila and we'll find out together."

"You're on."

Pike studied her creamy skin and brown eyes in the winter sun, no makeup wrecking how perfect she already was. "So, the school decision's been made, right?"

"Yup. Nothing fancy. Denver, so I can still drive home or catch a cheap flight if they need me."

"A flight?"

She nodded. "I'm trying to get better with that."

"Good for you. And business school, you were saying the other week?"

She shrugged. "I kind of think so, eventually, but I decided I'll just take whatever I want for the first year. Who knows what I'm any good at, I've tried so few things. Maybe I'm a chemistry genius or the next da Vinci."

"Maybe."

"I'm not in much of a rush to find out, in any case. I've given myself nearly a hundred grand to dick around with and it's not like I've got Ivy League tastes. Education bargain buffet. I'll try a little bit of everything."

"That's cool. Michigan's got some nice schools. You know, if you ever felt like transferring. Seeing where your folks are from and everything."

She shot him a grin and Pike smiled himself, insanely pleased she didn't mind him flirting so artlessly, so soon after reuniting.

"Maybe. We'll see." Mac stared at the road for a half mile then caught Pike's eye. "How about you? How's it going, being benched by your injury? And your mom's mortgage and everything?"

It was remarkable how they'd managed to chat on the phone two or three times a week, yet barely traded a hundred words related to the competition that had brought them together. The few they *had* exchanged had been heated—Mac's rigorous attempts to get him to accept half her prize money, and his adamant refusal. The subject had been dropped, mention of Alaska made unofficially but unmistakably off-limits.

What had they talked about then, for the past few months? Silly stuff—music and movies and daily nonsense, and the planning of this vacation. Hours and hours of the soothingly mundane. It had done wonders to keep Pike positive through his physical therapy.

"I think my time in the military's pretty much done now," he said.

"Because of your leg?"

"No, I think *I'm* just done with it. I fulfilled my mandatory active service last summer, before...you know. I think I'll just cross my fingers my reserve duty is quiet and go back to boring old civilian medicine."

"V.A.?"

He nodded. "Only place I can really see myself. It pays way better than the military. I should be able to get my mom's place paid off in eighteen months."

"Wow."

"Yeah, not as quick as winning the stupid prize money." He paused, unnerved yet relieved to have brought it up. "But I can bite that bullet. I'm thirty-two now. Time to grow up."

"Wow, thirty-two."

"I know, I'm ancient."

"I won't tease you. I'm twenty-six next month. I'll probably seem like some old grandma to the teenagers in my freshman orientation."

"Yeah, the army's like that too. I look at some of these kids and I'm like, what are you, twelve? They probably look at me and think I'm fifty."

"Nah. You're very immature."

Pike rolled his eyes. "Thanks."

"Don't worry. That's how I like 'em." She turned them off the highway and onto a quieter route, driving them through the living postcard that was New Mexico.

Postcard. A troublesome thought overtook Pike. He pictured the card he'd received in the mail the previous week. A wedding announcement, he'd been sure—a classy, embossed envelope. But inside, a folded note card boasting a painting of sprucey wilderness and the words, *Alaska in April...*

Upon opening, *It wouldn't be the same without you! Please save the date, and expect an information packet and formal invitation shortly.*

April seventeenth, it had informed him, along with the same address he'd hitched a ride to from the Fairbanks airport in August. He cleared his throat.

"Have you, um…" He trailed off.

"Yes?"

"Have you given any thought to going back to Alaska at all?" he asked her.

Mac laughed. "Maybe, but not anytime soon. Think I've had my fill for a few years at least." Her tone told Pike she'd not received a card of her own.

"Why?"

"No reason." He held his tongue. He was certain that whatever invitation he was in store for, he wouldn't be RSVPing. No fucking way. Not for any amount of money. Definitely not. Not after that first trip's finale…

Though if he was that sure, why did the impending invitation scare him so thoroughly shitless?

He couldn't tell Mac about it, that was a no-brainer. He couldn't guess what she'd suggest he do, and he was afraid, frankly, of how easily he might be persuaded to agree with her logic. Plus this trip should stay as free of all that nonsense as possible. Bad enough the question was dangling over his own head. He shoved the thought in a vault and buried the key, a worry for when he got back to Detroit and checked his mail again in March.

Glancing at him with a smile, she broke their silence. "I miss your mohawk, by the way. I'll need to get you stoned and go at you with some clippers."

"Have at it. How long 'til we're at your place, anyhow?"

"Forty minutes maybe."

"Nice."

"Yup, then just seven thousand miles and we're on vacation."

Honeymoon, Pike thought. Just without the marriage part. Hell, maybe he'd trick her into a crackpot elopement on the shores of some Philippine island. Weirder things had happened to him, many of those experiences being ones only Mac could fully appreciate.

Perhaps he'd see if he couldn't wheedle a blessing out of her brother while he was here, just to be prepared.

"Six weeks," she sighed. "How long 'til one of us murders the other, do you think?"

"Dunno, but kill me in my sleep. And take mercy on me and have sex with me first. Black-widow style."

Mac looked his way, biting her lip mischievously. Pike bet she had no clue what that did to him.

He echoed her pronouncement. "Six weeks. Man, that sounds so nice when it's not related to the service."

"I'll bet. For me it's six weeks of, like, the start of my life. My first time in a whole new hemisphere."

"And you decided to ruin it by inviting me."

"We'll see about that." Mac flipped the radio on, just a faint drone of pop to cover the engine's whines. Pike studied her from the corner of his eye, not quite believing he was really here, next to her, invited to share her life for the next month and a half. He realized it must go both ways, that she wanted to share his as well. Maybe she even found him half as charming and fun as he found her.

"Thanks," he said. "For following through with all this."

Mac laughed. "Sure. By the way, thanks for shooting yourself in the leg so I could win five hundred grand."

"I'd do it again," Pike said.

"Even after all that rehab?"

He nodded. "No question."

"Well… You know, there's a V.A. hospital in Santa Fe. In case you ever got sick of Detroit and felt like transferring."

Impractical or not, the invitation lit him up inside. He hid it well. "Who knows? Kind of dusty out here though, isn't it?"

"Not as dusty as the Middle East, I'm sure. Not as stabby as Detroit."

Pike made his voice stern. "Leave Detroit alone. My one and only rule, Machiniak."

"Fine."

"Hey, do I get to see your sparkly tap-dancing trophy tonight?"

"But of course. I'm sure my brothers will haul out every embarrassing photo and home movie we've got. And I had an unhealthy obsession with being on camera, so prepare yourself for an all-night film festival."

"Excellent."

"Speaking of photos—open up the glove box. Check out what's on top."

Pike pulled out a folded sheet of paper, finding two photos printed on it. The first was of Leah and Rory, both in snow-dusted winter clothes, heads close together as Leah snapped the selfie. Behind them loomed a giant Christmas tree and, beyond that, tall buildings. Beneath was a photo of Rory alone, looking down at the guitar he was playing, seated at a table in someone's cramped, colorful kitchen.

Pike laughed, feeling happy in a way he wasn't accustomed to. "That's awesome."

"She sleuthed out my business e-mail, just last week. Thought you'd get a kick out of those."

He nodded and stowed the paper, emotion thick in his throat.

"I didn't reply yet, since I wanted a shot of us together to really blow her mind."

"We'll have to arrange a reunion, complete with vacation slides," he said.

"Good thinking." Mac dug in the cup holder at her elbow and slid out a cell phone. She woke it up and held it out in front of her. "Get over here. I'll document the very first leg of our big adventure."

Pike unstrapped himself and leaned over, pressing his cheek and shoulder to Mac's. He felt her smile as he glowered.

He buckled himself back in as she checked it. "Oh, classic Pike. You going to wear that grimace in all our snapshots? Guess I'll just have to catch you off guard."

No problem there, he thought. Just a touch of her hand or a flirtation whispered and his brain would melt and leak out his ears.

Pike turned his attention to the landscape, the fascinating colors and shapes and the largeness of the sky of the place she came from. He imagined other landscapes, the blue of the Pacific, white sand maybe. White hotel sheets wrapped around her tan legs. He felt words aching to pop from his lips, feelings threatening to slip between his ribs and burst out his chest.

Save it. Save it for a beach or a dark, private corner of some exotic bar or the top of a hulking rock in the middle of the ocean, the two of them resting triumphantly atop it, pondering the vastness of the horizon.

Mac switched on the headlights as the sun sank low, and he studied her in the deep pink, dusky light. Worth five hundred grand, worth a weeklong head trip, worth a bullet in the leg. He rubbed the spot, the dark scar hidden behind his jeans, the ugliest love proclamation tattoo in Creation. All that time spent in a war zone and he gets shot on leave...

It ached in the cold, ached just as his heart had, marooned a thousand miles away from her. He liked that though. There was purity in that ache, and purity was beauty to Pike in a world so otherwise senseless and murky.

As the route turned arrow-straight, he reached over and stole her hand from the wheel, clasping it between the two seats.

She met his gaze and smiled before turning back to the road. "Thirty miles to go."

Then seven thousand more. Six weeks. Maybe another fifty years. "Take me home," he said.

She sang the cheesy lyrics under her breath, squeezing his fingers in time. "I don' wanna let—you—go—'til I see the light. Whoa-whoa-whoa-whoa, take me hooome tonight..."

Pike shut his eyes and leaned back in his seat, lost himself to the warmth of her hand and the rumble of the truck. Here, under this vast, darkening sky and beside his friend, Pike had no clue what his role was or what his orders were.

Fuck it. He'd just float. Floating felt good. He'd float right up into the stars, into that secret galaxy burned across her skin.

He gave her hand another squeeze. "Take me wherever."

10k por challenge + open + close

everyone allowed what they can carry   take bets
                    L's boyfriend has theirs

1   ∅ ∅ ∅   ○○○   ○○○   ○○○   Mac
race   * * *   * R Ⓒ   * L Ⓟ ·   I Ⓜ D   Leah
                                                          Chloe
         reveal I as treacherous, D as cutthroat, L out of her element   Pike
                  sabotage P & M as valuable I   Mac ♥

2   ∅ ⊙—⊙   ∅ ○ ○   ○ ○ ○   set up
Meat locker * L Ⓡ   * D Ⓜ ←   I C P   tension   Rory
                                                              Daisey
need to get Melissa   Marissa   think they can   Ian
C + D talking   elim. D & M   Leah
                                                              Chloe
         R and L in a fight to get kicked out   worthy Rory
3   ∅   ○   ○   ○   ⌒○⌒   ○   ⊙   Leah ♥
2/ ?   Ⓛ ←→ R   Ⓓ ←   M   I   P   Ⓒ   Mac
                                                              Daisey
                                                              Rory, chloe
                                                              Chloe

4   a bet - winner gets six
              ∅ ∅   ⊙○○   their way   ○ ○   Ian
              R Ⓔ   P ←Ⓓ ·   ⇒Ⓘ M   Mac
                                                              Daisy ♥

5   names
A bridge?   ∅—⊙   ○ ○   both want D out   Mac
                     D Ⓜ ←   I Ⓟ   Pike
                                                              Mac ♥

6   I says   a ruse
         "stop?   ∅—⊙   ○   I has more   Ian ♥
         seconds"   Ⓘ Ⓜ   Ⓟ   than anyone   Mac
         to P   Pike ♥

7   ⊙—⊙   Mac
                       Ⓜ Ⓟ   Pike?

Twenty-One Questions logistics

ABOUT THE AUTHOR

SINCE SHE BEGAN WRITING IN 2008, Cara McKenna has published nearly forty romances and erotic novels with a variety of publishers, sometimes under the pen names Meg Maguire and C.M. McKenna. Her stories have been acclaimed for their smart, modern voice and defiance of convention. She was a 2015 RITA Award finalist, a 2014 *RT* Reviewers' Choice Award winner, a 2012 and 2011 *RT* Reviewers' Choice Award nominee, and a 2010 Golden Heart Award finalist. She lives with her husband and son in the Pacific Northwest, though she'll always be a Boston girl at heart.

caramckenna.com
facebook.com/authorcaramckenna
twitter.com/caramckenna

ALSO BY CARA McKENNA

After Hours

Curio and the Curio Vignettes

Hard Time

Her Best Laid Plans

Shivaree: The Complete Series

Strange Love: Remastered Tales

Unbound

Willing Victim

THE SINS IN THE CITY SERIES

Crosstown Crush

Downtown Devil

THE DESERT DOGS SERIES

Lay It Down

Give It All

Drive It Deep

Burn It Up

AS C.M. McKENNA

Badger

AS MEG MAGUIRE

Caught on Camera
Headstrong
The Reluctant Nude
Thank You for Riding
Trespass
The Wedding Fling
Wild Holiday Nights

THE WILINSKI'S SERIES
All or Nothing
Going the Distance
Takedown